THE EMPTY

**Other books
by
Thom Reese**

The Demon Baqash
Chasing Kelvin
Dead Man's Fire
13 Bodies

For more exciting
E-Books, Audiobooks and MP3 downloads visit us at
www.speakingvolumes.us

THE EMPTY

Thom Reese

SPEAKING VOLUMES, LLC
NAPLES, FLORIDA
2014

THE EMPTY

ISBN 978-1-62815-192-3

Author's Note on the Expanded Edition

I can't begin to tell you how excited I am about this expanded edition of THE EMPTY. This book has always been quite special to me and now, for the first time, the public will be able to read it as it was meant to be. This is the full story, the complete manuscript. This is the tale I'd originally set out to tell. But, let me step back for a moment. Allow me to paint the backdrop. My first novel, THE DEMON BAQASH, was released by Speaking Volumes in 2011. But, prior to this, in 2010, THE EMPTY was accepted by another publisher. At this point I was still an unpublished author. First time authors are a risk to publishing houses. They have no track record. The accountants can't scan through sales numbers from previous efforts to determine how many units might be sold, there's no back catalog of books that might experience a sales boost as a result of a new release. First time authors are bright flashing question marks boasting the potential for great gain or loss. And so, in order to minimize risk, publishers often hold untested authors to a rather strict word count, this because longer books are more costly to produce. Such was the case with the original published edition of THE EMPTY. In order for it to see the light of day, I was forced to remove material from the manuscript, thus reducing the word count to an acceptable level. Soon after its publication, it became a favorite among my burgeoning loyal readership. Still, amidst the praise and excitement, I was sometimes told that it felt like something was missing, that there must be more to the story.

There was.

Recently, the rights to THE EMPTY reverted back to me and Speaking Volumes (the publisher of my other four books) immediately offered to rerelease it. I was thrilled, of course, but even more so when Kurt Mueller at Speaking Volumes offered to release an expanded edition, the full story, the tale I'd originally sought to tell. Allow me a moment to comment on this. I am still a new author. As of this writing, my first book was released just over two years ago. I'm not a household name. My novels aren't riding a wave at the top of the New York Times bestseller list. It's very rare for an author in this position to be asked to do an expanded edition such as this. These opportunities are often reserved for established authors on books that have been on the market for a decade or better. (Think Stephen King with THE STAND.) And so, I am exceedingly thankful to Kurt and Speaking Volumes for showing the confidence both in me and in this story to commit to this project.

Now, about the expansion: I've reinserted the material subtracted from the original published version and added content that had been outlined, that to me was always a part of the story, but was never incorporated due to looming word count issues. My hope is that the added material will offer a richer tapestry, a fuller telling of the tale. This is not filler material, but scenes that, in my mind, should always have been included, scenes that add flesh to the central characters and augment their particular trials. Without giving anything away, readers will now encounter events that occurred during the previously silent years between the early chapters and the present day story. You'll get a glimpse into Donald Baker's *Histories* which were mentioned frequently in the earlier edition, but never revealed. You'll learn about the people known as the reyaqc, and get a peek at their origins and early culture. The only thing I've omitted is a short segment that would have appeared as one of the interludes. It wasn't necessary to this tale and, as it hadn't been utilized in the original published version, I'd already reworked it, now utilizing it as a cornerstone event in a sequel. I think you'll find this was a solid decision.

But, enough about the process. This novel is for you, the reader, the book enthusiast. This is for those who enjoyed the original version of THE EMPTY and desire a fuller telling. And this is for the first time reader as well, for those who may never have picked up one of my books, but are just looking for a good yarn. I hope you find yourselves immersed in the tale of the reyaqc. I hope the reyaqc become real to you and continue to live and breathe in your imaginations. THE EMPTY isn't easily categorized. It's at once science fiction, horror, and fantasy. Certainly, it has elements of each. But, categories are limiting. Think of it how you will. My only hope is that you reach the final page and say, "I don't want it to end." To a writer, this is the greatest compliment. I'm excited about this project and hope you share in the joy. I believe this volume paints a much clearer picture of the tale, of the struggles and conflicts of the tormented race known as the reyaqc. I truly hope you enjoy reading THE EMPTY as much as I've enjoyed writing it.

Thom Reese
October 2013

Acknowledgements

With each book I grow as both a writer and as a person. Not because of any keen insight from within, but from contact with those who support and encourage me along the way. As with each project, my wife, Kathy, has been my biggest fan and most discerning critic. Her insights help me to strive for a better story, and my manuscripts would be lesser things without her input. Thank you, sweetie, for all you do. My girls, Trista, Amy, and Brittany, are a continual source of inspiration and joy. I could never adequately convey what each of you mean to me.

A very special thank you to Kurt Mueller at Speaking Volumes for making this special edition possible. Your encouragement and vision have been priceless. Thank you to my faithful reader and dear friend, Jeff Granstrom, for his feedback on this and all of my projects, to Deborah Lynn for her literary input, and to Dr. Edgar Cox for guiding me through some of the medical aspects of the tale. A big thank you to Lisa Rene Smith, Linda Houle, and Cindy Davis at L & L Dreamspell. I'd also like to thank Randall Dunn, Stephen Forbus, Travis Szynski, Crystal Neher, the Leeney clan, Ed Walczak, Gaylon Kent, Kym Low, Amy Densham, and all of the others who have cheered me on through those long hours at the keyboard.

To Kathy, Trista, Amy, and Brittany.
Without you I am truly empty.
With you, my life is rich beyond measure.

PART ONE

THE MOLTS

Chapter One

1897

Dolnaraq was only eight winters into existence, but knew the smell of prey. Oh, and he loved prey. Loved the hunt. Loved the kill. But this prey would be different. This prey would not warm his belly. His teeth wouldn't penetrate this flesh. The animal's blood would not dribble down his chin and onto his chest. No, this one was reserved for quite a different purpose, something nearly divine in scope and meaning. "Do you smell him?" whispered Dolnaraq as he drew in a long, sweet breath.

Tresset nodded, though the young male wore a curious expression. "Yes. To the east. Maybe over that next rise."

"We must be quiet," whispered Dolnaraq as he moved in the direction of the scent.

"Dolnaraq," whispered Tresset. "Are you sure?"

Only two winters Dolnaraq's senior, Tresset liked to assume superiority over his younger friend, over any who would let him, really. He would organize hunting parties with the young of the pack and direct their movements, deciding who should flank a beast and who should charge, which of them should scout ahead and which should ideally strike the killing blow. But this hunt belonged to Dolnaraq. He'd contemplated it for many weeks, determining which type of creature to seek, imagining what that animal might add to him. He'd thought of how proud his father would be when he first saw Dolnaraq anew. For Dolnaraq would have done what even his father feared to do. Oh yes, father would be proud. He also knew his mother would squeal like a baby pig. But that was what mothers did. She would adjust. She would one day approve. She would be forced to concede that Dolnaraq was no longer a pup, but had entered a state of maturity, which deserved respect and maybe even awe.

Dolnaraq paused, gazing at Tresset. "Am I sure?" he asked in response to the question posed him.

"It is a major step. One best come to with the counsel of your father."

Dolnaraq scoffed. "You never get counsel." He lifted his head again, sniffing at the air. "The scent grows weak. We must hunt before the creature finds its hole." Dolnaraq moved slowly toward the small snow-covered rise, and then glanced back at Tresset. "Do you come or stay? Either way, I go."

Tresset hesitated for only a moment, then nodded and went to march past Dolnaraq as if to take the lead.

"No," said Dolnaraq, holding out his arm to block Tresset's way. "This one is mine. I'll lead."

Tresset paused, narrowed his eyes, and looked to contemplate the request. Like all reyaqc, the youth's eyes were as mother's milk, devoid of all color except for the tiny black dot of a pupil at the center. Even so, this one had a dark intensity in his gaze that sometimes caused even adult members of the pack to pause. It went beyond the physical appearance of the eyes to whatever lay within. Unremarkable, yet anything but, Tresset was a strange one. But for all that, in this instance he gave a slow deliberate nod, allowing his younger companion to pass, taking the lead in this most precarious hunt.

Dolnaraq sighed within. He was glad the older youth accompanied him. For all his bluster, this was a frightening thing he meant to do, and having a companion beside him would bolster his resolve.

Both youth were accomplished hunters. Their pack was nomadic, living beyond the confines of the civilized world—of the human world. Like the prey they fed upon, they moved with the seasons, for the most part staying well hidden within forested areas. The land they inhabited was known by humans as Siberia, it was late in the nineteenth century, though Dolnaraq knew none of this, nor did he care. He often wondered though, why the pack did not move further and further south until they'd left this bitter cold land behind. But Dolnaraq's father insisted the more comfortable climes were fully inhabited by humans and that the reyaqc should fear unnecessary contact with these similar but very dangerous people. Humans are a superstitious breed, and could never understand the needs and drives of the reyaqc.

Dolnaraq did not care for humans. There was a need for them, yes. The reyaqc would always need to dwell within hunting distance of their towns and villages. But, nothing more than that. Just within hunting distance. Dolnaraq despised those reyaqc who comingled with the gypsies, wearing human clothing, singing human songs, living in traveling caravans that skirted the boarders of human civilizations. Most humans thought these gypsies strange, often believing them to have occult powers. But they believed them to be human. The majority of gypsies were human to be sure, but they often traveled in the same caravans as their reyaqc cousins. Dolnaraq couldn't understand why a reyaqc would feign humanity, no matter how similar in appearance. Dolnaraq was reyaqc, and he was about to become even more so.

They were over the rise now, gazing down into a small icy field. Dolnaraq saw it—the fox. His prey. Oh, how that shiny red coat gleamed. He could imagine that fur covering his own skin. How silky it must feel. Those eyes, so bright, so intelligent. And the teeth. Dolnaraq wanted the teeth as his own.

The two young reyaqc were silent, communicating now only through hand signals. Dolnaraq indicated that Tresset should circle around to his left. He saw his companion's expression tighten at the instruction— Tresset liked giving the orders—but still he moved accordingly.

Dolnaraq proceeded slowly, never allowing his quarry to leave his direct line of sight. He was upwind of the fox. The sly creature would not smell him. All he needed was to remain silent and invisible. He wondered if the fox would hear his heart beating. It seemed to be pounding so hard that surely every creature in the forest would hear its thump. He needed to calm himself. He knew that. But Dolnaraq had been dreaming of this moment for so many weeks now. How could he possibly hope to remain calm?

And frightened.

Dolnaraq would never admit this to Tresset, but he was terrified. Yes, he wanted this—more than anything—but if something were to happen, if Tresset stepped on a brittle stick and scared the thing away, well, Dolnaraq would be relieved. He would feel cheated and relieved at the same time. He'd be angry at Tresset, but thankful too. This was a huge step, and Dolnaraq wasn't yet all that huge.

Stop it, he thought. If he remained this distracted he'd scare the fox away himself and then Tresset would accuse him of doing it on purpose.

He was almost there now.

Just a little closer.

Just a little closer.

Just as Dolnaraq was about to lunge, the fox sensed him and bolted to the left. But, Tresset was there. It scurried right, but found Dolnaraq. It slipped under a fallen branch and then into some low brush, but both of the young reyaqc appeared, cornering it, driving it into their grasps. Dolnaraq lunged but lost his footing on a small patch of ice. Still, he caught a fleeting grasp of the tail, slowing the fox enough for Tresset to snatch it in mid leap. The creature struggled and snapped, piercing Tresset's right earlobe and drawing a surprising amount of blood. It wriggled and wormed, its sleek legs pumping frantically against Tresset's bare thighs, leaving scarlet ribbons across his legs. But still the young reyaqc pressed the thing close to his chest, using his forearm and elbow to trap it against his body, while squeezing its jaws shut with both hands.

"Dolnaraq, hurry! I've got him!"

6

Dolnaraq moved forward, but slowly. Did he really want this? There was still time. He hadn't done anything yet.

"Dolnaraq! I can't hold him forever!"

He had to do this. He had come too far. What would Tresset say if he backed out now? He would be an outcast. The others would never respect one who boasted of great things and fled the very same when opportunity appeared. This was his hunt. His time. There might be no other.

Dolnaraq moved on instinct alone. Almost mechanically, he scooted forward on the cold uneven ground, extending his right hand as if to pet the fox. The frightened creature enhanced its struggles, bobbing forward and back, whimpering, pedaling its feet as if running, though Tresset had adjusted so that the paws now found only air.

"Slowly," cautioned Tresset. "Not too much. Not too fast. Once you begin, there's no need to rush."

The fox's hair was slick to the touch, and cold, much colder than Dolnaraq would have assumed. But his skin was cold too. The Siberian climate was not a gentle one for any of its many inhabitants. Dolnaraq's palm now held the back of the creature's neck. The time was at hand yet still Dolnaraq hesitated. Maybe this wasn't right for him. Maybe he was too young. Maybe…

The fox broke free of Tresset's grasp. Dolnaraq's reaction was immediate. The bed of tiny pin-like spines emerged from his right palm, penetrating the fox's neck at the base of the skull. The connection was made. The world stood still.

Dolnaraq did not feel himself tumbling over as he drew the fox close to his breast. He didn't feel the jagged branch slice him just above his left elbow. He didn't hear Tresset's continued warnings to be slow, to only take a small amount during this first connection. No, all Dolnaraq knew was the essence of the fox as it coursed through his shivering form. He felt fire in his veins and knew that certainly his limbs must be about to burst open. He heard the echoing chime in his head, bouncing from one side to the other behind his eyes, muddling his thoughts, obstructing all else. He felt his muscles twitch and cramp and felt his stomach wretch, emptying its sparse contents onto the whimpering and terrified fox. He felt every fabric of his person stretch and separate and then pull together, before stretching yet again and again. He seemed to be twirling around, around, and yet he was certain that he remained still. He felt Tresset's pull as his friend sought to disengage him from the beast, but he clung closer. The fox was his. The fox was him. He felt the creature swoon, its heartbeat slow. He felt its breath grow shallow. He knew what this meant. He knew he had taken too much. He also knew he would never stop. The fox was him. The fox was him.

Then Dolnaraq knew nothing at all. Only cold, dark nothing.

Chapter Two

Dolnaraq awoke two days later, feeling strange—not himself. His arms jerked when he tried to wipe his eyes, causing him to strike the side of his own face. Every muscle seemed bound up in balls. His legs did not want to extend, his stomach was tight and gurgling. And his vision was strange—somehow the colors had become less vibrant, the images less true.

"So, you've decided to become a molt." It was his father's voice, from somewhere just behind him. The voice was as it always had been, but the tone was unfamiliar. Dolnaraq couldn't tell if it was anger, sorrow, or maybe even disbelief.

A molt? His father had called him a molt. The term referred to reyaqc who, in addition to drawing essence from humans, drew from animals as well, shedding some of their more human-like characteristics in favor of those of the animal. A molt. Yes. The fox. Dolnaraq vaguely remembered the hunt, the chase, the experience. Had he done it? Had he been successful? Had he truly drawn from the fox? He lifted his quivering arm to before his eyes. Where was the fur? Where was the sleek coat he'd envisioned?

He rolled his head in the direction of his father's voice. "The fox?"

His father moved forward. His skin and hair were darker than Dolnaraq was accustomed to seeing on him. A band of gypsies had recently settled in the area and many of the pack had drawn essence from these dark strangers, causing their own tones to gradually darken as well. "Yes, the fox," said his father. "It is dead."

Dead! No. He'd taken too much. When first drawing from a creature one must proceed slowly, taking small amounts of essence over several days. If too much is taken and the animal perishes, then another must be found—another of quite similar essence. Otherwise the reyaqc may become ill, the two essences not complementing one another, but rather battling for primacy. Dolnaraq sought to find his voice. It came in a harsh whisper. "Dead. But, have I…?"

"Changed? Yes, boy, you've changed." Dolnaraq's father closed his eyes, drew a long breath. "Why?"

"To be strong, Father. To be a great hunter." And then, after a pause. "To make you proud."

"Make me proud! How could you imagine this would make me proud?"

Dolnaraq had no words, no response. His young mind could not fathom the reasoning behind his father's question. Of course the elder reyaqc should be proud. Dolnaraq had shown courage. He'd taken risk in order to better himself. Why would a father not be proud?

Dolnaraq watched through unfamiliar eyes as his father drew closer yet. "Boy, have you never wondered why I have not become a molt, why so few of our pack have done so?"

Dolnaraq had assumed it was because his father and the others were too afraid to take such a bold step, but not feeling comfortable with this response, he remained silent.

"The reasons are many," began his father when Dolnaraq failed to respond. "There are risks in the way of the molt."

"Then, you were afraid," said Dolnaraq before he could stop himself from doing so.

"No," sighed his father. "Not afraid as you see it. The advantages of animal essence can be either great or minimal. Yes, you may acquire the hunting skills or the superior sense of hearing or smell. But you also may degrade your intellect, or you may become more rash and violent or more skittish and fearful. Your appearance will change making it more difficult for you to blend with humans."

"Why would I want to blend with humans? They stink."

Dolnaraq's father offered a momentary grin. "Yes, their odor can be off-putting. But we need their essence. We need to hunt among them. Like it or not, we depend on the humans for our survival."

"You're a human lover!" screamed Dolnaraq. He had expected his father to praise him, to tell him how brave he had been, to say that he wished he had the same courage as his young son. But, all he had done was to belittle Dolnaraq, making him feel foolish. "You're a human lover and a coward." Dolnaraq attempted to rise from the cave floor, but found he was unable to lift himself from his bed of straw.

His father watched his pathetic struggle for a few moments, and then said. "No boy, I am neither. The humans are not so despicable as you might think. And I am neither enthralled by them nor a coward, as you claim. But neither am I your father. Not any longer. You may rest here until you've regained your strength, and then you must find a dwelling of your own."

This was the last conversation the two would have; though the young reyaqc did hear his father weeping in long, guttural sobs from beyond the cave entrance and long into the night.

*****

Dolnaraq found his feet. He was now able to hobble unsteadily about the cave. His head still ached and his stomach would not yet tolerate food, but at least he was able to move about. Though, why he'd want to, he didn't know. His father had an old, palm-sized mirror he'd acquired from a human some years prior. Dolnaraq had taken this and viewed his image. He had changed, yes. But not as he had hoped. His nose was now dark, but still shaped as before with no other fox-like characteristic. His left ear was somewhat elongated and random shoots of red fur protruded from it. His left eye—though still milky white—had widened in comparison to his right. And, within his mouth, one long canine tooth had grown—again, on the left—and protruded stupidly from between his lips making it impossible for him to shut his mouth completely. This also caused some difficulty in speech. The fingers on his left hand were shortened and clumsy, and his left leg felt twitchy and uncontrollable. He had no sleek beautiful coat as he had imagined. His senses of smell and hearing had not been enhanced. All in all, he'd become a useless freak. As such, he'd determined never to exit this cave again. What possible use could there be for one such as he?

His father had ordered him to leave, but his mother would care for him, he was sure. And if not his own mother; if she fell sway to the same repulsion as his father, then one of the other females father kept, one of the childless ones would certainly show pity on this freak.

Pity. That was all he was worth—someone's pity.

Dolnaraq rolled over in the hay weeping. It was not supposed to be like this. He was supposed to be stronger, more able. He was supposed to be admired not pitied. Maybe he should die. Maybe he should refuse all food, take no essence whether human or animal, and allow himself to waste away. It would be painful, yes, but not so long lasting. He was already weakened, in need of essence. The process of becoming a molt had drained his system. In many ways he was already depleted. Surely, it would be a simple thing to die. Then his father would truly weep. He would realize what his rejection had done and he would fall to his knees in anguish. Perhaps he'd even take his own life. This thought heartened Dolnaraq. He only wished he could be alive to witness it. Maybe he could hold his breath, pretend to be dead, make his father realize how wrong he'd been, and then Dolnaraq could "awaken." His father would be so thankful Dolnaraq was alive that he would hug him and care for him.

Or maybe he would curse him. Maybe he would rather that Dolnaraq did perish. Then he wouldn't have the embarrassment of a freakish pup.

Nothing made sense. Nothing was right.

But then came the raid. And everything changed.

*****

The pack from the north attacked on the night of the smallest moon. The minimal light granted them cover as they swept in from three different points of attack. Reyaqc packs attack one another for various reasons—food stores, supplies, better positioning relative to humans and prey, sometimes to replenish their stock of females and youth, or other times simply out of pure savagery.

The commotion began well after sundown. Shouts and footfalls as reyaqc raced back and forth about the clearing, growls and shrieks, the sounds of struggle, the gasps of the dying. Dolnaraq knew the sound of a raid. There had been many in his short lifetime. This was part of reyaqc life. He also knew that even a pup such as he was expected to defend the pack. If he was old enough to hunt, he was old enough to fight.

Dolnaraq closed his eyes. It would be an easy thing to simply lay here and allow one of the raiders to come by and kill him. There would be no prolonged starvation, no pleas from his mother to reconsider. What of the others? What of his mother? Already he could see the females gathering armfuls of food and supplies and carrying them further back into the depths of the cave. The females were doing their part. Dolnaraq should do his. Perhaps he would die in battle. Then his father would have no choice but to be proud. Yes. Die in battle. Die a hero. Maybe even a freak could be a hero.

It was not an easy task to rise from his bed as his muscles curled into tight balls of pain. But Dolnaraq used the cave wall for support and

13

gradually attained an upright position. The first steps were particularly painful, but with each his muscles seemed to loosen. He hobbled some, his left leg remaining numb and twitchy, but he found he could move about in a slow uneven gait.

The scene beyond the cave was a mass of confusion. The northern pack had seemingly swept in from all sides, catching Dolnaraq's clan off guard. Already, bodies littered the cold snowy ground, many slashed open with entrails leaving streaks of red upon the pristine white. To his left a young female was thrown harshly against an ancient oak. Her head made a sharp cracking sound with each of three successive strikes. When she finally fell limp, the northern reyaqc bent to clutch her right ankle and then dragged her into the darkness. Directly ahead, two northern reyaqc—both molts—descended upon Mynig, the pack chieftain. These reyaqc had the sharp claws of mountain cats. Mynig did not cry out, nor attempt to flee. Rather, he bit and clawed until finally succumbing in a heap on the bloodied snow.

Most of the northern reyaqc were molts. But not molts such as Dolnaraq had become. These were fierce creatures, many with full long canines and razor-sharp claws. How had they done this? Why had they become amazing while Dolnaraq had become foolish?

He knew the answer to this.

In these more savage packs, those who did not achieve some level of strength or usefulness were simply slain and then consumed by the pack. In this way, at least, they contributed something to the wellbeing of the many. If Dolnaraq were found by these, he would be murdered. He'd be devoured. Dolnaraq now realized he didn't want to die, that whatever he had become, he still had reason to go on. But could he? Could he go on? The pack was under siege and Dolnaraq was still weak and uncoordinated from his ordeal.

Two reyaqc fell before Dolnaraq, scraping and clawing, causing the young pup to scurry to his right. All about him were scenes of carnage— limbs severed, throats bitten and ripped. Dolnaraq's pack was not large, only comprising some forty members. Dolnaraq knew each corpse by name. He had spent hours with each dying soul. An older reyaqc, Narmon, called out from where he lay on the icy ground. There was a gash in his side, and he was trying to force his innards back to within his body. "Dolnaraq!" he cried in a raspy croak. "Help me to put myself back together! Help me put these in!"

Dolnaraq stood horrified. What was he to do? Narmon was obviously beyond repair. How could he possibly expect young Dolnaraq to fix him?

"Dolnaraq, please!" croaked Narmon one last time. But Dolnaraq fled with a quick hobble. Still, he seemed unable to outdistance the carnage. Everywhere, he saw those he'd known for the entirety of his existence falling to this superior force. There was nothing he could do, no direction he could turn.

"Amazing."

The voice came from behind Dolnaraq. He spun to see Tresset standing before two males who were breathing their final breaths.

"Amazing," repeated Tresset, a broad grin on his pale round face, a look of shear awe in his milky eyes. "Can you see the strategy, Dolnaraq? Can you see how they swept in from the east, forcing our pack to retreat west? Then waves two and three, from the west and north, encircled us, cornered us against the caves. We were pathetic, with no plan, no countermeasures. But, these! These were magnificent. Our entire pack will have fallen within thirty minutes. It's amazing."

The youth was enthralled, hypnotized by the battle. But he was also correct in his assessment. Dolnaraq could see that now. His own pack was doomed. Even now, they were down to less than half the number of the invaders. The only hope was retreat. It was not brave to die for dying's sake, for this would only bring a greater victory to one's opponent. No. It was time to flee. Dolnaraq didn't know if this was logic speaking or shear cowardice. But he knew it was right, that it was necessary.

"Tresset," he called. "Tresset, come. We must flee. Our pack has fallen. Come. Now."

"Do you see the discipline?" asked his friend. "Do you see it? Even those few who have fallen do so with grace, with superiority."

"Tresset, please. We need to go."

It was then that a large bear-like reyaqc fell upon Tresset. The youth went down with a panicked yelp, but no serious injury had yet been inflicted. Dolnaraq had no time to think, which was well, because had he had that opportunity he surely wouldn't have leapt upon the brute, sinking his one long canine into the thing's neck, clamping it there, pressing it deeper, deeper. Dolnaraq felt the things talons as it dug into his side. He released his hold, but the brute of a molt did no such thing. Now Dolnaraq was on the ground, those claws raking at him. His own blood splayed across his foe's gnarled face.

Another joined the fray. At first Dolnaraq thought it might be Tresset, but the other youth was still on the ground, having scooted to the side after Dolnaraq had fallen upon the molt. Whoever it was, he'd somehow pressed himself between Dolnaraq and the other, and was now grappling with the larger reyaqc. Despite the molt's injury to the neck, it was still a lopsided battle, and the outcome predetermined. The molt would be the victor.

Dolnaraq moved to renew his attack but the other shouted at him. "Dolnaraq! No! Flee into the forest! Flee!"

It was his father's voice. And it was soon forever silenced.

Chapter Three

1897 - 1909

The two young reyaqc had fled their native pack the night of the raid. Dolnaraq had witnessed his father's murder. He stood horrified, nearly paralyzed with fear and fury. Tresset tugged at his younger companion, forced him to leave his dying father behind. Both youth had sustained minor injuries, and the pack they had known for the entirety of their short lives was no more. The surviving females would be carried off to the northern pack for sport and breeding. The adult males would all be slain and eaten, as would any youth old enough to hold revenge in his heart. Tresset had no desire to be consumed that eve.

The Siberian night was cold and harsh, with bitter winds that sliced through the flesh, and a deepening snow that made movement cumbersome and wearying. They spent the first night beneath the roots of a large tree that had been partially uprooted in some time past. The tree base, angled like a shed as the massive trunk leaned against adjacent trees and offered some small protection from the elements. The hole, left where it had stood, hid them from scouts searching for escapees such as themselves. It was a miserable night with Dolnaraq weeping for his dead father and for his mother, who by now had likely been dragged across the cold hard ground by some lusty molt. Dolnaraq was as bitter as the Siberian freeze.

Tresset had surely lost family as well. No, he had not physically witnessed his father's death, but surely the event had occurred. The forces of the northern pack had been too fierce, too well organized for any to have survived. And as for his mother—one of his father's numerous mates—well, she would have done to her what all females had done to them. As such, she would certainly soon bear Tresset a new brother or sister—only this pup, he would never know. Such was the way of the world. There was, he must admit, some small pang for the female. She had defended Tresset against his older brother—a pup born of another female—and had eventually driven the older one off when he'd become too cruel to the slight and fragile Tresset. She'd tended to her pup's every need, and given freely of herself.

These thoughts of family lost did not occupy his mind, nor did he ponder his own dilemma—that he and Dolnaraq were now on their own, responsible for their own survival in this harsh, bitter land. No, what drove Tresset's psyche were the scenes of battle. The strategy. The quick, decisive attack. The flanking molts. The way the northern pack had descended as if from nowhere, forcing his people into indefensible positions. There was a genius in the assault, a subtlety even within the fierce, grotesque brutality of it all. Tresset wished he could talk with their chieftain, sit beside him, learn of his strategy, and absorb his skill and ingenuity. This meeting was never to be. Tresset would eventually learn strategy, but the path was one he could not have yet imagined on that harsh, miserable night.

*****

Tresset led as the two reyaqc pups took to moving about the wooded lands of the Siberian wilderness, avoiding other reyaqc packs for fear they'd be seen as spies and executed on sight. Though the younger Dolnaraq often complained of proximity to the troublesome humans, Tresset made sure they always stayed within a two day's walk of human settlements as there was the ongoing need for essence. It was his duty, after all, to look after his younger, more timid companion.

Dolnaraq continued to draw from foxes as well as human beings, and with each infusion, became less the freak and more the molt he had dreamed of becoming. Tresset became a molt as well, choosing the fierce mountain cats as his sustaining species. On occasion they came upon one of the wandering gypsy tribes that dotted the region in the early nineteen hundreds. Some of these clans were most receptive, having lodged reyaqc gypsies before, while other groups cursed them as werewolves or vampires, chasing them off with torches and shotguns. Neither of the pups cared much for these foul-smelling humans, but living briefly with a traveling clan offered a respite from the continuous grind to survive. It also gave Tresset a chance to question humans and learn of wars and strategies previously unknown.

In this manner they moved about Eastern Europe, from Siberia to Belarus, through Poland, and eventually into Germany, traveling about the northern parameter near the Baltic Sea, nearing cities and towns such as Rostock, Lubeck, and Kiel. This time was a transitional one for the humans, a time of growing industrialization and of political unrest, but the two young reyaqc cared little of this. They were not of the people. They were of themselves alone. None else mattered.

One night, as they prepared to hunt the streets of a tiny German village, the two decided to split one from the other. This was not uncommon. Nearly naked, and resembling beasts as much as they did men, they were prone to draw attention. At least separately they were less obvious, able to blend into the surroundings, to flee with no concern for the other. As well, should one be captured or injured, the other would still be free to initiate rescue. This had been Tresset's strategy. Even now that they had each seen over twenty winters, Tresset was still the strategist between them, though Tresset sometimes wondered if Dolnaraq was only allowing him to believe he was making the decisions. The younger molt was clever and occasionally devious. He was capable of certainly subtle manipulations. These two were close, emotionally. Closer even than siblings. Closer maybe even than lovers, though there was nothing sexual about the relationship. Theirs was simply a bond born from living a difficult and brutal life together, where, for over a decade, they had relied only on the other in matters of survival, where each knew everything about the other, confided all, and would risk all for that sole individual that actually mattered in this world.

"I'll be back first," said Dolnaraq as he inched to behind Tresset, a playful chide to his tone. They were at the tree line where the forest met the village.

Tresset turned. "Is that a challenge?" he asked, some humor to his tone.

There was a smug glint to Dolnaraq's eyes. "There's no challenge to it. I'm swifter. I'm smarter. I'll infuse and return before you even begin to decide on a human." Dolnaraq gave Tresset a playful nudge. "I'll even sweeten it into a wager. I'll give you a first go at the two females if you beat me back to this spot after infusing."

Tresset's heart quickened. "Two females?"

Dolnaraq nodded. "Two."

"Reyaqc females?"

"Of course reyaqc females," said Dolnaraq with a snort of indignation. "We're not going to mate with those foul smelling humans, I hope."

Tresset laughed. "Where are these females and why don't I know of them?" No wonder Dolnaraq had been acting so peculiar this evening, all full of energy and giggles. He'd likely known of this all day.

Dolnaraq shrugged. "I caught their sent while capturing our meal. They occupy a cabin in the forest about two miles east of the human village?"

"And there are no males?

"No scent of them."

"And no humans."

"No. Though they do dress as humans. The villagers likely think they're just an odd pare of sisters and leave them alone." Dolnaraq paused, cocked his head, and added, "Though I don't know why we're even talking about this. It's not as if you'd know what to do with a female if you found one." He laughed, giving Tresset a playful shove.

"Me!" said Tresset. "It's not as if you've mated either, you little pup!"

"Little! Apparently, you've never looked at your own reflection!"

Tresset laughed. "So says the tall and mighty. You're only two inches taller than me. And as to the females, I know exactly what to do."

"And that would be run!" laughed Dolnaraq.

At this, Tresset dove on Dolnaraq, catching him off guard. They both tumbled down a small grassy rise, laughing and tussling, slapping and grappling. These were to be their last carefree moments together.

*****

Tresset moved through narrow alleyways, keeping low and to the shadows. He was slight of frame and stature, yet lithe and agile, quick of movement to both strike and flee. The two females were on his mind and he was annoyed at how distracted he'd become. They'd led a solitary life since the demise of their pack, with only casual encounters with their own kind. But, females. Females! Alone, where no reyaqc males roamed. Was it possible that…?

Forget that. He needed to put this from his mind. He needed to focus on the task at hand. There were two human males ahead at an intersection. It was autumn of 1908, and both wore light overcoats and flannel caps to ward off the light drizzle and the seeping chill. They appeared to be in dispute. Tresset understood very little of the language, but their voices rose, each attempting to out-shout the other. They spat as they spoke and waved their arms in grand gestures of proclamation all the while reeking of the drink that inhibited their capacities. Tresset smelled the adrenaline surge and the alcohol seeping from their pores as each man struggled simply to remain upright. There were other smells as well—sewage and sex, meats and perfumes, horses and swine. All of the detestable odors of humanity. How foul they were, these "civilized" people.

Stuttering something about "Abigail's honor," the larger drunk took an off-balanced swing at his companion. The other sidestepped the clumsy blow, but tumbled to his rump nonetheless. The big one, apparently believing he'd knocked the man to the ground, proudly crossed his arms at his chest, smiled stupidly down upon the other, and spewed useless verbiage. The smaller man, still seated on the damp cobblestone, kicked his right foot from one side to the other, tripping his gloating companion and sending him tumbling down. They rolled about, wrestling and punching and cursing. Tresset spat at the humiliating display. Would he be forced to procure essence from these pathetic creatures? Was that his lot?

He supposed so. As dismal as these two might be, they were hidden away from the crowds, and in their current conditions, quite easy prey. As well, it had been nearly three weeks since Tresset had last received essence and he could feel the withering from within his limbs. His skin had become pale, nearly transparent, his features dull. Attack now, infuse the needed essence, then later, select another and then another, each with strong intellect and solid stature. Survive now. Thrive tomorrow.

Now, one of the drunks was on his knees, vomiting onto the deep red bricks, his belly retching, and his throat gagging as he expelled the foul contents of his stomach in violent, splattering surges. Tresset moved as quickly as a mountain cat, slashing this one across the neck with his short but lethal talons, mercifully eliminating his misery. Then, kicking him aside, he clutched the other in his hands, jerking him to an upright position, and glaring into the clouded and confused eyes. His face was puffy and unshaven, lined with the deepening crevasses of approaching age. His eyes were bloodshot, with lids hooded and droopy. His lips were large uneven flaps barely concealing rotted teeth. The human stared down at his companion as death throes caused the lifeless form to shudder and squirm in the rank pool of vomit and blood. The human winced as the bed of tiny hollow spines emerged from Tresset's right palm, penetrating the back of his neck even into the core of his spine.

The electric tingle of essence raced through Tresset's form, burning as it dispersed about his body. His vision blurred, becoming dark and red. His mind screamed a thousand different insanities as his muscles curled and cramped. The drunk shuddered and then vomited. Tresset pulled free of him, turning to stumble up the alleyway even as the now-unconscious man fell face-forward onto the unforgiving cobblestone, his two front teeth shattering upon impact.

The agonized molt fought for clarity of mind. This was the most dangerous time, just after the infusion, while he was disoriented and nearly incapacitated by his body's sporadic acceptance and rejection of the new essence. Tresset lurched as he made his way around a corner, righted himself and then staggered forward. A gas streetlamp flickered, sending flittering shadows across the moist stone surface. Tresset fought nausea, vertigo. He steadied himself with a flattened palm against a tiny brick home. His stomach buckled. He slumped to his knees, retched a dry heave. Then, clutching an iron fence, Tresset pulled himself upright. He could not allow himself to succumb this close to the still-warm bodies. Until he'd recovered, distance was his greatest defense.

Sounds tickled his ears: laughter, giggling, a carriage drawing nearer. He heard the snort of a horse, and his glossy eyes perceived a lumbering form making its way up the uneven avenue. The recessed doorway of a small home was to his right. Tresset nearly fell into the tiny space, obscuring himself from the passersby. He considered rising again, but his body offered only sporadic quivers at his best efforts. His head lulled to one side, connecting with the hard stone wall beside him with a subtle *thunk*. It was only now, slumped and weakened, that he realized the drizzle had become a downpour. Tresset closed his eyes. Just a few moments. Just enough time to gather his bearings. Then he'd reunite with Dolnaraq and they could be away from this foul-smelling place.

*****

Tresset awoke the next morning. The fresh smell of moisture hung in the air. Despite the cleansing rain of the night before, he could still smell the man's vomit on his chest. He snorted and gagged, wishing he could scour the skin from his own form. Blinking several times, he attempted to focus on his surroundings. It was early, the sun not yet inching above the eastern horizon. Few of the humans had yet to wander from their shelters. Tresset's muscles were still cramped. His head throbbed and it was an effort to pull his vision into focus. He listened to the sounds of the village, his ears twitching at approaching voices—only three thus far, and a carriage, possibly two, beyond that, the unnatural sound of a motorcar far in the distance.

He rose, tripping on the still-damp cobblestone, and then angled his head first to one side and then the other, listening to the sharp clattering pops and cracks of his bones seeking alignment. He extended each leg individually, working out the knots. A wave of vertigo washed over him and he nearly stumbled. His muscles still twitched and his innards turned and retched. Something within the drunken man's essence did not agree with his system. It wasn't the alcohol. That foul substance which humans used to purposely muddle their own capacities was not held within essence, and therefore not transferred. No, this was something at a more basic level—an inherited defect or disease. Tresset would need to infuse again soon, attempt to dilute this one's effect on the whole.

But first Dolnaraq.

It was nearly daylight and the two had yet to reconnect. Tresset sniffed the air, drew in the invisible particles floating about on the gentle breeze. All of the obvious odors were there—sewage, sweat, meat cooking, moss, livestock, decay. No Dolnaraq. The breeze was from the southeast. It was possible that Dolnaraq was downwind and thus obscured. But this made little sense. Downwind would mean Dolnaraq had spent the night in the heart of the village, for the forest was to the south. It would not make sense for the young molt to move north, deeper into the confines of humanity.

Tresset sniffed at the breeze, cocking his head, inhaling in quick, short snorts. His ears twitched at every sound. There was nothing on the air. No musky odor, no low growl or whispered message. No sense that Dolnaraq had been near to this place. Tresset staggered several steps up the rocky boulevard, moving northward, nose lifted to the breeze. Dolnaraq could not be far. The village was small. Surely Tresset would find him within minutes. Still, moving closer to the populace, especially in his weakened condition, seemed little wise in any strategic sense.

He paused, sniffed. His ears twitched. Voices. Panicked. Back from where he'd felled the drunks. Now doors opening and slamming shut. Racing footsteps. More shouts. The shrill sound of a metal whistle, then an authoritative voice barking commands. Additional voices. A female's shriek. A gun cocking. Multiple footsteps spreading out in each direction. He had become the hunted.

Tresset glanced in each direction. To the right. The narrow alleyway. None had yet entered there. He turned to flee, but his legs were still weak. His movement was slow, awkward. He staggered through the trash-strewn alleyway. How foul these humans. A mangy canine emerged from between two structures. It growled and yapped until Tresset swiped at it with his talons, nearly missing the beast in his unbalanced state. But he did connect. Not a lethal strike, but a wounding one, enough to cause the small gray creature to scurry off with a terrified whimper.

There were footsteps and then shouts from immediately behind. "*Der werwolf.*" Werewolf.

Tresset turned, growling deeply and baring his long sharp teeth. If they wanted werewolf, he could give them werewolf. In fact, it was often these myths that brought fear into the human limbs, weakening them, causing men to doubt their ability to slay this strange foe. They believed that only certain blessed elements could kill the were-beast, and so frequently fled when in truth they had the means to fell the molt where he stood.

Tresset charged, not giving the humans enough time to logic through the situation. No guns had yet been raised, and no fool leader had yet mustered the courage or the wit to realize that they outnumbered Tresset seven to one. His movements were still slow and awkward, but the space was confined. In less than two second's time he had clamped his jaw on the nearest man's throat, thrashing from side to side as his teeth sunk deeper into the flesh. Then, in one fierce move, he jerked his head back in a splay of red and pink, nearly half of the man's neck still hanging from between his clenched teeth.

Spitting the warm meat onto the street, Tresset swiped his talons, catching the nearest man across the left side of his pudgy round face. There were screams, shouts, curses, but no gunshots. The space was too close, the risk of striking their own too high. Tresset used the confusion to his advantage, growling like a beast, slashing, biting, not giving the mob a moment to organize. Already, two of the men fled, weeping like frightened females. They were cowards, but would draw the attention of others. Adrenaline surging, Tresset's earlier weakness was forgotten. He bit another man directly in the face, leaving his ample nose hanging only by a thin thread of flesh. Tresset leapt over a fallen man, barreled into another, and sprinted out of the alley and around the nearest corner. He fled three buildings south and darted onto another avenue and then ran down yet another road, all the while moving toward the nearby forest.

There were continued shouts and screams. The air was heavy with fear and anger. Tresset roared at the wide-eyed cowards emerging from their homes, and slashed at any in his path. Finally, a gunshot rang out. The bullet whizzed past his right ear almost before he heard the booming report. He dived to his left, snatched a young human male of perhaps sixteen winters, and held him as a shield before him. The boy whimpered and fouled himself almost immediately, but Tresset held him close, dragging the struggling youth toward his goal. The tree line was less than a block away. Once there, Tresset could easily flee and hide. This was his element. If the humans sought him there, he could kill them off one-by-one.

Reaching the end of the road, he considered slashing the boy's neck, but remembered his need for essence. The drunk's core had been bad. It was corrupting Tresset's being. He needed another infusion soon. Keeping the boy would embolden the villagers. No matter how fearful they were, they would be obligated to find the lost lad. Still, Tresset had little choice, and so, pulling the wailing youth along, he entered the forest.

Tresset sprinted through the woodland for nearly an hour, dragging the lad over branches and stones. He lost his grip twice, each time, scrambling after the panicked youth and terrifying him back into submission with his fierce appearance. Eventually, the boy wearied, and allowed Tresset to pull him along the still-moist ground with a minimum of resistance. What weaklings these humans could be. Their world dominance surely had far less to do with any great intellect than it did with their propensity to procreate in vast numbers. Tresset knew that even with his whimpering burden, the villagers would not be moving as quickly as he. They would realize that he was now in his own element and proceed with caution, first tending to their wounded, then arguing over strategy, then, finally forming search parties. But even this they would do only past sunup. These humans, they may have the wit and guile to create technical wonders such as guns and motorcars, but they were superstitious and feared the creatures of the dark more than any logic should dictate.

Tossing the lad to the ground, Tresset paused, sniffing the air, listening to the sounds of his element—rustling leaves, birds, the lapping of the nearby lake, a wolf tracking a rabbit off to the east. No, the villagers were not close. He had time to recoup, time to draw the needed essence from the shivering youth. Tresset squatted, lowering himself to where he could gaze at the young man face-to-face. The lad was dark of hair and light of complexion. His nose was a bit straight, but not large. His mouth was small, but his lips reasonably full. All of this was bordered by a round smooth face with virtually no angles or juts. The lad was not so much handsome as he was pretty.

The boy renewed his flagging whimpers as Tresset slowly reached around to the back of his neck, placing his palm there, inserting his bed of tiny needles into the spine, drawing essence from within. Once again, the burning tingle raced through his weary form as he closed his eyes and welcomed the essence with a gentle purr. Oh, how it stung. The glorious pain of it all. This youth was unsoiled, so unlike that pitiful drunk of the night before. His young, vibrant essence would renew Tresset; recreate him in some small fashion. Tresset would be fresh and pure, the corruption of the other, diminished by the new.

The boy shuddered and retched. Tresset pulled away. He had nearly taken too much. This one must live. Tresset must draw from him again and then again until all that had come the night before had been eradicated. Tresset laid the boy back onto a bed of golden leaves. He would sleep. He would heal. Perhaps in another day, two at the most, Tresset would draw from him again. And then, perhaps a third time as well. By then the boy would be weak and useless. Tresset would allow him to succumb then. But only then.

After drawing the essence, the familiar waves of vertigo rushed over him. But this made him smile. The lad's substance was being integrated into his being, battling for supremacy over that of the drunk. Leaning up against a large bent oak, Tresset closed his eyes, allowing his body to work its wondrous miracles of recreation as he rested.

*****

When Tresset awoke, it was to a curious itching on his arm, and his leg, and on his other arm. He found that there were small red sores about his form that itched and burned.

The drunk!

The drunk had had such sores.

Tresset hadn't thought of it at the time—had barely noticed it really. But, upon reflection, Tresset could remember one on the back of the man's right hand, and another just under his chin. What disease was this? What had this foul human done to Tresset?

The resting place was beside a small lake. Tresset raced into the icy green water, scrubbing at his own rubbery skin with a jagged stone, drawing blood as he scoured the offending sores from his form. Again and again, he scraped at the things, allowing the frigid water to rush over the wounds. But the burning, the itching would not go away. He was unclean. He was unclean!

Racing up the small muddy beach with an anguished roar, he made his way to the still unconscious youth. "You humans! You are diseased. You corrupt all that you touch."

The boy came awake with a start, and howled in fear at the sight of his captor. With the subtle pleas of, "*Bitte, bitte.*" Please, please. He attempted to scoot back out of the monster's reach. Tresset had no patience for either the screams or the weak attempt at escape. His only thought was to dilute the drunk's influence. His palm found the back of the boy's neck. He pulled the lad to his feet, pressing him against his breast. There was a soft, moist popping sound as Tresset's tiny hollow spines once again punctured the boy's skin. He drew essence, and continued to draw.

The boy's eyes glossed over into a hazy gray.

Tresset continued.

The boy drooled thick yellow mucus, his head lolling to one side.

Tresset still continued.

The boy lost consciousness, his eyes rolling back, his tongue extending.

Tresset still continued. His entire being burned, but he continued.

The boy gasped twice, and then stopped breathing, his form becoming limp and useless even as Tresset pressed him even closer against his own chest.

Still Tresset continued.

Finally, when he could remain upright no longer, he dropped the withered corpse into the shallow lakeside water and collapsed onto the ground, quivering and burning, still scratching at the offending sores.

He awoke beside the shimmering lake. The boy's body had been pulled away as the tide had come and gone. This was a pity. The youth would have made a tender meal. Tresset blinked. It was again nighttime. But which night? Had he simply slept through the evening, or all the way into the following day? He was confused, disoriented—and dirty. He felt such an incredible filth about his form. The sores were gone. Or, at least, they were no longer visible. But still he felt an amazing uncleanliness. His legs wobbly, his bearings skewed, he tossed himself into the lake and began scouring his own offensive form.

He spent days like this. Alone in the secluded forest. The villagers had never found him, nor had Dolnaraq appeared. Tresset simply spent his days bathing, scrubbing, wearing his skin away. But still he was unclean. He must be. There was just a sense of it.

Eventually he was forced to move on. The need for essence was upon him, and there was still Dolnaraq to consider. Where had his companion gone off to? Why hadn't the younger molt come searching for Tresset and found him in his lakeside hideaway?

Perhaps he had.

Perhaps Dolnaraq had stumbled across him while he was riddled with disease and decided it better to leave Tresset to his own agonies. Anger welled up in the young reyaqc. Indignation. A sense of ultimate betrayal.

But, no. Not yet. Find the pup first. Then determine his guilt. Perhaps he too had been infected by that foul village and feared revealing his own disfigurement to Tresset.

The reyaqc swooned, a sudden vertigo upon him. Essence. First essence, then Dolnaraq. Tresset clawed at his own skin, picked at invisible scabs. He was now and would always be, unclean.

Chapter Four

Dolnaraq had heard the shouts, the cries, the panicked bustle as the townsfolk discovered the murdered drunks. He'd been toward the east end of the village, having drawn essence from a finely dressed man who claimed to be *der rechtsanwalt*, an attorney. The slight man with the large mustache and even larger nose had pleaded for mercy, begged for forgiveness, confessed of sins with someone called Abigail, and offered to handle all of Dolnaraq's litigations. The young molt understood very little of this and simply silenced the annoying little man by drawing essence and leaving him slumped on a sofa.

Dolnaraq had then discovered the man's icebox, nearly empty but for a glass bottle partially filled with goat's milk and a red slab of meat neatly wrapped in white paper. Dolnaraq quickly consumed the cold bloody flesh, ripping at it with his sharp canines, and grunting with pleasure at the bittersweet taste of blood. Still weakened from the infusion of essence, Dolnaraq then curled up on the patch of rug under the small dining room table, resting as his body worked to incorporate that which the man had given.

The young molt awoke to the sounds of panicked villagers. "Tresset," he whispered as he rose. "Tresset."

Dolnaraq cocked his head back, sniffed the air, his ears rotated, turning from side-to-side, attuned to the chaotic sounds. Within seconds, the young molt had discerned the scene. Tresset had slain a man and fiercely wounded another. The bodies had been discovered, his companion pursued. Dolnaraq was still weak. His limbs were sore and his vision clouded, but he was not incapacitated. He'd been slow in drawing the essence of the man, cautious. Unlike Tresset, he was still able to function at near full capacity.

Bolting through the doorway, Dolnaraq sprinted toward the rising commotion. But he was not alone. Humans seemed to pour from every home, alerted by these same shouts of horror. Dolnaraq was quickly sighted and pursued.

As had Tresset, Dolnaraq scrambled one direction then another, weaving between buildings, clawing at anyone who approached. There were screams and curses, cries of *"der werwolf,"* but Dolnaraq ignored all of it. He was focused primarily on the scents of the village, on locating Tresset. As he neared the wooded border of the town, a man stepped before him, lean, gray-haired, with the thin line of a mustache on his upper lip. He was old, but not feeble. Bare-chested, his biceps rippled as he lifted a broad two-sided ax above his head and brought it down, missing Dolnaraq by only inches as the frightened molt dived to his left.

Dolnaraq was young, agile, accustomed to the fights of survival. Instinctively, he buried his long sharp canines into his attacker's calf, bringing the man to his knees with a painful howl. Another quick chomp and the jugular opened, splaying a red fountain on the approaching mob and giving the young molt the opportunity to scamper away unimpaired as his pursuers gasped in horror.

Tresset's scent was on the subtle breeze. It seemed he had made the forest. Dolnaraq smiled as he sprinted forward, darting into the green sanctuary, racing between limbs and stones as only one of the forest's true inhabitants could do. Small black birds fluttered to the sky and a lop-eared rabbit bounded out of the young molt's path. The scents and sounds of the village diminished to near nonexistent and Dolnaraq savored the fresh aroma of vegetation.

But there was another scent as well. A foul smell, and one too familiar. No villager could have raced ahead of him. None could possibly have outpaced him in his own environ. Then why did he once again smell the rank human odor?

A shot rang out. The molt was spun around and thrown to the ground, his face buried in the brush. His left shoulder burned with a fierce fire that traversed the entirety of his arm. There was blood. Too much blood. He tried to rise but his limbs betrayed him. There were voices, but not those from the village behind. These were from ahead. Two brightly dressed men emerged from the trees just to the right of center. One was large, burly, with a belly that hung well over his belt. His slit-like eyes were shaded by unusually bushy brows, and his entire face reddened with the exertion of the hunt. The other man, thin and slightly hunched, was much younger, perhaps just exiting his teens. His loose brown hair spilled over his face nearly to the tip of his nose, and his mouth hung open in surprise and fear.

The larger man lifted the shotgun midway up his chest, apparently contemplating another shot at Dolnaraq. They inched closer, cautiously, one step at a time. Step, pause, step, pause. All the while discussing what they should do with this unique kill. Dolnaraq attempted to speak, but it sounded mostly like a growl and the larger man hoisted his weapon to his shoulder as if to let off another shot.

Dolnaraq heard the villagers approaching from behind. Obviously so could the two men for they jabbered even more, the larger man pointing toward Dolnaraq, then further into the trees. The younger man shook his head, a look of sheer panic on his elongated face. But the older, heavier man prevailed, marching over to Dolnaraq and giving him a swift kick in the ribs, apparently in an effort to prove that the injured molt was no threat. He proceeded toward the sound of the villagers as the younger man crept forward, cautiously grasping Dolnaraq by the ankles and yanking him into a patch of heavy brush. Dolnaraq's eyes, fuzzy and gray, saw the dark trail of his own blood as he was pulled across the uneven ground, over a large jagged stone, and down a subtle grass-covered slope. He gasped, attempted to move one last time and then the darkness overcame him.

*****

Dolnaraq awoke in a cage. He was lying on straw, which carried the overpowering odor of an unfamiliar creature. The floor was of unfinished wood planking, coarse and uneven. There were metal bars across the two long sides of the pen, and the two shorter walls were of painted wood, white and red. The young reyaqc rolled onto his back. The entire upper left portion of his body ached and throbbed. He angled his head in that direction and found his shoulder and upper arm bandaged in dirty white wraps. He attempted to lift the arm but only succeeded in producing a fiery pain that raced from elbow to jaw. Cautiously, leaning upon his right elbow, he managed a sitting position. His eyes were still blurry and he blinked repeatedly. But his nose worked as well as ever and he inhaled the cacophony of odors about him: horses, mules, sawdust, oil, humans. Too many humans.

The sun was low in the western sky. Dolnaraq realized he'd been unconscious for most of the day. Tresset. What had become of Tresset? Dolnaraq was sure his companion had made the forest. Certainly, he'd been able to avoid the villagers. But what of these ones? The men who had taken Dolnaraq. Had they captured Tresset as well? Or worse. Perhaps Tresset had been slain rather than wounded and caged. Dolnaraq reclined, staring at the paint-chipped ceiling and sniffing at the cool evening breeze. There was no hint of his companion's scent. True, Tresset could be downwind, but if he'd been captured by this same lot, surely Dolnaraq would identify some hint of his scent.

No. Tresset was not here.

Dolnaraq smiled. Tresset was not here now, but he would be soon. He would come to rescue Dolnaraq. And when he did, the two would ruin the men who had shot and captured Dolnaraq. Their blood and flesh would taste very, very sweet.

*****

The night came, and with it, movement. There was much commotion, some hollering, shouting of orders, the clanking of iron upon iron, horses neighing, and a handful of motorcars starting their sputtering engines. The large-bellied man appeared just prior to the leaving. He stared appraisingly at the confused Dolnaraq, nodding his head and grunting his approval. Another man, one Dolnaraq had not seen before, approached only moments later. He was short of stature, wore soiled clothes in need of mending, and had round eyes that seemed to twinkle as he spoke. "Food for you, my young friend," he said as he slid a bowl of fatty meat and raw vegetables through a small slot at the base of the cage. "Food for you," he repeated with a nod and a smile. Dolnaraq understood fragments of the human language known as German, enough to comprehend this simple statement. But he did not move toward the offered meal. Rather, Dolnaraq stared at the man with a hate known only between captive and captor. Dolnaraq would slay this little man one day. He would slay him and make a meal of him. "Food for you, my young friend." Oh yes, food for Dolnaraq, but not such as this man could have dreamed.

Dolnaraq's cage was built on a flat-bedded cart and pulled by a single horse—an old gray and white beast with a sunken back and the odor of rotting teeth. The cage swayed and jerked with the movement causing the still-full bowl of slop to spill over onto the bare wooden floor. Dolnaraq felt the jolt of each bump and dip throughout the entirety of his left shoulder and neck. The pain would shoot directly into his head, nearly blinding him with piercing agony.

They traveled for three days in total, but only this one time during the dark hours. Dolnaraq surmised that perhaps they were attempting to sneak from the nearby village where Tresset and he had hunted. This led him to conclude that they were hiding him, that for whatever reason, these humans did not want the other humans to know they'd captured the young molt.

When finally the procession stopped, it was in a large grassy area on the outskirts of another small village. There was an immediate buzz of activity as the many human workers assembled booths and gadgets, stocking flimsy shelves with brightly colored toys and candies. A beast, much larger than Dolnaraq ever dreamed possible, was roped off with a simple stake just a few feet from Dolnaraq's cage. The creature had dumb black eyes, floppy ears three times the size of a falcon's wingspan, tree trunk-like limbs, and a long gray snout that writhed like a snake. The brute surely had the strength to free itself by wrenching the puny wooden stake from the ground. But, why then, did it remain a captor? This made no sense to the pained reyaqc.

Once the general commotion had slowed to occasional shouts and curses, the small man with the worn clothing and the twinkling eyes again visited Dolnaraq. As before, he slid food through the opening at the base of the cage. "Eat, my friend. You must remain strong." Dolnaraq did eat, but he felt anything but strong. His shoulder still shot with blinding bursts of pain. The thought that Tresset would rescue him heartened him some, but even this seemed a foolish hope. The group had traveled many miles; there were numerous beasts and humans in the company. Tresset could easily lose Dolnaraq's scent in the foul-smelling blend. But Tresset would find him. He knew Tresset would do this. For surely, he would do the same for Tresset.

The big burley man with the slits for eyes came by as the sun inched toward the final quarter of its daily journey. He grunted and nodded, then barked orders to a young worker tending the huge gray beast. The youth nodded and ran off to Dolnaraq's left. The big man smiled and then nodded again, mumbling something to Dolnaraq, though the molt did not catch the meaning. He then ambled away, apparently quite satisfied with himself. Dolnaraq would be quite satisfied when he opened the fat man's bowels and spilled his innards onto the shiny green grass.

The young man returned with four buckets of water—two wire handles in each hand. Setting all four of his sloshing metal burdens on the grass, he then lifted one of these, approached the cage with a sly grin, and tossed the water directly at the surprised reyaqc, striking Dolnaraq squarely in the chest. Dolnaraq howled in protest, shaking his head furiously and hammering his palms in a staccato drum roll against the grainy floorboards. But the boy repeated the process, only this time, knowing what was coming, Dolnaraq dodged the throw and the water splashed uselessly onto Dolnaraq's sleeping area. Another quick splash to the right torso and Dolnaraq charged the bars of his cage causing the entire structure to shudder and creak, though the bars remained true and Dolnaraq stumbled backward in renewed agony as the fourth cascade doused him in the face.

The boy laughed and hopped about, pointing at Dolnaraq. But there came a voice from beyond the youth. "Boy, what do you do?" said the little man with the twinkling eyes. "Leave this one be."

"Wilhelm said it must be bathed," protested the youth.

"So you decided to make a sport of it?" shot the other. "Besides, this poor creature is still injured. You increase the chance of infection if you dampen the wound."

Dolnaraq comprehended only a portion of this exchange, but he vaguely understood that the older human was chastising the younger for his treatment of Dolnaraq. How small this man's mind must be. Did he treat Dolnaraq any better by being party to his capture and imprisonment?

This small dirty man then made his way to the cage. "My apologies to you, my young friend. The youth bears the stupidity of a poor upbringing. Perhaps I can get you a towel."

But the man had wandered too close to the cage and with too little caution. Charging the iron bars, Dolnaraq shot his right arm between these, slashing furiously at the man and ripping his left cheek. Dolnaraq did not have claws such as Tresset did. His sustaining species was the fox, and thus he had dark curved nails at the ends of his fingers, not talons. But these were enough to slice the flesh, enough to wound and rip. The man stumbled away from the cage with a yelp.

Dolnaraq glared at the injured man, eagerly licked droplets of blood from his fingers. The man glanced back, appalled, and then staggered away to tend to his wound.

*****

The night was horrifying.

Dolnaraq's cage was moved to a sawdust walkway lined with booths and mindless attractions. He had not noticed these before, but at the top of each side of the cage were rolled curtains which were now released to fall down before the bars, enclosing the confused reyaqc in near darkness. There was much commotion, hurrying about, shouts and curses as the crew rushed one way and then another in final preparation for, "the opening." Whatever that was.

Soon there were new sounds, new scents. Dozens upon dozens of unfamiliar humans crowded into the area—children hooting, females giggling, and men boasting and cursing. There was the strange sound of mechanical music warbling through the air. All the livestock became agitated. Dolnaraq could smell their heightened perspiration even in his shrouded pen. There were the pops of what seemed to be small guns, the creaking and protesting of machinery, and the smell of sweet foods wafted about the breeze. Two young males raced past, then paused, jabbering between themselves. One approached the cage, cautiously lifting the corner of the drape to peek inside. There was a shout, the voice of the obese slit-eyed man. The two children raced away squealing with mirth as the man who'd shot and captured Dolnaraq cursed and spat.

Soon a crowd collected near Dolnaraq's cage. There were mutters and whispers, talk of a scam and a phony. Then the slit-eyed man hollered above the crowd, quieting them. "Tonight," he said in a grand and husky voice. "Tonight, you will see something amazing, something raw, some-thing few human eyes have ever witnessed. You've heard rumors of lycanthropy, of men who turn to wolf. But you believe these to be folly, the foolish talk of the simpleminded. But, tonight! Tonight, you face the truth. For the first time ever, a true werewolf has been captured and caged. Tonight, for your pleasure, I present—the wolf boy!"

As the curtain rose, Dolnaraq was already pacing the length of his cage, his random tufts of fur on end, his nostrils flaring with the unfamil-iar scents, his ears twitching to the multitude of sounds. There were gasps and whispers. A young mother drew her two small children close and backed away from the cage in fear. A bearded man raised a bottle of golden liquid above his head, hooting and cheering. Dolnaraq was confused, frightened. Why were these people here? What did they want of him? Did they plan to make him their evening meal? Dolnaraq under-stood some of what the slit-eyed man said. He'd mistakenly referred to Dolnaraq as a wolf. He'd said Dolnaraq was here for their pleasure. What pleasure could that be? The hunt? No. Dolnaraq was already captured. But, consumption. They would take pleasure in consuming Dolnaraq, for surely he would take pleasure in consuming them.

In a rage of fright and anger, Dolnaraq growled, racing to and fro about his cage, swiping at the air with his curled fingers, cocking his head this way and that at the scents and sounds. The crowd applauded, but Dolnaraq did not understand this flurry of sound. Becoming more fearful yet, he found the sudden need to make water. The slit-eyed man stood just two feet in front of the cage, staring at the mesmerized crowd, nodding and grinning, so very pleased at what he'd done.

There was laughter and hooting as the slit-eyed man cursed and stumbled over his own clumsy feet in an effort to escape Dolnaraq's golden stream. His face red, his lungs heaving, the bulky man struggled to his feet, stumbling again and nearly knocking an old toothless woman to the sawdust ground. The crowd laughed some more. One man cried, "A toast to the werewolf!" Another responded, "I think he already toasted that fat carnie!" More laughter. More curses from the slit-eyed man. And the curtains suddenly fell, plunging Dolnaraq into darkness and causing the crowd to boo and hiss.

*****

Morning came and Dolnaraq had slept very little. The slit-eyed man, still reeking of Dolnaraq's scent, ordered the "wolf boy" to go hungry. Apparently, this was retribution against Dolnaraq's insult to his dignity. But Dolnaraq was not hungry and therefore did not miss the food. He was agitated, confused. What was the purpose of the crowd? What had they expected of him? He still wondered if he'd been an intended meal, and that only his attack—however flimsy and ineffective—on the slit-eyed man had delayed the feast. The sun was just inching over the horizon when Dolnaraq finally felt his eyelids becoming heavy and his limbs weak. Moving to the corner of his cage, he used his feet to scoot some straw together into a pile, and then lowered himself to the floor with a despondent moan. He understood so little of his situation and wished Tresset were here to guide him through this strange circumstance.

The cat was there when he awoke. It was nestled beside him, under the crook of his arm. Orange-brown in color, it bore alternating dark and light stripes. Its eyes were wide and green, and its paws a snowy white. Dolnaraq snorted at the creature, but the thing simply meowed and nestled closer yet. Dolnaraq considered slaying it outright, but was not yet hungry enough to bother. He was sleepy and the feline was simply not that interesting. He fell back into slumber, allowing the diminutive creature to remain.

The cat was still there three hours later when Dolnaraq awakened to the sound of the twinkle-eyed man. The small human wore gauze on his left cheek as a result of Dolnaraq's attack. But this had not altered his manner toward the reyaqc. "Good day, my young friend," he said as he arrived with a meager bowl of food. "It seems you've gained a new companion in the night." The man smiled and cooed at the cat and generally played the fool in his attempt coax the creature to him. Finally sliding the food through the small slot in the cage, the man said. "You embarrassed Wilhelm last night. He's been storming around the place ever since, cursing you and promising to kill you the first chance he gets. Don't worry. You've made him more money in one night than he normally sees in a week. He won't be harming you again, I'll promise you that." Then the little man leaned forward with a sly wink. "Only next time, please wait till I'm nearby before you piss on the big buffoon. I'd really liked to have seen that."

*****

The days fell into a dull routine. The little man, whose name Dolnaraq learned was Oskar, would bring food and chat for a few minutes about the happenings of the day. The cat became a permanent resident of the cage. It ran off from time to time, sometimes returning with a slain rat or sparrow clasped tightly within its jaws, but always it nestled beside Dolnaraq in the long cool nights. Dolnaraq had never understood the human propensity to keep pets, but he did find a certain comfort in having the curious little thing around.

After several days, each of which featured daily "performances" offering Dolnaraq up as a spectacle before an amused and skeptical audience, the carnival moved on to yet another village. Dolnaraq was agitated and restless. He had not been allowed out of his cage since capture and his muscles grew stiff and weak. Though Oskar would reach in with a rake each day and pull away waste, often slipping new straw into the space, and sometimes dousing offensive stains with water, the cage still became rank with the odors of Dolnaraq's own existence. After moving on to yet another town and yet another week's performances, Dolnaraq felt a familiar withering from within. It was rapidly approaching the time for another infusion. He now spent his days curled in a ball at the center of his cage, shivering and gasping, his skin becoming nearly transparent and taking on a bluish tone.

"You are ill, my friend. What is wrong?" asked Oskar one brisk morning as he set Dolnaraq's food dish aside and gazed in at his charge.

Dolnaraq's heavy eyes fluttered open. He stared at the concerned face just five feet away and knew he had not the energy to traverse the space. "Essence," he moaned in a hushed growl. "Essence."

Oskar's eyes widened. Dolnaraq had yet to speak since capture. "Why, you are full of surprises, aren't you?" The man moved closer, right up against the cold metal bars, probably for the first time since Dolnaraq had swiped at him. "What is that you're saying, now?"

"Essence," moaned Dolnaraq. At the sound, the cat purred and leaned against the feeble reyaqc's stomach as if to lend support.

43

"I'm sorry, my young friend. I do not understand," said Oskar.

Dolnaraq didn't know where the energy came from, perhaps sheer survival instinct alone, but in that moment he leapt forward catching the startled handler at the base of the skull, pulling him forward, and drawing deeply from him. Oskar stared questioningly into Dolnaraq's vacant white eyes, a look of fear and perplexity creasing his genial features. The caretaker's green eyes, normally so lively and bright, became dull and hazy. His jaw went slack. His form twitched then lurched. Dolnaraq released the limp figure, allowing the man to slump into a heap beside the cage. He then retreated into a corner, Oskar's essence burning as it raced through his body, renewing, reshaping, rebuilding.

Chapter Five

The rabbit was deft, agile, swift of foot, and Tresset was burdened with an ever-depleted form. Several weeks now, and still he felt the effects of the tainted essence. No sores could be seen—none besides the self-inflicted scratches as Tresset continually scraped rocks against his skin in an effort to purge his system—but still, the taint remained. It had become a part of him, a piece of his makeup. And so Tresset had come to despair his existence.

The reyaqc require—first and foremost—human essence. Their form is essentially human, their internal organs similar, their intellect comparable. None are certain of the reyaqc's origin; some say they are the product of unions between human females and demons, others claim they are a gross mutation; others, the next evolutionary step toward perfection. Regardless, it is safe to assume that there is some past human connection. But Tresset had forsaken human essence. He'd come to despise the need, to view it as inherently corrupt, and so refused to instill his system with this central component. Mountain cats, his sustaining species, were rare in this area and so he'd taken to infusing from simple house cats. The feline essence was similar enough that he had not suffered too greatly from incompatibility, but his body ached for the human component.

And so, as Tresset leaped at the rabbit, a simple feat, a near-mindless kill, his legs betrayed him. He fell far short of his mark as the frightened creature bolted from view, never to be found again. Tresset cursed and rolled onto his back. His stomach growled in protest. It had been six days since last he'd tasted meat. He thought again of Dolnaraq. Why had they not yet connected? Why was he not here in Tresset's time of need?

The molt's eyes fluttered in a vain attempt at focus. He sought to rise from his grassy bed, but found his limbs too weak. Better to rest. Later, food. Later, essence. Later, Dolnaraq.

*****

Tresset awoke to the smell of roasted boar over a crackling campfire. There were voices, laughter, the clanking of pots and pans, the mingled odors of both human and reyaqc.

Gypsies, or, Romani as they often liked to be called.

Tresset blinked.

The sky wavered.

Blink, blink. No, not the sky, canvass. A tent.

A lantern sat at the far end, its flame dancing about, creating spirit-like shadows upon the uneven fabric.

Now there was a face before him—young, female, dark of eyes and hair. Human. The young woman turned to her right. "He wakes," she said with a suppressed giggle. The girl could not have seen more than seventeen winters.

Another form appeared beyond the girl. Male, nearly elderly. Clothed in colorful gypsy garb. His milk white eyes glowed eerily in the flickering lamplight. A reyaqc.

"I am called Jisch." He spoke in the Russian tongue, one much more familiar to Tresset than German, though why this one did not utter the reyaqc's own language, Tresset could only guess.

"Human…lover," managed Tresset, though still he was weak from lack of food and essence. Even the simple act of forming syllables seemed an effort.

Jisch chuckled. "Perhaps. But this human lover is likely the sole reason you yet live." The reyaqc moved closer as the young woman scooted slightly to her left. "You are well depleted, young one. Far too much animal essence. How long since last you drew from a human source?"

Tresset stared at him, contempt in his gaze. He remained silent.

Jisch sighed. "I suppose that is an unnecessary question. The point is, if you are to live, you must infuse. And this you must do quickly." The senior reyaqc turned to his right, signaled to a young human male who had just entered the tent: tall, lean, a wry grin and intelligent eyes. "This is Carman. He is a willing giver."

"No," managed Tresset.

But Jisch paid him no mind. The young human stepped forward, kneeling beside Tresset. Jisch lifted Tresset's right arm. The young molt struggled against him, but all strength had fled. He had no recourse. Jisch placed Tresset's palm at the back of Carman's neck. The process was instinctual. Tresset could not will the needlelike spines to remain hidden within his palm. Not when the need was so great. There was a surge of heat as the young gypsy's essence flowed through Tresset's hand, down his arm, and into his core. Tresset's eyes went wide. His vision blurred. And unconsciousness took him yet again.

*****

The young human girl was there when he awoke. Her name was Lyuba, and she had volunteered to minister to the ailing reyaqc.

"It was I who discovered you," she said with a playful smile. "You seemed as dead, but Jisch concluded you could yet be saved." She dipped a rough cloth in a basin of water, withdrew it, and squeezed the excess fluid away. "Such a handsome one. It would have been a shame to lose you."

"Dol…naraq," muttered Tresset. "Have you found Dolnaraq?"

The girl seemed perplexed. "Dolnaraq? Is this another of your kind? Is he of your pack?"

"He is…my pack."

Lyuba nodded and patted Tresset's forehead with the damp cloth. "This one, we have not seen. Was he with you before you fell ill?"

Tresset shook his head. Already the human stench threatened to overcome him. "No. Have not seen in…long while. Lost. Separated."

Lyuba pushed a wavy lock from before her deep brown eyes. "I will ask Jisch and the others of your kind. If there is word of this Dolnaraq, I will let you know."

With that, she leaned forward, kissing him lightly on the forehead. Revulsion welled up within him as she rose, saying, "Now, rest, precious one. Rest and recover."

*****

Lyuba became Tresset's constant companion. Though her presence repulsed him, he found a certain comfort in her tender care, in her willingness to nurse him back to health. He was weak, much weaker than he first realized. And only after two weeks with the gypsy clan did he acknowledge how close to death he had come. The girl, though, concerned him at a deeper level. She was attracted to him. Tresset could tell this, not only by her constant and nonsensical attentions toward him, but also by the distinct odor of her sex as she became aroused. True, some reyaqc coupled with humans. The practice was not common, but neither was it forbidden. Offspring could not be produced, and for some reason this attracted certain human females. Still, Tresset wanted nothing of the humans, least of all further intimacies beyond the already degrading need for essence. And thus, he did his best to avoid the girl whenever he sensed the scent of her arousal on the evening breeze.

48

"You brood," said Lyuba one day as she came upon Tresset sitting atop a large boulder and staring out over the green expanse.

Tresset nodded and grunted. He'd hoped to avoid her by venturing away from the camp.

"I'm not quite as agile as you. May I have a hand up?"

The girl stood at the base of the stone, smiling up at him as she extended her hand. Tresset silently cursed as he reached down to draw her up. Could he never be rid of this one?

Lyuba scrambled up the rock and then seated herself to Tresset's right, nearly so close as to touch him, but not quite. "It's a nice view," she offered.

"I suppose," agreed the reyaqc.

"I paint landscapes. I think I'll paint this one. It's pretty."

Tresset did not respond.

"You're a quiet one."

Tresset glanced at her, still annoyed at the intrusion. "I have nothing to say."

"I was engaged to be married, you know. But the boy's family ran into problems with a town official. There was some trouble. It seemed best that they separate from the clan in order that suspicions not fall over our entire community."

Tresset snorted. "Gypsies always have trouble with law. What's so different about this one?"

Lyuba stiffened, perhaps taking some offence. "The *Romani* are good people, only misunderstood—like the reyaqc."

"You are not like the reyaqc."

The girl shrugged. "Maybe no. Maybe yes. And you, do you have a mate?"

"The reyaqc do not mate for life. It is…a different arrangement."

"But, have you mated? Is there a reyaqc woman who bares you children?"

Tresset rose. He'd grown tired of the conversation. "No woman. No children. My pack was decimated when I was a pup. Only Dolnaraq and I remain." With that he leaped from the stone and made his way into the brush, the scent of Lyuba's arousal lingering in his nostrils.

*****

The rape occurred four weeks into Tresset's stay with the Romani clan.

Tresset could not say why he intervened. The human girl meant nothing to him. At best, he tolerated her, at worst she repulsed him. But despite his hatred of humans, Lyuba had been kind to him, had tended his needs, had even cleaned him when, in the first days, he'd fouled himself.

The clan had settled on the outskirts of a small German village where they would remain for five or six days, selling their wares, entertaining with song and dance, reading palms, and generally profiting from the townsfolk. Three young human males, each perhaps in his late teens or early twenties, found their way into the camp on the third evening. The air was brisk and clear, a three-quarter moon illuminated the ground. Lyuba, despite Tresset's revulsion, was stunningly beautiful and habitually flirtatious.

They cornered her toward the eastern edge of the camp and, when she spurned their gross and overt advances, dragged her beyond the tree line. Tresset had just excused himself from the campfire where he'd discussed with Jisch and two young reyaqc females, the missing Dolnaraq. He was in a state of turmoil. His lifelong companion had seemingly vanished and here he sat among humans and human-loving reyaqc, both of which he despised. And yet they had each, human and reyaqc, shown him a kindness he'd never encountered among those more like himself. Worse, he'd come to realize that he could become complacent here, perhaps even comfortable. Tresset kicked the dusty ground. Cursed. Growled. He did not belong here, and yet he found himself unwilling to disappear into the night as he knew he should.

The scent assaulted him like boiling water splashed his face—adrenaline, testosterone, lust, fear. Lyuba's cry was stifled, but Tresset's catlike ears were keen. Instinctively, he loped toward the tree line.

Why?

She was a human. Miserable. Repulsive. By all logic he should let her be. What was she to him? Cattle. Nothing more.

But she had cared for him, nursed him back to health. She had stroked his face, brought him water. She'd shown him affection unlike any he'd yet known on this earth.

Foolish thoughts. She was human. Nothing more mattered.

Yet still, heedless of all logic, he moved to intervene.

Tresset found Lyuba pinned to the uneven ground, a dirty cloth shoved deep into her mouth, one assailant holding her arms, another her legs, her dress torn away, heaving breasts exposed, her legs spread wide to allow the third male access to her most private parts. Tresset extended his retractable claws, first pulling the lanky youth from between the girl's quivering legs and castrating him with two deft swipes before opening his belly and turning to the dying lad's startled companions. These, he disposed of with brutal finality.

In all, the strike lasted less than a minute. It took far longer to disengage the hysterical Lyuba as she clung to him, arms wrapped tightly about his neck, her face buried in his chest, her tears dripping onto his taut and bloodied belly.

"You came for me." Her words were broken by sobs as her form shuddered in the aftermath of the horror. "You came." She kissed him on the chest once, twice, pressing herself into him. Tresset sought to pull away—her human stench was near overpowering—but she clung to him all the more. At some point, he relented, hesitantly wrapping his arms about her shuddering form, attempting to comfort her. This was not affection, but rather a realization that only in this way could he calm her sufficiently that she would eventually release him.

"Tresset, Thank you. Thank you."

Another kiss, this one on the cheek. Tresset suppressed the bile rising in his throat.

The Romani clan was forced to pick up camp and move along quickly. They could not risk the village's scrutiny once the three lads were discovered missing.

If Lyuba had pestered Tresset before, she now harassed him tirelessly. Her injuries had been minor, but the rape had been consummated. Tresset had saved her life but not her honor. The young reyaqc had never understood the human fixation with sexual protocol. Sex was the most basic of biological functions and necessary for the continuation of the species, and yet complex rules and traditions clouded the simple issue. As to the Romani, they value virginity in a young woman above all else. Lyuba was now marked. It was unlikely that any amongst the clan would allow a son to marry one so defiled. This, despite the fact that she was a healthy specimen from good stock and likely capable of producing multiple offspring.

"We could be married, you and I," she said one night as she found Tresset returning from a romp in the woods.

"You know well, reyaqc do not marry," he said, turning away from her.

"But, you care for me. I can see it. You may not know it yourself, but you do."

Tresset remained silent. There was no use arguing this nonsensical point.

"You are alone, your one companion gone from you. I am now tainted in the eyes of my people. But we have each other."

Tresset turned toward her, anger rising in his veins. "We do not have each other. You at least have a family and I have...myself."

"Family?" the girl suddenly became furious. "Family? My father was too drunk to prevent the rape, and now he scorns me as if it was I who committed the act. My mother won't even meet my gaze. Everywhere I go, whispers, smirks. But, you..." She grabbed his arm, cradling it, hugging him even as he fought the urge to rip her face from her head. "You cared enough to come for me. No one else cared, but you. And now that I am unclean, it seems you are the only one to care."

"I...do not care."

She gazed at him at length, a peculiar twist to her lips. "Of course you do," she said finally. "I think it's time I prove it to you." She gave him a quick peck on the cheek. "I'll be in my tent—alone—soon after sunset. Come to me."

A firm hug, a wan smile, and she moved back toward the camp.

The smell of her sex lingered on the subtle breeze.

*****

Tresset did not go to Lyuba's tent that evening, but as had become his habit, bedded down amidst the trees at the outskirt of the camp. He did not feel comfortable indoors. Even the thin canvas tents incited some small claustrophobia in the often endless nights. And sleep was now deep, near deathlike, since he'd foolishly allowed himself to become so depleted. No more was he so attuned to his surroundings as he'd once been. No longer did the wisp of a scent invade his dreams and wake him to impending danger. True, these traits would return—with time, with multiple infusions—but at this point, on this clear star-filled night, he slept as the dead.

At first it seemed a dream. Lyuba's scent. Her arousal. But then, still dreamlike, it became something more. There was a tension in his loins, a tingling. Pleasant. Stirring. An unfamiliar warmth. Moist. Enticing. There was a subtle friction, rhythmic, pure. A building of glorious pressure.

And then he was awake.

And she was there, atop him, naked, straddling his pelvis, her hips in constant motion.

She giggled. "We are now mated, you and I. You the husband, I the wife. We'll have a ceremony. There will be no shame. No..."

The realization that she was defiling him came as a rush of anger and revulsion. Hissing deep within his throat, he released his claws, swiping right to left with such ferocity that he nearly detached the girl's head from her form. Enraged, he allowed the corpse to fall to the grassy ground as he leaped to his feet, screeching, scraping at invisible sores, his entire form itching and burning anew. Diseased. Diseased! The human contact had ruined him, damned him.

Hearing the commotion, someone moved forward from the camp proper, Jisch, the elderly reyaqc. Tresset's claws found his belly, twisted, pressed deeper. Jisch fell with a bewildered gaze in his salt-colored eyes. Another form in the shadows—human. Tresset did not hesitate, but bounded forward, slashing, growling, hissing. In all, seven members of the clan would fall before finally Tresset loped off into the forest where he would spend two weeks lying in a narrow river, scraping at sores that could not be seen. Only one thought held him to within a hair's width of sanity—Dolnaraq. Out there somewhere, Dolnaraq.

Chapter Six

When Dolnaraq awoke, Oskar was gone but the cat remained. The reyaqc's muscles were of knots and twists and his stomach protested in waves of nausea. But Dolnaraq's mind was clear. He remembered the incident, the taking of essence, the shocked and fearful expression on the little man's face, an expression aghast at the betrayal of a friend. Dolnaraq felt glum, but couldn't fathom quite why this mood had overtaken him. The man meant nothing to him. If he truly respected Dolnaraq at all, he would have freed him weeks ago. There was no bond, no friendship, regardless of how the simple man chose to address him.

The skinny young man who had accompanied Wilhelm on the day of Dolnaraq's capture brought his food dish for the next several days. The young lad, his dark brown hair perpetually flopping before his eyes, would rush forward in a hunched trot, slip the metal tray into the slot with a quick push, and then race away before Dolnaraq could move to within reach. More than once the young man became tangled in his own lengthy limbs and stumbled to the ground during the process, once spilling Dolnaraq's dish. The reyaqc went hungry that day.

The cat remained. He would nestle with Dolnaraq and then stroll away to a corner of the cage he'd claimed for his own. Dolnaraq allowed it this freedom and twice actually petted the thing. Its fur was soft, silky, much like the thinning fox hair that Dolnaraq bore in tufts about his own form. Dolnaraq considered infusing from the cat, but knew the danger of introducing yet another species into his mix. Human and one animal breed—that was the limit. One might attempt an infusion from similar breed, especially if most of the original essence was depleted, but even this was risky. Others had attempted drawing from more diverse species. Most had perished for their efforts. The few who survived risked becoming as imbeciles and lunatics, babbling and pawing, losing all power of reason and purpose.

*****

Oskar returned on the day Dolnaraq slew the cat. The creature had been irritable that day. Dolnaraq understood very little of feline behavior and only knew that the thing had become a pest. It raced back and forth across the cage, sometimes lunging at the flies that populated the space. It screeched for no apparent reason and would not leave Dolnaraq to peace or solitude. Finally, the slim creature leaped into Dolnaraq's lap, and, seeming to settle, curled up as if to sleep. The bemused reyaqc gazed down at the huddled ball of fur, the hint of a smile on his narrow lips. Just as he stroked the silky fur for the first time, the cat hissed and scratched Dolnaraq's forearm with its extended claws. Dolnaraq was quick, snatching the cat up and biting deeply into its neck. Blood splattered into Dolnaraq's left eye and oozed down his chest. Dolnaraq had not planned on slaying the little nuisance, but had acted on instinct alone. Now the thing was dead and there was nothing else to do but to consume the carcass. It had been long weeks since Dolnaraq had had truly fresh meat and he wondered why he hadn't thought to devour the cat sooner.

It was during this meal that Oskar returned. "Oh, no, no, no, my young friend. This is not right. We must talk, you and I."

Dolnaraq tore another piece of hindquarter free and chewed.

"What are you, my friend? I know you are not a werewolf as Wilhelm proclaims. But what are you, really?"

Dolnaraq cocked his head. The man was addressing him as one human would address another.

"You do understand me?" ventured Oskar as Dolnaraq spit fur from his mouth then swallowed a tough length of flesh.

Dolnaraq stared at the man. His grasp of the German language had increased with his time at the carnival and he comprehended most of what Oskar said. "You say it is wrong that I eat the cat. Why?" Dolnaraq's words were slow, some of his pronunciations poor, but his sentence was coherent.

Despite the bloody scene before him, Oskar managed a wry smile at the first true sentence uttered by Dolnaraq in his presence. "The cat was...not for eating," he replied, obviously a bit dumbfounded by the question.

"You bring me meat every day. You consume meat yourself. Why was this meat forbidden?"

"The cat was your friend, your companion."

"I did not ask for a companion."

"True, but often we do not have the luxury to choose our companions. We must make do with those we are given. Often we find camaraderie where none was expected."

Dolnaraq tore free another length of flesh. He had no reply to this.

Despite the grizzly scene, despite the recent attack on him by Dolnaraq, Oskar stepped closer, his eyes narrowing, his lips pursing into a peculiar frown. "Your face has changed. It looks..." he stammered, apparently formulating the thought even as he spoke. "It looks familiar, rather like... My young friend, what did you do to me? I thought that I would die."

"You might have," offered Dolnaraq between bites.

"But your face, in some small way... No. I am delusional. Forgive me."

With that, the little man shook his head as if in confusion, then turned and ambled silently away. This was fine with Dolnaraq. He was still eating.

*****

Oskar returned two days later, in his arms he held three tattered and worn books. He set these on the dusty ground, held up one finger indicating that Dolnaraq should wait, disappeared around a corner, and then returned with a short gray metal stool. Seating himself on the stool beside the books, he said, "It is time you made some progress."

Dolnaraq was leaning against one of the two wooden walls of his cage thinking of his carefree times with Tresset and wondering if the two would ever reunite. He cared little for what the man was saying.

"I suppose," said Oskar. "That we should begin with names. Mine, as I'm sure you know, is Oskar. What is yours?"

Dolnaraq stared at the opposite wall.

"What do you call yourself?"

Silence.

Oskar sighed. "All right, then I suppose it best that I myself give you a name. In youth I had a dear friend named Otto. I believe I will call you Otto."

Dolnaraq picked a piece of rotting flesh from between two teeth and flicked it across the cage.

"Now…Otto. If you are ever to live beyond the confines of a cage, you must be civilized. We cannot have you behaving like an animal."

Dolnaraq lulled his head in Oskar's direction. "I am not an animal."

"No, I don't believe you are. The very fact that we can converse attests to that fact."

"Still I am caged like an animal."

Oskar sighed. "Wilhelm thinks you a beast. He also seeks to become rich by owning you."

"And you? You could free me and yet you do not."

58

"You…" Oskar hesitated, apparently searching for words. "You are a threat," he said finally. "I sense a fine intellect, but you behave as a beast. You have attacked me twice since your arrival. On the morning of your capture, you had apparently slain several people in the nearby village. The attacks were savage—animalistic. Wilhelm lied to the villagers, convincing them that he had slain the werewolf. Otherwise, they surely would have tracked you down and slain you. I cannot, in good conscience, release you while I still believe you would behave as such."

Dolnaraq stared at the chipped paint of the wall before him, not meeting Oskar's gaze, not responding to the statements. Apparently the villagers believed there had been only one "werewolf." Good, perhaps Tresset had escaped.

After several moments, Oskar reached down and selected a pale blue book and dusted it off with a few swipes of his palm. "Language, Otto. I believe it best that we begin with language."

These sessions became a routine. Each day Oskar arrived with his armload of books, settled on his creaky little stool, opened a book, and began his lesson. At the onset, Dolnaraq responded to very little the man had to say. He simply leaned against the wall of his cage, picked at fleas, and listened as the man droned on. For all appearances, it was a wasted effort on the part of the man. But Dolnaraq was listening; he was allowing the words to penetrate his sharp and curious mind. Eventually, his resolve softened and he began repeating words given to him by Oskar and even conjugating sentences aloud. The spoken word held little difficulty for Dolnaraq. He already spoke the native tongue of the reyaqc, a fair smattering of Russian, and now German. But the written word was a peculiar and mysterious thing. The first time that Oskar passed a book through the bars and asked Dolnaraq to read, the reyaqc stared dumbly at the thing, then to Oskar's horror, ripped the pages free, allowing them to litter the floor beside him.

"No, no, no!" cried the man. "A book is a sacred thing. It is by this means that one generation may pass knowledge to another, that men who will never meet in this world can communicate deep and wondrous thoughts. A book is to be respected above all else."

Dolnaraq released the book, allowing it to tumble noisily to the floor, but said nothing.

Eventually, though, Dolnaraq did gain a grasp of written language, and in fact, learned he had quite an aptitude in this area. Soon Oskar moved on to other languages, first English, then French, then Italian. Oskar taught from great works of literature from various languages. Dolnaraq read Dostoyevsky's *The Brothers Karamazov* in the original Russian. He devoured a German translation of Homer's *Iliad*. He pored over Dickens and Shakespeare in English. Oskar began teaching him world history and discussing with him the politics of the time. Dolnaraq was a quick and able student, absorbing everything, questioning the reasoning of the authors he read, and debating the logic. Through all of this, Oskar would smile, nodding eagerly as the wordplay between them grew to the type that two university academics might enjoy over tea in some austere campus library.

One day, as Dolnaraq sat mulling over Dante, he peered quizzically at his tutor. "You're a carnie," he said.

Oskar nodded.

"You obviously have an amazing mind. You speak multiple languages; you dabble in philosophy, politics, the social sciences. You have a rich love for and grasp of literature. How then is it that you tend to the beasts in a rundown carnival managed by an inept tyrant?"

Oskar frowned, leaning forward on his bony elbows. "It is as you say. In truth, I am an academic, having spent the better part of my adult life on staff at the University of Heidelberg."

"What brought you to this place?"

"My younger sister, Frieda. She is married to the buffoon."

"Wilhelm? Your sibling is his mate?" Dolnaraq had seen the woman only in passing, a slight creature with thinning hair and sunken eyes. At some point she might have been attractive, but now only seemed listless and dull.

Oskar nodded. "My father passed when I was still a student. Consumption took him. Frieda married Wilhelm when she was sixteen. He is an abusive man and I have often been forced to intercede in their affairs. When my mother died four years ago, Wilhelm took my sister's portion of the inheritance to purchase this carnival. Due to the transitory nature of carnival life, I feared for Frieda. If I were to have remained at the university, she would have been traveling the countryside with no advocate. Wilhelm is rash, vengeful, jealous of her beauty, and prone to assault her should any other look her way. I knew I must remain nearby lest she be harmed."

"Why not simply kill Wilhelm and free your sister?"

Oskar seemed astounded. His face crumpled into a peculiar expression and his eyes narrowed so much so that Dolnaraq could no longer see the green of them. "Have you learned nothing of human society in all of our time together?"

Dolnaraq remained expressionless.

"Civilized men do not simply kill other men they do not like," added Oskar when it became clear Dolnaraq was offering no response.

"I have learned that civilized men do in fact kill one another for numerous reasons; many of which are less substantial than those you've just presented."

"It is illegal—immoral."

"And quite common," added Dolnaraq.

Oskar shook his head. "The point is this: Frieda is the reason a learned man scrapes up manure in this shabby little establishment. I signed on in order to be near to her. Now, I do believe its time you continued with your reading." Oskar rose, set the metal stool aside, and strolled off to tend to the elephant.

*****

The relationship between Dolnaraq and Oskar was more than that of teacher and student. Just over three weeks into their lessons together, long before Dolnaraq had much benefited from Oskar's teachings, the young reyaqc was, once again, depleted. His energy level dropped significantly no matter how much he ate and drank. His limbs shook and his vision blurred. Oskar approached the cage as Dolnaraq lay huddled in the corner. "Otto, you are ill, my friend."

"It is time. I require essence."

Oskar narrowed his gaze at this, obviously recalling the last time Dolnaraq had claimed a need for "essence."

"What is this essence? You've mentioned it before."

"It is…essence. I know no other way to explain it." The words were slow and difficult to speak. Dolnaraq was weak, and he was not yet fluent in the German language.

"The essence," asked Oskar. "Did you take essence from me when you attacked me last?"

Dolnaraq nodded.

"This is why your face has changed, why you've come, in some fashion, to resemble me?"

Dolnaraq nodded again, cradling himself in his own arms as a bone-deep shiver raced from one end of his form to the other.

"What will happen if you receive no essence?"

"I will die."

Oskar nodded and paced left and then right before the cage, his hands buried in his pockets, his fingers fiddling with the keys within. "If I should offer you essence, what would become of me?"

Dolnaraq stared blankly at the man for several seconds before speaking. "You would become my giver?" he asked, astonishment oozing through the syllables.

"Giver?" asked Oskar.

"One who gives freely of his essence."

Oskar nodded, continuing to pace, continuing to rattle his keys. "Again, what would become of me?"

With great effort, Dolnaraq pulled himself across the straw strewn floor and to the bars. "If you were to become my giver, I would become more like you."

"And me. What danger is there for me? I am told that I was in near coma for three days after your last... After you took essence."

Dolnaraq stared at Oskar. The green eyes bore both curiosity and fright. The generous mouth neither grinned nor frowned, but seemed taut with anticipation. Both hands were pressed deep in Oskar's pockets and Dolnaraq could hear loose change and keys clicking together as he worked them round and round the tiny space. The small man smelled of adrenaline, and Dolnaraq sensed Oskar was battling a very strong urge to flee. "If I take from you," said Dolnaraq. "If I am careful, you will most likely live."

"If you are careful?"

Dolnaraq nodded.

"And if you are not careful?"

Dolnaraq stared blankly forward.

Oskar rattled his change some more. "How very careful can you be?"

Dolnaraq did not answer immediately, but stared at the man for many seconds before saying, "I will try."

Oskar jiggled his keys. He paced left then right. Several times it seemed he was about to speak, but then remained silent. Eventually he paused before the cage. "You will surely die without my essence?"

"Yours or another's."

Oskar nodded and jiggled his keys.

"Free me," offered Dolnaraq. "I will seek the essence of another. You will remain unharmed."

"And that other, will he remain unharmed?"

Dolnaraq answered with a blank stare.

A turn to the left, three steps in that direction. A pivot, three steps back. Jiggle, jiggle. "All right," said Oskar. "This we will do, but please…" He trailed off, seemingly unable to complete the thought.

"I will take care," offered Dolnaraq.

Oskar nodded, hesitated, and then stepped to within Dolnaraq's reach.

"Relax." Dolnaraq reached out wrapping his right palm around the back of Oskar's neck. "I will draw it out slowly, and attempt to take only what I require." With that, Dolnaraq inserted the tiny hollow spines into the back of Oskar's neck. There was an almost indiscernible pop and then Oskar's eyes widened, meeting Dolnaraq's gaze, locking there for several seconds before closing. Dolnaraq withdrew his hand and crawled off into his corner without another word.

In this way, Oskar became Dolnaraq's giver. With time, Dolnaraq grew more adept at withdrawing essence in moderation and Oskar became more or less accustomed to the process, though invariably it left him drained and useless for the following day. These constant infusions from the same source did bring about changes in Dolnaraq. The obvious effect was that with each passing week, the young reyaqc more and more closely resembled his giver. As well, Dolnaraq had not had access to a fox in many months and his animal-like appearance diminished almost entirely.

This infuriated Wilhelm, who stormed about the carnival cursing and stomping, blamed Oskar for the situation. Oskar, for his part, never revealed the nature of his relationship with "the wolf boy." Truly, there was very little to tell. Dolnaraq had revealed to Oskar only what must be revealed. Never did he mention the word reyaqc. Never did he explain his origin, or the true nature of his species. Never did he even utter his true name. That was a name for the reyaqc. No human should be entrusted with too much. To Oskar, he would remain Otto the wolf boy.

One day, Dolnaraq and Oskar sat poring over a scholarly article about the current politics of Europe. Oskar contended that a rise in nationalism between many European states combined with an ever more complex series of alliances and treaties would inevitably lead to war—possibly a war such as the world had never known. He urged Dolnaraq that if ever he should be free, that he should flee to America, a growing nation across the great Atlantic. Powerful, but not yet fully aware of its potential greatness. "There is much opportunity there. With luck, they will remain detached from the problems of Germany and our neighbors. I fear our dear land, Otto, will be at the heart of the coming conflict."

Dolnaraq protested that he was not human, and thus not concerned with the battles of men. But Oskar countered, saying, "You live in a world dominated by humans. It will only become more so. You are bright, bright as anyone I have ever known. I have given you my face, the face of a man. You no longer resemble an animal. Adapt, learn, grow. Be who you are and what you are, but understand the world in which you live."

It was then that Wilhelm appeared as if from nowhere, a bundle of furs beneath his arm. These, he tossed harshly at Oskar. "Glue these to his face and arms," shouted the lout. "The crowds no longer believe in the beast."

"I am not a beast!" shouted Dolnaraq from his cage.

Wilhelm marched forward, but took care to remain beyond Dolnaraq's reach. "You are an animal. I hunted you, I captured you, I own you. No matter what this little man teaches you in his sissy little books, you will always be a stinking animal."

Wilhelm marched away as Dolnaraq glared at the man's flabby and disgusting backside.

Two nights later, Tresset appeared.

Dolnaraq sensed the familiar scent on the air and immediately gazed about the darkness seeking his long lost companion. His stomach jumped and a tiny crease of a smile overtook his stoic features. Oskar was with him, but knew none of this. He was once again expounding on the opportunities of America, saying that it was time he took his savings, gathered up his sister, and fled to this emerging giant across the waves. "Otto," he said. "Perhaps you should accompany us. Aside from that tuft of red fur on your left hand, you now look entirely human." Oskar paused. "Well, there are the eyes. But dark glasses should cover those. Think of it, Otto. A new life, a fresh…"

And then Tresset slew him.

There was a sharp ripping sound, a hiss of air from the now-opened windpipe. Oskar's eyes went wide, his tongue protruded, and his useless, bloodied form tumbled to the dirt.

Dolnaraq stared blankly at the corpse for perhaps five seconds, and then met Tresset's gaze. "The keys to the cage are in the human's pocket."

Within moments, Dolnaraq was free for the first time in nearly a year. Filling his lungs, he relished the purity of the air. He knew it was impossible that the air would be any different, for his cage had bars and so he breathed of the same air now as he had breathed before, but nonetheless it smelled fresher somehow.

There was a sudden commotion. Wilhelm had heard the disturbance, or perhaps he had simply happened upon the scene. Either way, he was there now, shouting with all of his bluster. "Beast!" he cried. "The beast is free! He has slain his keeper!"

Dolnaraq was upon him before the large man could hope to flee.

"See," stammered Wilhelm as Dolnaraq harshly grabbed him by the collar. "See, I knew it. You are an animal."

"I AM NOT AN ANIMAL!" bellowed Dolnaraq. Then, even though his once long and deadly fangs had reduced to human-like teeth, he plunged his mouth onto Wilhelm's neck, bit deep, and tore away a hunk of flesh nearly the size of a baseball.

Dolnaraq released the man, allowing him to stumble to his knees, clutching at the enormous gap in his enormous neck. He spit the meat of the man into Wilhelm's face, and turned, marching directly to Oskar's bloody corpse. Here, he knelt on one knee, slipped his hand into Oskar's left rear pocket and withdrew the man's wallet. He already bore Oskar's face. Now he bore the man's identification. A quick trip to Oskar's trailer and he would bare his banking information as well. Dolnaraq made to rise, and then glanced down at the corpse, truly noting it perhaps for the first time. "Dolnaraq," he said quietly. "My true name is Dolnaraq. I am in your debt."

With that he rose, gazing deeply into Tresset's eyes, wanting perhaps to hug him or in some other way express the joy he had in seeing him. But such affections were the things of humanity. Besides, there was little time. Surely someone had heard the commotion. Others would investigate.

"Come," he said in breathless excitement. "We go to America."

Chapter Seven

1910-1911

As it turned out, Oskar Kohler was a wealthy man. And as Dolnaraq had taken Kohler's identity, it was he who was now wealthy. This was not a fortune, but still enough to allow two young reyaqc a comfortable upper middleclass existence in the ever-expanding New York City of the 1910s. The late Oskar's money had not come from his years as a university professor; that position did not enable a man to accumulate significant sums. And obviously, the wealth had not come from his time serving in the traveling carnival. No, this was family money passed on after the death of his parents, and Dolnaraq was quite fortunate to have it. It's said that knowledge is power, well no less so is money. Dolnaraq was able to provide passage to America for himself as well as for the not-quite-conventional-looking Tresset with few questions and limited paperwork. As well, a few well-placed dollars allowed the two to bypass the barn-like immigration port at Ellis Island and its physical examinations which neither reyaqc would likely pass. Instead, they moved through a much less densely populated facility reserved for first-class passengers. Most of the normal bureaucracy had been skirted and the two soon found themselves happily situated in a fourth floor apartment near Columbia University where Dolnaraq enrolled for the purpose of attaining his first of many degrees.

Knowing the money was not infinite, he'd met with several brokerage firms, selected two, and invested his excess funds with the hopes of multiplying his investments. Dolnaraq proved to have a knack for increasing his holdings, and by the time the great depression came and went nearly two decades later, the young scholar had maneuvered himself into millionaire status.

While Dolnaraq loved his new life, treasured the verve of civilization, thrived on the fast-paced metropolitan experience, Tresset found a renewed hatred for his human cousins. Of course, there was the human smell, and in a city this size, the odor was overbearing. Additionally, though Tresset had now been over four months without animal essence, his appearance was still peculiar at best, thus forcing him to leave his dwelling only at night, to pull his homburg hat low over his forehead, and to flip the collar of his topcoat so few could glimpse his atypical features. Tresset detested the binding restraints of clothing, and loathed the needed subterfuge. Dolnaraq encouraged him, saying that soon these features would recede entirely and Tresset would be free to embrace all society had to offer. But what Dolnaraq had yet failed to realize was that Tresset had come to despise humanity, to loath these people to his primal core.

Though the city did offer one very strong concession for Tresset.

The hunt.

Never before had Tresset been in such a place. In the past, when he'd hunted villages on the outskirts of civilization, the death or injury of one person caused uproar throughout the entire settlement. But, here—here! Who noticed one missing from among over two million? The immediate family, of course, but few beyond. He quickly learned to hunt the lower east side of Manhattan where recent immigrants from Ireland, Germany, Poland, and Italy crowded into multistory tenement buildings. Frequently, two or three families squeezed into one three-room apartment. The people were mainly poor, many did not speak the language of the land, and they were easy prey for Tresset.

The displaced molt had tried to include Dolnaraq in these excursions, but his increasingly humanized companion routinely declined. Dolnaraq felt the need to maintain a consistent appearance, that of Oskar Kohler. If his features changed too drastically, even over a matter of months, this could elicit curiosity among his university peers. Thus, Dolnaraq was very picky about his choice of donors, for not only was he seeking a particular look, he also desired essence from those of above average intelligence. Dolnaraq had thus taken to drawing primarily from other university students. This, Tresset considered risky, as Dolnaraq was known on campus; but thus far he had been successful in his endeavors. He'd even shared that there was a particular student with whom he hoped to recruit as a voluntary and ongoing giver.

On this evening, Tresset had decided to hunt the Italian neighborhood on Mulberry Street. As was often the case, the process of getting to his intended destination was a nerve-racking event. Henry Ford's Model T automobiles were the growing rage so not only did Tresset need to dodge electric streetcars, pushcarts, and bicycles, but this new mechanical hazard as well. Garbage littered much of the overcrowded street and the odors of cesspools and humanity mingled, causing Tresset to breathe primarily through his mouth. There was a slight drizzle, and the unpaved street was a muddy slop. Tresset paused under an awning, surveying the row. The sun had receded, and with it, many of the outdoor vending tables had been cleared of their wares, carts pulled to alongside tenement buildings, and the general hubbub of the place had settled to a more palatable din. The lamplighter, a pudgy adolescent of about fourteen years in age, made his way up the street, igniting the sparse and unevenly spaced gas street lamps with a long unwieldy pole.

A red-faced man pushing a two-wheeled cart loaded with broken chairs and table legs, passed within about four feet of Tresset. Glancing at the reyaqc, whose face was hidden in the shadows, he chortled, "I come to America because they tell me the streets, they're paved with gold. When I get here, the streets, they aren't paved in gold; they aren't paved at all. And who do they expect to pave them? Me. That's who."

When Tresset failed to respond to the affable gripe, the old Italian mumbled a curse, and moved on repeating his clever grievance to the next person he encountered. Wiping his hands with a coarse cloth kept in his coat pocket, Tresset slipped around a corner and into a narrow alleyway between two buildings. He'd come too early this eve. The streets were still overly populated. He'd keep moving, not giving anyone a chance to get a good look at him, and then, in an hour perhaps, he could begin the hunt in earnest.

Toward the back end of the same six-story building, Tresset came across a young boy of perhaps ten years in age, urinating against the brown brick wall. Tresset sniffed at the fetid air and glanced in either direction. Miraculously, in a place crammed with thousands of souls per square mile, they were alone in the alleyway. Tresset did not often infuse from youth, but neither did he ignore the opportunity. What care did he have if he received from the young or from the mature? And what care did he have if the human was left intact, damaged irreversibly, or even dead? These were not his kind. Did the humans care how many cows perished to give them beef? No. And neither did Tresset care how many humans expired to grant him continued life.

The boy finished making water and glanced up at the approaching figure. His brown eyes were wide and round, his nose a button, his cheeks just now shedding the last vestige of baby fat. He gasped at the frightening sight of Tresset, but the reyaqc was fast, clamping one hand over the boy's mouth even as the other slid round to the back of the neck. Yet it was not the child that shouted an alert, but the mother, some three stories above. Her head and shoulders protruding from the window, she shouted, "*Mia figlio! Mia figlio!*" A moment later, an iron frying pan hurled down toward the startled reyaqc. The pan missed, clanking against the metal fire escape and bouncing harmlessly off to the left, but the mother's frantic and continued cries of, "*Mia figlio! Mia figlio!*" had alerted others, and now there were startled voices from Mulberry Street behind as well as thundering footsteps from above as three men in various stages of undress bounded down the fire escape.

But, Tresset did not flee. He was a creature of the wild, such as these poor immigrants had never seen in their precious urban kingdom. Blood was sweet and battle welcome. Too long had he crept about, hiding in shadows, cowering from the daylight. Tresset welcomed the conflict, embraced it even. With what was surely seen as amazing agility, he tossed the startled boy aside and leapt vertically, grasping the bottom of the still-suspended fire escape. The metal shuddered and groaned as it opened, allowing the reyaqc to bound up the structure with cat-like fluidity. Startled, the lead man hesitated, causing a blockage for those coming behind. Surely, these three had expected to chase the scoundrel off by the sheer fact of their presence. In no way had they expected a mugger to bound up the swaying structure like some cornered jungle cat.

Reaching the first of the three, Tresset easily tossed the man over the side and two stories to the ground. Landing with a thud and a sharp *snap*, the Italian now lay below, unmoving, and thus beyond Tresset's concern. The reyaqc still possessed his retractable claws, though they had shortened and weakened some in the past months. Swiping cleanly from right to left these proved quite effective in shearing the left cheek from the next assailant. There was a splay of blood and panicked shrieks from the gathering spectators below. Though he thrived on the hunt, Tresset detested the feel of the disease-ridden human blood against his skin and wished the drizzle would graduate to downpour and cleanse him of the sickness.

Realizing that there were now men racing toward him from both above and below, Tresset tossed the bloodied form toward those ascending, and then bounded off of the fire escape and toward an adjacent window some four feet distant. The window was short and narrow, and even with his catlike agility Tresset was unable to launch his entire body through in one easy move. But still, he'd managed to get head and shoulders through the opening while his lower body slammed against the brick exterior. Only three seconds later, the reyaqc had scampered through the window and now raced across the tiny apartment and out through the doorway and into the adjacent hallway.

Realizing his pursuers would assume he'd try for ground level, Tresset instead made his way up the nearby stairway. Arriving on the roof in just over a minute's time, he glanced in each direction, spied the nearest building, raced toward it, and leaped, landing deftly on the adjacent roof. The night air was cool and moist. The moon now illuminated the night sky and street lamps cast flickering shadows across the avenues. And though Tresset longed for essence, the ruckus below told him all he needed to know. For this night at least, he had become the hunted, not the hunter.

Chapter Eight

Bathed in the wavering light of a mercury vapor lamp, Dolnaraq dipped his pen in the ink well and jotted another line. He was hunched over his desk, three books open, each overlapping the other. Several pages of scribbled notes splashed across the writing surface. "Very curious," he muttered while flipping another page of the topmost book. Aristotle. There were some very interesting things in the ancient philosopher's background: some hinted anomalies, some missing pieces, suppositions about his parentage. Dolnaraq had come across the first of these while studying for a world history exam. At first, he'd dismissed his thought as fanciful. But the seed of an idea had been planted. And so he'd rushed off to the university library and returned to his small apartment with an armload of books on the man. The more he studied, the more he became convinced that he and this ancient man of wisdom might have a curious link. How very remarkable that one of the great human minds of history might not have been human. Dolnaraq would need to research further, of course. There'd be other sources to collect, Aristotle's own writings to dissect—possibly even scholars to interview—but if Dolnaraq's supposition proved true, how many others like the ancient philosopher might there be as well?

Dolnaraq's contemplations were interrupted by the sound of approaching footsteps in the adjacent hallway. The door swung open and the reyaqc was assaulted with a too-familiar odor as Tresset marched through the doorway. The molt's cloths were bloodied, and he wiped furiously at his hands and face with an old gray towel. "I assume the blood is not yours," said Dolnaraq.

Tresset grumbled something unintelligible and tossed the rag onto a small Victorian table adjacent the kitchenette.

"There was another article in the newspaper. They've dubbed you 'the Mulberry Street Butcher.'"

Slipping out of his soiled overcoat and hanging it on a wooden coat rack, Tresset replied, "Do you think I care about your newspapers?"

Dolnaraq closed the top book and turned toward his companion. "The newspaper is not the issue. It's the fact that you're drawing attention. They've increased the police presence on the lower east side. People are more alert, they're taking precautions. You'll be caught if you don't change your method."

Tresset snorted. "The humans are weak."

Setting his pen aside and rising to his feet, Dolnaraq glared at his companion. "Are you that stupid? Has that cat essence muddled your brain? There are tens of thousands of them, Tresset. Hundreds on every block. They have guns. And now they're looking specifically for you. Have you already forgotten I was nearly killed by humans, that I spent almost a year caged like a beast? We are not infallible, you and I."

Tresset straightened, the short hairs of his neck stood on end. "What is it you want me to do? I must have essence and so I must hunt."

"My need is the same, and yet I have killed no one since arriving on this continent. I've drawn no attention to myself. I lead a comfortable existence and my needs are met."

"You've become soft, just like your precious humans. Every month you think less like a reyaqc. If I didn't know better, I'd think you were one of them."

Dolnaraq drew close to his companion. How small-minded this molt could be. How shortsighted. "Understand this. I am not human. I do not desire to be human, nor do I idolize the race. But, I do acknowledge the potential gain from these people. We are few, but they are many. They have great knowledge, great resources. I will take advantage of these. In doing so, I will help our own people to rise above savagery." He paused, made direct eye contact. "When we lived in the woodlands, we drew from the essence of the beasts. But we also learned from them, how to hunt, how to survive our environment—how to thrive. We're in a different place now. We have new lessons to learn. But more than that, we have an opportunity to lead the reyaqc far beyond our present state of savagery."

Tresset turned from Dolnaraq, paced the room. Dolnaraq knew his companion resisted this line of thinking. He'd always wanted to do things on his own terms, had never been willing to see a grander design. Yet he was intelligent and often showed keen insight. If only he could be made to see his true potential, he could one day become a great leader of the reyaqc. But not if he continued in this manner. Not if he became nothing more than a brutish killer.

After several moments, Tresset turned, facing his companion once again. "None of this changes anything, Dolnaraq. I still need essence."

"Not with such frequency. There's no need to kill. Spread out. Hunt different neighborhoods. Draw essence in moderation. Leave your donors alive."

Tresset snorted. "You are not the reyaqc I knew before."

"Neither are you. Before my capture you took more care. You used logic. You understood the need for secrecy. Now it seems you have a vendetta against the humans. Not only do you have the physical need for essence, but you seek some senseless revenge upon them all."

"They are filthy creatures—diseased." Tresset grabbed his soiled rag and rubbed it furiously against his palms. "They—every one of them— deserve a swift journey to hell."

Dolnaraq sighed and shook his head as he placed a hand on his companion's shoulder. "Tresset, this is a war you cannot win."

*****

Tresset did not heed Dolnaraq's advice. The killings persisted. Tresset was simply too vengeful, too maddened by the disease he believed himself to have contracted from the drunk so many months gone, too enraged by the defilement subjected upon him by the girl Lyuba. Dolnaraq saw no sign of the blemishes Tresset battled. Perhaps they were real. Perhaps they were just below the surface of the skin and Tresset felt them itching or burning. But more likely, this impurity had long since purged from his system and Tresset fought a phantom. He would not hear this, of course, but it was Dolnaraq's opinion nonetheless.

The "Mulberry Street Butcher" did expand his hunting ground, though, thus making it more difficult for authorities to capture him. He found victims on Doyers Street in Chinatown. He attacked lovers in Central Park. Eventually he braved Sixth Avenue, plucking a shopper right off of the street and dragging him into an alleyway as the man exited a tailor's shop. The attacks became more brutal and more frequent.

Dolnaraq noticed a change in Tresset's temperament. His thinking became muddled, his mood continually foul. Though his true need of essence came roughly every three weeks, the attacks were now a nightly occurrence.

This could not continue indefinitely. Tresset now hunted closer to their home. Soon the authorities would sweep in on him, perhaps, in the process, ensnaring Dolnaraq as well. Though Dolnaraq loved the city, it was clear Tresset could no longer live in such a setting. So Dolnaraq initiated plans to move Tresset cross country. The western regions were still mostly open and only sparsely populated. Initially, Dolnaraq thought perhaps Tresset could escape to Montana or Colorado. But, upon reflection, he thought of how the molt had hated the Siberian winters. Perhaps he would do better further south, Utah, or maybe Nevada. Possibly, he could even align himself with a reyaqc pack. Dolnaraq was certain that if

Tresset did find such a community, and if he was not killed on first sight, he would rise to one day be their chieftain. For Tresset had a keen mind, a scheming mind, one full of strategy and will.

In reyaqc society, ascension was achieved through the killing of the present chieftain. In fact, it was a duty, a responsibility laid upon the victor to then assume that mantle, to care for the pack, to lead and to protect. Yes, this was Tresset's destiny. Dolnaraq could see this now. It had been foolish to assume otherwise. Dolnaraq would sorely miss his lifelong companion, but each must choose the path meant for him.

Then came that dreadful evening in late April. It was the time of Monday night washing. Row upon row of linens, undergarments, shirts, and trousers were strung between buildings from each and every window a full six stories high. Dolnaraq was seated near the window of his fourth floor apartment, a large book of early European history in his hands as he gazed out over the fluttering spectacle before him. Suddenly, he heard the clamor of shouts, the racing of feet. Sniffing the breeze, he smelled blood, sweat, adrenaline—and Tresset. The beast had finally come home to roost.

Moving quickly, Dolnaraq exited the apartment, locking the door behind him. He could not let Tresset lead the police to their home. If Dolnaraq were implicated, all Oskar Kohler's assets would be frozen. Dolnaraq's education would cease, he would quite possibly spend years imprisoned because of Tresset's foolishness. And what then? From whom would he infuse? How long before the prison guards learned his true nature? The two might be executed, or, at the very least, isolated, which, in reality would be just a slower form of execution. For without access to essence, they would each perish in little over a month's time, less perhaps.

Dolnaraq cursed himself as he raced down the stairs. He should have sent Tresset on his way months ago. Why had he kept him near? Why had he continued to battle with the muddle-brained molt? Tresset would not listen to reason—even in his most lucid moments he was as bull-headed as a charging rhinoceros. A strange thought occurred to Dolnaraq. He loved Tresset. Not as humans defined love. He wasn't even sure that reyaqc were capable of that emotion. But there was a bond they shared, perhaps akin to that of siblings. And if it wasn't love, per se, it was at least a comfort, a familiarity that glued them together despite their growing differences.

Dolnaraq exited a side doorway leading into the tight alleyway between high-rise apartment buildings. Hundreds of pieces of laundry fluttered above creating a low, almost thunder-like rumble. Leaning his head back, Dolnaraq breathed deeply. There. There was the scent. Tresset had not turned into the apartment building as Dolnaraq feared he might, but had continued past. Perhaps the molt had had a moment's lucidity and realized the folly of leading the police to his home.

Dolnaraq raced toward the scent. If asked, he couldn't have expressed what he hoped to accomplish. This was Tresset's fight. Dolnaraq had warned him of this inevitability for months. Yet still Dolnaraq raced through the crowded alleyways, bumping into pedestrians and bicyclists, nearly tripping over milk bottles and trashcans. Rounding a corner, he came face-to-face with the conflict. Tresset was on the ground, three uniformed officers over him, two of which pounded on the huddled form with nightsticks.

Had Dolnaraq taken time to ponder the situation, he might have slunk back into the shadows and let the outcome be what it may. But Dolnaraq acted on instinct—and so, before he could contemplate his actions, he pulled the nearest of the officers away from Tresset's huddled form. The man whirled on him, cursing, swinging his club, grazing Dolnaraq's scalp. Blinded by fury, Dolnaraq lurched forward, attaching his teeth to the man's ear and tearing away to his left. He pulled again, and then again, and now the member ripped free. The man howled as Dolnaraq spit the now-useless flap of flesh onto the gravel alley. But Dolnaraq wasn't finished. Pulling the frenzied man to him, Dolnaraq bit hard on the Adam's apple, chomped down, and twisted. The man's shriek turned to a pathetic gurgle as he dropped to his knees, clinging at his ruined throat, before finally losing consciousness in a widening pool of his own blood.

There was a sharp *thud* as a nightstick struck Dolnaraq. But, the reyaqc did not double over, did not cry in pain. A reyaqc's strength is not superhuman as such, but it is greater than that of the average man, perhaps closer to that of one of the great apes, a gorilla or a full-grown chimpanzee. Three swift maneuvers and a quick twist, and the assaulting officer lay at Dolnaraq's feet, his neck broken.

Suddenly it was over. Tresset had disposed of the third policeman. They stood, momentarily alone in the alleyway, onlookers gawking and shouting from both ends, but none willing to come forward. Rising out of his carnal haze, Dolnaraq glared at the carnage about him, at his own bloodied clothing, at the bodies sprawled at his feet, and then his gaze lit on Tresset. "Never!" he shouted. "Never again." He moved away, separating himself from his former companion. "I am not an animal," he cried. "I am not an animal!" Then turning, he raced through a nearby doorway, down a corridor, out into the darkened street beyond.

Chapter Nine

1943

The reyaqc community was small by human standards comprising just over sixty residents. Situated in the lush green woodlands of rural Pennsylvania, the reyaqc had adopted the appearance, manner, and even the common names of the Amish. Though they held none of the religious or social constraints of these human cousins, this guise allowed them to live a relatively secluded existence with little outside interference from neighboring communities. Most humans simply considered them reclusive – even by Amish standards – and respected their privacy. Among the true Amish they were seen not as one of their own, but as some aberrant offshoot. Some years earlier there had been heated discussions between pack chieftain Jeremiah Schrock and other local Amish leaders. The reyaqc were outsiders, and quite strange in manner and custom, with no connection to any known communities. Schrock argued that his group had been displaced by "non-believers" some years before and had taken to a nomadic lifestyle. Until now, they'd never remained in one locale for long, and sought only a place to call their own and a promise to be left in peace. They required no communion with other like-minded communities, nor did they desire any assistance. Schrock had quoted the Bible liberally, spouted the appropriate lingo, and even chided the legitimate Amish for being less devout than they. This rebuff was not taken well – as had been the plan – and the pack was soon left to fend for itself and its residents henceforth considered outsiders by both the general population and the Amish alike. This had been the desired outcome.

Dolnaraq had first learned of this group through his increasingly exhaustive research of the reyaqc, their history, and current state. Over the previous three decades, he'd become well known within the reyaqc community as an intellect and a voice for their people. Dolnaraq had become quite comfortable moving among humans and had from time to time championed reyaqc interests in land acquisition and even criminal legal issues, while never once revealing the true nature of the species. He was convinced that if ever the greater human community learned of their reyaqc cousins, that genocide would be the result. Case in point: the current war raging across the seas. Atrocity upon atrocity perpetrated against the Jewish population – against humans! – by other humans, simply because of differences in custom and belief. How could Dolnaraq expect anything less should the greater population discover that some among them were a different species entirely? Yes, there were those who knew. There had always been those who knew, but the reyaqc were adept at keeping this number to a minimum and in being very selective when revealing this crucial information to human individuals.

The reyaqc are longer lived than humans, having a natural lifespan of between ninety and one hundred-thirty years, though many never live to see a natural death due to the riggers and risks inherent to their oft nomadic or, in some instances, animal-like existence. Likely due to the regular infusion of new genetic material, civilized reyaqc remained vibrant and relatively youthful through most of their long lives. For those living amongst humans this meant the occasional retreat and initiation of a new human identity. This was one such time for Dolnaraq. He'd lived for three decades as Oskar Kohler, was over fifty years of age, and appeared to the humans to be in his mid to late twenties. As such, he'd spent the previous five years gradually transferring his substantial financial assets to his distant "nephew," Matthew Greene. Dolnaraq had desired a time of solitude to focus on what was to become his life's work, the compilation and writing of a comprehensive history of the reyaqc, and decided to live among this secluded pack for a time before reemerging in the human community as Greene. He'd now been there for nearly three years and was preparing to reenter human society, though, in truth, he felt a pang of loneliness as he made his preparations. It had been refreshing to live among his own kind. There was no masquerade, no need to display false emotions or present contrived expressions. Here, he was simply Dolnaraq. And in many ways he felt he could live the remainder of his years content and happy in such a place.

But this was not his lot and he accepted this reality. Dolnaraq was one of the few reyaqc to have made significant human connections – high ranking connections. Most did not know his true nature, but saw him only as a bright and inspired individual. As Oskar Kohler he'd been able to influence legislation and impact financial sectors, paving the way for secluded reyaqc communities such as the one he now occupied. He'd recently mailed numerous correspondences asking business and legislative connections to welcome his nephew, Matthew Greene, as they would himself. As a reyaqc, Dolnaraq's features were always subject to gradual change. At first sight of Matthew Greene, and after not seeing Oskar Kohler for nearly three years, most would likely feel he looked similar to their old friend Oskar, but would never believe him to be the same man. Simply a familial resemblance. Nothing more.

Dolnaraq was writing another such correspondence when Ruth entered the small corner room Dolnaraq used as a study. She was young, slender, appealing. Reyaqc do not marry. They claim no enduring love nor do they mate for life. It is not uncommon for a male reyaqc to have as many as five or, in the case of a pack chieftain, even ten established mates. Even so, Dolnaraq held a special affection for this one. She was vibrant and intelligent, infusing only from those she deduced to be of above average intellect. This was an approach Dolnaraq had practiced since first arriving in America. Physical health was important, of course. And Dolnaraq would never infuse from one sickly or infirm, but muscle mass and athletic prowess meant little to him. He spent his years within great institutions in vast cities, not in the forest fighting for daily survival. And while Ruth had spent her short life in this one reyaqc community only, she had a sense of greater things. She was someone with whom Dolnaraq could share thoughts and ask opinions. She was someone of similar intellectual capacity and with a sometimes surprising understanding of the greater world which she had never seen. He'd considered asking her to go with him when he departed the community, but feared the complications of such a move. Already she'd born him one perfect son, and Dolnaraq knew it would be difficult to raise a young and impulsive reyaqc among humans without great risk of discovery.

"Are you working on your histories?" asked Ruth as she strolled to behind him and placed her palms on his shoulders, gently kneading them as she spoke.

"Ah, Ruth. No. A correspondence to a contact in Washington. Though, I doubt he'll pay it much mind. Everyone there is focused on the war effort. Still, he'll likely remember receiving it if I show up on his doorstep claiming to be Oskar Kohler's nephew."

"Why not wait until the conclusion of the conflict to reenter human society? You would likely be more successful in your endeavors if your contacts were not distracted by war."

Dolnaraq angled his head in such a way as to afford him a view of Ruth. "If society made sense, that might be a fine idea. But, humans are volatile. This war will surely end, but another will follow, and another after that. There will never be a perfect time. As well, they have a propensity to live only in the present. Oskar Kohler has not been seen for nearly three years. Already his influence has likely dwindled. If I wait much longer, my connections and influence will be all but nonexistent. I'd rather not start from the beginning."

She leaned in closer, whispering in his ear. "Is that the only reason you're fleeing?"

"I'm not fleeing, I'm…" He paused, turning in his seat to better see her. There was another reason, one more personal. Ruth had guessed this. He could tell by the tone of her voice and the glint in her pale eyes. "I suppose I am fleeing," he admitted. "In a sense at least. Ruth, I have not lived among my own kind since I was a pup. I find it… welcoming, comfortable. But, I can't allow myself to be comfortable. I want to be productive. I can do much more for the reyaqc by working among the humans than I can by enjoying a life of solitude."

"What about your histories? You've made significant strides in your writing since you arrived."

Dolnaraq gazed at her for a moment before speaking. "In some ways, yes, I've recorded much of what I'd learned. I've sifted through documents, transcribed interviews, I've drawn new conclusions. But everything I've done was simply the synthesis of work I'd done in human society. In order to move forward, I need to have access to libraries and court records. I need to interview people, both human and reyaqc. I need to be free to travel about and meet with those who have the knowledge I seek."

This time it was Ruth who stared long at Dolnaraq before speaking. "What is it you fear?" she said at last.

"What do I fear?"

"Yes," she said. "You are perhaps the most motivated individual I have ever encountered. You have a passion for what you do, a relentless drive. But there's something beneath all of that. There is something dark and brooding at the core. You fear something. It must be something horrible to drive you so. What is it that you so dread?"

Dolnaraq did not hesitate. "Extinction." He paused, turned. "Yes, extinction. I used to fear our savagery, knowing that we could be so much more than we are, knowing that we have much to contribute. And this I still believe. But, the more I learn of our current state, the more I study our people, the more I fear the reyaqc are on the verge of extinction. The human population continues to grow and to expand into new geographic territories. At the same time, reyaqc populations dwindle. It becomes more and more difficult for us to live undetected by our human cousins." He paused, gazing into Ruth's soap-like eyes. "I'm not so deluded as to believe that I alone can save our race. And that is why I must be about my business. I must connect with other reyaqc. I must seek others who, like myself, have acquired influence within the human community."

"And this is why the histories are so important to you?"

"Yes. I desire to present the reyaqc with knowledge of our common histories and ancestries. The reyaqc need to understand the greatness within, that we have impacted the world for both good and ill throughout history. I'm hoping that if we, as a race, can embrace our common heritage that instead of living in isolated groups, battling over small patches of earth and diminishing our numbers through savagery, we can come together for the betterment of our people. We need to create a bond. We need to grow, and to reproduce. And eventually, in our own timing, we will present ourselves to the humans. But only when the appropriate groundwork has been lain, only when humankind has matured to the point where it can accept us for what we are. Judging by the current state of the world, this could prove a long wait."

"Speaking of reproduction." The voice came from behind. Dolnaraq and Ruth both turned to see Martha, another of Dolnaraq's claimed mates, standing in the doorway. "I'm ovulating," she said. "You'd instructed me to notify you."

Dolnaraq cocked his head. "Thank you, Martha. You'd best disrobe. I'll be with you momentarily."

As Martha unbuttoned her gown, Ruth gazed at Dolnaraq and asked, "Is it wrong to set all of your concerns and aspirations aside, just for a few hours, and do something for you? Or, at least, for someone you care about?"

Dolnaraq eyed Ruth and then glanced to Martha who was already near naked. The reyaqc are not fond of garments and tend to wear as little as possible. With the exception of times of inclement weather, this community wore clothing primarily as a pretense. It was never known when humans may traverse the rugged dirt road that led to this sanctuary, and it would cause uproar within neighboring human communities if it was discovered that these folks strolled about naked.

"You haven't answered my question," prodded Ruth.

Dolnaraq met her gaze, but remained silent. He had no answer to such a question and any response he might offer would likely cause only sorrow or anger.

Finally, Ruth allowed a curt nod and said, "Go to Martha. She's ovulating. You wouldn't want to miss this opportunity."

Dolnaraq hesitated for a moment and then rose. He had a brilliant mind and an honorable purpose, but interpersonal relations such as this left him befuddled. He sensed anger in Ruth's tone where there should be none. They were not humans. They did not mate exclusively, nor were they prone to great proclamations of endearment. He cared for her, yes, and likely more so than he had any individual since Tresset, but he found it near impossible to understand her temperament. "Would you like to join us?" he asked, thinking that perhaps she was somehow feeling put aside.

"I don't believe so," said Ruth, her voice soft and tight. "Martha ovulates. I have nothing so grand to offer."

Dolnaraq nodded, untied his robe, and allowed it to drop to the floor. He then moved to Martha, pressing her back against the wall, and took her there as Ruth tidied his desk.

*****

It was leaving day. Dolnaraq had packed his few personal items into one suitcase and all of his research materials and writings into four large crates. Jeremiah Schrock had offered to take him into the nearest town on his carriage where he could then obtain a bus ticket for the next stage of his journey. Ruth stepped forward as Dolnaraq prepared to climb up into his seat, her fingers knit as she held them before her breast; her pale eyes withheld some unknown emotion.

"I left you a twenty-four volume set of encyclopedias," he said, initiating the conversation. "Continue your education. You have a fine mind, don't allow it to atrophy."

She nodded and fiddled with her hair. "Encyclopedias, is that all you have to say in parting?"

He stepped closer, his gaze fixed on hers. "Do not doubt your significance in my life. It has been profound." With that, he turned and climbed onto the carriage.

"Will you return," she called as Schrock began to pull away.

"One can never be certain and I would not want to part with a lie upon my lips. I will write. That much I can promise."

As she nodded and turned to walk away, Dolnaraq found that he had a peculiar feeling in the base of his belly. Hollow. Unsettled. Perhaps he should have eaten before departure. He would now have to wait until Jeremiah Schrock let him off in town. That would suffice, he supposed. The place was less than two hours distant by carriage.

They'd been gone for less than five minutes when Dolnaraq heard the gunshots.

"Those came from the village," said Schrock as he pulled back on the reigns, first stopping forward movement and then turning back toward the settlement, urging the two aged horses into a quick gallop.

They arrived in time to see a young soldier standing in front of the white steepled church, a handgun raised above his head as he shouted at the residents. To Dolnaraq, it seemed the community was waiting to see if the man would do anything drastic. Most took cover behind walls, doors, even barrels. None approached him. None sought to disarm him. How different from the pack he'd known as a pup.

The man shot into the air.

"Where is she?" he screamed. "Where's Beverly? I know she's here! Believe me, I will kill you fat heads if I have to!"

The wind was moving south to north allowing Dolnaraq to catch the man's scent. There was adrenaline and other mingled hormones signaling fear and desperation. This one was near to losing control.

Without a word to Schrock, Dolnaraq slid from the carriage, slipped to the rear, and then ran to behind the church. Traversing the contour, he stepped closely along the far side, staying between the pristine white wall and the row of shrubbery lining the structure. He emerged behind and to the left of the soldier, making eye contact with Schrock who had since climbed down from the carriage. He was a large reyaqc, big bellied with a full head of steel wool hair and a matching beard that, in the style of the Amish, extended to below his shirt color. His eyes were narrow, barely revealing their peculiar nature. Schrock must have appeared intimidating to the soldier who was shorter by a full head, wiry, and rather insubstantial. Still, the man had likely seen combat. He wouldn't hesitate to kill if he deemed it justified.

"Ho, young man," said Schrock. "What are you doing waving that pistol about?"

Dolnaraq saw Ruth now. She'd exited his former dwelling and stood some twenty yards behind Schrock. What was she thinking? She was within the line of fire.

"So, what are you, the big cheese?" asked the man.

Schrock shrugged in a most human-like fashion. "I suppose I am."

Ruth began walking forward. Was she suicidal? Was she trying to make some sort of point to Dolnaraq by endangering herself?

"Where's my Beverly?"

Dolnaraq knew the young woman to whom he referred. She'd come to the community over a year ago. Her boyfriend was overseas and she'd sought a reprieve from talk of the war and of hatred and conflict. She'd met a young reyaqc woman, become friends, and eventually had been recruited to live among the reyaqc as a voluntary giver of essence. She was very well thought of among the community, and valued dearly as were all voluntary givers.

"Do you speak of Beverly Grey?" asked Schrock.

"Then she is here. That's just swell." He leveled the gun at Schrock, his long angular face twisted in a weird grimace. "You get her out here right now or I'll fill your fat belly with lead."

"I do not believe it would be wise to bring the young woman forward. Not if you insist on waving that gun around like some sort of lunatic."

"Beverly's my gal!" His voice was a hoarse holler, his hand quivered as he pointed the weapon at Schrock.

"Well," said Schrock. "That she might be and then again she might not. But, the young lady came to us voluntarily and has appeared to be quite happy as a valuable member of our community. I believe she has the right decide for herself just exactly whose gal she might want to be."

Ruth was closer yet, now less than thirty feet beyond Schrock.

Dolnaraq could smell the rush of hormones. The man was unstable and would likely fire the weapon if met with more resistance. It had been many years since Dolnaraq had played the hunter. Though, by reyaqc terms, he was young, he had spent his hours at a desk, not in physical activity or in life and death struggles. Still, the instinct remained. Those years spent with Tresset, traversing the countryside, raiding human villages, living only on what they could hunt or steal were decades gone, but suddenly seemed but a breath away. He calculated the distance to the man, the amount of time it would take to cover the ground, the angle at which he would need to strike in order to prevent a stray shot from hitting an innocent – from hitting Ruth. He was in motion nearly before he'd made the decision to act.

Dolnaraq traversed the ground in under five seconds, tackling the man just as he sensed Dolnaraq's approach. The soldier went down, grappling with the reyaqc. The gun discharged, once, twice. There were screams and shouts. In particular, one shrill female cry pierced Dolnaraq's brain. Infuriated, terrified at potential loss, Dolnaraq punched the soldier repeatedly in the face, but he was not so strong as he'd once been, though healthy, he was easily winded while this madman was combat hardened and in peak physical condition. The soldier clawed at Dolnaraq's face, kneed his groin. The gun came up as Dolnaraq loosened his grip in response to the pain below. The soldier wrestled free, Scrambling to regain his footing. Dolnaraq lunged, vaguely aware of shouts and screams in the distance. Someone had been shot. Who? Was it Ruth? It had to have been Ruth, she was right there.

He caught the soldier's heal, causing the man to stumble back to the ground. The man hit hard, with a loud thud, but somehow the gun remained in his hand. Even as Dolnaraq clutched him at the shins, he twisted, turning onto his back, then quickly raising into a sitting position, the gun held in a two handed grip, finger on trigger, barrel aimed at Dolnaraq's face.

He fired.

*****

The soldier's name was Harry Fraser. He'd just returned from active duty in the European theater to learn that his girlfriend, Beverly, had run off to live with some fringe Amish sect. In an act of arrogance and lack of forethought displayed primarily by young males, he'd immediately decided to rescue her from her own poor judgment, never considering that she might have found a place where she might thrive and grow. Dolnaraq stared at the young man, studying him, watching his movements as he sought to free himself from the restraints. His head throbbed where the bullet had skimmed him, his vision was slightly blurred. Fraser hollered and swore, shaking left and then right, nearly toppling the wooden chair to which he was bound. He was full of wisecracks and putdowns. His beaklike nose provided him a somewhat vulture-like appearance and his dark narrow eyes revealed only anger and venom. Dolnaraq had encountered many men like this before. His type was volatile and aggressive, likely to leap toward violence at the slightest perceived threat to his manhood. It would be difficult to reason with one such as this.

The man presented quite the conundrum. What were they to do with him? They couldn't simply allow him to leave. He'd likely return with cohorts and shoot up the settlement in search of his beloved. They could contact outside law enforcement, but this was always a final option. The reyaqc wanted as few prying eyes as possible. Their ruse worked perfectly well for the casual passerby, but close scrutiny would certainly reveal the true nature of the community's residents. These were not molts, wild and untamed, that might simply slay the man and devour his flesh. These were what Dolnaraq considered a purer breed, what he hoped were true reyaqc: separate from humanity, but wonderfully civilized and intelligent, contributing to the greater world in their own unique way.

"You present us with quite a quandary, Mr. Fraser," said Dolnaraq. "We are a nonviolent people and yet you bring violence to our home."

"All I want is my gal. Bring Bev to me and we can go in peace."

Dolnaraq shook his head. "I don't believe it to be so simple. You discharged a gun. You shot one of our own. A defenseless female. We could press charges. We should indeed press charges. After which, I'm sure you would be court-martialed and dishonorably discharged. Your prison term would likely be lengthy."

"Listen, I don't know what you people want from me. I'm here for Beverly. That's it."

"And then what?" asked Jeremiah Schrock who stood behind and to the right of Dolnaraq. "Suppose your little lady doesn't want to come along with you, then what? Will you shoot her too? Will you take her by force? Pardon my straightforward speak, but you don't seem like the rational forgiving type."

"She's my gal!" hollered Fraser.

Dolnaraq, who was seated in a chair directly opposite the man, leaned closer. "She may have been your gal. But it's her decision whether she chooses to remain your gal. Can you understand this concept, Mr. Fraser?" Dolnaraq had never fully understood the human notion of one's ownership or possession of another individual. Certainly he theoretically understood the concept of life mates, but that didn't imply the forfeiture of one's individual rights. Why was it that so many humans felt they had the right to dictate the actions of others? What was it in the human psyche that allowed a person to think he could dominate another through sheer force of will? And as to life mates, it was true that most marriages survived until the death of a either man or woman, but Dolnaraq had seen relatively few truly happy marriages, and extramarital affairs were much more common than society cared to admit.

Fraser sneered. "She's my gal. You'll see. She's too good for a bunch of backwoods religious zealots. She's Presbyterian. I don't know what she sees in you. She's Presbyterian!"

"And do Presbyterians condone shooting unarmed females? Because that is what you did, Mr. Fraser. What moral tradition gives you the right to fire upon innocents?" Dolnaraq paused, awaiting an answer that was not forthcoming.

The large arched door to the church, which, in actuality, was not used for worship, but rather as a meeting hall and open barracks, swung open. Ruth strolled in followed by a young human female. For the second time this day, Dolnaraq felt a hollow sensation at the base of his belly. What a strange and unwelcome feeling.

"Bev!" shouted Fraser as he resumed his pulling and rocking.

The human girl stepped forward, slowly walking up the narrow center aisle and halting before the bound man situated at the front of the small sanctuary. "What was you thinking, Harry?"

"Me? You ran off to live with this bunch a crazies. What did you expect me to do?"

Dolnaraq glanced at Ruth as she came to beside him. "How is Dorcas?" he asked.

"The bullet struck her thigh, shattering the femur. Mathias is tending to her wound, but he fears she may lose the leg."

Dolnaraq nodded, his head still throbbing from the bullet wound. This would be a shame. Dorcas was a fine female specimen and still in her prime reproductive years. He turned his attention to Beverly, an attractive young human female: golden blond hair, well proportioned form, with a satisfactory intellect and cheery disposition. She'd been an asset to the community, acting as a giver for five of the reyaqc. "Beverly, this man insists he has a claim on you. Are you in agreement or do you dispute his claim?"

The young woman hesitated, glancing first at Dolnaraq, then to Ruth, and then finally to the bound and struggling Harry. "I'm… not sure. I just needed to get away, is all. There was too much talk of the war, and Harry, I don't know about us. You're a swell guy and all, but… I don't know."

For the first time, Harry ceased straining against the binds. "But, I bought you a ring. I was thinking that maybe you would… You know."

"A ring? Really?" There were tears emerging from the corners of her eyes.

"Yeah. A solitaire – like the one your ma has."

"Harry, that's so very sweet of you, but…" She paused here, biting her lower lip and dropping her gaze to the wood planked floor. "I'll need to think on it. This is all so sudden. The girl you shot, she was a friend of mine. These people have shown me nothing but kindness and acceptance and you march in here shooting up the place. I… just need to think on it." With this, the young woman turned, marching from the room, a handkerchief in hand, dabbing at her eyes.

*****

Dolnaraq determined it would be best if Ruth spoke with the human woman. He understood that females generally responded more openly to other females, and he was also aware that humans sometimes perceived him as stern or peculiar. He wasn't entirely certain that he agreed with this assessment but it was a fact nonetheless. Ruth returned after perhaps an hour with the woman, baring little more information than she'd had in the beginning.

"She's contemplating the engagement," said Ruth as she slid onto a high-backed wooden chair across the table from Dolnaraq. He'd returned to the dwelling they'd shared before his near departure. A large square gauze bandage was taped to his left temple and partially obscured his left eye.

"There is no logic in that," said Dolnaraq. "The man is volatile. He treats her as a possession. Doesn't she understand that this will only increase should they wed? Human males believe that their strength and aggression makes them superior to their mates. Beverly has much more to offer than this thug would ever allow. It would be a terrible waste of potential."

"She doesn't see it that way. To her, he's a sweet, handsome man. They grew up together."

"It would be a shame to lose her. It's so difficult to find female givers. She is admired and accepted here. Long term givers are considered full members of this community, equal in nearly every way."

"Almost the way human males treat their woman it would seem."

Dolnaraq grunted a grudging agreement.

Ruth nodded. Beverly was her giver. They'd developed a deep and enduring bond. "I will not try to influence her decision. In areas such as this, a woman must follow her heart."

"You're talking like a human."

Ruth offered the hint of a human-like grin. "We are talking about humans. They have their own way. And who is to say it's any worse than ours. Perhaps having a life mate would be somehow fulfilling."

"It's impractical. Based on my research, I've determined that the reyaqc population is steadily decreasing. What is needed is for two thirds or better of all infant reyaqc to infuse with females, thus becoming female themselves, in order that we have a large breeding population. By doing this, each male could fertilize multiple females simultaneously, thus strengthening the chances of survival for our species."

Ruth's face was emotionless, her eyes a virgin canvas. "Perhaps. But, I still think there is value in the concept of life mates."

Dolnaraq noted an underlying tone in Ruth's words but was uncertain of her meaning. Females of any species were a strange breed, he'd determined. This day's events had done nothing to change this opinion. "And so what of the man?" he asked. "Do we free him simply because the woman loves him?"

"Actually," said Ruth. "I believe that might be the best course of action. He came for her. If she chooses him as a mate, he will care little for us, and will likely only desire to steal Beverly away from this place. He's yet to discover our true nature, and I'm sure he would rather flee before we seek to punish him for shooting Dorcas."

Dolnaraq contemplated this. She could be right. Fraser had yet to learn the true nature of the reyaqc. Better to allow the woman to cloud his mind with thoughts of love and marriage than to prolong his stay and risk exposure. "So be it," said Dolnaraq. "And let us hope this is the last we see of Harry Fraser."

✻✻✻✻✻

The letter arrived nearly five months later as Dolnaraq sat in his recently acquired Washington DC estate, enjoying the warmth of the crackling fireplace in his expansive study.

Dear Mr. Matthew Greene,

I hope this correspondence finds you well. I will attempt however inadequately to speak plainly, though with discretion. As you know, the young woman, B, left our community in order to marry her suitor, the young and impetuous Mr. H.F. We had not heard from her since her departure, and in truth had thought little of the incidents leading to her exit. After a lingering struggle, Dorcas healed of her wound. I am happy to report that she was able to keep her leg, though she walks with notice-able limp and has considerable pain, particularly in the cold of night.

I have never had a sustained relationship with a female, and find such pairings mysterious and confusing, but I suppose it is common for lovers to share the most intimate details of their lives. It would seem this was the case with B and H. At some time, some intimate and carefree moment, B revealed to H the true nature of our community. Knowing her as I do, she likely did so with enthusiasm, exclaiming how wondrous we are, how amazing and unique. I'm certain she intended no harm. She truly loves our kind and had she not wed the man, H, I think it possible she may have lived the remainder of her days among us. But, as you are painfully aware, hers is a rare gift among humanity, to embrace and love those so different from herself even when her understanding is and will forever be limited to that of an outside observer. On whole, humanity fears what it does not understand. On whole, humanity seeks to subdue, or better, to destroy that which it does not understand.

At this point, I must say, Mr. Greene, please do not fret too deeply. Our community survives. And it appears that that which we hope to conceal is again concealed. But, there was an attack and there were casualties. H.F. attacked at night, which, in truth was likely to our advantage. Our senses of night vision, hearing, and olfactory are much better than there's and once we were aware that an attack was underway we were able to quickly subdue this lunatic and his three like-minded companions. Yet still, we did not respond with such speed as to prevent several fatalities. Among those lost were: Amos, Claudia, Caleb, Esau, and, it pains me to say, your dear friend Ruth, pregnant with your pup and due to birth in less than two months time. My understanding is that she'd kept news of the pregnancy from you, not desiring that you feel an obligation that would prohibit the continuation of your work.

The intruders were slain, their bodies deposited in a wooded area adjacent a tavern some twenty miles distant from our home. The place is known as a site of violence and lawbreaking. There are frequent brawls, illegal gambling, prostitution, and the occasional murder. When and if the remains are discovered, the authorities will surely make the proper assumptions and our community will be spared undue scrutiny as a result of these events.

I am saddened to write with such unhappy news to one I consider so dear to my being. I miss you, my friend, and long for you to one day return to us, though I understand and appreciate your efforts in the world beyond. Be at peace and take heart, the female, Martha, will soon birth you a pup and she has promised a female as this is your desire.

May the world treat you with kindness and understanding,
Jeremiah Schrock

It was perhaps a half hour's time before Dolnaraq released the page, allowing it to drop to the floor in a subtle swaying descent. That strange hollow feeling in his belly, nearly forgotten during the months since his departure, had returned with a suddenness and ferocity he could never have anticipated. He rose, staggered, and moved to the window overlooking a finely manicured garden. "Ruth," he said in a strangled choke. "Ruth."

Chapter Ten

1968

Brian Hazelton didn't particularly like Las Vegas. Sure, the palm trees were a rather exotic change, and the mild winters beat the nearly sub-arctic Minnesota. The entertainment wasn't bad. The Beatles had been there, Elvis loved the place, Sinatra and his pals were regulars. Of the bunch, Brian preferred Elvis. The Beatles' music was okay, but their hair was too long and he'd heard rumors they used drugs. As to everyday necessities, his home was centrally located. The grocery store was only three blocks east. The post office was within walking distance. But the heat. Triple digits – 105 on Monday, 107 Tuesday, 109 Wednesday. Even after dark the temperature only managed to inch down into the nineties. No end in sight. It was mid August and the long-term residents all agreed there was another month of this. He wasn't all that pleased with the work environment either. Casino work was nothing he'd ever envisioned. He'd spent most of his adult life repairing washers and dryers. Now he repaired slot machines. There was other work in Las Vegas, true, but the best available job at the time – the best paying job that he'd found – had been as a slot tech.

The casino floors were smoke-filled and poorly ventilated, aggravating Brian's asthma, and drying his eyes to a sandpaper texture. It wasn't as if there wasn't smoke in every work environment, but the gray haze was considerably thicker on the casino floor of the Sahara than it would be in, say, an auto shop or a Laundromat. At least those places had windows. As well, the casinos were loud, with the rattle of slot machines, the often distorted overhead music, the boisterous drunks. By nature, Brian was a loner. He'd enjoyed the general solitude inherent to fixing home appliances. It fit his temperament. But, this… Well, this was where he was. At least until Deanna's father kicked the bucket.

That sounded harsh, he knew. But it was a truth. Brian's wife of thirteen years had an ailing, elderly father. The man was too stubborn to uproot and move to Minnesota where he could be with the family, and too ornery to move into a "home" where he could have proper nursing care. He wouldn't consent to allowing Deanna's younger brother, Charlie, to come stay with him. "Your brother's a drunk and a doper," he'd said. "I'll not have some drunk and his lowlife, draft-dodging hippy friends hanging about my place." He'd then stated that if she really thought he needed tending to – and he wasn't all too certain that he did – well, then it would just have to be Deanna and "her man" that came to Las Vegas to do the tending.

Barry and Kenny, Brian and Deanna's twin sons, now aged eleven, had handled the move with relative stoicism, and had soon made plenty of friends. They seemed well-adjusted. Deanna had settled into a comfortable routine of volunteering at the church and selling Avon to the locale housewives. And Brian had…

Well. Brian was just waiting for the old man to kick the bucket, wasn't he?

Brian set aside the dog-eared paperback he'd been reading, rose with a grunt from the quicksand-like clutches of the couch, and ambled through the narrow living room and into the small kitchen. The family's cat, Uhura, named after a character of the television show, "Star Trek," was hunched in the corner just beyond the dining room table. Strange. The cat seemed to be spooked, hair on end, back arched, tail erect and twitching. Brian shrugged. Crazy creature. It was always skittish about something. Brian yawned and glanced at his Timex. Nearly two a.m. Still another three hours or better until sunup. He'd had a restless night and had finally given up on sleep, deciding instead to read the Ian Fleming novel, "You Only Live Twice." Now it was too late to go back to bed. He needed to be up in another couple of hours and going to sleep would just cause him more harm than good.

Brian opened the cabinet to the left of the refrigerator and withdrew a large red can of Folgers coffee. Might as well start pumping the caffeine. He was going to need it.

What was that sound?

Had it come from the garage?

He glanced toward the cat. Uhura was now pacing one direction and then the other, back forth, back, forth, fur on end, tail held high. The feline let off a low growl, the likes of which Brian had never heard from this typically docile creature.

There it was again, a rustle followed by a soft *thunk*.

Brian set the coffee tin on the counter and made his way through the narrow kitchen and into the tiny laundry area. He leaned his head against the door leading to the garage.

Several seconds went by.

Nothing.

Brian almost let it go. But he was curious now. And there was his family to think of. Deanna and the kids were still asleep, and Brian didn't entirely trust the neighborhood. It wasn't awful, he knew. It was older, but well kept, and centrally located. But there had been crime in his area and it seemed someone was always having a very loud argument or inciting police activity of one sort or another. It wasn't that Brian lived in a hotspot of criminal activity; it was just that no matter how nice the neighborhood, this simply wasn't suburban Minnesota.

Brian leaned further into the garage door. Still nothing. Assuming he'd simply heard a stray dog or a garbage can knocked over by a wind gust, he opened the door into the connected one-car garage and flipped the light switch to his left. He squinted as he scanned the space. It was cluttered with bicycles and tools. A twin-sized mattress leaned against one wall. There were several cardboard boxes filled with toys that the boys had outgrown. There were skateboards lying across the narrow walk-space, daring Brian to step between them all without somehow breaking his neck. There were two broken window air conditioners, a lawnmower, several brooms and lawn care tools, but no car. That item had been relegated to the driveway.

Lit by a single bare light bulb situated amidst the ceiling rafters, the garage was a sea of shadows. Brian took one step in, scanning left to right. The place was so cluttered that it was hard to distinguish much. He really needed to commit a day to organizing this mess. Brian took another step, and then another. There was nothing here. He was sure of it. He'd probably just let his lack of sleep coupled with the fertile imagination of Ian Fleming get the better of him. Still, he was here. He was curious, and would never be satisfied until he'd made absolutely sure that there was no intruder. Brian stepped over a homemade skateboard made from plywood and discarded casters and then over another adorned with a roughly painted shark. He glanced behind the leaning mattress thinking that perhaps he'd find a rodent or a stray cat that had somehow wandered in.

Nothing.

He peered around the numerous cardboard boxes. Did they really need all of this stuff? If they hadn't bothered to unpack the boxes by this time, they probably never would. Or, maybe he was subconsciously hoping they could simply reload the boxes onto a moving van and flee this hellhole.

Another half-dozen obstacle-laden steps and he was at the small exterior door leading to the side of the house.

Brian gripped the door handle, but before he could twist the knob and open the door, someone knocked on it from the other side. Two knocks, very deliberate, spaced apart by about three seconds. Brian hesitated, removed his hand from the knob. His heart was racing, and the perspiration on his forehead had nothing to do with the Nevada heat. "H... Hello?" he stammered in a hushed near-whisper.

Silence.

Brian stood, not breathing, his ears attuned to the slightest of sounds, remaining this way for close to a minute. Just when he was nearly convinced that he'd heard nothing at all, it happened again. That same deliberate knock, one, then a pause, and then the other.

Knock... Knock.

"Who's out there?" he asked, his voice barely above a whisper. It seemed his heart had leapt into his throat.

Again, silence.

Brian waited, breath held, muscles taut, sweat dripping down his face. He stood there for what seemed five minutes or better, just staring at the wooden barrier, noticing the first signs of peeling paint, and the subtle patterns of the wood. Not a sound, not a twitch of the knob, not even the rustle of a breeze.

"Stupid kids," he finally concluded. Neighborhood kids pulling a prank. Kids. Yeah. That was it. Just kids.

He allowed the air to flee his lungs. Had he been holding his breath all that time? Brian reached out, hand still trembling. He grasped the door handle. It was slippery from his sweaty palm.

He twisted.

The door pulled open with only the hint of a groan. Even at two in the morning, the heat coming from the outside was stifling.

Brian's breath caught short in his throat.

His heartbeat quickened.

No one was there.

Brian exhaled, shook his head. His chest actually hurt. Had he nearly given himself a heart attack because of a stupid prank?

A sound.

Just a few feet to Brian's right.

It seemed to be coming from the row of overgrown shrubbery lining his home.

Brian swallowed. Someone was there after all. And suddenly, he wasn't so certain that it was just kids.

There it was again, a rustle, this time accompanied by a gasp. The kind of gasp someone made when in pain or in shock. Had someone been hurt? Had there been a mugging?

Almost against his own will, Brian took a step away from the doorway and to his right. A step closer to the sound.

There was something there, partially obscured by the shrubbery.

It was a foot. A naked leg and foot. Just beyond a toppled garbage can.

Brian traversed the short distance in five quick steps. There knelt a man – naked – situated amidst the scattered garbage on the dry and dusty ground. He was pale, his skin almost transparent. Even in the Nevada heat, he shivered and shook.

Another step closer.

Brian leaned in. "Hey, buddy, are you okay? What are doing here?"

The naked man offered no sound, made no move.

"Hey, you can't stay here like this. Are you hurt?"

The man cocked his head emitting a low purr. Obscured by shadows, Brian couldn't get a good look at the man's face. Cautiously, Brian reached out, touching the man on his left shoulder.

There was that purring sound again. It reminded him of the sound Uhura made when he petted her.

Just as Brian began to retract his hand, just as he was about to mumble something about calling the police, a hand shot out. The grip was strong. Stronger than anything Brian had ever known. He heard his wrist bones crumble into tiny slivers even before the pain registered in his shocked and confused brain.

The naked man was up now, at eye level, his right hand whipping around to the back of Brian's neck. If Brian had had the opportunity to think, he would have noted that the movement was faster than a Ron Santo pitch. The pain was sharp, deep, searing. It seemed something had penetrated the back of his neck even into the core of his spine. And Brian's final thought as a living breathing man, even as his limbs quivered and contracted, even as fire erupted in his veins, even as the contents of his stomach blew out from between his lips and his bowels opened in an incredible stench, was that this face before him, this strange feline-like face, was not the face of a human being.

Chapter Eleven

Tresset closed his eyes inhaling deeply before releasing his breath in a long steady stream. There was a surge and then another. His entire form shuddered as he received the essence. Beginning at the fingertips. Electrifying his palm, nearly bursting through his arm and into his torso, head, and other extremities. His eyes opened slowly – an eternal moment – meeting those of the involuntary giver. Wide with terror and incomprehension. A whisk of empathic connection. An intelligent being just like Tresset and yet worlds removed. What did this person, this human, know of the struggle to survive? He of the two car garage and middleclass environ. What did he know of loneliness or disappointment? What did he know of the need, the burning, all-encompassing desire, the compulsion to invite the very fabric of a hated being into one's own body, into one's own cells, into the very makeup of one's own molecular foundation? What could he possibly know of Tresset? How could he even begin to comprehend?

And what if he did know? What if he was to learn of the reyaqc with their peculiar need? What then? Would he embrace them? Would he claim understanding or compassion? Would he recognize Tresset's value as a fellow being?

No. Not impossible, but unlikely in the extreme.

No more than Tresset had sympathy for him. Though Tresset absorbed the man's very makeup, the two were undeniably, unforgivably different. Similar, yes, in form. Similar in drives, similar in emotional needs.

But different always.

Should this man and those like him learn of Tresset and his kind, he might argue compassion but only in that the reyaqc be treated humanely once corralled into camps and prisons. He would claim that he held no ill will toward these bizarre creatures, but he would claim that for the public safety they should never be allowed freedom, maybe never even be allowed to reproduce. Yes, humanity would go through the motions. Humans would debate and deliberate. They would argue about how to best deal with the situation, but in the end fear would be the beacon in the night. They would follow that fear down the road to unspeakable atrocities, all the while proclaiming that they meant no ill will and wanted only what was best for all.

It was the story of human history. Tresset was certain it would be the story of the future.

Another surge, a gasp, a shudder. More, more.

A stench.

Another.

The man's eyes, wide, wider, and then…

Lifeless.

Tresset stepped back, suppressing a quiver as the essence stuttered through his form. He stared down at the fallen human and wiped the man's perspiration from his hands with a soft cloth he carried in his front pocket. He hadn't intended to slay him. He'd known his need was great. He'd known the level of depletion. But he also disliked moving among the humans and so had delayed his journey into the population center. He despised the odor. He despised the arrogance, the assumption that they alone were the heirs to all the earth had to offer. He'd established a relatively comfortable, if solitary, existence living among the hot and stony foothills adjacent the Colorado River which fed Lake Mead.

Lake Mead!

Another example of human arrogance. This body of water existed only because the humans had chosen to build that ridiculous dam which disrupted the natural flow of water.

Much of the area Tresset roamed was sparsely populated and thus unsuitable for the hunt. It was never wise to forcefully infuse in small communities unless one planned to move on immediately following the taking of essence. There was simply too great a risk of exposure should the human develop complications or even parish as a result of the taking. It was so much easier to locate a culprit among dozens than it was thousands. As well, while a person's family and loved ones might press to locate an aggressor within a good sized city, the pressure usually ended with those few individuals; where in a small community, everyone became involved in the problems of everyone else. And so, when his need became great, when his skin thinned and paled, when his limbs began to quiver, and his veins to protrude, Tresset would wrap himself in human attire, don sunglasses and a floppy hat to better disguise his peculiar features, and make his way to the nearest bus depot some fifteen miles distant where he would board a westbound bus heading toward the cesspool of human depravity called Las Vegas. The population was greater there and geographically distant from Tresset's cave, which overlooked the river. He could enter the town, usually targeting a residential district, find a suitable donor, infuse, and leave town before the attack became known.

That was, unless, as in this instance, the human perished. A murder would always draw attention, even though, less than a week later, it might be forgotten by the community at large. Humans lacked focus. Or, perhaps, it wasn't so much that they lacked focus as they focused primarily on their own needs and circumstances, thus allowing the trials of others to dribble off like dew from a leaf. Though, if he was to be honest, reyaqc could be accused of the same. It was survival instinct, he supposed. And as Tresset had a well-developed survival instinct, he would exit town well before the body was discovered. The sun was three hours distant, and Tresset had pulled the corpse away from the garage and into the backyard, leaving it between the home and a row of flowered bushes. Certainly the man's spouse would wake and wonder where he'd gone off to, but her instinct would be that he'd taken a walk, or gone to the market. She wouldn't be poking around the lawn searching for a body. He would be discovered, certainly. And soon. But, likely not in the first hours. Assuming the woman wouldn't rise at least until six AM, Tresset was comfortable that he'd be well on his way before anyone began looking for the culprit.

Tresset noted the scent on the subtle breeze seconds before her heard the voice. Even thus alerted, he was startled. "That was sloppy," said the reyaqc.

Tresset turned to face the looming form before him. A molt. Large, perhaps six foot three in height, maybe more. He was bulky and round with broad shoulders and beefy arms ending in large paw-like hands. His facial structure was more or less round, featuring small intelligent eyes, a somewhat elongated nose, and a broad expressive mouth with a bit of a cleft at the center top. His canines were long and curved but not so predominate as to cause difficulty in closing his mouth. The right canine was perhaps an inch longer than its companion, creating a somewhat unbalanced appearance.

Obviously noting Tresset's cautious gaze, and likely smelling his sudden rush of hormones, the bear-like molt offered a broad, endearing, and very human-like grin. "No need for fear, friend. We are too few to fight when there is no cause."

Tresset stood tall as though at attention, though this still left him better than a foot shorter than the other. He was still weak and somewhat dizzy following the infusion, but wanted to give the impression that he was at full capability. He didn't know this molt and had no clue as to his purpose in approaching him. "Who are you?" he asked, still at the ready for deception and attack.

"Bremu Oleirg," said the other, offering a knowing nod.

"A pack chieftain?" said Tresset in response. He knew this because reyaqc had no surnames. The only time a second name was added was when one slew a pack chieftain, thus attaining the leadership of the slain leader's pack. The new leader would at this time add the slain chieftain's name to his own. This molt, Bremu, had slain his predecessor, Oleirg, as surely Oleirg had slain his predecessor, adding his name to his own. "How did you find me?"

"We were traversing the neighborhood on the way to a hunt. Your scent was upon the breeze. I smelled you even through the open window of a moving vehicle."

"I was unaware that there was a Las Vegas-based pack."

Bremu's massive head moved slowly side to side. "No, not Las Vegas. Never Las Vegas. Too many humans. Far too civilized. We roam the desert beyond, some seventy miles distant." The molt spoke with a slight impediment, likely the result of the cleft. It was the kind of thing that could lull someone into believing him a halfwit. But already Tresset sensed no such lack in this massive molt. Angling his head slightly right, Bremu added, "May I suggest we take our conversation elsewhere, or would you prefer we both be apprehended for your lack of control?"

Tresset felt anger surge through his limbs. True, he had blundered in slaying the human, but having this other comment on it made him feel small and foolish.

Obviously sensing Tresset's anger the other offered a hearty chuckle. "Take no offence, little one. We all have needs. Sometimes those needs cloud our better judgment. Can any molt claim he's not done the same?"

Little one! This hulking, lisping, beast had the audacity to call him little one!

Bremu chuckled yet again, deep, resonating. "Have I offended you yet again? I called you little one, that's it, isn't it? Give me a name then and prevent further such gaffs."

Tresset studied the molt, silent and brooding.

"Oh, let it go – please!" chortled Bremu. "Let's not start this relationship with animosity."

"I never said I desired relationship."

"Our association then – our introduction. Call it what you want. We reyaqc are too few to quarrel over imagined slights and well-intended overtures. Now, what do you call yourself?"

Tresset wanted desperately to dislike this one, but Bremu was right in all he'd said. It was only Tresset's anger at being caught unaware that rankled him so. "I am called Tresset."

"Tresset," said Bremu. "And are you aligned with a pack?"

Tresset hesitated before speaking. "I have not been aligned since I was a pup."

"And you've existed alone all these years?"

Tresset swallowed and paused before speaking in slow deliberate fashion. He wanted no emotion to be obvious in his words. "Not all. I had a companion. We parted company some years ago." A wave of vertigo passed over Tresset but he willed himself to retain his stance. The new essence tingled and burned. He didn't need such a distraction just then.

Bremu nodded, either unaware of or ignoring Tresset's incapacity. "Well enough. Tresset, the solitary, tonight you will hunt with Bremu Oleirg and those of my pack."

"I have already infused and have no desire to join your pack."

Bremu chuckled. "And I have not offered you a position in my pack. But, we'd best leave this scene and I've got transportation. Ride with us tonight. Share your stories and I'll share mine. If in the end we part ways, we'll both be richer for what we've learned from the other. If we decide otherwise, well, we'll worry about that then, won't we?"

*****

Bremu's transportation was a decade old school bus, modified to serve the pack's needs. A thick wall had been erected behind the fourth row of seats. This front area was where the reyaqc rode. The rear section, beyond the wall, was for humans. In this section, the windows had been covered with sheet metal, the cushioned seats replaced with two wooden benches, each bolted to the floor along the two long walls. The exterior of the bus had been painted a light brown, nearly a tan, with random swatches of olive green spattered about the thing. It gave the bus a quasi-military appearance as the coloring was obviously intended to camouflage the vehicle when it was parked in the desert. In apparent contrast, a peace sign was spray painted onto the driver's side wall. A different type of camouflage, supposed Tresset. Urban camouflage. Bystanders would assume the bus was owned by those of the so-called hippy subculture, a movement that apparently grew by the day.

Even camouflaged such, even moving about only in the wee hours when few humans moved about, discovery was always a concern. Molts were peculiar to the human eye. That said, it often surprised Tresset how seldom they were discovered. Tresset had given this topic much thought and had determined that their seeming invisibility came about for several reasons. One was that humans were prone to dismiss their own senses rather than accept something that challenged their concepts of a well-ordered world. A passing glance at a molt in the dark was usually rationalized away and soon forgotten. Another factor was that the reyaqc were secretive and very jealous of their anonymity – their survival depended on it. Thus, midnight raids, guerrilla tactics, and the establishment of packs only in non or minimally populated areas. As well, the reyaqc were few in number. All of the reyaqc about the globe would only fill a midsized town. And spread about as they were, it was very difficult for the human population to interact with many of this rare people. Even so, there had been many discoveries throughout time. Often, the reyaqc were thought to be some sort of supernatural monsters: werewolves, vampires, even bigfoot legends evolved from reyaqc/human encounters. Aside from this, there were human sympathizers, people who did know and were willing to aid these seemingly peculiar cousins to their race. Those not sympathetic were most often eliminated before they could stir together a mob or movement. The reyaqc had no choice but to be brutal and efficient.

Tresset hesitated upon climbing aboard the bus. Bremu had four companions, all male, all molts. Was this truly wise to trust these unknowns? True, they were of his kind, and he detected no odor of rising adrenaline, no racing hormones which might signal an impending attack. He was likely safe. But he'd spent nearly half of a century alone, living in various outlying areas, remaining only so close to humanity as to have a source of essence. True, he'd encountered other reyaqc along the way, some individuals such as himself and, on three occasions, packs, but he'd never felt compelled to spend more than fleeting moments with them. It was true, he'd mated with several of the females he'd encountered, likely producing offspring, but he'd never remained long enough to be sure of this. His last true companion had been Dolnaraq. It would be weak to admit, even to himself, that Dolnaraq had hurt him by abandoning him those many years ago, but in sullen moments, the emptiness flitted about his soul. It was usually after such thoughts that Tresset hunted with a greater fervor and aggression than at times when his mind was more placid. And while at some level Tresset longed to once again be with those of his own kind, he was leery of them as well. Leery not so much of physical injury, but of the emotional variety. That kind had a much longer duration.

Tresset chided himself. Foolish thoughts. Foolish fears. He was not some weak and emotional human. These ideas had no place in his mind. He was accepting a ride from these reyaqc, nothing more. And it would be good to spend an hour or two among his species. It would be refreshing, perhaps even therapeutic.

Therapeutic. Forget that!

Again, thinking like a human. He truly had been away from his kind for far too long.

"I've found a lone molt," announced Bremu as he climbed onto the bus, gesturing for Tresset to follow. "Apparently his need was great because a human perished during the taking. I've offered him transportation."

Tresset followed Bremu onto the bus, nodding first to the lanky molt in the driver's seat and then to the other three, each sitting alone on a seat along the left side of the bus. Bremu slipped into the front right seat indicating that Tresset should take the seat immediately behind him. They all, with the exception of the driver, sat, not forward in the seats, but with their backs against the metal walls, feet extended across the bench-like seats. This meant they each faced the center aisle and were face-to-face with those seated across from them. "Hello," said Tresset as he lowered himself into a like position. In truth, he didn't know what else to say. His solitary life had not given him much cause to maintain communication skills. Already he felt uncomfortable and questioned the wisdom in this decision.

"Hey," waved the driver in greeting. His hair was long and dark and could have belonged to a human hippy. He wore a tie-dye T-shirt, bell-bottom blue jeans, and a stainless steel chain adorned with the popular peace symbol. Despite the human clothing his face was pure molt, extending into a near-muzzle. His arms were long and wiry, and all exposed areas were covered in coarse brown and black fur. The left arm appeared to be perhaps six inches shorter than the right, the fingers shorter as well, more human-like than those on the opposite hand. Tresset suspected monkey essence, likely spider monkey to be precise, but he could be wrong on the breed of simian. He wondered where the molt had found monkeys from which to infuse. Likely they'd stolen these from a zoo. Monkeys were not native to Nevada.

The molt seated directly behind the driver was dressed more conservatively, wearing only black, likely in an effort to remain unseen at night. He nodded a greeting as well. "Hello lone wanderer," he said with a nod and a flourish of exaggerated hand motions. His essence was of the fox and Tresset was forced to turn away from him for fear he might show weakness; for this one reminded him of how Dolnaraq had appeared when still he infused fox essence. Tresset did not like to be reminded of Dolnaraq.

The next molt sat directly across from Tresset. He cocked his coyote head to the left, eliciting a low tone, not a growl, nearly a hum. His eyes were dim in the way of the mentally impaired. Tresset was not naïve to the cause of this deficiency. One hopes that when infusing animal essence to acquire desirable traits such as enhanced hearing, night vision, olfactory sense, and perhaps speed and ferocity. But a reyaqc has no control of the essence and sometimes it is the animal's lack of intellect that is received. This poor creature was obviously one such instance. Tresset could see in the pained expression that he desired to speak, to be included as an equal, but this might never be the case. Once animal essence is received the core characteristics take hold. In some instances, such as with Dolnaraq, continued infusions diminish negative characteristics granting desirable effects, but often these traits remain. In fact, they are often, if anything, augmented by additional infusions. The only sure way to reverse the process was to cease infusing animal essence altogether. With time, and as the animal characteristics fade, there is hope of regaining a more superior intellect, but this reversal carried risks of its own. The molt returned Tresset's gaze for several seconds, emitted a low rumble from deep within his throat, and then lifted one leg, bent at the waist, and began licking himself.

Tresset nodded at this poor specimen and then turned to see the final member of the group. The molt sat across and to Tresset's left, and studied the newcomer long before speaking. "What are you called?" he asked.

"Tresset."

The molt nodded. He was tall, sleek, and young, with dark canine fur covering his form. Tresset could see this because this one wore no clothing. His muscles rippled beneath the fur, his stomach was taut and well muscled, his arms bulging with strength. His expression made it clear that he was unhappy to welcome a newcomer.

"Tresset it is!" said the simian driver. "Nice to make your meet. They call me Spider, but my real name's Treleq." The driver then punched a button on the dashboard and loud music blared from speakers mounted in the upper front right and left corners of the bus. It was some blaring human music, something about "in a gadda da vida, baby," whatever that meant. It gave Tresset a headache, but the driver bobbed in his seat and tapped the rhythm out on the steering wheel as he pulled away from the curb.

The fox-like molt across and to Tresset's right studied him for a moment before speaking. "I'm guessing mountain lion, is that right? At first I was thinking pussy cat, but no. You look too angry for that." He offered an exaggerated wink.

Tresset nodded but said nothing.

The fox angled his head. "Unless I've missed something, there aren't many of those in town. Where do you live?"

Here, Tresset pondered his response. Should he give an honest answer? Was there a danger in these molts having such information? "The foot hills," he said eventually. "Near the Colorado River. I have two captured and caged lions. I infuse from both."

"Whoa!" said Spider. "That's far." Still, he pounded the rhythm to that annoying human noise. Tresset wanted to sever his neck.

"Don't be an idiot. It's no further than we come," snapped the sleek canine molt across left from Tresset.

"Whoa!" exclaimed Spider. "Lighten it, huh? It's just small talk."

Bremu chuckled. "Enough! Think of the impression you leave." His gaze settled on the sleek, canine molt. "Is that understood, Kyorl?"

The canine molt called Kyorl snorted in response.

"So, tell me, Tresset," this from Bremu. "You hunted a quiet neighborhood at night. How did you know you'd find a source?"

Tresset allowed a slow stream of breath to exit his lips before responding. He was in no mood for questioning. "Simple. I look for a dwelling with lights on and someone moving about within. I then make enough noise to cause curiosity, and wait for the male to investigate."

"Tricky. How do you know it will be the male?" asked the fox molt.

"He knows," injected Kyorl, "because the male defends the household. Females don't investigate strange noises in the night."

The coyote molt nodded as if he understood the exchange, which was doubtful.

"But, why go to the trouble?" asked the fox molt. "Why not hunt a commercial street where people are outside for the taking?"

Tresset stared at him. Was this one as stupid as his companion? "I am a lone reyaqc. I have no transportation that will spirit me away after an attack. I have hunted populated streets in the past. I've learned that eventually this leads to discovery."

"I get it," offered Spider with some enthusiasm. "You pick a place and time of night where no one's outdoors and then lure your prey into your trap."

"I believe that is what I said, yes." Tresset felt the urge to withdraw his cloth and wipe the filth from his hands, but suppressed the impulse. Too many eyes were on him and none would understand the need.

"As you will see, our methods are not so subtle," said Bremu. He added nothing more.

Tresset soon learned the meaning of his words as Spider pulled the bus onto a commercial lane, slowing as he did so. The reyaqc stared through the windows judging their options. "We could go to Fremont Street," said the fox molt. "There are always humans meandering around."

Bremu shook his head. "No, Anesch. Too soon since we last raided the area. Besides, there's a heavy law enforcement presence there."

The one called Anesch nodded. "Hey, that's okay. No argument here."

"I told you already. The Pioneer Pub," said Kyorl. "It's been over two years since we last hunted there. It closes in less than thirty minutes. The humans will file out in twos and threes. Easy picking. Isolated parking lot. Not much light. Set back from the street. I don't see why we're even debating this."

Bremu nodded. "I know what you've suggested, Kyorl. And the suggestion is valid. I was simply getting additional input."

Kyorl glared at Bremu.

Tresset felt renewed apprehension. It seemed these molts had no clear plan. As well, he sensed friction between Bremu and the one called Kyorl. Perhaps this Kyorl wanted to add Bremu's name to his own.

Tresset had no desire to become involved in pack disputes. He simply wanted to return to his cave and continue his solitary existence.

Maybe.

In truth, though each molt was annoying in his own right, it felt good to be among other reyaqc. It had been far too long since he'd been with those of his kind. Far too long. And in truth, he felt a pull. Nothing substantial. In fact, it was nearly indiscernible. But it was there, a longing, a desire, a need. Tresset closed his eyes pushing the ridiculous thought from his mind. He needed no one. He wanted no one. And any thoughts contrary to that would bring him nothing but pain. He wanted none of it.

Spider broke Tresset's contemplations with a shouted announcement. Even so, Tresset barely heard the molt over his blaring music. The tune was now something about riders on the storm. "Pioneer Pub coming up on the left, my hairy comrades. We going for this?"

Bremu nodded. "Why not? It'll give Kyorl one less thing to brood about and it's as good a spot as any. The parking lot works to our advantage."

Tresset understood immediately what Bremu meant by this. The building was fairly isolated, set back perhaps twenty yards from the road with vacant lots on either side. The small gravel lot had no lighting of its own, but relied on the distant streetlights. Spider was able to pull the bus along the west side of the building where it was almost completely obscured in shadow. The building itself was no larger than a medium sized ranch home and made to resemble a log cabin. As soon as the vehicle rolled to a complete stop, Tresset's companions filed out of the bus. Anesch, the fox, turned before exiting. "Tresset," he said with a jovial tone. "Join us! That is unless you have something against good sport."

Tresset allowed a low growl to slip from his throat, but he rose and followed his companions into the near-dawn night. This was a mistake. He could feel it in his bowels. It was a mistake and he had no reason to be here. None whatsoever. But, then why was he climbing down into the lot? Why was he walking along the side of the bus, following Anesch?

"You're not actually going to allow this one to participate," said Kyorl to Bremu. "We know nothing about him."

Bremu turned to Kyorl, his tone even and forceful. "We know that he is more like us than not. That will suffice."

"He could be from a rival pack. We don't know."

Anesch the fox turned to Kyorl. "Really? That makes sense to you? That another pack would send a spy all the way out here to infiltrate us? You might want to check your paranoia at the door, dog breath."

The dull-witted coyote molt gazed from one to the other, nodding as if to agree with both.

Tresset was about to walk off into the night and leave these bickering beasts to their squabbles when Spider called out in an urgent hush. "I know you girls want to prove who has the prettiest dress, but the door's opening."

Bremu moved forward with a fair amount of grace for a being of his bulk. Peeking around the corner, he nodded. "A male and female. Both young."

"Both drunk," added Spider.

Before Tresset could ask the plan, Bremu offered one almost indiscernible nod and Kyorl and Anesch rushed forward and around the corner. The attack was swift and nearly silent. The two young humans, both with long wavy hair and red headbands, were attacked from the rear, each molt pouncing on his target bringing them down before they could comprehend that they were under attack. Each molt blocked the human's air passages with their palms rendering them unconscious. Almost in unison, they flopped the still forms over their shoulders and carried them to the bus where Spider opened the rear door. The humans were dumped onto the metal floor and the door closed and locked, all of this within less than a minute of first contact. Tresset couldn't help but to be impressed with the efficiency of the attack.

Already, Spider was back to his lookout corner. The molt moved with a peculiar gate. His long narrow legs and too long arms seemed to sway out of sync with each other and several times he leaned forward in simian-like fashion using his arms to propel him before returning to a nearly upright crouch. The shorter arm obviously caused him some difficulty with balance, but the molt seemed all but oblivious to this. "I like it, I like it," he said hopping about as if dancing to one of his idiotic human songs. "Give us some more, baby."

"Keep it down, Spider," warned Bremu. "We're not done yet."

The coyote nodded.

"How many do you seek?" asked Tresset as he stepped to beside the bear-like molt.

Bremu chuckled. "Why, as many as we can fit in the bus, of course."

Tresset was taken aback. These molts intended to abduct perhaps a dozen humans. "But won't the disappearance of so many cause suspicion?"

"And what if it does? I'm responsible for a pack. And this pack roams the desert some seventy miles or better from this place. If I don't provide, then each pack member will need to venture out to satisfy the need. Wouldn't you agree that this continual stream of attacks would create a greater chance of capture and discovery? We do periodic sweeps, targeting different areas of town – sometimes venturing further into other communities. No two hunts are ever too close together in timing or geography. Our way is sound."

Tresset wasn't entirely convinced at the soundness of the system. Surely the humans would eventually see a pattern to these disappearances. "How long do you keep the humans before returning them?"

Bremu chuckled. "Return them? So that they can tell strange tales of abduction? No, no. These will remain until they are depleted."

In other words, they kept the humans until they perished. "Do you have no willing givers?"

Again, a chuckle. "Willing! Tell me, have you ever had a willing giver?" Tresset did not answer and so Bremu continued. "No. Of course you haven't. Such things are fables. I've never known a human to care if a reyaqc lived or died."

"I did have one," said Tresset after a moment's hesitation. He disliked sharing things of himself.

Bremu's eyes went wide. "You did? An actual willing giver? Tell me more."

Tresset pursed his lips, staring at the stony ground before raising his head to meet Bremu's gaze. "Long ago. In Europe. A Romani clan found me near dead. They nursed me to health. It was a mingled people. Reyaqc and human lived together." Tresset withdrew his cloth, rubbing this against his palms before jamming it back into his pocket.

"Well, that explains it," said Kyorl. "This one is weak. He's cohabitated with humans."

"I have not!" shot Tresset. "They were despicable, the reyaqc weak, the humans filthy, diseased." He knew this had been a mistake. He should not be with these others, and he certainly shouldn't be sharing pieces of his history.

"Hey, motley ones," said Spider. "I hate to break up the party, but we've got more."

This time it was a group of three, all males, all in their forties or fifties. Bremu indicated that they were not ideal, but that they should take them anyway. There was no way of knowing how many more would exit the building and dawn was not too far distant. They might not have the opportunity to acquire all that they needed.

"Let's see if our human loving friend can handle one," said Kyorl. And before any could respond, he pushed Tresset into the open.

The humans turned at the sound and Tresset had no chance to contemplate his attack and so simply leapt at the closet man, this with catlike strength and grace. The humans could never have imagined that a being could move with such ease and quickness and were caught off balance. For a flicker of a moment Tresset thought of his recent infusion of essence, of how this had left him weak and slightly disoriented, but apparently his current adrenaline rush had suppressed the inadequacy. He felt as fine as ever. The goal was to subdue, not to kill and not to draw essence, and so Tresset suppressed his natural instinct to claw and bite. The first man was easy as the element of surprise belonged to the molt, but though Tresset knocked the man to the ground, disabling him with kicks and punches, he was not rendered unconscious and so grabbed at Tresset's feet as he turned to defend himself against the other two who, over their momentary shock, now rushed him.

The men were not young by human standards, but they were healthy and strong, with the bulging arms of laborers and the no nonsense attitudes of men who had fought many fights, usually attaining victory. They each wore the black leather vests Tresset had come to associate with motorcycle riders. Their hair was long and greasy. They reeked of tobacco and beer and Tresset smelled animosity, even hatred, seeping from their pores. The oldest of the trio, a leather-skinned Caucasian with a long angled scar traversing his face, drew a knife as another punched Tresset in the belly. Tresset was not large, only five foot three, but he was strong and quick. And he was fierce. It was now three against one as none of his reyaqc companions had seen fit to aid him.

The claws came out.

All of his senses were attuned. He smelled every breath, heard every grunt, saw every twitch. The world became almost as a series of still photographs, each that Tresset could examine at length before responding. And yet it was simultaneously a blur, a red haze of anger and violence. Tresset clamped his teeth on the knife-wielding man's arm and ripped away a sizable chunk of flesh, almost simultaneously swiping at another, leaving four deep gashes across his chest. Another swipe and the third was incapacitated as well. It was then that the other reyaqc interceded. Tresset felt Bremu's large arms wrap around him from behind. "Now, now, little one. That's enough. We need them alive if they're to do us any good."

Tresset stared down at his work. One man was on his knees, cradling his belly in a futile effort to keep his intestines where they belonged. Another stomped about cursing as he held his injured arm. The third simply rolled to and fro on the gravel surface whimpering like a puppy without a bone. Tresset was disgusted. He could feel their blood on his hands and arms. He needed his rag. He needed to cleanse himself of the filthy human moisture, but his arms were restricted by the bear molt.

Even as Bremu pulled the kicking and spitting Tresset back into the shadows, the others moved forward to pull the humans toward the bus.

"This one's dead," called Anesch, indicating the man who had, moments before, been battling his innards.

"Bring him anyway," said Bremu. "He will provide a good meal." To Tresset he said. "Has your fury subsided, or should we continue this absurd dance?" There was humor in his voice. It seemed a barely suppressed chuckle lurked within his massive throat.

"Release me. I have no desire to soil myself further with human blood."

Bremu chuckled as he released Tresset, giving him a hearty pat on the back. Tresset withdrew his cloth and began wiping the sticky human blood from his hands and arms. He caught Bremu eyeing him curiously, but the bear said nothing. As Anesch and the coyote hefted two of the men into the bus, Tresset heard voices at the doorway to the pub. "Others come," he announced, turning to Bremu.

Kyorl pushed harshly past him nearly causing Tresset to stumble. "I'll do this. We don't need any more screw ups."

Even as two young females exited the structure, Tresset grabbed Kyorl's arm. "Enough," he said.

"Let go of me, human-lover." Kyorl's sleek dark face was taut with hatred.

Tresset may not have attacked. He may have let the slights and the tension go without retaliation. He might have walked away and left this misfit clutch of molts to their own fates. But, something clicked. Something hammered within Tresset's brain. It could be that he'd simply had enough of this posturing pup. It could be that he was tired and in a populated area, the foul odor of humans wafting on every breeze. It could be that he hadn't tested himself in battle against another molt for many long years, or that the thought of being called a human lover disgusted him at such a basic level. It could even be that he didn't want to appear weak in front of these, his own kind. It could have been none of these. It could have been all of these. Often one never truly knows the deeper purpose behind his own actions. Sometimes one just acts. There is no explanation, none, at least that can ever be verbalized. The mind is a tricky devil, the soul all the more so. Who can truly say why we do anything at all? At best, for human and reyaqc alike, our understanding of motivation is incomplete and shrouded in shadows and rationalizations. All of this to say, Tresset did act. He didn't care that there were now two human females to witness the encounter. He didn't care that he and his companions were in the open and therefore in danger of both exposure and capture. He didn't care that Kyorl was large and strong and filled with youthful aggression. In that moment Tresset didn't care about anything but his own fiery rage.

And so he pounced upon the larger molt, claws fully extended. Kyorl was tall, lean, with rippling muscular. He was perhaps six foot one in height. His body was solid, youthful, well developed. Still he stepped back in surprise at this initial assault. Tresset swiped at his face, but Kyorl deflected the move with a quick duck and block. Tresset adjusted, literally climbing the molt, scrambling up his form, clawing and biting as the other snarled and snapped. Tresset had his knees on the other's upper back, one arm across the face, the other the chest. He bit Kyorl in the right shoulder, eliciting a startled yelp.

The canine twisted and flipped, throwing himself back-first onto the hard gravel surface and trapping Tresset beneath him. Again, Tresset bit. He clawed at the face, drawing blood and flesh. Kyorl arced his back, pressing Tresset fast against the ground. With a fierce growl, he flipped. Tresset had not been prepared for this maneuver and so failed to fend off the first bite. Kyorl's teeth penetrated just above Tresset's left nipple pressing deep into the musculature. Another bite, this one where neck met shoulder, an inch further up and an artery might have been severed. Another bite. Another. Tresset squirmed and shook, but could not free himself from the larger molt's hold. Panic churned through his veins. He was helpless – helpless. He could die here. In this filthy human place, he could die!

Tresset thrashed, attempting to shake the beast off or to at least unsettle him, but Kyorl held firm. Another bite, this one to the neck proper. This was it. These were Tresset's last moments alive. He was about to die. Kyorl's head came down again, his mouth open, revealing his long curved canines red with Tresset's blood. He was helpless. Helpless. The canine outweighed Tresset by fifty pounds or better, what hope did he have in such a situation?

No. This was bad thinking, human thinking. Tresset had lived the life of a hunter, tracking and slaying many species, even bears and mountain lions, for his sustenance. Kyorl should not be the victor here. Why then did Tresset have such difficulty freeing himself from this molt's grasp? Perhaps he was still feeling the effects of the infusion. Tresset was pinned, arms held to the gravel surface, legs incapacitated by the molt's weight. Helpless.

No. Not incapacitated, not helpless, only subdued. Battle was not only of the body, but of the mind as well. A defeat usually occurs first in the mind and is then followed in the physical. Tresset had nearly allowed defeat to flood his mind. Nearly, but not quite. He refused to be defeated by this sniveling pup.

In a frenzy of anger and frustration, Tresset shifted right and then left, utilizing only his upper body and thus forcing his opponent to focus on this. In one swift move he freed a leg, and brought his knee up, connecting with Kyorl's groin. Seizing the momentary release as the canine responded to the pain, Tresset freed his left arm from the other's grasp and swiped viciously across the neck. Kyorl fell to the side as Tresset leapt onto him, reversing their roles of only a moment before. Kyorl's eyes went wide as, without hesitation, Tresset stabbed a single claw into his belly and then drew it all the way up his torso and into the neck, leaving a long jagged gash which seeped an expanding gush of blood.

Kyorl blinked. He gasped, attempting to say something, perhaps, "Human lover," and then he went still.

Tresset expected to be rushed by the others of Kyorl's pack, but all was silent save for the roar of distant traffic. For no reason, he thought of the two human females that had exited the pub. Had they run inside, screaming and telling others of the incident? Had they fled to their vehicle? And then, from somewhere deep within his consciousness, he remembered Bremu and Spider subduing them and dragging them to the bus as Tresset battled his foe. There had been another human as well. A male had emerged only to be restrained by Anesch. Peculiar how the brain worked. All of this he had seen yet none had registered as, in the moment, the information had no use. Tresset sat, still straddling the body, chest heaving, limbs aching from both fatigue and injury. Still, why had the others not descended upon him? He'd killed one of their own.

Tresset exhaled slowly, rose, and then turned to face the others.

"It seems our pack has reduced by one," said Bremu, his eyes fixed on Tresset. They remained this way for several seconds, each molt studying the other, the only movement being the rising and falling of chests. "Alright," said Bremu finally. "We can't afford to diminish our number. You proved yourself. Throw your mess into the bus and climb in. You're part of the pack now.

Tresset would never fully understand why he did it. He could have easily disappeared into the night to continue his solitary existence. He owed nothing to these molts. He wasn't even sure he liked them much. Likely Bremu had allowed Tresset to slay the canine because Kyorl challenged his leadership. Tresset had been used as a tool. This was almost certain. But the soul is a tricky devil, and for whatever reason, Tresset nodded, bent, lifted the still bleeding form and carried it to the bus.

Chapter Twelve

2009

Shane Daws had a nervous energy, a desire for excitement, maybe even a little adventure. Instead of returning to his room at the Pulitzer Opera Hotel, he'd decided to check out the Paris nightlife, and so landed at a little club only a few blocks from his hotel. The music was vaguely Latin style, the setting neo-gothic. Three large screens flashed scenes from about the club—couples dancing, beautiful girls giggling and drinking, a band playing on a small, mostly-dark stage, bartenders serving drinks. Shane settled at a small round table in a corner and took in the scene. The place was not large; it was very dark, quite smoky, and too crowded. But aside from that, it was very, very French. It just had that feel. This place was true Paris.

The girl was standing perhaps ten feet distant, talking with a thin, olive-skinned man in a gray beret, and, of all things, sunglasses. Shane wasn't particularly looking for a girl, but he wasn't particularly *not* looking for a girl either. He was in his late twenties, newly single after his second divorce, and seeking adventure. It was only natural that a girl as attractive as this would catch his eye—or had he caught hers? It seemed she may have been studying him before his gaze had landed on her.

Before Shane could contemplate his approach, she'd moved toward him, now smiling down at him as he sat in his little corner. *"Bonjour."*

"Bonjour," he replied. He knew very little French and had just exhausted about a tenth of his vocabulary. *"Comprenez-vous anglais?"* he added, asking her if she spoke English.

"Bien sur." She nodded. "My English is passable. You are American?" Her pronunciation was accented, but quite clear.

"Yeah, American. Guilty as charged."

"You are here alone, an attractive man such as yourself? Do you wait for others—a girlfriend perhaps, or a wife?" She tilted her head coquettishly and offered a wry grin.

"Alone. No wife, not any more at least." He chided himself immediately for saying the last. "And you?" he added quickly. "Looks to me like you're with someone." Shane inclined his head toward the young man with the beret.

"Oh, Eudo. My cousin. Do not concern yourself with him. He is here looking for… someone as well."

Shane smiled and nodded. *Looking for someone as well?* Was this beautiful woman trying to tell Shane that she was looking for someone— perhaps a blond American someone? He reached into his pocket, withdrew a stick of spearmint gum, unwrapped it, and slid it between his teeth wishing to God it was a Marlboro. "Well, here's to hoping you both find what you're looking for." Shane lifted his glass in a mock toast.

The girl smiled. It was that wry smile again; a smile that seemed to hint that there was another more dubious smile behind it. Though this registered at some subconscious level, Shane was too enamored to pick up on subtleties. In retrospect, he would note that her facial expressions had a somewhat plastic feel about them, that her accent, while French, held something else behind it, something exotic and truly foreign. And of course, the eyes. Those beautiful brown eyes were only as brown as the brown contact lenses she wore. All of this registered, and none of it did. This was a stunning young woman, and she was interested in him. All nuance was lost in a swirl of hormonal haze. "My name's Shane," he said. "I'm here on vacation."

"*Enchante*, Shane. I am Gisele. And I am not on vacation." She cocked her head. "You travel alone, or alone only tonight?"

131

"Alone. I had some time off coming and Paris seemed far enough away from home that I might just relax." Shane withdrew the gum from his mouth, placed it in an ashtray, and then replaced it with another. He'd picked a terrible time to quit smoking.

"Time to one's self is very important to the French," smiled Gisele. "Did you know that the French work only thirty-five hours per week, and vacation for five weeks each year? Attending to personal time is vital to us."

"I didn't know that."

"I'm sure there are many things you do not know about us." A cock of the head, and that coquettish smile again. "You have money to travel; your attire is new and well made. You must have a professional occupation."

"I sell insurance. I do okay."

"Insurance. There are licensing requirements, no? Schooling as well. You must have some intelligence."

A nervous chuckle. "Well, licensing, yeah. Before that, I eked through college."

A nod, a cock of the head. "And you are healthy?"

"Um… Healthy, uh, yeah. I mean, as healthy as anyone, I guess." What was this girl doing, screening for a husband?

"No familial illnesses?"

"Wow, okay. This is a little weird."

Gisele laughed an embarrassed laugh. *"Excusez-moi.* I am rude. Accept my apologies. It just seemed…" She trailed off as if embarrassed.

"What?" prompted Shane.

"Well, you seem—what is that phrase?—too good to be true. You are handsome. I have friends who would love to have a face such as yours. And intelligent. I'm sure those same friends would benefit from your intellectual capacities. As well, you are well-to-do, and yet, somehow single."

Shane blushed, but could think of nothing to say.

After an awkward moment Gisele said, "The air in here is stale and it's too loud to have civilized conversation. Would you like that we step outside, perhaps to where it is more private?"

"Um, sure… More private." Was this really happening?

Gisele smiled a full smile this time. "Good. Allow me to inform my cousin of what we do. He can become over-concerned."

"Of course," nodded Shane. And the course was set.

*****

Shane and Gisele strolled south from the club. She had her arm hooked in his, giggled like a teenager, and laughed—perhaps a little too hard—at his jokes. It was drizzling now, a thin mist that wafted through the air, adding a fresh scent to the urban environment. Gisele directed Shane around a corner to the left. Two or three blocks later, they angled right at an intersection. She continued probing, asking about his close acquaintances and family, if anyone in his family had ever had this disease or that. She threw in vague facts about herself, enough, Shane later supposed, to deter him from feeling like he'd been given the third degree. As well, she named streets as they wove from one to another. "We're now on *Rue Montorgueil*. The bars are wonderful—very friendly. Oh! This is *Rue Cler*. The best cheese shops in Paris. Ah, Shane, *Rue Poncelet*. There is a tea room you must try someday." It seemed to Shane that perhaps they had been walking in circles. But, he was a foreigner here. Everything seemed different and everything seemed the same. He wasn't sure, at this point, if he could even begin to backtrack. And as it turned out, this was exactly as Gisele had intended. She'd named several frivolous boulevards, none of which were even in the same *arrondissement,* or neighborhood, as they traversed. This way, when Shane was released—assuming he survived—he would be disoriented and confused, and in no way capable of directing authorities back to Gisele and her companions.

Eventually, they made their way to a small, brick, two-story apartment building that sat near the top of a rolling avenue. "This is my home. If you are interested, you may come inside."

Shane was interested, and followed her down the two concrete steps and in through the narrow wooden doorway. The entranceway was dark, the smell musty. Paint peeled from the plaster walls, and a single flickering bulb illuminated the space from a narrow corner alcove. A young man wearing too-large clothing squatted against one wall smoking a filterless cigarette. He stared at Shane and smiled as the couple crossed the threshold. The lighting was poor, but there was something about the man's eyes. Something that seemed...

"My apartment is on the second level," said Gisele before Shane could complete his thought. Then she led him up the steep staircase. For the first time, Shane wondered if perhaps this hadn't been such a great idea. Here he was in a foreign city, essentially lost, and following a stranger into her apartment. Gisele was beautiful. She was exotic, exciting, but also somewhat odd. It was now that Shane began to think about her oft-peculiar or forced facial expressions, about her numerous questions concerning his health and finances, about the circuitous route they'd taken to her apartment. He opened his mouth to offer some lame excuse as to why he should leave, but she was already pulling the door open, smiling back at Shane with that oh-so-beautiful smile. She took his hand in hers and drew him in.

It was then Shane knew without doubt that he should have fled when he'd had the opportunity.

There were five of them—four men and one woman, all very peculiar in their bearing, all staring at him with eyes that might just as easily have been pearls. In addition, the young man Shane had seen in the entrance-way now stood behind him blocking his exit.

"These are my friends." Gisele stepped away from Shane. "They are pleased to meet you."

Terror seized Shane as he gazed from one to the other to the other and each stared back at him as a lion would an injured gazelle.

All were young. All wore loose-fitting clothing, nothing stylish, nothing that would draw attention to themselves. They were thin, hungry looking. A couple seemed too pale to be healthy. Of course there were the eyes, those strange, strange eyes staring at Shane through pupils barely larger than flecks of pepper. One of the males, an unshaven youth with straggly brown hair and a missing front tooth smiled at Shane from the old threadbare couch on which he reclined. "*Bon soir,*" he said. Good evening.

Eudo, Gisele's "cousin" from the club, was the first to approach. He no longer wore his sunglasses and his white soapy eyes confused and frightened Shane. Eudo was not tall, nor was he bulky. Shane was athletic, and felt he may be able to "take" Eudo in a fair fight. But the odds weren't fair, and Shane knew better than to aggravate the situation.

"This will hurt," said Eudo. The voice was heavily accented and not without compassion. "I apologize."

Shane made to move, to bolt from the scene, but the one in the door-way anticipated his move and grabbed him from behind in a fierce bear hug. Eudo stepped closer, his murky white eyes intent on Shane.

Even as Shane screamed and thrashed, Eudo seemed to contemplate his face, to study his features. "Gisele was right. I would like to have your face." With an almost boyish smile he then extended his right arm, and reached behind Shane's neck. There was a sudden puncturing sensation, the quick snap and burn as something penetrated his spinal column...

And there was most definitely pain.

*****

Shane found consciousness a very dubious commodity. It would come, and then flee. It would tickle at the edge of his mind, but never come fully into being. It seemed red clouds swirled before his eyes, drawing near, and then dispersing into haze, then reforming at the edge of his vision, only to repeat the process. A single dull tone sat in his ears, neither increasing nor decreasing in volume, simply remaining, unceasing, maddening. Strange scents tickled at his nostrils, something of the sea it seemed, oysters perhaps. But no. Something more peculiar. Something unknown. His entire body ached. Even the slightest movement seemed beyond his ability. But worse, he could not... seem... to... stay... awake.

His eyes fluttered open, perhaps for the twentieth time. His stomach knotted. He retched, but there was nothing to expel. Someone sat beside him, patting at his forehead with a cool damp cloth. She came into focus. Gisele. But a different Gisele. Her eyes were as white as had been her companion's. And her face was...different. Not much, just... The lips, perhaps a bit fuller, the ears, a tad larger.

Shane chided himself for stupidity. He was delirious. A person's features don't change. Not without surgery or with the passage of time. She patted his head again and smiled her black widow's smile. *"Ca va?"* she asked. "How are you?"

Shane attempted to respond, but could accomplish nothing more than a grunt, which was probably for the best. For if he'd had the ability to speak, the words would have been less than gracious. Once again, she patted his forehead with the cloth, and then Shane was gone.

Chapter Thirteen

When Shane awoke next, Gisele was not to be seen. The scruffy guy with the missing tooth stood in the small kitchenette frying bacon—naked. The aroma was pleasing. Suddenly Shane realized how very hungry he was. How long had it been since he'd eaten? How long had he been here? Somehow it seemed it may have been several days—or had it been weeks? There were so many hazy half images, so many... memories? Gisele beside him talking, people in and out of the room, Gisele tending to him, coaxing him, muted conversations from just beyond the rim of reality. He blinked, attempting to bring his eyes fully into focus. Shane was on a couch. There was a plastic bucket on the floor beside him. It smelled of vomit. A wool blanket covered him, and...he was naked beneath it. What was going on here? Shane attempted to rise to a sitting position, but his muscles refused. There was a strange coppery taste in his mouth, and his head felt as if someone had dropped a building onto it.

Sensing the movement, the naked fry cook glanced at Shane and smiled. *"Bonjour."* Then, raising his voice, he shouted toward a bedroom door. The words were French, but Shane understood a reference to "the American." A few moments later, Gisele appeared from beyond the bedroom door. She wore an oversized men's polo shirt and nothing more. Shane recognized the shirt as the one he'd worn the night of his attack.

"Ah, you are awake." She came forward and seated herself on the edge of the couch, placing her palm against his forehead. "Good. The fever is gone."

Shane shook his head in an attempt to keep her from touching him. "What did you do to me?"

Gisele smiled. "All of that in due time. Now is the time to recover." She turned and said something to the naked guy in the kitchenette. A moment later he was handing her a glass of water. "Here. Sit up just a bit. You need to drink much."

Before Shane could respond, she had placed a hand behind his back, and gently pressed, helping him into a sitting position. Shane did not trust her, but he was thirstier than ever in his life, so accepted the water. It was lukewarm, slightly cloudy, but tasted like life itself. Gisele attempted to slow the rate of his drinking, but he shrugged her off, downed the glass— much of it dribbling onto his chest—and then said, "More."

Gisele smiled, nodded, and then called her companion, asking for a refill.

Shane glanced at the approaching cook—at his state of undress—and managed to croak the word, "Naked."

Gisele laughed. "My people are not ashamed of our bodies. They are to be celebrated. Not hidden beneath layers of fabric." She paused, cocked her head, offering that wry grin of hers. "But you are uncomfortable. I will ask Alard to dress."

She did so. Alard chuckled and pranced around playfully for a moment, brought Shane his water, and then disappeared into the same room from which Gisele had emerged.

There was a moment of awkward silence as Shane and Gisele were left alone in the room. Finally, Shane spoke. "You set me up. Your friends mugged me."

Gisele shook her head. Her expression blank, unreadable. "Mugged? No. Something different."

"You're telling me that if I were to find my wallet right now, all the money would still be in there?"

"No. The money is gone."

Shane gazed at her for a moment, studying her eyes. "You and all your friends—your eyes?"

"They are different. Yes."

Shane nodded. Gisele had made a reference to "my people." Shane was coming to realize she wasn't referring to the French. He was just about to comment on this when the front door opened. It was the other young woman Shane had seen in this apartment the night he'd been attacked. She had a young, eager-looking man on her arm.

At that same moment, Alard emerged from the bedroom and Eudo appeared in the doorway behind the couple, blocking the exit. Shane recognized the scene immediately and made to warn the young man. But he was too late. Alard moved swiftly. He smiled, said something in French as he reached out placing his hand on the back of the confused man's neck. Then the man's brown eyes went wide, his long limbs trembled and bucked. Alard and Eudo lowered him to the floor as his legs gave out, but never once did Alard release his grip on the back of the neck.

Shane began to scream in protest, knowing that this was exactly what had been done to him, but he was weak, his system still healing. As he tried to rise, a wave of vertigo overtook him. He would have fallen from the couch, but Gisele caught him, pressing him back down onto the frayed cushions and into a reclined position. Shane protested, but his strength fled him—consciousness as well.

*****

When next Shane awoke, there was no sign of the other victim. Had he been killed? Had they moved him to another room? What was happening? What were these people doing to him—and to others? How long had this been going on? And why was he still here? Why were they tending to him? If this was a mugging, why hadn't they simply dumped him on a street corner and been done with it? Shane had the unsettling feeling that he'd stumbled into something very, very weird.

Voices intruded from the adjacent room. Shouting. A male and a female. The words were in French, and Shane could understand almost none of it. But there were continued references to *"L'Americain."* Obviously, he was the topic of the debate. Shane shuddered at the implications. He'd witnessed the attack of another—he'd seen too much. He must be disposed of. The way he saw it, his only real chance of survival was to get out of the apartment before it was too late.

Slowly, very slowly, Shane rose to a sitting position. His head swam, and for several seconds he braced himself with the arm of the couch. He felt nauseous. His vision moved in and out of focus. There was still that low hum in his ears. But it seemed his strength was returning. Good for that. He needed it.

Shane wasn't given the chance to flee. For it was then that Gisele and Eudo strode into the room. Eudo glared at Shane as he sat there on the couch, a blanket covering his nakedness, his limbs still quivering from the ordeal of sitting upright. There was something about the man's face, something strangely familiar. He was still Eudo, yet there were subtle changes which Shane knew he should key in on. Still the truth of it evaded him. He knew those features, but not as they were. The face was similar to, but not the same as… What? Who? It seemed so obvious, and yet so distant. Shane scowled in frustration. Did Eudo now resemble Shane's younger brother, Chris?

Gisele gazed from one man to the other, and then said something to Eudo in French. Eudo seemed to contemplate for a moment, and then marched silently to the front door and out of the apartment.

"Time to dispose of the witness?" asked Shane with some bite to his voice.

"You are perceptive." Gisele stepped forward.

Shane's stomach dipped and spun. It was one thing to contemplate the worst, it was another to hear it confirmed. He began to rise as she approached, but even as he struggled to his feet, he fell back onto the couch.

Gisele chuckled. "Silly Shane. I am not the threat." She sat beside him on the couch and laid her hand on his kneecap. "But, yes. You are a concern. It was never intended that you be here so long, or for you to see what you have seen."

"The other guy, the one Alard attacked, is he dead?"

Gisele shook her head. "No. Like most, he handled the process well. Alard and Eudo were able to leave him unconscious at on a public bench. He will not know what was done. Within a few days he will feel entirely himself again."

"And me?"

"You did not respond well. Your system rejected the process. That is why you are still here. It is very fortunate you survived. But now you present a larger problem. You have seen enough to become a danger to us. What are we to do with you?"

Shane stared at her for a moment. "Tell me what's happening here. What 'process' are you talking about? What did you do to me? Maybe if I understand, I won't be as much of a threat as you think."

Gisele glanced at the door where Eudo had exited, and then back at Shane. She sighed, placed a hand over his, and then she told him of a strange species known as the reyaqc, of their need for "essence," of how they rob genetic information from their victims in order to survive. Oh, and if Shane thought Gisele and her companions were inhuman, then he'd best pray he never encounters those known as molts, for those… those were something altogether different.

*****

Several days later, Shane was finally off of the couch and standing before a cracked mirror in the tiny bathroom adjacent the living area. His hair had turned gray, or more accurately, white—the stark pure white of a cotton ball. Not the slightest hint of color. Twenty-eight years old, and he had the hair of a centenarian. And all because of this…genetic theft! Eudo had taken something from Shane—DNA, stem cells, something. And that process had gone awry. It had somehow damaged Shane, nearly killed him. But he was better now. Much better. His strength was returning. Except for the occasional swirl of lightheadedness, the vertigo was gone. He still had the low tone in his ears, but it had become less troublesome. But his hair! The shock to his system had apparently been too much.

Shane was still coming to grips with the reality of the reyaqc. That such a species could live alongside humanity, unknown, undiscovered, except by a select few, seemed amazing to him. Yet, he had no alternate explanation for what he'd seen and experienced. Apparently, this entire apartment building—all four units—were occupied by reyaqc. They came and went from one unit to another. Some were more or less permanent residents, others only occasional. According to Gisele, the place was owned by an old and wealthy reyaqc who offered it as a safe haven for his kind. She and her companions had taken to luring potential donors to the place, usually young men and women seeking a night of excitement. As best they could, the reyaqc would perplex the victim as to the true location of the place, infuse the "essence" from the people, and then dump them someplace where they would awaken, weak, but essentially unharmed. Wallets and purses would be gone. The victims would assume it had been a simple, if not elaborate, mugging, and go on with their lives. Many were so embarrassed by the foolishness of walking into the trap in search of sex, that they never even notified the police.

Things had not gone so simply for Shane. His system rebelled—he'd nearly died. From what Gisele told him, Eudo had wanted to dump him in the English Channel and be done with it, but Gisele had argued that Shane was a foreigner, an American, and should his body be found, there would be increased scrutiny. She'd promised to nurse him back to relative health, after which, they could deposit him on a bench some- where, none the wiser. But Shane had seen things. He'd witnessed an attack. Eudo worried that this information might interest the authorities should Shane report it.

Now the question still remained—what to do with Shane.

In truth, Shane was simultaneously terrified and exhilarated. Natural- ly, he feared for his life. But in truth, he didn't see these people as killers. Even Eudo, the most rigid of the bunch, grudgingly allowed Shane to remain yet another day—each and every day. It seemed to Shane that Eudo didn't want to kill Shane, but rather that he felt there may be no other option.

Truth be told, Shane had no inclination to turn these people—he sup- posed he should call them people—in to the authorities. What had society done for him? Two failed marriages, a disenfranchised family, a job that paid well, but, hey, money was only that—money. If nothing else, at least these reyaqc were different, exciting.

"You seem to be in contemplation." It was Gisele. She'd come up be- hind him.

"Yeah. My hair. Not quite the same look I had when I met you in that club."

Gisele smiled that still-wry smile of hers. "It makes you look more the man. Not a boy."

"Just what I wanted. To go gray before my dad. Maybe someone will give me an AARP card and I can get discounts."

Gisele cocked her head, obviously not understanding the reference.

"An organization for retired people. I look old."

Gisele grinned and looked at him head to feet. "No. *Blanc* hair or no, I don't think any persons will think you old—especially not the ladies."

Well, that was a curious comment. Shane was taken aback and searching for a response when a commotion came from the living area. Peering out of the bathroom, he took in the scene. The other female reyaqc, her name was Monique, had brought home a young man, a donor—a victim—for one of the more transient male reyaqc, Franc. But the intended prey had had a switchblade in his pocket. Franc was huddled on the ground to the left of the doorway, blood seeping from his shoulder. Monique was being held, back to the man's chest, the switchblade at her neck. Eudo and Alard were on hand, but drew no closer for fear of frightening the man into harming Monique. As Shane stepped into the small living area he saw the apprehension on Eudo's face, in his posture. Surely he thought Shane would side with the other human and complicate matters further. For the life of him, Shane couldn't say why he didn't.

Shane stared at the man, at his clothing, his bearing. He wore a Boston Red Sox cap and Gap blue jeans. "You're American," Shane said as he moved further into the room.

The man narrowed his eyes and drew Monique closer yet. "So?"

"So am I. Cleveland." There was a pause. Every eye glancing from one person to another. Each wondering what the other would do. "You can put the knife away. These people won't hurt you."

"The chick set me up. She said we'd be alone, have some fun. Then that freak came at me."

Shane shrugged. "Now he's on the ground bleeding and you have a knife. There's me and two other guys standing here. That knife can't get all of us at once. Let her go. Leave. Forget this ever happened. If you come back with the cops, we'll all swear you pulled a knife and tried to rape the girl. That's what, six against one? And you a foreigner. Cut and run, pal. It's better for all of us."

The man glared at Shane, then at each of the reyaqc. His eyes were wide, his expression grim. He had to know Shane was right, had to know he was outnumbered. But logic doesn't dictate every action. In times of stress it often becomes less than a whispered voice riding the winds of a gale. And so, with no more consideration than one would take when grabbing one more potato chip from a half-empty bag, the man drew the blade across Monique's neck. She screamed and everyone moved. There was chaos. Eudo tripped over Monique as he attempted to rush the man. Alard dropped to beside her and pressed his palm against her wound. Shane rushed forward, tackling the assailant in the hallway and tumbling with him down the narrow wooden stairway. Shane's shoulder hit the railing, and then his head connected with the corner of a stair. The other man's knee jabbed him in the gut.

The two embattled men hit the floor with a thud. The bloodied switchblade skittering across the tile and out of reach. Shane slammed his fist into the Boston guy's face four times in rapid succession, subduing him. Shane was still not at full strength, but a lot could be said for adrenaline. Eudo and Alard were upon him in moments, dragging the American ruthlessly up the stairs in a series of staccato *thumps* and *thuds*. By the time Shane made his way back up into the room, Alard and Gisele were on the couch tending Monique's wound, and Franc, bloodied but not lethally injured, was on the wood planked floor, bent over the man, his palm pressed firmly at the back of the guy's neck.

The process seemed to go on forever. At first the Bostonian shuddered and twitched, yellow muck seeping from the corner of his mouth. Twice, he made feeble attempts to shrug his assailant off, but eventually he became still. Yet Franc continued, his eyes narrow, his tapered jaw set firm and unforgiving. Soon there was the rank odor of defecation. Alard attempted to pull Franc off, obviously warning him of some danger, but Franc shrugged him away, continuing until all knew that the man was dead.

*****

Shane stood in the tiny bedroom gazing out of the window at a neighbor's laundry fluttering in the breeze. Gisele entered the room, approached him from behind, wrapped her arms around him mid-torso, and laid her head against his back. "You defended Monique. You captured that man before he could flee and give us away."

"And then we all stood around and watched Franc murder him."

"Franc is gone. He is not like most of us." Gisele gently turned Shane so that he was facing her. "Emotions were… I'm not sure how to say it. Escalated. There was fury. It is regrettable, but it is done. This is not the normal way of things, but it is not unheard of either."

Shane shook his head. "If I hadn't tackled the guy, he'd still be alive right now."

"And we would be in danger."

"The guy had a switchblade. He wasn't the kind to go to the cops."

"No. But he might have been the type to return here with associates who also bore switchblades, or maybe guns."

"He was American. I doubt he had a gang with him."

"Monique says he spoke French with little difficulty. He claimed to have been here for more than a year. He could have friends."

Shane remained silent for several moments. His emotions were in turmoil. Guilt weighed on him, but excitement as well. He wanted to believe Gisele, that this was just something that happened occasionally. The man obviously wasn't a model citizen—he had a switchblade, after all—and used it. It was pure luck that he hadn't found Monique's jugular vein, or some other crucial spot. The girl had a cut, but that was the extent of it. Still, had Franc really needed to kill him? And why hadn't Shane stepped in and pulled the reyaqc off once he'd realized what was happening. Alard had done as much. Perhaps if Shane had joined the effort…

Shane closed his eyes. The Boston guy was gone. True. But Shane was still here. And these people were fascinating. In particular Gisele. She'd been nursing him over the past several weeks. They'd talked, even laughed some, bonded. She was beautiful beyond description, and he believed she was genuinely attracted to him as well.

But she wasn't human.

He looked down at her, at the concern on her face, and yes, in those so-strange eyes. He didn't know what made him do it. Perhaps it was the tangled emotions, the fear, the adrenaline rush, maybe simple hormones, but he lowered his face to hers, slowly, so slowly, and brushed his lips against hers. At first her response was tentative, but only momentarily. For then she pressed closer to him. Their lips connected again, but this time there was no hesitation. They stayed this way for several moments, standing before the window, caressing, kissing, loving. At some point, Gisele lost her shirt. Shane wasn't sure how that had happened, but greedily cupped her left breast in his trembling right hand. Finally they moved toward the bed. It was small, barely more than a metal-framed cot. But it would do.

*****

The next several months were a kaleidoscope of emotions and ex-citement. Shane took an extended leave of absence from his job—and in doing so, lost his current position. But his boss hinted that they might want him in a new region just launching in Las Vegas. That would be fine—eventually. At the moment he wasn't sure if he'd ever return to the states. If he did, it was nice knowing he had a job awaiting him.

Shane and Gisele were in love. Soon he was fully accepted by the other local reyaqc as well. These young reyaqc were not wealthy. In fact, most stole for food and money, though Shane did meet two who had jobs, and one who attended University. Soon Shane helped fund their lifestyle. His bank account was healthy, but not endless. It took only a few months to deplete it entirely. Then it was back to stealing—this time with Shane's involvement. Most often, they stole from the "donors." After bleeding them of their DNA, the reyaqc took the victim's wallet. The cash, of course, was easy and untraceable. But Eudo seemed to have the whole identity theft thing down to an art. He'd use credit cards online, and even at ATMs, as he had software designed to reveal a person's PIN. It was an exciting life that Shane felt would never end.

But all good things do end.

Often, tragically so.

Shane discovered Eudo first. He lay on the floor, perhaps four feet to the right of the door, neck slashed open in a jagged tear, a pool of blood spreading across the years-old carpet. Alard was in the kitchenette, his naked body lying in a twisted lump, limbs spread at awkward angles, white satin eyes lifeless and staring. There were shuffles and thumps coming from the bedroom. Shane heard a familiar feminine voice, strained and cursing, then silent.

"Gisele!" he screamed. "Gisele!"

He had no time to think as he sprinted across the small living area and into the bedchamber beyond. He didn't stop to ponder who or what might have done this. He didn't pause to find a weapon, perhaps a butcher's knife or some heavy object that could be used as a club. The creature was one such as Shane had never seen—never imagined. Gisele lay sprawled upon the floor, her lovely face bruised and distorted with swelling. Her sightless eyes seemed as two pearls floating in hot red wax. There was blood, far too much blood. Shane couldn't determine specifically from where it had come. The beast crouching above her turned, its face contorted, features uneven and indistinct. There was very little that resembled anything human in form or manner. Still, there was recognition, however faint, however impossible. Only the slightest semblance of a face Shane had not seen for several months.

"Franc?" Shane whispered.

Then the thing was upon him. He was unconscious. And Gisele was forever gone from his life.

*****

Shane awoke in a spacious hotel room. His head swam, that low hum sitting somewhere deep in his ears had returned. His mouth was parched, his lips cracking. A figure sat at a small table across the room, typing on a laptop computer and occasionally gazing out through the nearby window. He seemed to be of about middle age, was not tall, and wore a tight reddish brown beard. Shane instantly identified him as a reyaqc. Having spent so much time with them, he recognized the rubber-like skin, the contact lenses, the slightly unusual facial expressions.

"My name is Doctor Donald Baker," said the reyaqc. "I own the apartment building you've inhabited for the past several months. It's commendable that you have befriended my species. But your companions are no more. I think it best you leave this country." Donald Baker smiled his practiced smile. "But first, we must talk."

For the next three days, Shane told Donald Baker everything he could remember about his time with the reyaqc. Donald recorded each conversation on audio, as well as jotting copious notes. He asked clarifying questions, covered the same ground many times over, and occasionally divulged tidbits of information from his own life. Shane was familiar with Donald Baker by reputation. According to Gisele, Baker was a historian. Never before had someone attempted to chronicle reyaqc history, and Baker had done so meticulously, researching legends, genealogies, first-person accounts. He interviewed numerous subjects, both human and reyaqc. There were journal entries, correspondences, court records, even a translated excerpt from one of the Dead Sea Scrolls, in his writings. Some of his information dated back to as early as 1400 BC. During the course of his meetings with Baker, Shane wondered if perhaps these interviews would make it into a future volume of this ever-expanding project.

Shane pestered Baker about the creature that had killed Gisele. It had been Franc, he was nearly certain, but Shane had never seen a reyaqc such as this. Could this be the mysterious "molt" Gisele had warned him of? Baker remained quiet on the topic, revealing nothing, and responding to questions with questions. Shane would later find the answers he sought, but not from Donald Baker or from any other reyaqc. His sources would be much more mundane.

At the end of these few days, Donald rose, extended his hand, and offered Shane an airline ticket and a business card. "I reside in Boston. Do not hesitate to call should you once again become involved with my kind. Of course, your discretion will be much appreciated." He paused, cocked his head, and then added, "You may from time to time hear talk of me by my given name, my reyaqc name."

"Yes?" Shane said.

"That name is Dolnaraq."

With that, he left the room. Shane would not see him again for over three years.

The First Interlude

From Histories Volume One, an ongoing chronicle of the reyaqc

*The following report is a correspondence between a household serv-
ant and her sister, who obviously lived at some distance. I have pinpointed the date to between 1832 and 1835. The country is China, the locale,
an insignificant community located some two hundred miles west of the
eastern seaboard. The event involves a young human female, Yi Min, and
a reyaqc pup, nearly depleted, all but empty. This is an interesting study
in that the servant, a woman named Dao-Ming, did not report the incident. Her confession indicates multiple fears and superstitions as her
motivation for allowing this process to go unchecked. In pondering the
events documented here, I have found that I will never truly understand
the human psyche. Perhaps this is to be expected; for it seems few
humans understand human emotions any better than do I.*

Dearest, Chu-hua,

Here I am at the beginning of this correspondence and already I do
not have words. There is a tale I must tell. No, not a tale, for to call it a
tale might imply that it was a fable, and that it is not. I have told no one
of this and ask that you do the same. For I fear for my safety should the
master learn of what I have seen, and more even, that he discover that I
did not report it at the first. In truth, I do not know why I have remained
silent. It is fear, I suppose. Yes, fear. But you do not yet know what it is I
fear so greatly and so I will explain.

Yi Min loved flowers. She loved the colors, loved the scents. She
loved tending to their soil, nourishing them the way all living things

should be nourished. She loved watering them, pruning them, making them happy. Yes, she believed that she made the flowers happy, that they responded to her, that they knew her voice and recognized her scent. As Yi Min's caregiver, I often scoffed at this. It seemed such nonsense. Yi Min would chastise me. "But what does a caregiver know? You spend no time in the garden. You are too busy puttering about the home doing whatever things grownups do when out of the sight of children."

Yi Min was only six years old and already so full of opinions.

She lived with her father, myself, and two male servants who tended to the grounds. The young girl's mother had died in child birth. Her father, my master, was a high-ranking military official. I must confess, I spent very little time with Yi Min, instead busying myself with cooking and cleaning, rarely offering the girl an opportunity to participate or to learn. This, among other things, is to my shame.

But, Yi Min had her flowers. And they loved her. She was satisfied with that.

The other girl first appeared on an autumn morning. Yi Min was busily tending to her flora, a small batch of powdery blue bulbs that only bloomed for about three weeks at this time each year. Yi Min did not know the name of the flowers. In truth, she did not know the true names of any of them, but graced each breed with names she'd herself created. She called these flowers blue sunlight because of the way they brightened the garden in a time when many blooms had gone to sleep for the year.

The other girl was at the eastern border of the garden, just within the tall wooden fence, near the yellow-tinted flowers named smiling fans. I did not know how long the girl had been standing there, or how she had entered the garden. My master always boasted of how secure his property was. But what did he know? He was not here on this first tragic day.

Yi Min did not appear frightened of the girl, though certainly she considered her peculiar. The stranger's skin was pale, almost white like the petals of the flower Yi Min called snow bird. Her eyes were whiter yet, with only a tiny black spot at the center of each. Her face was bland, with no distinguishing features, her lips thin, her cheek bones barely noticeable at all. The girl's pale hair was longer than Yi Min's, extending to just below her creamy white shoulders. Strangest of all, the girl wore no clothing, but stood still, staring at Yi Min, entirely naked.

I wish I had chased the girl away during this first, so peculiar, encounter. But I, standing in the distance, was transfixed by it all. And, yes, fearful. I must admit this, if only to you, my dear sister. I was frightened of this waif of a child, though, in that moment, I could not have understood why.

"Hello," said Yi Min, as she bowed. "I am called Yi Min."

The girl said nothing, acknowledged nothing. Her expression, so neutral, did not change. She did not move forward nor retreat, but simply remained staring at Yi Min.

"Are you lost?" asked Yi Min. "Has someone stolen your clothing?"

Again, the girl said nothing.

Yi Min stared at her, examining her plain featureless face, her pale colorless skin, and asked the same question that held me stone-like and inadequate. "Are you a ghost?" she asked.

The girl remained expressionless, apparently assessing Yi Min. The two stood silent for many moments, until finally, without a word, the girl moved forward until she stood before Yi Min. It was now evident that this girl was slightly taller, not by much, but just enough for Yi Min to tilt her head in order to meet the girl's gaze. "My name is Yi Min," said Yi Min a second time, for she must not have known what else to say.

The girl examined her for a moment more, her strange white eyes moving up and down Yi Min's tiny form, seemingly evaluating her. Finally, the girl extended her right arm, slowly, with subtle grace, touching Yi Min lightly on the back of the neck and saying, "My giver has gone."

The girl was back the next day, and the next. Each time she was silent, never speaking another word since uttering that one mysterious sentence on that first morning. She remained unclothed, always appearing as from nowhere, but always on the east side of the garden. The girl would stare at Yi Min, who would then stand and bow, introducing herself each time as if the two had never met. Eventually, the girl would move forward, extend her arm, touch Yi Min on the back of the neck. Always, I watched from my perch beyond the foliage, not wanting to disturb the two. In truth, I'd come to believe this girl to be one of the many poor orphans to wander the streets. Yi Min, who came from a family of some means, showed her grace and mercy and I did not desire to in any way interrupt such behavior. The elite so seldom find it in their souls to think of the unfortunate as having dignity or even basic rights.

On the fourth day Yi Min was ill, feverish, and feeling devoid of any strength. She drank quite a bit of water. For some reason she was always thirsty now. She told no one of the girl, of this new "friend," obviously afraid the adults might chase her away, accusing her of being a beggar or a thief. Yi Min was likely correct in this. Besides, as much as she loved her flowers, it was nice for her to have someone more like herself, even if the girl never spoke. I was foolish enough to have been happy that she'd made a friend.

On the fifth day Yi Min found a small hole under the fence on the east side of the garden. "Ghosts don't need to crawl through holes," she said aloud. This was when, I believe, Yi Min determined that this girl was truly human, and as such, had needs just like anyone else.

The next time the girl appeared, Yi Min had clothing for her, an old smock, one she no longer wore; one that would not be missed. She'd brought food as well, a plate of fruits from the garden. Surely this girl who was not a ghost must be hungry. Obviously, she had no caregiver to tend to her needs.

The girl had more color now, more like Yi Min's own golden skin tones. Her lips seemed broader as well, her face more defined, and her hair was now a healthy black, though her eyes were still as white as the snow bird flowers. "Yi Min," said the girl in a strangely familiar tone.

"Yes, Yi Min," agreed Yi Min with a nod.

"Yi Min," said the girl again, this time as she reached around to the back of Yi Min's neck, and pressed her palm against the young girl's spine. A peculiar practice, I thought. Certainly it was an expression of endearment.

Yi Min became sick and weak. She vomited frequently, and slept much later than she should have. She was always thirsty, and became a nuisance as she constantly pestered for more water. Her hands often shook and she claimed the world appeared fuzzy. It was at this point that I should have alerted someone. But I could not see how the girl could have caused Yi Min's illness. Surely these things could not be related. This was simply a girl. Some poor orphan in need of a friend.

Often, the other girl would be waiting as Yi Min made her way to the garden. She wore the old smock Yi Min had given her, and she'd even cut her hair to about the same length as Li Min's. Her color was much better now, just about the same shade as Li Min's, and I wondered how I had ever thought this girl a ghost.

There came a day when Li Min could no longer get out of bed. She was so weak and so thirsty. She tried to call to me, but her voice was so small as to sound almost like a whisper. Still, I did hear, and was nearly to the room when I heard the other girl speak. "I will get the water you need," she said.

When had the girl entered her room? How did she get into the home unnoticed? The dwelling was not so large that a person could walk about and never be seen.

Peeking through the door, I saw the girl gently brush Li Min's bangs aside and smile a very familiar smile. "I will get the water," she repeated.

Secure behind the door, peeking through the tiniest of cracks, I watched as the girl strolled across the small room and into the larger room beyond. "I would like some water, please," said the girl to, Enlai, the gardener.

"Oh, Li Min," replied the man. "Your color is so much better. But, why do you wear that old rag? Your father will think Dao-Ming neglects you."

"I will change," said the girl.

"But what has happened to your eyes?" asked Enlai. "They are so white."

"Perhaps I stared at the sun too long."

"Strange," said the gardener. "Well, here's your water. Now, go dress in something better. Your father may be coming home today."

Certainly, Li Min was frightened when the girl returned. For I know the fear that gripped my breast. Perhaps her stomach turned this way and that like mine; likely our heads were afire with similar questions and horrible imaginings. She stared at the stranger, at her own face on the other, her own hair, even at the shape of her body. It must have seemed she looked into a mirror. The girl truly had become Li Min. Only the eyes remained as they had been. The two soulless eyes, white except for a small black spot at the center of each. How had I not seen this before? Am I so blind; am I so cold as to ignore that which is so obvious?

"There cannot be two of us," said Li Min as she accepted the water from the girl. "Someone would surely see. And my father is due home.

He will know the difference." I was proud of her then. She seemed so brave. How I wish I could have summoned some of her courage.

"Perhaps," said the girl in Li Min's own voice. "Perhaps." The girl sat beside Li Min on the bed, took the now empty water glass from Li Min's hands and set it on the end table, then reached around to the back of Li Min's neck. "Do not worry," she said. "I still need you, just as your flowers need you." Li Min started, her eyes wide and then it seemed the energy withdrew from her form. This was the first time I'd been so close when the girl touched my charge, and I will tell you I nearly found the courage to enter the room, to pick up a broom and to beat this phantom away. But, my dear sister, here lies the truth. At this point, in this moment, I returned to my belief that this girl was otherworldly. Perhaps a long deceased ancestor coming to claim a living body, perhaps some wandering spirit desiring a host. I did not know which then and I do not know which now, but I do know that great fear has the power to paralyze. I do know it has the power to wean a soul of all integrity and to leave only selfish wishes and an unhealthy desire to preserve oneself. I will forever regret what happened next. I will forever remember my cowardice as, again, I remained at a safe distance, observing but never interceding.

The next time I saw Li Min, she was in her garden. But, not on the little stone path that wound throughout, but far at the back, beside the fence, near the flowers Yi Min called smiling fans. She was in a hole, beside the fence, the place where the girl came and went. It was a place not easily seen from the home, or by anyone not specifically tending to the flowers. It was a place not easily seen by anyone but Yi Min. I saw only because I crept among the vines with hopes of discovering the truth about this ghastly stranger.

Yi Min had been buried from the neck down. In her weakened state she could not push through the blankets wrapped about her or through the rich soil that covered her. Neither did her voice have the force to carry but a breath's distance away. Yi Min looked up at her friends, the smiling fans. "I am planted beside you, my friends," she said, attempting a weak smile. The flowers did not respond, nor did they seem to smile now, but simply swayed uncaring in the gentle breeze, ignoring this brave and precious child. I have much in common with the smiling fans.

The girl brought water, steamed vegetables, and rice. She fed Yi Min much the same way a mother would feed an infant. Yi Min had no strength to protest. All she could do was to eat, drink, and stare up into the face that had been stolen from her.

There was a sound of horses, of a carriage. The master, Yi Min's father, was home. My heart raced. Surely he would know. Surely he would understand that this girl was not his daughter. He would set this right. He would do what I had not had the courage to do. It seemed Yi Min tried to move. But she was obviously so very, very weak. The phantom girl smiled a gentle smile, stroked Yi Min's forehead, and then slipped her hand around to the back of her neck.

"No," said Yi Min in a voice barely audible. "No more."

The girl smiled and then continued.

After the girl was done, she rose, brushed the dirt from her clothing, and then moved slowly away. I heard the master's cry of joy, "Yi Min! Look at my girl. You've grown. Only three weeks, I've gone, and you've grown." I fled then, through the garden and into the courtyard beyond, exiting the property at the rear. I have little money and no hope of employment. But, dear sister, I could not face my master. Never could I face the man whose daughter I had so grievously betrayed. Daily, I think of returning, of slipping under the eastern fence and stealing Yi Min away. But, what then? The girl would desire to be returned to her father. She would incriminate me further. I might be executed for such a grievous sin. And so, I remain distant and in a perpetual state of dread. Sister, I fear I have blackened my soul. Forgive me for I am weak beyond words.

Your grieving sister, Dao-Ming

The Second Interlude

From Histories Volume Two, an ongoing chronicle of the reyaqc

The following document dates back to the first Iron Age, roughly 1200 BCE and is one of the earliest documents known to use the South Arabian alphabet. It was found in the form of a leather scroll, rolled, and sealed within a ceramic pot, and is incomplete. The location of the find was southern Egypt, though the language and content of the document might imply that its origin lies elsewhere. Some territories are named within the document, though most were not previously known. Small states tended to rise and fall with some rapidity during early history and this is likely the instance in this case. Canaan is mentioned, and this is a well known land, as is Phytelaqc, a name rarely known by humans but quite familiar to learned reyaqc. Though much is still unknown concerning its inhabitants, this Phytelaqc was the earliest known reyaqc community and thus important to our history. Unfortunately, this fragmented document gives little new insight concerning this heritage. The author is anonymous, but was likely a scribe to the king mentioned in the document. Whether this is a first person account or a tale told to the scribe is also a mystery. As of yet, there is no additional source material to corroborate the account. But when coupled with other known facts concerning the time, and that it was found amidst other documents of value such as civil records and verifiable histories, it seems likely an honest telling and not a fiction. It is unlikely that we have the beginning of the account as it seems to start abruptly and with no note as to authorship or origin. Still, this is a valuable piece, and, though obviously written by a human, contains interesting nuggets, giving us a glimpse into the lives of early reyaqc.

The sword fell. The wall was breached. Shouts cried out into the night. Shadowy forms burst through the battered doorway, their outlines huge, lumbering, and fierce. Orders were barked in a dialect unknown. A small company of defenders raced forward, blades drawn, prepared to stay the intruders. But the invaders were swift and quite fierce. A head was severed. Another man's chest crushed beneath the massive boot of an intruder. "Sound the trumpet!" cried one. "We are under siege!" But then his voice was forever silenced by a cold iron blade through the belly. Another defender fell, and another. Shouts and cries could now be heard throughout the city as other walls were breached. Flames arched into the night, glowing orange against the hovering mist as torches fell upon frail wooden structures, igniting them in bursts of red and yellow.

There was a loud clang and the sound of [*missing material*] ...he fell, as the beast warrior knelt, reaching to behind his neck and [*missing material*]

The door to the king's chamber was thrust open. It was a modest room with a gravel floor and uneven walls lined with linen and fur. "Sire!" shouted the aid. "We are besieged! The city is aflame, the wall fortifications breached!"

The aging monarch rose unsteadily from his bed, wiping the sleep from his puffy eyes, attempting to blink off the night's wine. "Where? How many?" he asked as he rose, wobbling to his feet, and glancing at the empty goblet beside his bed.

"From all about," answered the aid as he glanced back through the doorway making sure the intruders had not yet made their ways down this corridor. "Numbers unknown, but great."

The king reached for his old and scarred leather tunic which was lying on a dais beside the bed, and slipped it over his red and sweaty head. "Who? The Shabti? I thought we'd bested them finally?"

"Not the Shabti," offered the other.

"The Uri? The Egylithians? [*Editor's Note: this could be a misspelling of the word Egyptians, an alternate name for them, or reference to a different people entirely. D*] Certainly not the Canaanites! What need would they have of us?"

"Not the Canaanites, sire. It is, we believe, the beast warriors of Phytelaqc."

"Beast warriors!" cried the king as he slipped his right foot into a tall leather boot and tied it with unsteady fingers. He stumbled, righted himself, shook his head. "Impossible. I do not believe in these half men. It is a legend, nothing more." He stretched out a shaky arm for the other boot. "Tell me something of importance [*missing material*] …bowed his head in contemplation.

Just then, shouts and swordplay could be heard in the short hallway leading to the king's chamber. Metal struck metal with deafening clangs, there was a guttural gurgle and a scream of sudden death. The king's eyes went wide as the intruder made his way into the room, stooping in order to pass through the too low doorway. The warrior's skin was gray and leather-like, his milk-white eyes set wide. His limbs were as tree trunks, his bulk great and ponderous. His nose was like the trunk of an elephant. Not near as long, perhaps nine inches in length. It did not seem to have the capacity for independent movement, no musculature within, for it simply swung this way and that as the hideous creature moved about.

[*Editor's Note: It is not unheard of for a reyaqc to infuse elephant essence, but it is quite rare. For one thing, full adult height is determined soon after birth during the first infusion which must always be from a human if the pup is to survive. Thus, infusing elephant essence will not increase height, though it can most definitely add to bulk. (Likely this molt's mother purposely had the new born pup draw from a very large human with the intent of him taking on elephant essence and becoming one of these so-called beast warriors.) As well, elephant essence is found to be one of the least compatible sources. These molts are often deformed. Many become simpletons. Often their bulk makes it quite difficult to maneuver. This is not always the case, as each reyaqc responds differently even to the same essence, but the problems are common. Apparently, though, in this instance, the molt was well formed and in complete possession of his senses. – D]*

"I don't believe in you," said the frail king to the monster of a man as he gave up his struggle with the second boot, and instead, found his battle-worn scabbard, wrestling to remove the blade before his head could be separated from his neck.

His aide, a devoted young man of perhaps thirty summers, with deep brown eyes and a shaggy mane of black, had his two-handed sword at the ready, and swiped wildly at the invader, who, too large for the room, was forced to stoop and crouch, his movements inhibited both by ceiling and wall. But still, the man's trunk-like arms held his blade firm, and he easily fended off these frantic blows with quick flicks of the wrist and sudden furious parries. The beast warrior was obviously accustomed to fighting in close quarters and had adapted his form to suit the need. Almost before the exchange had begun, the aid found himself to be on the defensive. A desperate parlay, a thrust. The intruder's leather-like arm spewed red. But the wound was not deep, and the limb remained useful. Still, these warriors of Phytelaqc, it seemed, bled the same as anyone else.

The king hobbled forward, still wearing only one boot. He thrust, but his blade was deflected. The aid attacked from the opposite side, but the intruder leaned back, avoiding the blow. The aid was now off balance due to his missed thrust, and the beast-man easily gutted him in the side before the determined defender could regain balance. The young man tumbled to the floor, his two-handed sword slipping from now lifeless fingers and landing with [*missing material*]

With a shout, the king thrust again, striking the huge creature square in the abdomen, but the intruder's thick pelt held true, and the king's blade did naught but bruise his massive opponent. There had been a time when the might of the king's arm would not have been stayed by even supernatural flesh, but that time was long since gone, and all he could now hope for was to stay this thing until additional defenders arrived.

As he deflected another blow, this one nearly ripping his sword from his grip, the king heard more shouts and footfall in the corridor, and the clanging of metal on metal. There were cries of pain, and orders barked in a foreign tongue. "We are overrun!" cried an anguished voice that, in the end, evolved into a death scream.

"What do you want?" screamed the king to his attacker. "We are but a tiny kingdom, with no wealth to speak of. What gain do you seek?"

The enormous thing answered with his sword. Though confined in the small chamber, and denied the freedom of unrestricted movement, the beast warrior was still swift and incredibly agile. Blade met blade, sending a shudder through the king's entire form. Their swords met again, this time the intruder's strength had proved too mighty for the aging king and the monarch's blade tumbled useless to the floor. There was a small wooden stool beside the bed. The king grabbed it, brought it over his head, attempting to smash it into the intruder's face. His opponent simply knocked it aside and out of the king's grasp with one swipe of his massive arm. The king backed up, stumbling, then righting himself, his back now firmly against the wall. "I do not believe in you!" cried the king as the giant's blade passed through his generous belly.

Moments later, three defenders rushed into the room, prepared to lay down their lives for their [*missing material*]

The kingdom was taken in less than a [*missing material*]

All of the human subjects were [*missing material*] … the situation was [missing material]

…of the humans have been captured. Those of healthy form and sound mind are used in some bizarre ritual involving the laying on of hands, which always leaves the human depleted and ill, oftentimes unto death. The females are often defiled. The substandard are slain. If the imperfection is simply that of small stature or simple mindedness, these castoffs are consumed as livestock. If it is an infirmity then they are burned alive. The surviving humans are kept in a [*missing material*]

As stated earlier, this document is incomplete. I have entered all that remains with the exception of some small fragments containing only a word or two each. None of these could be reassembled in such a way as to gain further insight. We do know that Phytelaqc existed in this period, though there is no record of it during the second Iron Age (1,000-550 BCE). This does not mean that it did not survive into this time, but likely this is the case. The inhabitants were obviously molts. They were aggressive and warlike. As the reyaqc population has always been far smaller than that of our human cousins, it is likely that their warlike ways led to their demise. Likely the humans aligned forces and destroyed the city and its occupants. This, I fear, even in this so-called enlightened age, is the potential fate of contemporary reyaqc settlements unless humans can be made to understand us and accept us as valuable and deserving of life.

PART TWO

THE ROGUE

Chapter Fourteen

2012

A cry of pain and frustration came from across the room as Donald Baker slid a page from the report and placed it atop the walnut end table beside him. Moving his hand about six inches to the right, he clasped his lukewarm cup of Earl Grey tea and drew it to his lips before reading the following page aloud. "Madigan's account is, of course, fictitious. The ravings of a lunatic mind. That this survivor was subjected to unspeakable horrors is undisputed. His physical and mental conditions alone attest to this. Yet the nature of these horrors we may never know."

Donald offered a barely perceptible grin. "We know precisely what horrors the castaway faced, don't we, Arec?"

A grunt. A tug. No verbal response.

Donald slid another page onto the end table and savored his tea. This story from the late seventeen hundreds was intriguing. The sole survivor of a shipwrecked crew on an uncharted isle in the Indian Ocean, Gavin Madigan had been emaciated, weighing fewer than ninety pounds at the time of his rescue. His hair had fallen out and most of his finger and toenails had detached from his digits. According to the report, his eyes had been sunken and hollow, the dark circles beneath a stark contrast to the pale blue tint of his skin. The man had strange scars over most of his body. It had taken nearly two months for Madigan to offer coherent speech, and even then, the tale he told was quite suspect.

"Do you feel no pity for this man, Arec? Do you not recognize the great wrong visited upon him and his companions?"

There was a guttural rumble. "Your stories are monotonous, Dolnaraq."

Donald shrugged.

Arec responded with a snarl and a curse. "My father will kill you for this." There was venom in the voice, a cool, seething hatred.

Donald sipped off the remainder of his Earl Gray, placed the last few pages of the report face up on the end table, and rose with a subtle moan. He was feeling depleted but shrugged it off. Crossing the small but elegant living room, he stared out through the eastern window toward the tree line that edged his property. The sun was yet in hiding, but the first hint of a morning glowed tentatively, inching over the vast green expanse. Donald bent slightly, releasing the latch, and then gave a subtle tug. The window slid open with a whispered creak. The morning air danced over his features as he cocked his head back and inhaled deeply. He loved the smell of the morning dew on the New England breeze. He could smell the faint wisp of salt water on the air. Perhaps after he'd concluded the day's lectures he'd find his way down to the beach.

Turning only slightly, he inclined his head toward Arec. "It was your father that contacted me. This process, this detention is at his request."

There was a curse, a roar of protest, a violent tugging at the leather restraints. "Liar! My father is like me."

"Yes, but he is also intelligent and understands the realities of this modern world. He recognizes the need for change."

Arec cursed and spit.

Donald admired the creeping light upon the treetops. There was a subtle buzz at his hip and he slid his slender hand into his front pocket to withdraw his BlackBerry. "Good morning. Donald Baker here."

The voice was youthful but dry. "Dr. Baker, it's Shane Daws."

"Shane Daws?" The name was familiar, but Donald couldn't quite place the voice.

"Yeah, Doc. Paris three summers ago. There were…issues. An apartment building, some deaths."

Donald nodded. Of course. Gisele's young man. The affair had ended horribly, tragically even, as nearly all such affairs should. But the seemingly flighty young Daws had shown a peculiar maturity through it all. At the time it had seemed the young man might one day prove useful, though now, Donald couldn't quite fathom why he had thought this. "Yes, I remember. Mr. Daws, you do realize it's not yet dawn."

"Yeah, Doc. I'm in Vegas. It's not three a.m. here. But you'll want to hear this."

Donald's wife Elena entered the room, tying her blue bathrobe as she glanced at Arec, who sat tethered to a heavy wooden chair—thick, weighty, tall-backed, the finish worn thin in many spots. Arec grunted and growled, his ears lying back against his skull with a subtle twitch.

Donald held up one finger, indicating Elena should wait before asking who had called. "What seems to be the problem?" he asked into the phone.

"It looks like we have a rogue in Vegas."

"How can you be certain?" Donald moved across the room to his roll-top desk where a yellow legal pad and a ballpoint pen sat neatly beside one another on the otherwise bare surface.

"By my count, there've been three deaths. The cops haven't put anything together, but they don't know what I know."

Donald allowed a low rumble to escape his lips. These people—the groupies, the hangers-on—they always thought they knew so much. But they tended to jumble fantasy with reality. They made wild suppositions, conceived theories and radical assumptions. It often took hours to get to the truth of a matter. "Details, Mr. Daws, details. Everything you know. No guesswork. Simply report what has happened."

Over the next thirty minutes Donald grilled Shane Daws, asking and then restating each question, rewording the responses, looking for anything that would prove the young man wrong—anything that could point to another possibility. But Shane's information was solid, his conclusions sound.

"There's one more thing," said Shane. "The rogue was admitted into the hospital tonight."

"The reyaqc, what is his condition?" Donald glanced to Elena who now sat on the deep leather couch, her eyes narrow, the corners of her mouth downturned.

"He was brought into the UMC ER, I don't know, maybe a couple of hours ago. He attacked an attending EMT, infused from him, and then fled the hospital naked."

"How many witnesses to the attack?"

"Hospital staff. I don't think anyone has a clue what really happened."

"Was the reyaqc empty?"

"I don't think so. The only unusual characteristics reported were the eyes and the palms."

"Was he a molt?"

"I don't know, Doc."

Donald marched toward the window, gazing out over the now sunbathed tree line. "And the EMT? His condition?"

"In and out of a coma. They haven't figured out if he's going to make it."

Donald inhaled deeply of the morning air, closed his eyes, and then turned to face his wife. "I suppose I'll be on my way."

Donald sensed a slight pause before Shane Daws spoke. "Listen, Doc. You're in Boston, three time zones away. I'll follow up on things out here and keep you in the loop."

Donald snorted. "I'll call you with my flight plan. Meet me at the hospital emergency room one hour after my arrival."

"Um…okay, Doc. I didn't mean to…"

Donald disconnected before Shane could finish his sentence. He found Elena staring at him, her brown eyes contemplative, sad. She glanced at the still-struggling Arec and then back to her husband. "You can't save them all, honey. No matter how you try."

Donald grunted as he moved toward the bedroom. "Book me on the first available flight to Las Vegas. I may be several days. Arrange for three to attend me. Call the university. Inform them that I'll be out for the remainder of the week, possibly beyond." He paused, glancing at his still-struggling captive. "Olcott should tend to this one in my absence."

Elena stared at her husband's narrow back and sagging shoulders as he disappeared into their bedroom.

Chapter Fifteen

Dr. Julia Chambers cursed the man she'd married, shoved the still vibrating *iPhone* into her lab coat pocket, and gazed into the detective's pale eyes. It would have been nice if someone had the decency to tell her she was entering the worst week of her life.

Julia wouldn't have thought the man a detective. He just didn't fit the well-established pop cultural mold. Steve Glenn was neither noir rustic nor Hollywood handsome. If anything, his most defining characteristic was that he was amazingly nondescript. His was the face that one could see in a cafeteria or pass in the hallway on a daily basis and yet never remember from one encounter to the next. His hair was a business cut. His build was average, not thin, but no paunch. His lips were narrow, his face unlined. His sun-deprived skin seemed stark in comparison to Julia's rich dark chocolate variety. How could even a Caucasian live in the desert and remain that pale? Even the tie he wore over his white business shirt—ironed but not so crisp as to draw attention—was an uninspired solid navy.

"Do you need to take that call?" he asked while jotting a note in his small spiral-bound notebook.

Julia fingered the phone in her pocket. "No. It was just my husband."

"It's very late. If he's calling at this time, it might be important. I can wait if you need to take the call."

Julia shook her head. "Trust me. Anything he has to say can't be important."

Detective Glenn nodded his understanding. The truth was, he didn't understand. No one did—least of all Julia. "I'm told you know the victim personally. Something about Monopoly."

Julia allowed a micro-smile. "Monopoly Mondays. We have a weekly game."

"He's an Emergency Medical Technician. Is it common for physicians to become friends with EMTs?"

What an asinine question.

"Jimmy's a friend of the family. We've known each other for years."

Glenn scribbled something on his little green pad and then flipped over to the next page. "The man who attacked Mr. Harrison, he was a patient?"

"Yes, a John Doe found lying in the street. Jimmy and his partner brought him in."

"His condition at the time?"

Julia closed her eyes, attempted to focus. The events of the past day—Charles, Jimmy, this pandemonium. She forced herself to remain calm, unemotional. She was a professional. This was important. There'd be time for a mildly cataclysmic meltdown later. "He was a male, mid-twenties. Found unconscious. Vitals, all over the board. We had trouble getting accurate readings. His B.P. was erratic. Temperature, only 95.2. The patient experienced ventricular fibrillation. Pupils fixed, but not dilated. No color at all to the eyes. Just white. Almost as if he had no irises."

*****

Those eyes.
White, milky, soapy eyes.
Pin-prick pupils.
Staring. Staring.

*****

175

"Anything else you can remember about the man?"

"Um, yes. He was naked. They found him naked."

"I'm told you pronounced him dead."

*****

Julia tilts the man's head, checks the airway, puts her ear to beside his mouth checking for effective breathing. There is no tidal volume. Arms locked, hands overlaid, she presses on the man's chest again and then again. The patient's skin has a strange rubbery feel to it. The temperature is wrong, far too cold for someone who'd been breathing only seconds before.

And those eyes.

She can't escape those strange pasty eyes, staring sightlessly into her face. Locked. Unmoving. Empty.

*****

"Yes, dead. He flat-lined only two or three minutes after arrival." Julia crossed her arms. Why were her hands shaking? She could handle this. She dealt with life and death situations every waking day.

Glenn flipped another page, scratched his nose, and licked the tip of his ballpoint. "You attempted to revive him."

*****

The minutes click by, time simultaneously becoming no time and all time. It is a non-entity.

Julia's arms ache, sweat emerges on her brow. She blinks the moisture from her eyes. A nurse, she doesn't notice which one, dabs the perspiration from her forehead.

Press. Press.

Still the heart monitor offers only a single level tone. The soulless melody of the dead.

Press. Press.

Julia can't give up. Not yet.

Press. Press.

Those eyes.

Press. Press.

Staring.

Press. Press.

The gray-white of soapy water. No irises. Only the tiniest of pupils.

Press. Press.

Unresponsive. Dead.

Over twenty minutes, now. No response.

*****

"Yes, I tried to revive him. We worked on the patient for over twenty minutes, maybe longer."

"And you were unsuccessful."

Julia's phone buzzed. She ignored it. "I pronounced him dead at 12:47 a.m."

"Do you need to take that call?"

"I'll worry about the damn phone. You just worry about the investigation."

Glenn raised his eyebrows at the overly-terse response, a near miss at allowing character to invade his uninspired features. "All right. Next question then. How is it that a man pronounced dead was able to leap from the gurney, attack a healthy EMT, fend off other hospital personnel, and flee the scene without capture?"

*****

Julia gazes into the deceased man. She studies the now-lulling lips, the strange eyes, still open, but vacant. Her eyes narrow. The man's right hand lays face up on the gurney. What is that on the palm, that strange texturing?

Jimmy Harrison moves closer, noticing Julia's furrowed brow.

Julia runs her fingertips across the palm. Even through her rubber gloves, she can feel a strange uneven quality. She presses, only slightly. There's something just beneath the surface of the skin. It almost seems prickly.

Jimmy leans closer, his lips curling into a curious twist.

Without warning, the dead man's arm shoots up, his hand pressing into Jimmy Harrison's neck. There's a moist popping sound, almost like that of a pin penetrating a rubber balloon. The startled EMT releases a gurgling croak as his eyes roll back and his tongue extends. The naked man rises, still cradling Jimmy by the back of the neck, his pale, nearly translucent skin gleaming in the harsh lights, his strange eyes focused intently on the struggling man.

Julia lunges forward, grabs the naked man's arm and pulls. But the man is fierce and quick. Julia is thrown backward, colliding with a nurse, Lisa. They both fall to the floor; the instruments that Lisa carries skitter across the tile.

Shouting for security, Julia scrambles to her feet. Jimmy Harrison flops about the floor as if in seizure. Shedding his I.V. and other appa-

ratus in a flurry of jerks and grunts, the naked man races through the nearest doorway and down the adjacent corridor.

Gone.

*****

Inhaling deeply, Julia brushed her short bangs back with both palms. "I don't know how he did it. Medically, it makes no sense."

Glenn stared at his notepad, not making eye contact with Julia; his face expressionless. Julia couldn't interpret him. She sensed disbelief, but the man was simply unreadable.

"Detective, I know this sounds preposterous. I find it hard to believe myself. But the patient had been dead for nearly thirty minutes at the time of the attack."

Glenn looked up from his notes, his pale eyes meeting with Julia's own. "Mm-hmm."

Julia's *iPhone* sounded yet again. Cursing, she reached into her pocket and turned the phone to off.

"Your story matches that of the other hospital staff," said Glenn after a moment's pause. "I'm simply trying to determine if there's any sense to be made."

Julia opened her mouth to speak, but then caught the eye of a young man standing just beyond the doorway. She'd noticed him earlier, milling about in the background, not touching anything, not interfering; simply being there. At first she'd thought him a plain-clothed police officer—perhaps he was. But now she didn't think so. He interacted with no one, falling into the background whenever someone drew near. His eyes were cold and penetrating, his hair slightly long for an officer.

And white.

The man couldn't be much over thirty and his hair was as white as the night was black.

She looked back at Glenn, intending to mention the man, but when she looked up again, he was gone.

Just like everything else in her life.

Chapter Sixteen

Donald Baker marched down the brightly lit corridor, weaving between hospital staff, patients, and visiting family members. Inhaling deeply, he drew in the fragrances of humanity—perspiration, perfumes, powders, antiseptics—all the day-to-day things no one thinks about, though they reveal the world in its truest, most basic form. Drawing near, Donald apprised Shane Daws, who sat in a molded plastic chair against the far wall. At over thirty, Shane had a face that longed to be boyish with eyes that had seen far too much to ever be considered innocent. The young man wore a gray blazer with charcoal business slacks, a black collarless T-shirt, and black and white Converse All-Star tennis shoes—business casual, sort of. A man who inhabited the adult world, but refused to give up his tenuous hold on youth. The young man's hair was the one feature that contradicted his post-adolescent look. Though he had allowed it to grow out some since their last encounter three years prior, it was still as stark white as an Alaskan snowball.

Shane rose as Donald approached, slipped a stick of Wrigley's into his mouth, and extended his right hand. "Hey, uh…Doc, I'm sorry about the thing on the phone. I wasn't trying to imply that you weren't needed."

Donald dismissed the comment with a wave of the hand. "Of course you were, Mr. Daws. But that's not my concern. Please update me on the developments."

"Okay." Shane gazed down at Donald, a shorter man by two or three inches. "The EMT's name is James Harrison. He goes by Jimmy. Things are still iffy but it sounds like he's stabilized. They moved him to I.C.U. about two hours ago. The emergency room physician is staying on as his doctor. I guess they're personal friends."

Donald nodded. "Is he still comatose?"

Shane shrugged and rolled his hand in a doubtful gesture. "Not sure. It sounds like this could still go either way. The reyaqc hit him pretty hard for such a short contact—maybe ten or fifteen seconds. I'm guessing he must have been pretty well gone to risk infusing so quickly."

"Reckless would be my assessment." Donald paused, and then glanced just beyond Shane's left shoulder.

A tall, thin, young woman stood behind the young man. Hugging a thick black binder, she'd risen from the seat adjacent to Shane, and had remained a respectful distance behind. She grinned nervously under Donald's gaze and seemed to hunch her shoulders, perhaps self-conscious of her unusual height. "Who is this woman?" asked Donald.

Shane withdrew another stick of gum from his jacket pocket, un-wrapped it, and slid the slender stick into his mouth. "Uh…yeah, Doc, I was going to mention her. That's Terry."

"Theresa Alice Zimmerman." The young woman stepped forward, extending her hand in greeting. "Call me Taz. It's a huge honor to meet you, Dr. Baker. I've had the pleasure of reading snippets of your *Histories*, though complete volumes are nearly impossible to come by."

Donald directed his comments to Shane. "Why have you brought an-other into this?"

"He didn't bring me into it," said Taz as she ran nervous fingers through straight black hair. "I brought *him* in. We're on the sites. You know, tracking potential sightings, sifting through articles. I caught the pattern here in Las Vegas and called Shane because of his experience and prior contact with you."

"It's true, Doc. Taz is the one who keyed in on the rogue."

"I had to meet you, Dr. Baker. I've heard so much about you."

"Whatever you've heard is either false or grossly exaggerated, Miss…Taz. I'd ask that you keep what minimal information you've acquired solely to yourself. None of this is for public consumption—

especially not on some website frequented by the socially inept and dangerously curious." Taz bit a nail and Donald redirected his attention to Shane. "The patient? His room?"

"That's right behind me, Doc. I managed to cop three visitor's passes from the front desk, you know, in case someone tries to give us a hassle." Shane paused, glanced at the floor. "Hey, I'm sorry about... Um, Taz. It's just the way things worked out. I hope this doesn't make you think that I'm not able to help you, here."

"My opinion of you, Mr. Daws, has long since been established." Donald paused for a moment, sniffed at the stale recycled air. Shane was perspiring, obviously embarrassed to be seen with his young associate. Donald contemplated dismissing them both outright. Youth could be so...flighty. Daws was a sincere young man, it was simply that his judgments could be considered questionable. And this Taz... Her type frightened him. They were too eager, too infatuated with the idea of the reyaqc. Still, the two already possessed an unhealthy sum of information. Perhaps it would be best to allow them a controlled access, thus gaining their discretion and loyalty. "This is a serious business," he said. "Not some spurious UFO sighting or a vampire cult wearing plastic teeth and sipping red wine. Lives are at stake. Both human and reyaqc. The need for containment of information is critical. Is that understood?"

Shane nodded. Taz shrugged, still clutching her black binder to her chest.

"None of what you see or hear goes beyond us."

"That goes without saying," said Shane.

"Absolutely," agreed Taz.

Donald glanced to the doorway just beyond Shane. "This room?"

"Yeah, that's the one."

Donald moved toward the door.

"Um, Doc?" Shane was perspiring heavily. He was ill-at-ease, probably about to offer something he deemed confrontational.

"Yes, Mr. Daws."

"You do understand, this isn't necessarily the reyaqc's fault."

Donald closed his eyes and released his breath in an extended exhale. "Of course it is. The reyaqc have needs, yes. They have fierce primal drives. But they also have a great intellectual capacity. There are other ways. More civilized means. This rogue, he behaved like a beast, putting himself and others at great risk. Do not forget, premature exposure is the gravest danger to this already-endangered species."

Donald sighed. Shane's concept of the reyaqc was incomplete, romanticized. He both idolized and feared them. The young man needed to have a more realistic understanding of the species, otherwise he'd be useless to Donald, and worse, might become seriously injured or even killed in the process.

*****

Jimmy Harrison lay in a fitful sleep, his eyes moving from side-to-side beneath tightly closed lids. His skin tone was pasty, revealing blue veins barely hidden beneath the epidermis. Strands of lost hair peppered the pillow, and the man, though unconscious, gritted his teeth as if in great pain.

Donald approached with the detached demeanor of a physician examining a patient. Though, internally, his thoughts were less clinical. A reyaqc had done this. Hadn't they all learned by now? Couldn't they understand the ramifications of these actions? Couldn't they understand the risk?

Donald had wrestled with these same questions again and again and never once come to a satisfactory conclusion. Best to take a mental step away, remain unmoved, think of the solutions to this specific problem. He sighed, refocused on his task. The discoloration was accentuated below the eyes, on the cheeks and neck. Donald lifted both of the man's hands in his, rubbing Harrison's fingers between his own thumbs and fingers. "Fingertips, cold to the touch, stiff, and only marginally responsive." He moved to the foot of the bed and repeated the process on the feet. "The same would be true of the feet. Discoloration extends to just above the knees." Moving again toward the patient's head, Donald gently opened the jaw, then lowered his face to within an inch of the man's now-open mouth and sniffed twice, inhaling his stale breath. "Mr. Daws, what type of I.V. have they prescribed?"

Shane shrugged, offering an uneasy grin. "I'm not a physician, Doc."

Donald sighed and moved past his two companions to examine the I.V. drip. "Typical saline drip. He's in desperate need of electrolytes and is suffering from dehydration." He stepped around the I.V. stand and leaned over the patient, giving him three light pats on the left cheek. "James, James, can you hear me?"

No response.

"James!"

Nothing.

"Young lady, would you please stand near the doorway. Alert me should anyone approach this room."

"Of course, Dr. Baker." Taz nodded as she strode the three paces to the door, and then withdrew a pen from her blue jean pocket, opened her binder, and began to scribble notes.

Donald withdrew a small rolled pouch he'd concealed in the breast pocket of his tweed sports jacket. Laying it on the bed beside Harrison's left thigh, he untied and then unrolled it, revealing three syringes and three different medications. He then withdrew a small plastic zip-lock bag from his right hip pocket containing a gauze pad already dampened with rubbing alcohol. The gauze was then removed and he swabbed an area on Harrison's left bicep. From his pouch, Donald selected the needed medication and a syringe, removed the syringe from its plastic wrapping, and inserted the long needle into the tiny bottle, withdrawing three ccs of the pale pink liquid. He then tapped the syringe lightly with one finger as he depressed the plunger insuring that no air bubbles remained. He injected Harrison in his left arm, and then carefully re-placed his apparatus, rolling the pouch shut, and tying it tightly before returning it to his inner pocket. He spoke to Harrison in a low, furtive voice. "James, you must regain consciousness. You are in great danger." He patted the unconscious man's cheek. "James, it is imperative that you wake."

Jimmy Harrison moaned and rolled his head in the direction of Don-ald's voice.

"That's it, James. Now try to focus. Can you see me?"

The man's eyes fluttered open. The pupils were unusually wide for someone whose eyes had been shut for so long, and the stark neon light obviously bothered him. He closed them in a tight squint.

"Miss Taz, dim the overhead lights, please."

Nodding, Taz moved to do as Donald had requested.

"There. Is that more to your liking?" Donald bent, keeping his face only inches from that of Jimmy Harrison.

"Who... are...you?" asked Harrison.

"My name is Donald Baker. I need to ask some questions about the man who attacked you."

The patient's face screwed in confusion. "I was attacked?" Harrison seemed disoriented, glancing from side to side as if trying to determine just where he might be.

"Yes, James. You were attacked by a patient. The naked man."

"Naked guy. Yeah, I remember him."

Donald nodded. "Tell me what you remember."

The patient hesitated and rolled his eyes upward. "Not much. We, uh…responded to a call just north of Washington, a couple blocks. I don't remember, E Street, F Street, somewhere up there."

"It was E Street," offered Taz taking a step closer to the bed and grinning at her ability to be of assistance.

"Okay," agreed Harrison. "E Street. The guy was in the middle of the street." The patient paused to catch his breath. Even the exertion of talking seemed to put a strain on him. "Um, unconscious. Skin tone kind of blue-gray."

"Can you describe the man, his characteristics, anything unusual?"

"H-he was strange."

Chapter Seventeen

Dr. Julia Chambers was weary. She'd been on duty over thirteen hours. This wasn't by the hospital's direction. In fact, regulations forbad shifts of this length. But Julia felt a responsibility. Jimmy Harrison's case baffled her. She'd been present during the attack—had seen the whole thing. Still she couldn't ascertain just what had occurred. From her perspective, the patient—flat-lined, no tidal volume, no B.P. whatsoever—had reached up and choked the startled EMT. Contact had been minimal, no more than a few seconds. The naked man had then knocked Julia to the floor, leaped from the gurney, and fled down the corridor, leaving Jimmy Harrison quivering in seizure. None of Jimmy's symptoms had been consistent with strangulation. The windpipe was intact, not damaged in any way. He had not been held long enough to suffer from lack of oxygen. But still, he slipped into coma; his skin color became blue as if he was deprived of oxygen. His vital signs became erratic, and only in the past two hours had he shown hints of returning consciousness.

And there were those strange pale white puncture marks on the back of his neck. Almost indiscernible. How had those come to be?

Julia blinked, attempting to focus on the test results she held. She would need to sleep soon or risk becoming counterproductive.

Soon, but not yet.

She needed to check on Jimmy one more time before leaving. Besides, the only thing waiting at home was a lonely bed, and she wasn't sure that even now she was sufficiently exhausted to deal with that. Six years of marriage, and suddenly she was alone. They weren't necessarily six good years, but well, the marriage hadn't been Boardwalk, but it wasn't Baltic Avenue either. Something more middle-of-the-road: Indiana Avenue, or Illinois.

Apparently her soon-to-be ex-husband, Charles, thought differently. He complained about her long hours, her "marriage" to her work. He wanted children, longed for them, craved them even. Julia wasn't sure she'd ever known a man to desire fatherhood so fervently. He would make a good father. That was evident every time Charles' brother came by with his three boys. Julia wanted children too, but not yet, not until... Well, that was it, wasn't it? Not until when? Julia had to admit that she could have made adjustments. She could have eased back on her duties, could have conceded and joined the ranks of working mothers. She wasn't exactly in her twenties any more. If she was going to do it, it needed to be soon.

She loved Charles. She really did. Or was it that she loved what Charles represented—having someone waiting for her when she arrived home, no matter how late in the evening or early into the next morning it had become? Charles had been good to her. He'd tried to be flexible. But in the end Julia had made an unspoken choice to put her work first and Charles second. That was something he just couldn't accept. He was still a reasonably young, good-looking man, with a solid income. With that Denzel grin and those Fishburne eyes, there were always other options out there—and he'd found one. Or, she'd found him. Either way, the damage was done.

All for the cause, she'd thought many times. All for the cause.

The irony was that Julia was unsure that she still believed in the cause. She'd been full of self-importance. She was saving lives, she was wresting people from the hands of death—she was prescribing cough syrup and antibiotics to every illegal alien who walked through the door and detoxing the same homeless men over and over. She was doing the same things both vital and trivial that any other competent physician could do—and would do—if she weren't here. Was this worth losing her marriage over? Or was the marriage the same as the position? Was it just another facet of Julia's master plan, that, when examined in the light of her life, held little or no true significance? Did anything have meaning? Anything at all?

Jimmy had meaning.

Jimmy Harrison lay inside that room, fighting for his life, waiting for Julia to bring him back. If nothing else had significance, this did. This one patient, right now, in this very moment. Maybe that was all she could hope for, significant moments. And if there were enough significant moments, would that add up to a significant life? Most likely not. Julia seriously wondered if there was such a thing.

She closed her eyes, inhaled deeply, cleared her thoughts. She was bogged down in what-ifs and lunchroom philosophies. This was probably natural concerning her life circumstances. But none of it belonged here— not ever. Another cleansing breath and she walked through the door.

Jimmy had three visitors: a tall young woman standing midway between the patient and the doorway, a man of perhaps thirty with pure white hair—yes, *that man*, the one from earlier—and a fortyish red-haired man, leaning over the bed talking with Jimmy.

Talking with him.

Jimmy had regained consciousness. Why had no one alerted her? "Excuse me. Who are you people?" she asked, probably with more of an edge than necessary. Most likely these were simply concerned family members.

The red-haired man angled his head in Julia's direction, his bearded face void of expression. "I'm Donald Baker. This is Mr. Daws and Miss...Taz. I assume you're James' physician." The man had a distinctive upper-crust Boston air to his voice; but there was something else in there as well, something foreign, eastern European perhaps.

"Yes. I'm Dr. Julia Chambers. Are you related to Jimmy?"

"No, Dr. Chambers, there is no relation." The man wore tinted glasses, but even so, his gaze was unnerving. "Tell me, were you present at the time of the attack?"

Was this man with the police? Was he a hospital administrator? "Yes. I was there and have treated him since."

The man moved forward a step. "Actually, your treatment is inadequate. Massive amounts of electrolytes are required. He must be hydrated to beyond standard tissue saturation. Don't worry about over hydration. In this case, that should not be an issue."

"Excuse me, Donald. Are you a doctor?" If the hospital had sent an outside physician to check on her, well, they would hear about that. This was her patient—her friend—and she was doing everything in her power to help him recover.

Donald Baker cocked his head slightly to the left and smiled a haunting, unnerving smile. A smile that should not have been, thought Julia. She didn't know exactly what this notion could mean, but she held to it nonetheless. "A doctor, yes. A physician, no. My expertise lies in other areas. Though I do have considerable experience with cases such as these."

Now Julia was truly confused. Who was this man and what gave him the right to imply that she was incompetent? "Are you with the police? The media?"

"We're concerned for James and seek information on his assailant."

Well, that answer was no answer at all. "I'm sorry. But, unless I'm missing something, you have no official reason to be here."

Donald offered a tight, close-mouthed grin. Again, wrong, artificial, not a true grin at all. "Official? No. Ours is a moral obligation."

"Well, I've got a moral obligation to kick your skinny ass out of here."

Finally the young white-haired man spoke. "Dr. Chambers, this probably seems strange, but we can hel—"

"That's enough, Mr. Daws," said Donald Baker, cutting him off midsentence. "We'll be on our way, Doctor. Once again, my name is Dr. Donald Baker. I'm staying in a suite at the Venetian should you have need of me."

"Can't imagine why I would," said Julia as Donald nodded and strolled past her and out through the door.

"Sorry about that, Doctor," said the young man as he moved awkwardly toward the door. "He can be that way."

"Yeah, but he's still awesome," grinned the tall, black-haired woman. "Donald Baker! Can you believe it? Donald Baker!"

"Mr. Daws. Miss Taz," came Donald Baker's voice from the hallway. "Say nothing further."

"Coming, Doc," said the young man with the hair of a person thirty years his senior. He paused in front of Julia. It seemed he was searching her face with eyes that sang a sad and bitter song. "Listen," he said in a near-whisper. "Donald Baker's a pain. No arguments there. But he's an expert in this area. I can't say much, but he *can* help your patient."

With that, he turned and disappeared around the corner.

Chapter Eighteen

Tresset Bremu stood in the downtown Las Vegas bus station wiping his hands with a soft alcohol-dampened cloth. He hated the smell of the place. He hated the human livestock herding from one end of the terminal to another. He hated the drunks half passed out on the wooden benches and the security personnel who allowed the drunks to remain. He hated the tearful reunions and the even more tearful goodbyes. He hated the audacious sounds: the overhead speakers, the obligatory *iPod* in each young ear, the beeping of text messaging and the manufactured melodies of cell phone ring tones He hated the dumpy street people with the weary eyes. He hated every stinking little thing about this place.

Still, the bus station was a good place for Tresset. Well, maybe not good, but advantageous at least.

Inching forward, he scanned the crowd now departing a just-arrived bus. This one, he believed, had made its way from Chicago, across Iowa and the remainder of the Midwest, before angling southward in Colorado, eventually making its way to Las Vegas. He liked the ones that had come through the Midwest. The Midwest was dull, plodding, dotted with hundreds of tiny rural towns that offered the youth few distractions beyond school athletics, bowling alleys, skating rinks, and drugs. The latter being the most popular of the options.

But even that became old, at least for the ones who boarded the bus. These kids wanted out. They wanted adventure, excitement. They wanted something so unlike the routines of their lives that they were willing to climb onto one of these metal monstrosities with no more than a few dozen dollars—and of course their *iPod*—in their pockets and head west to adventure, to thrills, to Tresset.

Many of them made Los Angeles their destination. These hoped to become movie stars. Tresset had little interest in them. They were shallow bobble-heads with little sense and slim chance of accomplishing much beyond enhancing their currently anemic police records. The ones who made Las Vegas their goal were probably no less dull, but they at least didn't think they'd be the next Brad Pitt or Angelina Jolie. These kids weren't looking for fame; they were looking for adventure. They wanted some sort of stimulation that could shock them out of a lifeless existence. They wanted to take a chance, experience risk.

Tresset would offer them that opportunity.

Tresset normally left this task of "recruitment" to a subordinate, but as of late, the selections brought forward had been duller than most, many of them outright addicts or diseased—either of which were useless. There was a need. But the need was specific. The pack required more than warm bodies if they were to flourish. They needed healthy prospects, with strong genes, intelligent minds. It took some skill to identify these from among the lesser chattel, but after over a century of existence Tresset had skill in abundance. He preferred to hunt at the university, UNLV, where he could find much better stock. But those youth took time to cultivate. Oh, they could be swayed. With their youthful exuberance and ideological thinking, they could be grand recruits. And for his own personal use, Tresset wouldn't think of another source. But these took multiple visits. They had families who knew where they were, instructors who would miss them in class, roommates who would know they hadn't returned to the dormitory. One had to be so very careful with those. But these, they'd already fled their former lives, in most cases giving little or no indication as to where they might eventually land.

Tresset wiped his hands once again, then folded the alcohol-drenched cloth neatly and inserted it into the right pocket of his faded red sweatshirt. The sweatshirt, of course, was far too hot for the Las Vegas summer, but it had a large floppy hood, which was perfect for concealment.

Concealment was a high priority for Tresset.

He pulled the hood further forward, pushed his sunglasses up, and maneuvered through the crowd of people. Those he sought would not have luggage. At most, they would have backpacks—some might carry guitars in "gig" bags. They would be in their late teens or early twenties. They would be thin, hungry, edgy.

And they would be lost.

Having finally made it to their long dreamed of destinations, they would realize that their plan had been no plan at all. Where would they stay? How would they get money? How long could they last on the fifty dollars and twenty-two cents hidden away in their pockets? They could come in either gender; though Tresset's greatest current need was for females. Still, a healthy male with a competent mind and a solid physique would always be a welcome addition.

But none departing this bus fit these descriptions. Most were geriatrics, perhaps on a field trip or group outing, he supposed.

Useless.

Not only did the elderly smell bad, but they hoarded resources better used on those with the potential to contribute. How small-minded was a society that would acquiesce to the needs of the weak and inept. And as a greater and greater percentage of that society achieved advanced years, so would that society weaken accordingly, until one day, whether from internal faults, or outside intervention, it would collapse in upon itself leaving room for the strong and fit, for those worthy of the land's great resources.

Tresset withdrew his cloth, wiped his hands again. This was a filthy place.

A voice came from behind. A security guard. This was always a risk. The hood pulled low obscuring the face, the large dark sunglasses, the amount of time Tresset had been loitering—a security guard might mistake him for a predator—a different type of predator.

Tresset squeezed the damp cloth still clutched in his hand as he half turned toward the guard, still keeping his head lowered despite the man's eight to ten inch height advantage. Tresset hated avoiding the gaze of an inferior, which from his perspective, was nearly everyone. But he couldn't risk exposure.

Like most such men, the security guard was a buffoon. The buttons on his light blue shirt strained in a losing battle against the man's massive belly. He held a large black walkie-talkie as if it was the key to salvation. The man's face was round and poorly shaven. He was in need of a haircut and his greasy locks popped up in a subtle anarchy. "You been hanging around here a long time now," said the guard in a voice an octave too high for his burly form. "What's your business?"

Tresset could kill this useless human being before he knew that he'd been attacked.

"I said, what's your business?" repeated the guard.

Tresset clutched his cloth tighter yet. One quick swipe. The man would be dead or maimed.

"Sir, I'm gonna hafta ask you to leave."

A quick pounce, a snap! Did this useless slab of meat have any idea that Tresset held his very life in his hands?

"Sir! I said, you're gonna hafta leave."

"My cousin is on a bus from Des Moines," said Tresset in a tightly controlled voice. "I wasn't sure of the arrival time. It will be soon, I hope." Tresset paused, allowed the man to take a breath in preparation to speak, and then added. "The sweatshirt probably seems rather odd in this heat. I have a skin condition and must protect myself against exposure."

Tresset reached up, patted the man on his sweaty back saying, "Thank you for your concern," and then strolled away, feverishly wiping his hands with his cloth and glancing in each direction as if in search of someone quite specific—which in a way he was.

"Sir, I'm not done with you yet." The guard had attempted to make his high, tight voice sound authoritative, but had only succeeded in bringing forth a squeak on the word "done."

Tresset continued to move forward through the crowd.

"Sir, I am going to hafta ask you to leave."

The man was nearly upon Tresset now. He reached out to grab Tresset's shoulder with that pudgy disease-laden hand. Tresset would tolerate no such insult. He whirled, his right hand shooting up to the man's neck. But he did not draw anything from this man. No. None of this man's lowly essence would course through Tresset's veins. This was self-defense. Nothing more. The guard emitted a subtle gasp as Tresset, nearly a foot shorter, lowered him into a nearby molded plastic chair.

"You are an imbecile," said Tresset as the man's wide eyes finally took in the inhuman face before him. "You are an imbecile who has relinquished the right to draw breath." With that, a retractable claw from just above Tresset's index fingernail extended into the man's neck. Avoiding the jugular, Tresset cut directly into the windpipe. There was a sudden sputtering hiss of expelled air, and the man's eyes showed panic as he grasped at his throat. His mouth moved, but no sound came forth. Tresset calmly turned away, wiping his hand with his cloth. The strike had been swift and silent. He was nearly halfway across the room before he heard the first scream.

Humans, he thought, so predicable, so weak.

Chapter Nineteen

Jimmy Harrison's eyes, though still cloudy, were responsive and alert. He'd regained his customary smile and even a bit of his wry humor. But his color was poor, his respiration shallow, he was losing hair. Julia concluded her examination with a smile and asked how he felt.

"Weak," he said, his voice raspy. "But alive. For a while there I wasn't so sure about that."

Julia nodded, resting her palm gently on his forearm, her mocha skin a sharp contrast to his near snowy complexion. "Can you tell me anything else about your experience? Anything about the attack or what you felt afterward?"

Jimmy sucked a piece of crushed ice from a paper cup and shook his head. Even this seemed an effort. "The attack, no. Just a blank. Afterward, after I'd started to come out of it, I felt swimmy, like everything was moving at a different speed than me. My throat was dry. Very dry. Still is."

"What about your neck where the man grabbed you?"

"Feels like a rash. Burns. Itches."

"You look better. Your vitals are more or less stabile, your fluid intake and output are beginning to normalize."

Jimmy eyed her curiously. "Except?"

Julia pursed her lips. This was the dicey part. "Jimmy, you're my friend. You're also an EMT. I'm going to be straight with you."

Jimmy nodded. "Gotcha."

"Your hemoglobin is all wrong. Your white blood cell count is so low Dracula would probably try to give you blood. You're losing more hair by the hour. We still don't know what happened to you. Some freak briefly grabbed you by the neck. He did no damage to the windpipe.

There was no bruising as with strangulation. Yet, you fell into a coma. You displayed a strange pattern of puncture marks on your neck where you were grabbed, yet your tox screens reveal no foreign substances. But, at the point of contact, we've discovered some damage at the cellular level. Minimal, nothing cancerous. But, it exists. Truthfully, we've found nothing to explain any of this."

Jimmy seemed dazed for a moment. Julia thought perhaps he'd drifted off to sleep again. But then he blinked, made eye contact, and nodded.

Julia bit her lower lip and considered what she was about to say. "Jimmy, when you first regained consciousness, there were three visitors in your room. Do you remember them?"

Jimmy furrowed his brow as if attempting to access the memory. "I was still pretty foggy. Why? Who were they?"

That, thought Julia, was exactly what she wanted to know. "I'm not sure. One of them was a pompous Harvard type. Mr. Chips meets Night of the Living Dead. Strange guy. He seemed quite knowledgeable about your condition. He told me his name, where he was staying, but evaded my questions as to why he was here and what he knew of your attack."

"I don't know. I really don't remember."

With this, his eyes fluttered. He offered a weak grin. And then he was asleep.

*****

Once in the hallway, Julia exhaled and massaged her temples with her right hand. She was missing something, some key element. None of the normal causes for any of these symptoms panned out. Jimmy was not stable, his condition much more volatile then she'd led him to believe. And she had no clear diagnosis. Her iPhone vibrated. She lifted it from her right lab coat pocket. It was Charles, her husband. She slipped the phone back into her pocket letting it ring through.

Twenty minutes later Dr. Raul Martinez found Julia seated at the nurse's station as she pored over Jimmy Harrison's File. Raul was a young intern, bright, dedicated, with an offbeat sense of humor. Julia liked him. He was a thinker, willing to question established assumptions. Medicine needed people like him. "Yes, Raul, what is it?"

"I just learned about your case. Jim Harrison, the EMT."

"Yes. What about him?"

"I think you'd better take a look at these files. Both are fatalities I handled earlier this week.

*****

Julia groaned at the sight of Charles leaning against her silver Lexus LS Hybrid. She didn't have time for distractions. Especially not this distraction. She'd gone over the files provided by Raul Martinez, questioned the young intern doggedly, done some additional research on her own, and become more perplexed than before.

"It's late," he said with his Denzel grin. "I was wondering if you'd ever get out of that place."

Julia unlocked the car via remote and marched past him to the driver's side door. "Go take a dive off the Stratosphere, Charles. See if you can make some pretty spatter patterns on Las Vegas Boulevard."

"I've been calling. You haven't responded."

"Huh. Can't imagine why that would be."

Charles rolled his eyes. "Okay, maybe you don't want to talk. But that doesn't mean we don't need to talk."

The car door stood open, but still Julia turned to face her soon-to-be-ex-husband. "What could we possibly need to talk about? Oh! How's your new girlfriend? She going to give you a baby yet? Hey, here's an idea—why don't you get ten girlfriends, and then they can all make you a daddy in the same month."

Charles didn't respond. Rather, he simply stared at her, moisture creeping into the corners of his eyes. He looked good. He always looked good. Wasn't that part of the problem? There he stood, dark close-cropped hair, bushy black eyebrows that could dip into intensity or arc into wonder in a second's time. His deep brown eyes were somehow accentuated by his forest green polo shirt. There was something in his expression, though. Something unfamiliar. Something very un-Charles-like. Somehow her cocky, self-assured man looked lost.

Julia moaned. "What is it, Charles? What is so important that you need to stalk me in a parking lot at night? Do you want to start negotiations already? Are you angling for the HD TV, or are you going straight for the jugular and asking for the house?"

"I'm not sure we should go through with it."

"Go through with what? What shouldn't we go through with?"

Charles looked down, possibly focusing on his booted feet, a sure sign that he was uncomfortable. The last time she'd seen him this ill-at-ease, he'd proposed. In a way, that's what he was doing again now. "The divorce, Julia. I'm not sure we should go through with the divorce."

The man had to be out of his mind. "Charles, you initiated this. You said it wasn't working, you swore there was no other option."

"Maybe I was wrong."

"Maybe you were wrong."

"I mean, you know, maybe we should rethink—"

"Get out of here. Just get out. You have no idea what I'm going through."

"Will you at least—"

"Go! Now! Before I plow you down." Julia threw the stack of files onto the front passenger seat, plopped into the driver's seat, slammed the door shut, and started the engine.

Charles Chambers decided it best to move.

Chapter Twenty

Shane contemplated Taz from across the table—her lively darting eyes, her intense, yet energized expression, the way she folded her lower lip beneath her teeth while concentrating. It was now early evening. They sat in a booth at a small Chinese restaurant on West Charleston Avenue after parting company with Donald Baker some two hours earlier. Taz alternately sipped egg drop soup and scribbled notes in her ever-present binder. Despite himself, Shane couldn't help but smile. The girl's infatuation, her dedication to the reyaqc was endearing.

"What are you grinning at?" she said as she lifted the spoon to her lips.

"Nothing." He paused. "Okay, at you. Sorry. I just think it's cute. You haven't stopped scribbling in that thing since we sat down."

"I'm trying to get everything entered before I forget it. I've described Donald Baker. I've attempted to quote all he said with as much accuracy as possible. I've also described the patient, his condition, what Dr. Baker suggested."

Shane nodded. "Like I said, cute."

She smiled. It was broad, warm, full of vigor. This girl embraced her passions like few Shane had ever seen. She wasn't the type of girl he normally fell for; she was too… unpolished, perhaps, maybe too quirky. But the more he looked at her the more he studied her eyes, so vibrant, so full of vigor, the more he thought… No. He was just tired, excited about the events of the day. There was no real attraction.

"You're next, you know," said Taz.

"Me?"

"You've got a great story, Shane. Your experience with the reyaqc, someone could write a book about it."

Shane shook his head and then pushed his soup bowl away. He'd never cared much for the stuff. "I don't think my story would fill a chapter—definitely not a book."

"Well, whatever. It's still interesting." She leaned a little closer, her deep brown eyes locking with his, her lips curling ever so slightly at the corners of her mouth. Her right hand twitched. It seemed she'd almost reached across to clasp his fingers, but decided better of it. "I want to hear it. I want to know what it was like."

Shane grinned. "What if I tell you all about it in the car?"

Taz cocked her head and offered a curious smirk. "What are you thinking, Shane?"

"I'm thinking that maybe I know how to find the rogue."

*****

Shane Daws turned the same corner for the fourth time. This was the neighborhood where Jimmy Harrison, the EMT, found the naked reyaqc. This was where the rogue had been hiding, where he'd chosen to hunt. Shane was hoping this was a habit and not simply a one-time event. There had been the three attacks on humans as well, not in this specific neighborhood, but nearby. If he didn't find any sign of the reyaqc soon, he'd move on to the closest attack site, and then the next. The reyaqc had gone somewhere. A rogue would resurface. Shane hoped he could be there when this occurred.

Taking a sip of Pepsi, Shane glanced at Taz, seated in the passenger seat, and biting at a nail as they rounded another corner. Until this morning, the girl had never actually seen a reyaqc face-to-face. She'd longed to do so for several years, ever since her uncle had regaled her with stories of strange encounters in the jungles of Vietnam. And now, largely through her own intuition, she had landed in the middle of a rogue hunt. Taz's brown eyes were wide, scanning the shadowy streets with excited, wary, exuberance. Her binder sat in her lap, her pen in hand as she documented each step of the search. Who knew how she would respond if they actually found the thing? Who knew how Shane would react either? Despite his previous experience with reyaqc, this was new to him as well.

Shane didn't know Taz well. It had begun as an online relationship. They'd only met face-to-face a handful of times prior to this day. He didn't regard her as pretty, at least not in any traditional sense. She was too tall and leggy. On some woman these attributes might launch a successful modeling career. On Taz it simply made her appear awkward. Her hair was lifeless, her face unremarkable. She wore no make-up. Her choices in clothing did nothing to accentuate what natural beauty she might hold. But as he looked at her now, in the dim light, her eyes wide and curious, her bottom lip curled under her upper teeth in rapt anticipation, he felt a sudden stirring for her. He couldn't quite explain it. Maybe it was simply that she was a kindred spirit, someone whose admiration for the reyaqc rivaled his own. But she suddenly seemed, well, appealing.

"Are you staring at me again?" she asked with a sly grin. "That's the second time I've caught you in one day."

He shrugged and flushed. "Do you think the rogue will be able to communicate?" he asked, ignoring the question. "Or will it be too far gone?"

"Most believe that rogues have reverted to a more primitive state of being, leaving intellectual capacity dormant."

Shane nodded. "Probably because they infuse from too many sources. Compatibility issues, right?"

"Maybe. Though, I doubt there's any scientific data to support the thought."

Shane nodded. "But, what caused this reyaqc to land in the hospital? There were no signs of injury, no blood, no wounds. Was he empty?"

Taz flipped back through her notebook pages, scanning for the incident, though Shane had a feeling the girl already had the answer lodged in her head. "Not empty," she said finally. "At least, not if we can believe the witness statements." Taz read from her notes. "'The naked man admitted to the UMC emergency room, though with unremarkable characteristics, appeared entirely human to the hospital staff. He had nose, mouth, ears, even hair. His skin tone was pale but not translucent.'" Taz looked up from her pages, offering Shane a subtle grin. "The reyaqc may have been depleted, but not entirely empty."

"Exactly," said Shane. "What caused him to lose consciousness in the middle of the street? Think about it. The EMTs get there. The rogue's examined, transported in an ambulance. He had IVs inserted into his veins. He's pronounced dead, Taz. Dead. Then all of a sudden, in the emergency room, poof! He comes to. Had he infused something poisonous? Had one of his victims had bad blood? I don't know—maybe a drug addict or AIDS victim? What happened to him?"

Taz shook her head and scribbled something in her notepad. "I'm not sure if something like that could affect a reyaqc. Maybe something occurred at a cellular level. Donald Baker's Histories detail accounts of reyaqc falling into a state of near hibernation after receiving what he referred to as bad essence."

The two fell back into silence as they rounded another corner. Three tough-looking young men stood huddled together at the next intersection. One of them, a tall black kid with a tombstone tattooed on his left cheek, looked up as Shane rolled past. The tough whistled and waved, attempting to get Shane's attention, but he, Shane, continued forward. No, he wasn't in the market for crack, thank you.

Two more passes through these rundown streets, another drug offer, and the sight of a homeless man urinating on a fire hydrant, and Shane was ready to move on to the next neighborhood, the scene of the most recent attack. It wasn't far, just north on D Street past Owens, then another few blocks, and west into a subdivision.

They were there in four minutes. The neighborhood was old, but not in the state of abject disrepair as had been the previous. The streets were dark, not well lit. Only occasionally did Shane see another car. He slipped a stick of Wrigley into his mouth. "This would be good hunting ground for a rogue," he said. "Only a few cars. Not much foot traffic."

Taz nodded in agreement as she worked a sliver of errant nail between her teeth. "A rogue could stalk a pedestrian or just hide in the shadows between houses."

"Yeah, then *bam*! He strikes!"

"Bam?" she asked with a coquettish grin.

"Well, yeah. You know, uh…bam."

She giggled at his unease. Obviously, she thought it was cute.

Though only just past 9:30, it was a very dark night and Shane felt exposed. It was a frivolous fear, he supposed, possibly brought about by the character of the neighborhood he'd just left. But while that place, only a few blocks away, offered known dangers: drug pushers, addicts, random acts of violence, Shane had no such specific concerns here. No, this was more of a feeling. Something just wasn't right. He told himself that he was being silly, like a child afraid of the dark after seeing a B grade horror film, but he couldn't rationalize himself out of the feeling.

Something was wrong here. And whatever it was that he sensed, was well hidden, but close, so very close.

And then there was a sound—sharp, quick, shrill.

"Taz, did you hear that?"

"What'd you hear?" A tight grin of anticipation crept across the girl's face.

"I dunno. A scream, I think. Not right near us. Maybe on the opposite side of the block." Shane accelerated, scanned the darkened streets, turned left at the end of the block, then left again to go back down the opposite side of the same block. Now he slowed, scanning from side to side. The night was still; there was no obvious movement on either side of the street. Shane and Taz rolled down the car windows in an effort to better hear the exterior sounds. Even in the late evening, the Nevada breeze felt like a blow dryer on Shane's face. He'd grown accustomed to it over the past three years, but still didn't care much for triple digit summers.

There were shadows. Everywhere shadows. Most people don't think about shadows, but they're with us always. Everything animate and inanimate casts a shadow. Even vapor casts a wavy, pulsating shadow of sorts. Shane found it difficult to see beyond the shadows. This night they seemed all encompassing. How was he to distinguish a figure amongst the shadows of trees and homes? How was he to detect the subtle movements of a stealthy reyaqc from the swaying shadows of palm tree fans in the darkened night?

Shane slowed to less than ten miles per hour. He was certain he'd heard the scream. He knew he had. But it had been so short, just a burst, and then it was gone as if it had never broken the still night air.

Coming to the end of the block, Shane performed a U-turn and proceeded to move back up the same street. He saw the same shadows, heard the same distant sounds of traffic. He slurped the last of his drink through the straw and wished for another.

And then it was there—the rogue.

It stood nearly naked in the street, bathed in his headlights, wearing only an unbuttoned Hawaiian-style shirt. Having just bolted out from between two single story homes, its too-pale flesh was damp with perspiration, causing earth and grass to cling to its clammy skin. The chest heaved from exertion and drool dribbled from the corners of its lips. Its eyes were wide and white, featureless and void.

Adrenaline raced through Shane's limbs as he simultaneously rolled up the windows and applied the brakes. He sat still, staring at the reyaqc as it stared back at him. They both, each of them in their own manner, peered into the other, searching, seeking some basic understanding. Taz, for her part, grinned widely as she withdrew her cell phone from her pocket, flicked it to the video feature, and began recording the event. Almost unconsciously, it seemed, her free hand moved left, finding Shane's own hand. Their fingers intertwined. He squeezed. Her smile broadened.

Here it was, thought Shane, the rogue. Where had it come from? What drove it? What had it just done? There had been a scream. Where was the victim? Shane studied the thing, tried to memorize all there was to see. This was such a rare opportunity. He didn't want to do anything to scare it away.

Suddenly, he felt foolishly unprepared. This reyaqc was a killer, a danger. Shane had retraced its previous movements, hoping this would lead him to his quarry. And he'd been successful. But he hadn't followed through to the next logical step. He was face-to-face with the rogue, but with no means of capturing it. He could attempt to run it down, he supposed. But this was an intelligent being, magnificent in many ways, with every bit as much right to live as he. How could he ever think to plow it down? That would be murder.

Nearly reading his thoughts, Taz whispered, "You did bring a tranquilizer gun, right?"

Shane shook his head.

"A Taser?"

Shane shrugged and reddened in embarrassment. The truth was he hadn't honestly thought he'd find the rogue. Sure, he'd told himself that his logic was sound, that the reyaqc had obviously hunted a rather tight geographical area until now, and that logically it would continue to do so. But had he really believed?

The movement caught them both off-guard. The reyaqc charged, leaping onto the hood of Shane's teal blue Acura. The milky eyes focused through the windshield glass on Shane and then on Taz, then back onto Shane. Taz nearly giggled with nervous delight as she recorded the encounter. "Awesome," she whispered.

Shane could now see the tiny pinhole pupils directed at him. The reyaqc's nostrils flared, sniffing, seeking his scent. Its mouth widened in what may have been outrage or mirth, revealing a landscape of broken and missing teeth. The face was not symmetrical. The right cheekbone was high and sharp, while the left was sunken and hollow. The left eye appeared slightly larger than the right. Even the nose seemed to be confused as to which shape to hold, appearing more as a small blob above the lips than anything structured or purposeful. "His face," said Shane in full voice. There was no longer a need to whisper.

Taz nodded. "I think he's infused from too many different sources in too short of a period."

Suddenly, the reyaqc's fists came down on the windshield. Shane and Taz jumped in their seats, but the glass held. The rogue screamed a high, agonized squeal and hammered the glass again.

"Amazing," said Taz, still clutching her phone just inches from the glass.

The reyaqc leaned closer, its misshapen nose pressed against the windshield, saliva dribbling down onto the clear surface. It struck the glass again, this time jagged white lines snaked out in each direction. The reyaqc's hands were bloodied, but still he pounded again, again, creating snowballs of shattered glass with each successive strike. Shane cowered back in his seat. Another blow or two and the glass would shatter.

The reyaqc screamed something—gibberish, unintelligible—as he smashed his right fist down, finally penetrating the windshield, sending shards splaying across the interior of the cab. The hand was bloodied, a large jagged piece of glass protruding from just below the wrist. Shane had no time to think, only to react. He took his own palm and pressed the shard deeper into the reyaqc's hand, slicing his own in the process.

A howl.

A screech.

The reyaqc jerked its arm back through the glass and scurried over the top of the cab and off the trunk end of the car in a metallic thunder that echoed in Shane's ears.

"Taz, you okay?" he asked between hurried gulps of air.

Taz nodded. She'd dropped her cell phone and was hunting for it between her feet. "Your hand, how bad is it?"

"Not too bad. The reyaqc got the worst of it."

"What now?"

"I don't know. The reyaqc was behind us. Maybe still in the street. Maybe hiding between buildings."

"We've got to find it." Taz sat upright, her cell phone in her palm.

Shane shook his head. "No. You were right. We need a tranquilizer gun or a Taser. Something. We have no way of stopping a rogue." Shane pulled the gear lever to drive. He'd seen the thing, found it. He could do so again. Only next time he'd come prepared. He'd have a plan. A real plan. Shane took his foot off of the brake pedal, allowed the Acura to roll slowly forward.

And then stopped.

"What?" asked Taz as she scanned the street for signs of the rogue.

"We heard a scream. There must be a victim. There's someone out there who might be dying." Once again, Shane cursed himself for his stupidity. If he had had even the slightest forethought he would have brought a weapon. Any weapon. Something!

"The victim's probably dead," he rationalized.

"It's already too late," agreed Taz.

"It would be crazy to get out of the car after what just happened."

"We could call the cops."

"And tell them what?"

"No one would believe us."

"The victim might die while we're waiting for the police to arrive."

"If he's even still alive now."

But, he might be alive. Just maybe. An outside chance. But not for long if no one did anything. Not if Shane did nothing.

Closing his eyes with a muttered curse, he took three deep breaths, summoned what little courage he had to command, and threw the door open. Stepping toward the back of the car, he scanned the darkness.

"What are you doing?" whispered Taz, as she climbed out of the car as well.

"Get back in the car," ordered Shane. "No use both of us risking it."

"Forget it, buddy. No, 'Me Tarzan, you Jane' crap."

Shane nodded, but his mind was on the reyaqc. Where had it gone? No lights had come on at the sound of the reyaqc's shrieks, nor at the pounding on or shattering of the windshield. This was a neighborhood accustomed to crime. Its residents knew better than to intrude where they didn't belong. Shane turned around, suddenly frightened that the rogue may have circled back to the front of the car. He only now realized how hard he was breathing, how his chest heaved, how his breath stung the back of his throat. How close had he come to death?

How close was he still?

He scanned the darkness again.

Nothing.

But there was something. He knew that much. The reyaqc was close, hiding, waiting. Shane's mind cleared as his adrenaline levels subsided to sub-nuclear levels. His flashlight. Yes, his flashlight. Shane moved to the trunk.

Taz came to beside him. "You come up with a hot new plan?"

Shane held up one finger, indicating that she wait as he inserted the key into the lock and quickly lifted the lid.

There it was, long and black. He lifted it triumphantly.

"A flashlight? You're plan is a flashlight?"

Shane shrugged. It did seem ludicrous on the surface. "Hey, we need to see—right? And this thing's long, solid, it has weight. We might be able to use it like a club, fend off the reyaqc."

"What about a tire iron?"

Okay, the girl was thinking. Flicking the flashlight on, he gave a quick scan of his trunk. Nearly empty, just a half jug of coolant, a quart of 10W30, and a glow-in-the-dark Frisbee. "No tire iron. It's probably in a sunken compartment with the little dummy tire. No time to dig around for that now."

Shane stepped away from the car and pressed the lid shut as he scanned the night. Where was the reyaqc? Where was the victim? Taking a tentative three steps forward, he moved the flashlight beam slowly from left to right, attempting a logical search pattern. He tried to focus his ears on every nuance, every breath of wind, every tiny movement, but mostly what he heard was his own heart beating much faster than he believed to be healthy.

"Which side did the reyaqc first appear from?" asked Shane. He had been driving slowly. The reyaqc appeared as from nowhere. But it had to have come from somewhere.

"The right," whispered Taz. "It came from the right."

They were on the driver's side of the car, so Shane marched slowly around the front of the vehicle and toward the passenger side, still scanning the darkness with the flashlight. This was Vegas, the desert. The yards were small, the landscaping sparse. Many of the homes were xeroscaped, which basically meant stones and cacti—not much watering required. In short, there weren't many bushes and only occasional trees. The only true hiding place would be the spaces between dwellings.

But all seemed empty.

Had he been mistaken?

Perhaps the scream had not been a victim, but the rogue itself.

Shane took another three tentative steps forward. He was leery about straying too far from the relative safety of the vehicle. Though, with the windshield shattered, that safety was probably more in his mind than in reality.

Another few steps.

Nothing. No sign of a victim.

Shane realized that Taz was no longer beside him. He turned to his left, then to his right. "Taz," he whisper-yelled. "Taz, where are you?"

"Right here. At the back of the car. There's blood on the street. I think the rogue came this way."

"Okay, stay there. I'm coming to you. We need to stick together."

It was then the reyaqc struck.

Chapter Twenty-One

Donald Baker's eyes rolled back and then forward. He gazed over the young man's right shoulder, but saw very little of the room. Colors seemed to condense, to collide upon themselves, and then to break apart like watercolors doused beneath a faucet, running off the page in rivers of swirling dissolution. Donald squinted, his eyes rolled again. He drew in breath as the electric tingle raced up his arm, through his shoulder, and into the torso where it then dispersed throughout his body. Adjusting his hand, he curbed the flow, measuring it, controlling it. Though his very being screamed for the stuff, he knew he must direct his need, dominate it, subdue it. He was the master over his own body. The primal side could hold no sway.

Donald's breath was cut short as the essence burned like liquid steel in his veins. He tried to focus on the suite, on the Italian décor, the high definition TV, the picturesque view of the Las Vegas strip, but none would come into focus. "Yes, all right," he hissed. "That should do it."

Donald withdrew his hand, squinted, blinked, and then gazed at the young man before him. "Much better." Another sharp intake of breath and then a weak smile. "Thank you, Ric. Are you stable?"

The young man was seated on a recliner directly in front of Donald. He blinked, shook his head, and then twisted his neck as if trying to relieve a kink. "I'm well, Dr. Baker. Only weak. A little dizzy."

Donald reached forward, patting Ric on the kneecap. "Go. Lie down. Drink plenty of juice. I'll remain here and allow my system to adjust."

Ric twisted his neck again, blinked, and then rose unsteadily to his feet. "I'll be in my bed if you need me." The young man turned, taking slow deliberate steps toward his bedroom. He was not tall, perhaps five eight or nine. His hair was brown with just a tinge of red, and his face a symmetric oval. Ric was one of three such men who had accompanied Donald on this trip. Donald appreciated each as he would a son. How fortunate he was to have such loyal ones to tend to his needs. Donald truly didn't know how he would survive without such as these. Certainly he wouldn't return to what he had once been. No. Donald Baker had long since determined to die rather than to revert to his baser drives. He glanced down at the small patch of orange hair on the back of his left hand and then closed his eyes. No. Never again.

The sound of a door knock brought Donald Baker back to the present. He blinked, breathed deeply, and rose unsteadily to his feet. "Mmm, that burns," he said to no one. "Such a barbaric curse we bear."

He moved slowly across the plush carpet, easing into a fully upright position, and slipping his slightly tinted glasses onto the bridge of his nose before reaching for the door handle. "Yes. Who is it?"

*****

Julia knocked again. She was probably waking the guy, but was beyond caring. The things she'd learned in the past hours—the things she'd seen—well, some answers just couldn't wait. And Julia was nearly certain that Donald Baker—whoever he was—had some of those answers, or, at the very least, knew where to find them.

There was movement now, on the opposite side of the door, and then Donald Baker's voice. But weak, a bit shaky, asking who it was. Julia responded. She heard the latch flip with a quick *schlict*. The door opened slowly at first. Just a crack, a cautious peek, and then it swung open revealing Donald. Not a tall man, perhaps five foot eight, only an inch or so taller than she. He wore a navy bathrobe over silk pajamas and pale blue corduroy slippers on his too-white feet. He offered the same plastic smile as the first time they'd met. "Dr. Chambers," he said as he waved her into his suite. "I was afraid you'd have need of me. May I offer you a drink?"

Though the man was acting pleasant enough, he seemed ill, drawn out. "No. I'm fine, thank you."

Donald turned from her, assuming she'd follow. Julia hesitated. She didn't know this man. At the very least his actions this morning had been peculiar, some might say suspicious. There was something odd about him, something unsettling, but Julia sensed no immediate danger. Still, entering a strange man's suite—alone. Not exactly brilliant. She wished she'd thought to ask Raul Martinez, the intern, to accompany her. But she hadn't. She'd come alone. She'd come on a mission and would learn nothing if she turned and fled like a frightened teenager. Julia slipped her right hand into her purse, palmed the small can of mace, crossed the threshold, and closed the door. She followed Donald—who either hadn't noticed or had ignored her hesitation—into the expansive sunken living room. He pivoted, seemed to think for a moment, and then said, "You've been doing research, I presume."

Julia eyed Donald. His movements seemed forced, almost as if he contemplated every action, every gesture, before performing each maneuver. Julia strolled past him and seated herself on the slick golden-colored sectional sofa. She'd never been to a suite before. It was definitely *sweet*. "Yes," she said to Donald. "Research." That was an understatement. What she had seen…

Donald lowered himself into the matching recliner before her. "You found other cases, one's similar to that of James Harrison."

Julia nodded. "There have been at least three related attacks; two of these were fatalities. I was able to see the coroner's reports, along with photographs of the bodies. They were horrible, withered. Dr. Baker, what is going on here?"

Donald Baker's expression remained neutral. He gazed at her through tinted glasses. Was he wearing contact lenses as well? Strange. "Are you sure you don't wish a drink, Dr. Chambers? It seems we have much to discuss."

"Call me Julia. We're not at the hospital now." As well, it wouldn't hurt to be cordial. The man seemed stiff, a bit ill-at-ease. She wouldn't get the information she needed if they plodded about calling each other Doctor.

Donald nodded once again. "Julia, then. Very good." He held up one finger signaling her to wait, and then called out, "Bradley! Bradley, would you get Dr. Chambers a drink, please. Perhaps a Bordeaux."

A young man appeared almost instantly from an adjoining chamber. He was rather slight, light of skin, with an oval face similar to Donald's and a wire-like mop of hair nearly identical to the man's. A son perhaps. "I'll bring it right away, Dr. Baker." Okay, referring to Donald by title. Perhaps not a son, unless Baker was an extremely militant father—which didn't seem entirely out of the question based on Julia's first encounter with the man. She wondered where the young man and woman who had accompanied him to the hospital were. Donald had ordered them around mercilessly.

Donald turned back in her direction, offered another grin. She noticed Donald's right hand trembled slightly as he draped it over his left; he seemed extremely drawn out, nothing like he had just this morning. "Donald, are you all right? You look ill."

He waved it off. "It's nothing. I've just received a treatment. Now, Julia, tell me about the other victims. How did you connect these to Mr. Harrison's attack?"

The young man, Bradley, brought her a deep red wine. She allowed her can of mace to slip back into the purse, accepted the glass, and then, without tasting the beverage, placed it on the marble coffee table situated between them. "There were numerous similarities. The pallor of the skin, the sunken features, dehydration. Also, in each case, there was a bed of small pinprick-like punctures in the skin. Jimmy had the same."

"Yes he did," agreed Donald, but he offered no further comment.

Again, something irritated her, something about his facial expressions or lack of. It almost seemed she was conversing with a mannequin. This man was not what he seemed. Regardless his idiosyncrasies, it was time she learned something about the problem at hand. Julia leveled her gaze at Donald and leaned forward, elbows resting on her upper thighs. A casual yet authoritative posture. "Donald, obviously you know something. I'm guessing you came to Las Vegas specifically to investigate these cases. Tell me what's happening."

There was that smile again, that same manufactured grin that so unnerved her. "Well, you see, I'm not sure I can entrust that information to you just yet." His voice was soft yet commanding, a voice accustomed to giving orders.

"Okay, listen." Julia could be commanding as well. She hadn't come down here just to get the runaround from this pompous creep. "Crimes have been committed. You obviously know something about this. I'm a doctor. I need to understand what's happening to these patients—in particular Jimmy Harrison, who is my personal responsibility."

Donald nodded, this time forgoing the smile. "There are some things best kept from the general public. Surely, you understand this."

Julia's stomach took a dip and a twist. Was this guy with the government? Was this some sort of terrorist scenario? "Are you talking about a bio-weapon?"

Donald shook his head, his expression blank, emotionless. "Nothing like that. No conspiracy, no intrigue."

"Then what? I've got a patient to treat. Obviously, whatever this is has lethal potential."

Donald stared at her for a long moment, though he didn't seem to be scrutinizing her. Julia wasn't even sure that he was contemplating a response. He just simply stared. The guy gave her the creeps. She wanted to break his gaze, to flee from the room, but she calmed herself, controlled her breathing. He'd done nothing the least bit threatening; he'd simply been…odd. When finally he spoke, it was as if there'd been no pause at all, as if she'd just posed her question less than a second before. "Again," he said. "I'm not yet comfortable speaking of this. Though, I would be more than happy to assist you in developing a treatment plan. This I can do."

Julia narrowed her gaze. Forget about his idiosyncrasies, about her momentary ill-ease; take charge the way she'd planned to from the beginning. This was her parade, and she'd lead it where she meant it to go. "You're not a medical doctor, Donald. At least that's what you've led me to believe." Her tone was crisp, nearly accusatory.

"No, my doctorates lie in other disciplines."

"Then I'm not interested in your treatment suggestions—*Doctor*. I am, though, quite interested in what you know, what connection you have to these attacks—especially anything relating to my patient."

"Dr. Chambers, Julia, once again—"

"Once again, nothing. I need details. I need facts. You are somehow connected. Talk with me or I'll have Gil Grissom, Dirty Harry, Inspector Clouseau, and every cop in Vegas pounding down this door. Your choice."

Expressionless, Donald Baker was a hard man to read. There was no outward appearance of anger, no downturn of the lips, no furrowed brow, no reddened flesh. His voice was as it always had been: even, unemotional, authoritative. "I have one stipulation."

"And that is?"

"That you not question my sanity; that you not try to disprove my account until *after* I've completed my explanation. At which time, I will cease to concern myself with your opinion."

Julia blinked. What an oddball. "So, you're not going to swear me to secrecy, force me to take a blood oath?"

Donald remained emotionless, either not sensing or not caring about her sarcasm. "I wouldn't trust such a promise made in advance of this revelation. We'll save the oaths for later." He paused, but only for a moment, and then leaned forward in his seat. She could smell his cologne, something musky and nearly overpowering. This close, she could see that his skin was smooth, much smoother than she would have expected for a man his age, which she took to be mid to late forties. It seemed almost glossy, rubbery. Like a seal's skin might appear if it were a pale gray or peach rather than midnight black.

"Tell me," he said. "Have you ever heard of the reyaqc?"

"The what?"

"Reyaqc. Some claim the word to have Greek origins, others Scandinavian. There is also a theory that it springs from the Hebrew word reyqam, which means empty or void. The subtext is appropriate, I suppose. The reyaqc are sometimes referred to as The Empty, which is perhaps apt."

Julia waited for him to continue, and when he did not, she prompted him saying, "Your point is what?"

"This naked man of yours, the one who attacked James Harrison; he is a reyaqc."

This was becoming ludicrous. Why had she wasted her time with this man? "Donald, you're losing me."

Donald Baker simply gazed at her through his tinted wire-rimmed glasses. "No doubt I am. The reyaqc are an ancient race, one which has coexisted with humanity from nearly the beginning, but whose presence has rarely been made obvious."

The man was some sort of cult fanatic or psycho UFO-chasing geek. "You're saying this man is not human."

"No, Julia, not human. Though the more civilized reyaqc are quite capable of passing for human, and even functioning within human society—given certain conditions."

The conversation had become ridiculous, and truly, Julia considered simply marching from the room, leaving Donald Baker to his delusions. But she sensed he did know something. He might be seeing it through some weird fantastic lens, but if she remained calm, respectful, if she humored him, she might be able to get something of substance, something that would help her to ensure Jimmy's full recovery and shed light on the deaths of those other men. "So, assuming I decide to believe you, what's the difference between a human and one of these…reyich?"

"Reyaqc. Ray-ack. They have no DNA, or as they refer to it—essence of their own. The infants are born sexless, featureless. They have no hair, no eye color, only small openings at the nasal passages. The reyaqc must infuse genetic information from other living beings, most often, but not exclusively, human, if they are to live."

"No DNA. That's impossible."

Donald drew closer yet, gazing directly into her eyes. Once again she noted that behind his glasses he wore green-tinted contact lenses. "Impossible is a concept for small minds, Julia. Allow yours to expand."

"Sure. Fine. But no DNA? All life is built on DNA."

Donald nodded. "There is a genetic matrix of sorts, yes. Obviously there must be some basic foundation, but it's incomplete, unstable." A pause. "Allow me to rephrase. The haploid human genome contains an estimated twenty-thousand protein-coding genes. The reyaqc possess perhaps fourteen-thousand, yet, like humans, they have need of the full twenty. To complicate matters further, a reyaqc's chromosomes are unstable. They break down within weeks. Thus, there is a need to replenish."

The man actually sounded sincere. He truly believed this bunk. Had she stumbled into some crazy cult or radical group? Donald certainly had the blank expressionless look of a brainwashed Moonie. Inhaling deeply, she attempted to maintain her calm professional demeanor before this obviously deluded individual. "Okay, so—not that I believe any of this—but, how do they infuse genetic information from others?"

Donald nodded and seemed to remember to offer his stock smile. "Of course, as a physician, you gravitate toward questions of a practical nature. There is a bed of needle-like protrusions lodged just beneath the skin on the right palm of each reyaqc. When the reyaqc seeks to infuse, these tiny hollow spines surface and puncture the skin of the donor—or 'giver' as the reyaqc call them—extracting genetic material. A careless reyaqc can severely injure or even kill a donor."

"So, what then? The reyaqc has the victim's genetic code, does he then magically start to resemble the donor? You know, I think this might be a good plot for Doctor Who."

Donald cocked his head, offered a curious indistinct expression, and then rose, pacing before Julia like a college professor expounding on a pet topic. "Think of the reyaqc as an empty glass. Soon after birth, the glass is filled with water. This is the first infusion. Now, reyaqc chromosomes are unstable. They break down. So, to use our analogy, the water begins to evaporate. But, say we never want the glass to become empty. So we add more liquid. But this time we top off the glass with orange juice. Now the glass contains a mixture of juice and water."

"Then more liquid evaporates and you add some tea and then some soda, and so on," offered Julia in an effort to move him along.

"Correct," said Donald, for the first time offering an expression, however obscure, that might border on genuine. "So, with each infusion the reyaqc acquires some characteristics of the new, but retains whatever was left of the old. Obviously, the first infusion is the one to establish the basic foundation of the reyaqc's form—gender being the most obvious, full adult height being another. From that point onward, the reyaqc must infuse from this one sex alone or risk serious complications."

Julia rose. The guy was creative. She had to admit that. But this was giving her nothing of use. It was late. She was tired, frustrated, and more than a little perturbed at herself for pursuing this obviously useless lead. "It's a great story, Donald, but I think you're full of it."

"As promised." Donald paused. "Consider Eduardo Kac."

"And he is…?"

"A Frenchman. The title he prefers is Bio-artist. Kac spliced fluorescent genes from a jellyfish into a rabbit embryo. Quite creative really, though borderline ridiculous. This modified embryo was then planted in a female rabbit. Once born, the bunny glowed neon green under ultraviolet light. Julia, the ability to splice foreign DNA into another species is the basis of all biotechnology. Do you find it so hard to believe that that which is done in the laboratory might also exist in nature?"

"Well, that's a compelling argument," she said, though her tone was doubtful. "Listen, I appreciate your time, but I've been running nearly non-stop for close to forty-eight hours. I really need to be going."

Donald moved in her direction, hands clasped behind his back, lips pursed. Once again—manufactured mannerisms. "How do you hope to proceed? What is your plan for James Harrison's care? What will you do for the next patient of similar circumstance?"

Julia paused. How did she plan to proceed? Jimmy Harrison had slipped back into coma. She had no leads, no ideas on how to help him.

"Allow me one more statement," said Donald. "I realize this is quite difficult to accept. You most likely think me some fringe fanatic. And truly, in many ways it is better that you don't believe. It's far safer for the reyaqc that few humans know of them. But something is happening here in Las Vegas. In your position as an emergency room physician at the most centrally located hospital in the city, you may have need of further information. I will remain available to you should you need my services."

Julia offered a smile as artificial as Donald Baker's own. "Thank you, Donald. I'll certainly—"

There was a sharp rap on the door, a muffled voice from the hallway beyond. "Doc, it's Shane. Let me in. We've got trouble."

Chapter Twenty-Two

Donald made the door in three quick steps. As it swung open, Julia saw the young man who had accompanied Donald at the hospital. His white hair was tossed and unruly. His right hand was wrapped in a bloody white rag. His clothing was dirty and unkempt; his overall appearance being that of someone who'd barely survived a barroom brawl. But most shocking was that he supported a young woman, apparently unconscious. The girl's left arm was draped over Shane's shoulders; her head was slumped forward, her black hair spilling over her face. Shane looked as if he was about to lose his grip on her waist.

"A little help here, Doc. She's about to drop."

Both Donald and Julia moved forward, but Julia quick-stepped back as Donald reached them first. There just wasn't enough room for both to assist.

"It's Taz, Doc," said Shane as they moved the unconscious form down into the sunken living room and toward the couch. "She's still alive, but not in good shape. I told the hotel security guards she was drunk. I think they bought it, but don't be surprised if they come knocking."

"Bradley, my bag," said Donald, calling the young man who had served Julia the wine. "It's in the kitchenette." Two young men appeared, one of which was Bradley. The other seemed remarkably similar in stature and facial structure, though his hair was dark where Bradley's was light.

"Julia, a pillow please. No, two. Place them beneath her feet, prop her legs."

"Donald, I'm a physician. I should be the one to—"

"Not now, Julia. This woman has little time."

Bradley handed Donald what looked to be a medical practitioner's bag as Julia grudgingly slipped two throw-pillows beneath the young woman's calves. Already, Donald was wrapping a blood pressure cuff around the victim's arm. As he pumped the small rubber bulb in his right hand, Donald checked the victim's pulse with two fingers of his left. "Pulse is erratic," he said after several seconds. A minute later, "Blood pressure dropping steadily."

Donald withdrew an IV bag from the case. Julia was amazed at Donald's skill as he found a vein and inserted the IV needle. "Julia, hold the IV bag." He shoved the bag into Julia's hand before she could protest. Once again—she was the physician here!

"Mr. Daws, in the refrigerator you'll find three medications. I need you to bring me the pale yellow liquid. Bradley, take the IV bag from Julia, hold it above the girl's head. Julia, the hypodermic needle in my bag, quickly. Shane, the medication."

Suddenly, the girl heaved, shaking violently and nearly flopping off the sofa. Gasping now, grayish bile dribbled from her lips. Her breathing was labored and shallow. Her pupils fixed, but not dilated. Julia had been shocked into tacit compliance by the sheer force of Donald's personality. True, it was obvious Donald was prepared for this type of emergency, but now the victim was in crisis. Enough was enough. "Donald, you're losing her. Get out of the way."

Julia pressed in as Donald scooted back without protest. She went to work, recognizing the situation—the bloodless pallor, the hollowed cheeks, the muscle spasms. Yes, there they were, the white rash-like marks at the base of the skull. The pupils were still non-responsive. Breathing was shallow. Almost silently, the young woman expelled a final foul-smelling breath, and then went limp.

Julia's heart leaped. Instinct birthed in years of experience took control. "She's stopped breathing. Donald, do you have epinephrine in that bag?"

"I'm getting it now, Doctor." Donald's voice was even, emotionless.

Julia ripped open the woman's shirt, put her right ear against her chest, and, not hearing a heartbeat, checked for breath. None. Cocking the girl's head to the side, she inserted a finger in her mouth and cleared the remaining bile, thus ensuring an open airway. Julia then straddled the woman, locked her hands one over the other and began chest compressions. "Donald, the epinephrine."

"Ready, Julia." Again, Donald's voice was far too calm. The strange blank-faced man had seen this scenario played out far too many times before.

The syringe in hand, Julia injected the patient, listened for a heartbeat again, and then continued her efforts. Press, press, press. Listen. Press, press, press, press...

The woman did not respond.

"Breathe, girl. Don't you want to live?" Julia nearly screamed at the woman. How dare she give in so easily? Didn't she understand the value of life?

"Come on, Taz," urged the white-haired man. "Hang in there."

Press, press, press, press. Listen. Press, press. Longer. Longer. Time became evasive. Had she been at this only several minutes, or maybe an hour?

Press, press, press. Listen. Press. Julia was becoming weary. Her arms aching, the space between her shoulder blades stiff and cramped.

"Come on, Taz." She used the name the young man had spoken. "We've got to do this. You need to live."

Press, press, press. Her arms were cramping. Press, press, press. She was sweating, little dots of moisture traversing her forehead, down between the eyes and across the nose, dripping onto the patient.

Press, press…

Suddenly the woman's eyes opened. Her teeth clenched. She lurched upright, nearly smacking her forehead against Julia's own. A gray-black vomit erupted from the girl's lips like water from a fire hose, dousing the upper third of Julia's body. Julia gagged, tumbled to the floor, as the woman went limp, slumping to her left, motionless, silent, dead.

*****

"You saw the rogue," said Donald as he pulled Shane into the kitchenette. Julia was in the adjacent bathroom showering away the vomit.

"Yeah, Doc. Saw him, got attacked by him, beat him off with my flashlight."

Though Donald's face remained impassive, he roughly clasped Shane's arms at the biceps. "You beat him? Was he injured? What did you do to him?"

Shane, surprised by Donald's emphatic reaction, took a step back, shrugging off the grip. "I don't know. Like I said, he was attacking me and Taz. I was panicked. I beat him away. Taz was hurt. I had to do something."

"But, the reyaqc—what damage did you inflict? Is he in need of medical attention?"

Shane raked his fingertips through rustled white hair. "It was dark. Taz was already down. The rogue pounced on me. I swung my flashlight, pounded him off. He was going to kill us both. Do you get it? Can't you see what he did to Taz?" Shane wanted nothing more than to leave right now, leave Donald Baker to his own devices and walk away.

"Did you draw blood?" Donald was only inches from Shane's face; his right hand gripped Shane's shoulder with an amazing strength. For the first time, Shane feared Donald Baker. The ferocity of his gaze, the near manic tone of his voice, these were so far removed from the civilized doc that he'd come to know. There was something primal in his expression, something hiding just below the surface, screaming for release.

Breaking the gaze, Shane contemplated the question posed. Had he? Had he actually injured the rogue, or had he just frightened him off? He closed his eyes, tried to visualize the encounter. "Doc, honestly, I don't know. The reyaqc cut his hands while bashing in my windshield. Beyond that…I mean, he was able to run off on his own. He couldn't have been hurt too badly. It was just a flashlight." Shane purposefully omitted his own act of pressing the glass shard deeper into the reyaqc's hand. No need to anger the doc further.

Donald released his grasp on Shane's shoulder and stared vacantly at him. Shane felt a strange unease. This night, these things that had happened, now the doc's reaction, he'd never experienced such as these. With the exception of his time with Gisele, so much of his knowledge of the reyaqc was far removed, hypothetical, disconnected. There were chat rooms, websites, and of course, Donald Baker's *Histories*. But those tomes were closely guarded. Shane had only seen one volume—and that for a very brief time. But these past several hours, these were something different entirely. Amazing, true, but different, much different. Very frightening.

Taz. What about Taz? She was dead. Shane had taken her with him and now she was dead. She was what, maybe twenty-five at the most? She'd been alive, vibrant, curious, smart. Now she was dead. And it was Shane's fault. If he'd been more prepared; if he'd refused to let her tag along. Anything! If he'd done anything different, she'd still be alive right now.

Suddenly Shane realized the doc was speaking. He blinked, brought himself back to reality. "I'm sorry, Doc. What'd you say?"

"The rogue, he infused from Miss Taz. How long was the connection?"

Shane pulled a stick of chewing gum from his pocket, unwrapped it, and slipped it between his teeth. He hadn't wanted a cigarette so badly in nearly four years. "I don't know. I was just trying to get him off her."

The doc nodded. "It's important to know. Cross-gender infusions are inherently dangerous. The rogue must have been quite desperate."

"Well, it sure was dangerous to Taz. She's dead, Doc. In case you didn't get that. She's dead."

"Yes, she is. Was he a molt?" asked the doc, oblivious to Shane's rage. "Was the rogue a molt?"

Angered, but resigned that the moral outrage of the situation was lost on Donald Baker, Shane closed his eyes and tried to recall the encounter. He could still see the milky eyes, the wide gaping mouth with the missing and broken teeth, the near-translucent skin. There was hair, but very little of it. Shane envisioned the creature as it had been on the hood of the car. Was there anything else, anything to indicate animal essence in the rogue? "Doc, I don't know. I don't think so, but I don't know for sure."

The doc slammed his palm against the nearby wall, rattling the china stacked in an adjacent cabinet. "I need to know, Mr. Daws. I need to know so I can properly tend to him."

"Tend to him? Like, fix him? He killed Taz! Killed her just because she was there. Doc, what we've got to do is stop him." Did he not get it? Did he not understand that this girl was dead and the rogue was to blame?

The rogue, yes. And Shane as well. A shared responsibility. A collective guilt.

"Of course, he must be stopped," said the doc. "And *we* must be the ones to do so. The authorities cannot have contact." He paused, glared at

Shane. "Perhaps you don't yet understand. The reyaqc are on the verge of extinction. With the ever-expanding human population and continual technological advances, we find it more and more difficult to live undetected. Our numbers, already few, are dwindling at an alarming rate. So, yes we must stop this rogue—both to save his potential victims and to ensure the reyaqc species as a whole are not discovered prematurely. Soon the world will know of us, whether by our own design, or by exposure to one such as this rogue. It's imperative that we are introduced to the world in a non-threatening manner or our cause is lost."

"Doc, we're modern, civilized people. I don't think you need to fear exposure. There might be a boom in tabloid sales, but I don't think there'd be any action against the reyaqc."

"Nazi Germany believed they were a modern, civilized people, Mr. Daws. Rwanda. Iraq with their Kurds. I've seen how humans react to those who are different, however subtly. There is much need for caution." He paused, breathed. "As to this rogue, all reyaqc are precious. All are needed. We must help this one, heal him, lead him to his right mind."

"This one's pretty far gone."

The doc looked as though he might lunge at Shane. "How could you possibly know that?"

"Because I was sitting in the driver's seat watching him bash my windshield with his fist. Tell me that's rational behavior."

The doc stared blankly at Shane, his eyes screaming some mute and suppressed emotion. "Of course he was irrational. But, why? What brought him to that condition? Infusions from a genetically unbalanced donor, genetic material from too diverse a pool, infusions from multiple non-human species? There are numerous possibilities, but based on what we've witnessed, these three seem the most logical. He infuses from random humans with no clear selection process. But, is there more? His behavior seems animalistic, beastly. Thus, the question, is he a molt, Mr. Daws? It's important that I know."

Shane nodded. Was there anything, anything at all that he could pull from his memory? The teeth, though broken, seemed entirely human. The ears were not elongated or malformed. The nose was flat, oddly shaped, with large flaring nostrils, but again, human in appearance. The rogue had run upright, with no slouch or unease. He had no fur. His hands had been balled into fists most of the time, but even so, they hadn't seemed claw-like or peculiar.

Shane blinked, squinted, uttering one simple word. "Cell."

"Pardon me?"

"Taz had her cell phone. It has a video feature. She recorded some of the encounter."

He rushed into the adjoining area to where Taz still lay sprawled on the couch—cold, silent, dead, her black hair spilling off of the cushion, her eyes still wide and sightless, dried bile caked to her lips and chin. This did not have to be. If Shane had only thought things through...

Blinking back tears, he knelt, gazed at her face. Taz had never been gorgeous, cute in her own way, yes, but not classically pretty. Now, she seemed the very face of death, as if the grim reaper had not even allowed her the dignity of burial before sucking the form from her face. She was left hollow and dry, as if he'd already sent his legions of maggots to gnaw away her musculature, to rob her of even the final dignity.

"Oh, Taz, I am so sorry." She had not been Shane's lover. They'd never had an actual date. Though Shane had been blind to it, there'd been a connection between the two. Taz had realized it. Only now, in its absence, did Shane realize what they might have had, what he'd truly lost.

"Mr. Daws. The phone."

It was the doc, calling from the kitchenette.

"Coming."

Shane closed his eyes, drew a long breath. "I'm sorry, Taz. I've got to do this thing for the doc."

He felt like a ghoul, as if he was defiling her as he reached into her front blue jean pocket. The pocket was tight, and the phone crammed deep within. It took some wriggling, but Shane was able to pull it free. He'd have to come to terms with his emotions later. Right now he had to deal with the immediacy of the doc's pressing questions. "Here you go, Doc," he said as he marched back into the kitchenette and held the phone before them. "That's what we're dealing with."

They watched the tiny screen in silence as the rogue pounced onto the car hood. The corrupted face stared down again, only inches away. Shane felt his stomach tighten at the memory. He heard Taz's voice, tiny from the small condenser microphone.

"Awesome," she'd said in a hushed whisper. Shane felt tightness in his throat, moisture at the corners of his eyes. This was wrong. This was so wrong.

"Whiskers," said the doc.

"Excuse me."

"Whiskers, Mr. Daws. The rogue has three long feline-like whiskers protruding from either side of the mouth."

After several moments, the doc shifted his gaze toward the bathroom door where Julia showered. "Two things," he said. "Dr. Chambers is in need of reassurance. She knows much and has seen more. We cannot allow her to report what she knows. I fear I may have misjudged her acceptance when I revealed to her the truth of the reyaqc."

Shane worked his chewing gum. "What was the other thing? You said there were two things."

The doc nodded, his expression remaining solid, masklike. "Yes. I require that you dispose of the body."

*****

"Hey, uh, Doc Chambers."

Julia looked up. She'd been dialing her cell phone. "Yes. Shane, isn't it?"

"Yeah, Shane."

"Julia."

"Cool. Okay, Jules, you got a sec.?"

"Can it wait? I'm calling 911."

"Yeah, give me just a minute first, okay?"

Julia hesitated, and then lowered her phone. "A minute. No more. I've already waited longer than I should. This is all so bizarre."

"It is," agreed Shane as he slid a stick of gum between his teeth. "Hey, uh, sorry you had to be here for that. You did everything you could."

Julia blinked and wiped her face with a damp cloth. She now wore one of the doc's white business shirts instead of her own vomit-stained blouse. "I'm so sorry. Were you and the girl a couple?"

Shane thought about this night, of the attack, and of Taz, cradled in his arms. She'd been barely conscious; her last coherent action had been to pull his face to hers, to kiss him gently, meaningfully on the lips, to whisper, "We could have been great together."

"Um, no," stammered Shane. "We were...I'm not really sure. She was— There was something about her, you know?"

Julia nodded. "Is this real, Shane? Are there really creatures running around sucking DNA right out of people? This girl, Taz..."

"Terry was her name."

"Okay, Terry, it was as if her entire form just collapsed in upon itself."

This was true. Since death, her skin had tightened like shrink-wrap around the skeleton and musculature causing an almost mummified appearance in a corpse not yet an hour old. It was not a pleasant sight. Still, despite his swirling emotions, Shane had been given an assignment—he needed to make Julia understand that this was not the norm, that most reyaqc were not monsters—not entirely at least. He thought of the doc, his even, composed demeanor, and then the change he'd seen in the kitchen just minutes before. Was he really as civilized as he purported to be? Or had Shane misjudged him—misjudged the entire reyaqc species? No. He believed. He had to believe. He'd poured too much of his life—too much of his soul—into the reyaqc to change course now.

Shane met Julia's eyes. All he wanted to do was to crawl off into a corner and cry. But the doc had dumped this in his lap, and now it was up to Shane to minimize the fallout. "The reyaqc that killed Terry is a rogue. You've got to understand, most reyaqc are very careful not to damage their donors. A lot even have willing contributors. They call them givers. And they're nearly cherished among the reyaqc."

Yeah, and some kill wonderful, innocent young girls who want nothing more than to learn more about the species!

"Willing donors? Suicidal cult freaks, maybe."

"Nah. The givers understand that the reyaqc aren't evil by nature. The infusions are a matter of survival."

And some kill just to kill. Some go mad and ravage the most pure, the most childlike among us.

Julia threw the rag to the floor. "That girl was not willing. Those dead men were not willing."

Of course they weren't. Who would be?

"No, she was not willing." It was the doc this time, approaching from behind. He'd now changed from the bathrobe and pajamas into his tweed and bowtie college professor look. "These attacks are barbaric and must be stopped." He stepped to Shane's right. "I only wish I'd had the opportunity to confront this reyaqc before any of this happened. Perhaps I could have reached him somehow, appealed to his intellect."

Shane shook his head. The doc had not seen the rogue, hadn't witnessed the sheer lack of intellectual capacity. "This reyaqc's a bad apple, Jules. Most of them aren't like this. Some live in reyaqc communities away from human civilization, but a lot live right here with us. Most people don't even know it."

Julia narrowed her eyes, cocked her head just slightly to the left. "If they appear so human, how can you identify someone as a reyaqc?"

Shane glanced at the doc who nodded his approval. "Okay," began Shane, uneasy about revealing so much to this woman. "They don't *all* appear human. Not even close. But for the ones that do, the eyes give it away."

"The eyes?"

"Yes, the eyes are pallid, colorless, only a small pupil surrounded by a creamy white." Donald's voice was warm, soothing, yet purposeful. "Those who have embraced civilization often wear colored contact lenses in order to obscure their true nature."

Shane watched as Julia narrowed her gaze, stepping closer to Donald, gazing directly into his eyes. He liked her style. "Donald, it looks to me like you wear colored contacts."

"That I do, Julia."

"Your pupils are almost nonexistent."

The doc remained silent and expressionless.

Julia threw her arms up in frustration. "This is insane."

Shane moved closer to Julia, hoping to offer some sense of comfort. "Hey, this is difficult. I get that, but—"

"Difficult. There's a dead woman on the couch. Don't you think difficult might be an understatement?"

Shane caught a glimpse of the doc. He was maneuvering slightly to his right, closer to Julia, but slightly askew to her center so she wouldn't see his right hand. "Obviously something must be done," he said as his hand slipped into and then out of his jacket pocket. "Quite honestly, there's a bit of a quandary. You see, knowing what you've seen and learned, I'm not comfortable leaving you unattended."

The move was quick. A hypodermic needle to the lower neck. Shane barely had time to catch Julia's limp form before she hit the floor.

Chapter Twenty-Three

Tresset Bremu sat at his old wooden desk. The finish had worn thin years ago, and there were subtle grooves on the center right where most of the writing was performed. He was not writing now, but reading a dog-eared biography of Alexander the Great. The office looked as worn and battered as the desk. Originally, the space belonged to the foreman of the defunct silver mine, which Tresset's pack now occupied. The room was forever dusty, an unavoidable condition as gaps in the walls and windows allowed sand and dust to whistle through the grooves, coating the unfinished wooden floor and peppering the sparse furnishings. Tresset dusted his paintings constantly, each of which hung on the uneven pressboard walls upon completion. Most depicted a reyaqc society as he envisioned it—strong, dominant, sophisticated. One day this art would be proven the work of a visionary. Today it was merely a hopeful fiction.

It was just past dawn. Already the temperature had climbed into the upper nineties. In many ways Tresset resented the desert with its harsh dry winds and spiraling sand devils, with its snakes and scorpions, and dried up riverbeds. Though lush in places, he'd hated his native Siberia nearly as much. The bitter cold could be just as vengeful as the searing heat.

Both locales were refuges, places for the reyaqc to hide from the eyes of man. But the reyaqc were a strong species, truly superior to the humans, infinitely adaptable, intelligent, capable. The fact that they'd been forced to spend century upon century in hiding, blending into the background, masquerading as humans, or hiding off in barren wastelands, was anathema to Tresset. One day soon the reyaqc would unite. When they did, they would claim their proper place at the helm of the world.

Tresset wiped the dust from his hands with an antibacterial cloth, and then sniffed the hot dry air. Someone was approaching. Ordool, by the smell of it, a molt who had selected the western yellow bat as his sustaining species. A curious choice, thought Tresset, who drew his animal essence from the fierce and formidable mountain lion. But the selection had some small contributions. Though neither Ordool nor any other reyaqc had ever attained flight by infusing from a species capable of such, Ordool had acquired the bat's acute hearing and sonar-like abilities, thus making him an accomplished spy and hunter. Though, another species of bat might have been a better choice, as the yellow fur was nearly canary-like in its brilliance.

There was another's scent as well. Ordool was not alone. Tresset did not recognize the other, and so rose from his seat. "Ordool, you may enter," he said as the footsteps drew near. There were three sets, not two. Interesting. The yellow bat's companions must each be of comparable essence to smell so similar.

The ill-fitted wooden door opened a moment later, and Ordool entered followed by two young molts, each with thick, powerful legs and tiny noses that twitched continuously. "Spies," said Ordool with no preamble.

"Messengers!" blurted one of the jackrabbit molts. "Messengers, not spies." The noses twitched, and each shuffled nervously in his place.

"Where were they?" Tresset moved to inspect the intruders. He could smell their fear, sense their muscles tightening in preparation for flight. What cowards.

"They were over the eastern ridge. Just beyond the abandoned mines," said Ordool. "I monitored their movement for several minutes before sending Rethis and Frym to retrieve them. They were not coming forward as messengers might, but were stationary, simply gazing down upon our compound."

Tresset nodded and moved to just before the two. Both molts were several inches taller than Tresset, but this was not unusual. Most everyone was taller than he. But stature was not what made Tresset imposing. It was the very force of his will, of his intellect, of his potential savagery that gained him respect. "Is this true? Were you spying on my compound?" He kept his tone even, controlled, soothing even. These molts had inherited the rabbit's natural fear, and would need to be comforted in order to be of use.

"No," said the one on the right.

"Not exactly," said the other.

"Explain 'not exactly,'" coaxed Tresset.

"We are messengers," said one.

"But, we were frightened," added the other.

"We wanted to wait for an appropriate time."

"We were afraid of disturbing you."

"So, we waited."

"And watched."

"But, we're not spies."

"Just messengers."

Tresset held up his hand. "Stop. Please. You make my head spin." He turned his attention to the molt to his right. "You are from Bytneht Noavor's pack."

"Yes, that would be right."

"Bytneht sent us," agreed the other.

"Did he receive the supplies we provided?"

The two looked at each other. Tresset smelled the dread rising between them and feared they might foul his office. "Do not fear me. Simply answer the question."

"The supplies were received," said one.

"They arrived."

Tresset nodded. "Very good. And you claim to be messengers, so I assume Bytneht has a response."

Their noses twitched; their thick powerful legs became jumpy. They were about to flee. A quick glance to Ordool and the yellow bat shifted to his left, blocking the doorway. He was not particularly strong, but the bat essence had given him a peculiar appearance that many found off-putting. His nose was small and black, his face and body spattered with bright yellow fur. His eyes were wide and round, far from blind as many falsely believed of bats. His arms, though human-like, bore leathery drapes that may one day resemble bat wings, but now only added to Ordool's macabre appearance. His fingers were long narrow claws capable of opening an animal's throat with one vicious swipe. Surely, these two would find him fearsome and remain in place.

"Bytneht's response, messengers. That is why you're here, isn't it?"

"Y-y-yes, we are messengers," said one.

"We bring a message," added the other.

"From Bytneht Noavor."

"It has to do with the supplies."

"And with your offer."

"Yes," said Tresset, his voice becoming tight as his patience for the two cowards drew thin.

"He thanks you for the supplies," said the first jackrabbit.

"But...he declines your offer of an alliance," sputtered the second.

"He says... He says he has no desire to be directed by you."

"But he means no disrespect."

"No disrespect at all."

Tresset nodded. "In that case, I have a reply for Noavor." He used the second name, Noavor, the name of the previous chieftain which Bytneht had slain in order to attain his position. This usage indicated his lack of respect for the upstart.

"Yes?"

"Yes?"

The two jackrabbits nearly stumbled over each other's word.

"Tell Noavor that I am disappointed that he continues in his small-minded ways. Tell him the only hope of reyaqc survival is to pursue legitimacy, to secure a territory, establish our own nation. And that legitimacy can only be achieved by banding together, by creating a sizable force. Tell him that perhaps soon, his pack will need to find a new leader because his days are few." Tresset paused, smiled. "Did you get that?"

"Yes, yes," nodded the molt on the right.

"I fear the message may not be well received," added the one to the left.

"Of course it won't be well received," agreed Tresset. "But thank you for showing at least the small courage it took to stammer that flimsy protest." Tresset returned his gaze to the other molt. "As for you, you are useless."

Having the essence of the mountain lion, Tresset had retractable claws that emerged from just above his fingernails. As well, his teeth were long and sharp. His attack on the jackrabbit molt was swift, bloody, and immediately fatal. "Go," he said to the remaining messenger as he dropped the dead molt to the blood-spattered floor. "Deliver my reply. Now!"

Ordool stepped away from the doorway, and the frightened molt nearly leaped through the opening and was gone before Tresset could breathe another breath. Spitting a piece of flesh from his mouth he said, "Bring me some antiseptic. And then clean up this mess."

Chapter Twenty-Four

Tracy Taylor was twenty-one and she was hitting the Vegas strip. A college junior from Nebraska, her friends Sasha and Mindy—both a year older and likely four years more experienced—had swept her away, nearly bullying her into the trip. Not that she minded, of course. She was a grown woman now, and it was time for her to experience…things. But Las Vegas scared her. Oh, she would never admit this to her friends. They already thought her too conservative and uptight for her own good. But this was "Sin City." Certain things would be expected here. Not that these expectations didn't occur on campus. But this was different. At school, she was there for the purpose of education, and as for relationships, they were more of the long-standing type. Here, well, here she could expect a different brand of education.

It was sometime after eleven p.m. The girls were on the corner of Las Vegas Boulevard and Tropicana Avenue, standing amidst a sea of people, and bathed in the emerald glow of the MGM Grand Hotel and Casino. They'd just left the second night club of the evening and had decided to hit the strip in search of "action." Tracy had been glad to leave the club. It was much smaller than she'd anticipated, very crowded, dark, and loud. The constant *thump thump thumping* of club music had given her a headache worthy of a three-day hangover. On top of that, one of the guys she'd danced with, Dan, she thought his name was, had his hands all over her, constantly trying to coax her up to his hotel room. Eventually, Mindy had lured Dan away and the two spent the next half hour making out in a darkened corner.

Tracy wasn't sure that any of this was for her, but was determined to loosen up and have a good time. She was only young once, after all, she should enjoy it. Still, the idea of floating from club to club, making it with some random guy—or guys—she wasn't sure that was for her. Was that so wrong? Sasha and Mindy seemed to think so. And they were happy, carefree, enjoying the Vegas experience far more than she. Still…

Just because she was in a different setting didn't mean she had to be a different person.

Tracy glanced across the street to the New York New York, with its faux Statue of Liberty and artificial skyline. The trio had hit the Coyote Ugly bar earlier and Tracy had felt the good-spirited atmosphere at Coyote Ugly was a bit more to her taste than the outright club scene, but Sasha and Mindy were constantly on the prowl, in search of bigger and better. They only had three days and wanted to squeeze every last ounce of excitement out of the city. The three debated crossing kitty-corner to the cartoonish Excalibur, a mock castle with brightly illuminated red and blue spires, and then on to the neighboring pyramid-shaped Luxor. They'd heard there was a hot club there. But instead, they moved north on the strip with the vague notion that they'd make their way to Caesar's Palace—it was, after all, the most famous place on the strip, it had to be hopping.

There was a sudden stir in the crowd—shouting, whooping. Tracy turned to see a long white limo inching past on the bumper-to-bumper boulevard. Two girls of about Tracy's age were standing in the sunroof. One of the girls had removed her top to the raucous approval of the crowd. Mindy whooped in Tracy's ear, lifting her drink in a toast to the floozy. Sasha did her one better and lifted her top, exposing her own breasts to more cheers and roars.

"Great," muttered Tracy. "Now every creep on the strip will be hitting on us."

"Wooo!" whooped Mindy.

"Wooo wooo!" agreed Sasha.

Tracy figured she either needed another strong drink or an invisibility cloak—if only there was such a thing.

The girls continued northbound on the strip. There was plenty of jostling as revelers moved about, squeezing between clusters of tourists and hawkers. But the general atmosphere seemed relatively calm. It was just people having a good time. Nothing too drastic. Nothing too daunting. For the time being, everyone was fully clothed, though Tracy suspected that could change at any moment.

She was amazed at how bright it was even in the middle of the night. It seemed every building let off a glow of one kind or another. The Monte Carlo stood austere and majestic to the left, its architecture classic and refined, a subtle contrast to the more brazen feel of Planet Hollywood a bit further on the right, with its bright neon red "P.H." sign illuminating the way. Rows of Hispanics, both men and women, lined the crowded sidewalk and slapped glossy pictures of naked women into the hands of passersby.

Sasha accepted one and read the script aloud, "Hot babes to your room in fifteen minutes."

Tracy wasn't in the market for a "hot babe."

Another ten minutes and they came across a showgirl in a glittery pink and white costume with tufts of feathers on both head and rump. She was offering a free pull on a giant slot machine. Giggling at the ludicrous size of the flashing, flickering contraption, Tracy stepped forward and took a pull. She didn't win anything—nor did Sasha or Mindy, but the two girls, *"Wooo-ed"* anyway.

A block later and Sasha was feeling sick to her stomach. She'd been partying hard since eight p.m. and her system had finally decided to revolt. The three girls seated themselves on the edge of a large concrete planter containing a squat, pineapple-shaped palm tree, two beer bottles, and several of the "Hot Babes" cards. Tracy and Mindy encouraged

Sasha to breathe deeply and slowly. She'd be fine; she just shouldn't overdo it.

There was another commotion in the crowd. Tracy looked up expecting to find another half-naked woman flaunting her stuff, but this was nothing of the kind. The disturbance seemed to be on the sidewalk up ahead. Standing, Tracy saw the crowd parting. There were screams now. Not shouts of raucous frivolity, but real screams. Panic. Fright. Suddenly a figure burst through the throng—a man, naked, and swerving this way and that. At first Tracy giggled, embarrassed, but then she saw the figure more clearly. His face was wrong. The teeth were too long, too sharp, the nose too dark. One ear seemed slightly elongated and more triangular than the other. There was a thin matt of fur on his left thigh, and… Did he have one female-like breast?

And blood.

There appeared to be dried blood on his face and arms. The man seemed disoriented. His blank eyes darted to one side and then another as he twitched involuntarily, his limbs giving an occasional flip and shudder. He was vocalizing, but it seemed gibberish.

"Come on, we've got to get out of here," said Tracy with some urgency. She wasn't quite sure what she was seeing, but knew it had undesirable potential.

It was then that Sasha chose to empty her stomach into the large concrete planter. Tracy tried to move her along, but the girl was oblivious to all but her own personal agony.

"Come on, Sash. There's some kind of lunatic over there."

Sasha replied with another horrific retch that caused both Tracy and Mindy to avert their eyes.

Shouts.

Screams.

General chaos.

Tracy turned. The naked freak had bitten a middle-aged woman just below her left elbow. The woman's companion, a short overweight man of about fifty, attempted to pull the lunatic away, but the freak's jaws held firm. A font of blood sprayed upward. Apparently the guy had bitten through an artery. Another man joined the brawl, then another. Finally, the naked man was pulled free of the now-severely wounded woman. He hissed and spat and jabbered unintelligible syllables in a guttural animal-like voice.

One of the good Samaritans was thrown to the ground, striking his head sharply on the concrete. The naked man held another of his attackers by the back of the neck. The man's face seemed to go blank—his body shuddered. There were shouts of protests, screams of terror. Panicked tourists ran in every direction. The fifty-year-old man knelt on the ground, attempting to stop the woman's bleeding. No one came forward to help the other, now-captive, man who seemed close to losing consciousness.

Mindy tugged at Sasha's arm, attempting to get her up and moving. A frantic woman carrying a young boy of perhaps six years old, plowed into Tracy, nearly knocking her off of her feet. Tracy staggered but maintained her footing. What was a child doing out on the Las Vegas strip at nearly midnight?

Sasha retched again.

People ran this way and that, knocking into one another, shouting, cursing. Others stood, slack-jawed, hypnotized by the spectacle. Still others snapped photographs with cameras and cell phones.

No one helped the man held by the freak.

Tracy had a fingernail file. It was in her purse. She fished through the contents of her bag. Where was that thing? There. No. That wasn't it. What about… No. In frustration, Tracy inverted her purse, dumping the contents onto the sidewalk. There was the file, beside her lipstick. She snatched the thing from the ground, clutching it like Norman Bates would his prized butcher knife.

"Tracy, No!" screeched Mindy, who was finally pulling Sasha off the planter and in the direction of safety.

There was no time to respond. Tracy didn't know what the lunatic was doing to that man, but by the looks of it he might be killing him. Maybe he'd stabbed him in the back of the neck with an unseen weapon. Maybe he was strangling him. In any event, Tracy couldn't just stand by and watch a murder. She was probably crazy for attempting this, but so be it.

"My wife!" screamed the man tending to the fallen woman; his hands and sleeves were now covered in her blood. "My wife! Someone call an ambulance!"

Tracy moved to her left. She heard Mindy's hollered protests, but the voice was already distant. Circling to behind the naked lunatic, Tracy lifted the fingernail file high and drove it down into the man's neck, just to the edge of his right shoulder. The file bent and broke. The first inch or so of it remaining embedded in the man's flesh.

The lunatic whirled around, slamming into Tracy with his right fist and forearm. She was struck across the face, the force of the blow causing her to topple onto the sidewalk scraping her elbows and jarring her back.

Her attack, however feeble, had the desired effect. The freak was distracted, the victim free. He stumbled three or four steps forward, turned slightly to his left, as if to look back over his shoulder, and then dropped to all fours as he gasped and gagged, a yellow custard-like matter dribbling from his lips.

It seemed Tracy was now the target, as the lunatic moved toward her with small quivering steps. Blinking continually, he appeared disoriented, possibly having difficulty focusing. His arms flopped about, his legs jerked and kicked. Her heart pounded at a painful rate. Tracy scooted backward on the concrete, whimpering for the strange man to stay away from her. Wasn't anyone going to help her? Would all of these people just watch her die? Somehow it didn't occur to her to stand up and take flight.

With sudden coordination and speed, the naked freak bent, grabbed Tracy by the back of the neck, and pulled her toward him. Her face was crushed against the man's chest. She could hear the thumping of his racing heart, smell an odd, almost onion-like perspiration, feel the thick rubbery texture of his skin. She squirmed and screeched, but his grip was as iron. Then there was penetration. At the back of her neck, something had pierced into her very spine. An electric chill raced through her form. She felt herself shudder, but had no control over her limbs. She was going to die, right here, right now, on the Vegas strip. This was it. The end.

Something dark and brown flew through the air. It smashed against the back of the freak's head in a crash of amber and suds. Tracy felt the spray of beer on her face as the lunatic released her, rising to his feet with a wavering howl.

Tracy heard a familiar, "Wooo!" as another bottle found its mark.

Then there was another bottle, and another.

Still on her knees, Tracy glanced beyond the now-besieged freak. Mindy and Sasha—the latter appearing more pale than a bleached sheet—were grabbing impromptu missiles of all shapes and sizes—shoes, purses, beer bottles, cameras—and hurling them at the naked man. The rest of the crowd caught on and joined in.

With an inhuman roar, the lunatic bolted into the crowded street, sideswiped a car, but continued to move.

There was a shrill whistle. A bicycle cop racing toward the man. Wearing a bright yellow shirt and black shorts, he looked like a giant bumblebee as he weaved through the halting and honking traffic.

Instead of fleeing, the freak charged the cop, knocking him from his bike and onto the hood of a cab. The cop fumbled for something—his gun, a Taser? Whatever it was, the officer never had a chance to utilize it, for the lunatic smacked him hard across the face, and then lifted him over his head. It wasn't like some super baddie in a comic book movie. The crazy didn't lift him in one easy sweep. Tracy saw the man strain, saw the muscles tense beneath the too-pale skin, saw the clench of the lunatic's jaw and the perspiration on his brow. More than once he nearly dropped the dazed and incoherent cop. But somehow, with tremendous effort, he managed to lift the officer over his head and hurl him into the next lane where he struck the side of a metallic blue corvette. The sports car swerved, hit an adjacent cab, and stopped. The cop was now somewhere on the pavement between vehicles, and out of sight.

Traffic stopped. Cars honked. As Tracy eased herself back into a standing position, she saw the freak weaving between cars, scrambling over some of them, colliding with others. A double-decker bus came to rest in front of her, and by the time she'd moved around to get a better view, the freak was gone. After a moment of near-vertigo, she glanced back onto the sidewalk. Two men and a woman were now attending the bleeding woman. It seemed they might have applied a makeshift tourni-quet. Two more men knelt beside the male victim, who was still on all fours, and trembling as if in the first stages of seizure. To her left, Mindy and Sasha were approaching, Mindy pumping her fist in the air. "Vegas, baby! Woooo!"

Chapter Twenty-Five

Julia's head throbbed, her mouth was dry, her vision blurry. She moved to sit up, but a wave of vertigo swept over her, nearly causing her to vomit. Laying her head back into the velvety pillow, she blinked. The room was unfamiliar. Very classy with its light golden wallpaper, fine art prints, and sleek silk sheets; but despite all these, it held the smell and feel of a hotel room. Where was she? Her thoughts, her memories were so fragmentary, so fleeting. It was as if she could almost grasp one and then it would turn to vapor, flitting away on some gentle mind breeze. Why was she here—wherever here was? Why was she so groggy? Why was it so difficult to form even the simplest of thoughts?

She lulled her head to the right. Red luminescent numerals read one o'clock. It was light outside. She could see that even through the drawn curtains. One in the afternoon, but of what day? Why couldn't she think? Her eyes fluttered. She was sleepy still. Maybe she should just sleep it off. Maybe she'd be more coherent in another couple of hours. But, sleep what off? She wasn't a heavy drinker, she didn't do drugs. She certainly wasn't the type to get blitzed and land in some strange guy's hotel room. Where was she then, and why?

But, sleep. Sleep called to her. It would be so wonderful to sleep. This could all wait till later. Something floating on the fringes of her mind told her that just this scenario had already occurred several times. How often had she wakened disoriented and groggy and then fallen back into whatever haze she was experiencing?

No.

She was awake. She might be fuzzy around the edges; she might feel like emptying her stomach into the nearest toilet, but she was conscious now, and that meant she needed to act. She needed to find out where she was and why.

It was there, just at the corner of her muddled brain, she could sense it.

She blinked.

Had she just seen movement?

She blinked again, wishing she could focus. Her vision was just fuzz and shadows, nothing concrete.

Blink, blink.

Yes, there was a form, probably male, standing at the foot of her bed, just staring at her. How long had he been here? Who was he? Had she been drugged? *Had she been raped?* Julia's heart raced. She tried to lift herself into a sitting position, but nearly lost the contents of her stomach for the effort. "Wh-who are you?" she stammered as her head flopped back onto the pillow.

The shadow stepped to her left, moving around the bed and closer to her face. "My name is Ric. We haven't met yet—at least not while you've been conscious."

Julia squinted. The image cleared some, but there was still enough blur to make the young man appear as fuzzy as a newly-hatched chick. "Ric? Who's Ric?"

"I'm one of Dr. Baker's students."

Dr. Baker? Dr. Donald Baker. The name came clear as one she'd recently known, but there was no context. She couldn't recall who the doctor was. "I don't remember," she said. "Why am I here?" She was very weak, and the effort to speak created new waves of vertigo. Still, she fought to keep her stomach under control. It wouldn't help her situation to vomit on the young man's shoes.

Ric stepped closer. "You'll remember everything soon enough. Dr. Baker said you need to be brought around. I've set a pitcher of water and a glass on the nightstand. You'll want to drink as much as you're able, flush your system of the drug."

"What drug?"

"Dr. Baker will explain everything once your mind has cleared." With that he turned, strolled across the lush carpet, and let himself out. Julia heard the click of a lock turning after he'd closed the door.

Chapter Twenty-Six

Charles Chambers placed the phone in its cradle and then turned to the case file spread across his desk. It was tax litigation—his specialty—but it meant nothing to him at this moment. He'd file another brief, petition the IRS, agree to concessions. He knew the drill. The Feds knew the drill, except in the rare instance of some monumental fraud, both sides knew where the other would likely land before the first conversation occurred. In many ways the job of a tax attorney was robotic, just keep the system moving and rake in the money. It wasn't that Charles disliked his profession, even in its monotony; it was just that he had other things on his mind.

Julia, in particular.

He'd screwed up. The woman was amazing, vibrant, exciting. She was in love with him. Or had been. Still, for some inexplicable reason, he'd strayed from her. He couldn't say why he'd done it, couldn't even reconcile it to himself. He'd simply acted without thinking, maybe naively believing there'd be no consequences, or that everything would work out the way things always had. He'd never been unfaithful—not once. Never entertained the thought. It amazed him how quickly he'd allowed himself to slide toward the thing.

He really hadn't thought that the girl, Rachel—the other woman—would ever come into his life. Rachel was an administrative assistant for another attorney who rented space in the same office complex as Charles. He and she had crossed paths enough times to have established a comfortable, though seemingly harmless, casual relationship. Though, Charles now wondered if he'd simply been unwilling to acknowledge it for its true nature, for its underlying danger.

On the occasion in question, they had come upon each other in the parking lot. As usual, Julia was working beyond her scheduled shift and so Charles had decided to dine out. He hated dirtying all of those pots and pans to feed one person. As such, he'd found himself eating out more and more frequently. Rachel's car was parked next to Charles' motorcycle. She'd commented on his bike, said she'd never been on one, and hinted that she'd like to take a ride. Charles had Julia's helmet attached to his bike, and so nervously offered to take her for a quick spin.

He'd enjoyed the feel of her body as she'd hugged up against his back, as she'd wrapped her arms around his mid section, and leaned her helmeted head against his shoulder blades. He enjoyed the attention, the excitement. His body tingled with stimulation, with anticipation, and even with an electrified fear. How long had it been since Julia had really noticed him, much less desired him?

They ate at a steakhouse that night, a little hole-in-the-wall place off Maryland Parkway that Charles had frequented back when his office had been the next block over. Dinner was over quickly. They'd both ordered only salads. Perhaps both were nervous, and therefore not hungry. Perhaps they were anxious for something else, something looming on the eve's horizon. Afterward, once he'd returned her to her car, Rachel had suggested he follow her to her apartment, only a few blocks distant. They could have a couple of drinks, she said. Charles gazed down into her pale green eyes, feeling an unmistakable surge race through his body. She was beautiful, this one. Young, vivacious, witty. She and he had definitely clicked. Their conversation over dinner had flowed naturally. They shared many of the same interests, enjoyed the same music, had even, apparently, attended two of the same concerts.

Unlike Julia, this woman clearly desired Charles. There was no career between them, no other "love" competing for his space.

He'd stepped closer, extended his arm, gently brushed the side of her face with his fingers, and then slipped his hand to the back of her head, running his fingers through her golden hair, before drawing her to him. Wrapping his arms around her, he cradled her. He could feel his heart thumping against her, could feel her drawing closer, even closer. He leaned toward her upturned face, watched as her lips parted in anticipation of a kiss. God, this woman was beautiful. Sliding his hands to her arms, just below each shoulder, he pulled back to arm's distance. "Thank you for a wonderful time," he'd said. "I'll see you in the office."

Charles felt terrible after his infidelity, nauseous even. He couldn't sleep, couldn't eat. He spent most of the next day pacing back and forth, slamming his palm against whatever wall happened to avail itself. He'd nearly done it, nearly slept with that woman. And why? Because he was tired of going to bed alone? Tired of sharing Julia's affections with her all-important work? Tired of waiting for Julia to decide she was ready to start a family? He couldn't remember the last time they'd taken a weekend getaway together—or even gone to a movie. He realized that there was no relationship left to damage, and he'd told Julia as much when she'd arrived home late that evening. Told her everything. Charles wasn't one to sneak around. If he was that tempted, if he'd come that close, well, it would be better to make a clean break before his resolve weakened further and he did something unforgivable.

But now, just days later, he knew he'd made a terrible mistake. True, Julia was too involved with her work. If the marriage were to survive, something would have to give. But, even in these short few days he'd realized just how special Julia truly was. If he had to share her with her patients, then he would need to learn to be less selfish. She was his true life-mate, none other. How could he have ever thought otherwise? He only prayed the relationship wasn't damaged beyond repair.

The phone rang, jarring Charles out of his contemplations. Massaging his forehead with his left hand, he reached for the receiver with his right. His office assistant, Chloe, informed him that he had a call from UMC, the hospital where Julia worked. His heart leaped. Finally! He'd begun to think that she'd never return his calls. "Hello," he nearly shouted as Chloe put him through. "Julia, I've been trying to reach you. Listen, I've…"

"I'm sorry, Mr. Chambers," came a male voice. "I'm not your wife."

"Who is this? Where's Julia?"

The voice on the line was hesitant, perhaps nervous. "This is Dr. Raul Martinez. I work with Dr. Chambers."

"Yes?" prompted Charles, wondering where this was going. Was Julia now sending messages through an intermediary like some middle school girl?

"I'm trying to locate Dr. Chambers," said Martinez.

"Locate her? Hasn't she been at work?"

"Not for nearly four days. I received a text message stating she was tending to family out of town, but that was the last—"

"I received the same text." Charles cut the young doctor off mid-sentence. He'd thought the text strange. Julia hated text messaging, and often complained about how no one communicated like human beings anymore. To the best of his knowledge, she'd never once sent a text. When he received this one, he'd assumed she used it as a device to avoid having an actual conversation with him. "So, she hasn't been to work, and hasn't called?" he asked.

"No," said Martinez. "I was concerned. I went to her house the past two nights after my shift. She wasn't there."

Charles nodded, though Martinez couldn't see this. Julia had kept the house. Charles had been exiled to one of those pay-by-the-week "suites" the night he'd told her of his intentions. "You think something might have happened to her?"

There was a noticeable pause before Martinez continued. "There was…" Martinez hesitated, and then dove into it. "There was a patient, earlier this week. Dr. Chambers had been working on him. He attacked an EMT, almost killed him, and then fled."

"They caught him, didn't they? Hospital security?"

"No. Somehow he slipped away. The thing is, the attack was unusual. I came across some files of other victims that seemed to match the attack on the EMT. I showed these to Dr. Chambers. She was very curious and took the files. She said there'd been some people in the EMT's room that day. One man in particular, she said, seemed to know more about these attacks than he'd let on. I think she went to see him."

"Raul, you'd better tell me everything you know."

Chapter Twenty-Seven

The cleansing process was long. Julia couldn't say if it took hours or days. She slipped in and out of a hazy half-consciousness, downing as much water as she could, somehow willing her stomach to accept the liquid. Eventually she was forced to make trips to the attached bathroom. The first of these was a misery that left her stumbling to the floor, weeping as she fought unsuccessfully to keep from dribbling upon herself.

As clarity inched back into her life, she realized that, in addition to her bra and panties, she wore only a man's button-down shirt. The realization made her feel newly violated. She fought the temptation to rip the shirt from her form, and only restrained herself because this would leave her more exposed. Still, the feel of the fabric against her skin, the knowledge that whoever had done this to her had worn this same shirt, had perspired in it, made her want to retch.

The young man, Ric, returned only twice that she was aware of, though the water pitcher seemed continually full. He remained silent, not answering her questions about why she'd been detained, what type of drug had been used, or what was going to be done with her. He smiled a nearly familiar grin and went about his task of refilling the pitcher. After which, he placed the newly-filled container on the nightstand and left the room, always locking the door, never uttering a word.

Once, as the door opened, she'd rushed him, hoping to surprise him. But her legs had been unsteady, and she stumbled three paces from the bed. Ric entered to find her sprawled on the floor, sobbing in frustration. He extended a hand, which she grudgingly accepted; then he'd helped her to her feet, and led her back to the bed.

Eventually Julia felt well enough to move about the room. Her stomach had settled, and she even experienced hunger pangs. She investigated each closet and drawer and found no clothing. Her own garments had not been left at her disposal. She did, though, find a phone cord, disconnected, with no phone left in the room. She wondered what had happened to her cell phone. She'd obviously been here for some time. She must have missed work. Someone had surely tried to call, to find out where she was, if she was okay. She was furious. Her life had been interrupted. She'd been kidnapped. No one knew where to find her. With a scream built of pent-up anger and frustration, she launched herself at the door, pounding and hollering, demanding to be set free. Only moments elapsed before a voice came from beyond the wooden barrier.

"Julia, I must ask that you refrain from screaming."

The voice was accented, familiar, it was Donald Baker.

"Let me out of here! You have no right!"

Baker's voice remained calm, unflustered. "Perhaps you are correct. Yet the door will remain closed until we can speak civilly.

Julia pounded the door one more time in frustration. Pain shot up her forearm. She'd probably sprained her wrist, or at least bruised herself. Stepping away from the door with a muttered curse, she paced the room. The man wanted to talk civilly. He'd drugged her, kidnapped her—and who knew what else! But now he wanted to talk civilly. Julia refrained from screaming at the door, telling him where he could shove "civilly," and tried to think. What were her options? She moved to the window, pulled the draperies back, and looked down some twenty stories or more onto the Las Vegas strip. There was The Mirage with its white frothing waterfalls and lush tropical foliage, and Treasure Island—now simply called TI—and its two pirate ships facing each other from across a large, arcing, manmade pool. She was in The Venetian, she remembered with sudden clarity. Far too many stories up to attempt any ridiculous escape.

Donald Baker's voice came once again from beyond the door. "Julia, are you prepared to have a reasonable conversation?"

"I'm not sure how *reasonably* we can converse if I'm half-naked," she hollered from her spot by the window.

"Your garments are laundered, and folded, waiting for you just outside the door—which I've now unlocked. We'll be waiting for you in the living area."

*****

They were all there when she emerged: Donald Baker with his disturbing plastic smile; Shane, who avoided direct eye contact and shuffled uncomfortably in his seat; and the three young men she'd seen at one time or another throughout her stay, Bradley, Ric, and another now introduced to her as Phillip. These three, remarkably similar in stature, facial contours, and hair texture, stood silently in the kitchenette as servants might. Donald and Shane were both seated on the sectional sofa, Donald leaning forward as if in eager anticipation.

She remembered everything now, or near enough. A handful of cumulous floated about the contours of her brain; she wasn't as quick as she liked to be, but she was herself again. And she was not at all pleased with what she recalled. Hoping to throw the creep off balance with a bit of twisted humor, she reached into her purse and withdrew a Monopoly "Get out of Jail Free" card—which she always carried as a kind of joke— and tossed it on the coffee table.

Shane offered a wry smile; Donald acted as if he hadn't seen the thing.

"Julia, you look much better. Please, sit. Phillip has prepared some lattes. The caffeine will do you good." The man acted as if he was hosting a tea party.

Julia had counseled herself to remain calm, that outbursts would do no good. But this smug, arrogant man pushed every button. "You scheming little s.o.b., you drugged me."

Donald smiled.

"A woman died here. Where is her body?"

Shane looked down and away as he fidgeted with his fingers, but Donald maintained his cordial, this-is-all-run-of-the-mill tone. "Certainly you wouldn't expect us to keep a body in this suite for four days," he said, his mannequin face unchanging, his manner relaxed.

Four days? She'd been drugged and incapacitated for four days. What was this man thinking? And then she remembered anew. This was no man. At least not if all he claimed had been true. This was some creature masquerading as a man. His motives were not the motives of a man. His drives were unnatural and therefore suspect. His very appearance was stolen from those he exploited—apparently, in Donald's case, the three young men standing stone-faced not fifteen feet from where she stood. If all that she'd been told—or even some of it—was true, this was someone as inhuman as any space alien or monster from the worlds of science fiction and horror. The worst of it was that she did believe. Her rational mind wanted to deny it. Her clinical bias sought alternate explanations for all she'd seen and heard. But somehow she couldn't give any of these much credence. It was Donald Baker himself that ultimately convinced her—his very being, his aura, his presence. It was the false expressions, the rehearsed mannerisms, the rubber-like skin hidden behind a neatly trimmed beard, and the eyes disguised behind tinted glasses and colored contact lenses. It was the essence of the man that spoke of something other, something not right.

"If it's been four days," she said finally. "People will be looking for me. I should have been at work. I haven't been home."

Donald grinned that despicable grin. "Three people have attempted to contact you via your cell phone. A Dr. Wise, a Dr. Martinez, and a man named Charles, who, I'm guessing by his frequent calls and pathetic pleas, is an estranged spouse. I've returned each call with a text message from your cell phone indicating that you were called out of town on a family emergency and will be unavailable for several days."

Julia took a quick step forward. "You arrogant, controlling, son of—"

"Now, now, now," he cut her off, indicating the three young men already moving to intercept her before she could touch Donald. "We are civil people, you and I. We must act as such."

"There's nothing civil about you," she said as she stopped her advance, signaling to the three Kool-Aid drinkers that she was no threat to their beloved master. "It's all a façade. Somehow these sheep of yours don't see you for what you really are."

Donald inclined his head slightly to the left. "Actually, it is you, dear Julia, who have yet to understand the complexities of our race. Please do not think me evil. What I do is done with the purest possible motives."

Giving up on Donald, she angled her gaze toward the young white-haired man seated beside him. "Shane, you cared for that girl. Where's her body? What's really happening?"

Donald didn't give Shane the chance to respond. "The body has been tended to, Julia. And if you'd be so kind as to have a seat, the rest will be explained."

"You kidnapped me. I could have you arrested."

Donald Baker extended a hand, indicating where Julia should sit. Apparently, he was not about to proceed until everyone was in the proper place. Sighing, she dropped into the offered seat, just around the bend in the couch from Donald and Shane. "Very good," he said. "Now, the latte, please drink." He indicated the mug before her on the low rectangular coffee table.

What a control freak. "I'm not thirsty." Her tone was harsh, final.

"You suspect the drink contains drugs or poisons. Neither of which is the case. I'm simply being a good host."

A good host! This man—*this thing*—had to be delusional. "Oh, stick it, Donald. A girl died here. Other people have died. You've kept me against my will for four days. I deserve an honest explanation."

Donald Baker remained still for several long moments before speaking, his face an unreadable mask. "Four days ago you threatened to go to the police, telling them that I have some connection to the strange deaths here in Las Vegas. Rather than risk that particular complication, I concluded it best to tell you of the reyaqc. I had hoped you would receive this admittedly difficult explanation as the truth that it is, and perhaps even become an advocate as the reyaqc one day soon go public. You were not fully convinced, most likely thinking me crazy. But that, you see, was an acceptable state as well. If you had left me then and contacted the authorities, your story would have seemed fantastic. Depending on your approach, they would have thought one of us mad, and dismissed the entire episode as not worth their time. Then Shane arrived with that poor girl, the victim of the rogue reyaqc, which I have come to stop. Now you were more intimately involved. You had witnessed something that could connect me and mine to these deaths. Yet you did not trust me. In fact, your sense of duty demanded that you report what you'd seen. I had no choice but to detain you."

"And now?"

Donald leaned forward, tweed elbows resting on corduroy knees. "Now there have been additional developments. The rogue continues to attack the innocent. Where before he hunted in a rather tight geographic locale, thus allowing Shane to locate him, he now moves randomly throughout the city. In fact, last evening he attacked and killed a police officer right here on Las Vegas Boulevard in clear sight of dozens of witnesses." Donald paused, took a sip of his latte, and then continued. "There are other issues as well. Suspicions best left unspoken. Consequently, I find that I must confer with another of my kind."

"Where does that leave me?"

"You, once again, dear Julia, are a conundrum. I see that you now believe the reyaqc to be real. But you don't trust me. As I see it, this leaves us two options. One, we again drug you and leave you in the care of my young friends. Or two, you accompany me to a reyaqc settlement, where you can do no harm, and where, with luck, you'll grow to appreciate our dilemma." He paused for just a moment, and then added, "I see something in you. I'm not sure what it is just yet. Perhaps a longing or a seeking of purpose. Give me an opportunity to show you something wondrous, and perhaps we can help each other in our quests."

Julia was incensed. "How could you possibly think you see something in me? You don't know me. You know nothing about me."

The grin returned, that emotionless, artificial contour of his lips. "Julia," he said in as near to a sincere tone as she'd yet heard. "I may not be of your species, but I am a diligent student of the human race. I know you far better than Jane Goodall knows her chimpanzees, far more intimately than Pavlov knew his dog. You are experiencing a chaotic marital rift; that much is clear from simple phone messages. Therefore, you are in a transitional period, a state of unease and confusion. Aside from the estranged husband, the only calls you've received have been from colleagues. No friends, no family, even though you've suddenly dropped from sight during an admittedly stressful period in your life. You came here alone, having confided in no one as to your suspicions. Julia, clearly you are alone in the world. In many ways, perhaps it is you who are empty."

Chapter Twenty-Eight

Charles Chambers had drilled Dr. Raul Martinez concerning Julia's whereabouts. He'd made some other calls, tried to locate her through friends and colleagues—even through the police. Now, he took a more direct action.

"Venetian Hotel and Casino. My name is Juanita. How may I help you?"

"Yes. I'm calling for a guest, a Donald Baker. I'd like to be connected to his room."

"Thank you, sir. Just a moment." There was a brief pause, and then the operator returned to the line. "I'm connecting you now, sir."

Well, that was good, at least. The man did exist, and, as Martinez had stated, did have a room at this hotel. Charles heard three short clicks, and then the phone rang. It was answered after only two of these. "Hello." The voice was that of a young male.

"May I speak with Donald Baker, please?"

"Who may I say is calling?"

Charles had thought about this question. If he gave his true last name, Baker might too easily connect him with Julia. "This is Charles Douglas," he said, substituting his middle name in place of his surname. "Is Donald Baker available?" This man sounded young. Raul Martinez's impression, based on his conversation with Julia, was that Baker was a more mature man. Charles was fairly well certain that this wasn't he.

"May I ask the purpose of your call?"

"Yes, I'm an attorney with Dahl, Chambers, and Levin. I have some papers for Mr. Baker to sign."

"*Doctor* Baker is not available right now," said the young man with a bit of a snit. "I suggest you call back at a later time."

"Sure. But, listen. This has to do with a certain patient that fled UMC. *Doctor* Baker asked me to do some work on this situation. I'm sure he'd like for me to reach him as soon as possible."

There was a long pause. Charles hoped he hadn't over-played his ruse by claiming to have been hired by Baker. He hoped the reference to the wanted man might gain him some sort of ground. He ached to simply ask if Julia was there—if she'd been kidnapped, or worse—but feared that might just earn him a dial tone in the ear.

Finally, the young man responded. "Dr. Baker hired you?"

"Yes," lied Charles.

"Are you a reyaqc?" asked the young man in a nearly inaudible voice.

Reyaqc? Charles had never heard the term. "Yes," he said almost immediately. "I'm a reyaqc."

Another pause, but shorter this time. "Dr. Baker left about fifteen minutes ago. I don't expect him back for several hours, perhaps not even until tomorrow."

Charles was out of his seat now, pacing one way and then the other before his mahogany desk. "Where did he go? Is there a way for me to reach him? The information I have is important."

"He's gone to meet with Tresset Bremu. He'll be out of reach."

Charles cursed silently, but kept his voice calm. "Okay," he said through a sigh. "Oh, one other thing," he added almost as an afterthought. "Was the ER doctor with him? The lady, Julia something?"

"Yes, Mr. Douglas. She was taken as well."

"Taken? Is she all right? Has anything happened to her?"

Charles had dropped the ruse at this point. The click followed by the lifeless dial tone only confirmed this conclusion.

The Third Interlude

From Histories Volume Two, an ongoing chronicle of the reyaqc

The following is an interview I conducted with the reyaqc, Cheirves, a noted anthropologist and longtime professor at a prestigious European University. His human name will not be revealed as his true nature was never discovered by the school's faculty or administration. This conversation took place in 1987, only months before Cheirves's death. It is necessarily short as Cheirves was one hundred-twenty-seven years of age and already quite ill.

Dolnaraq: Thank you for taking the time to meet with me, Doctor. I know you are ill and I won't take more time than necessary. That said, I'll get directly to the point. What is it you'd like to share?

Cheirves: [*multiple coughs*] Thank you, Dolnaraq. The truth is, I'm concerned about the future of our people.

Dolnaraq: How so, Doctor?

Cheirves: As you know, I've studied the population patterns of the reyaqc for some decades. This has not always been an easy task as most reyaqc groups are scattered and have little communication. Even now, there are certainly some packs and communities still unknown to me.

Dolnaraq: And what concerns you with the population patterns?

Cheirves: Now, understand. An accurate census has never been taken of the reyaqc. That said, throughout this century, through efforts by those such as yourself, by Rynkall, by Heigisch, we've come a long way toward determining an accurate number. [*Cheirves pauses to cough*] Excuse me.

Dolnaraq: Certainly.

Cheirves: As I was saying, the reyaqc have always been scattered. By necessity, they've been quite secretive. Those living within homo sapien metropolises were easier to track, but these tend to blend in with the general population and so become as invisible. Still, I've been able to detail drastic declines in reyaqc populations in specific areas.

Dolnaraq: Which areas are most depleted?

Cheirves: Due to exponential human population growth, Europe and North America have had the most drastic declines in reyaqc populations. South America the least. This is interesting in that it is believed the reyaqc originated in South America where homo sapiens believe their origins to lie in Africa.

Dolnaraq: Of course, continental drift should be part of this discussion.

Cheirves: And by this you imply that the reyaqc and homo sapiens share a common ancestral root.

Dolnaraq: It would seem evident that there is a biological relationship, yes. Do you deny this?

Cheirves: No, no. Not in the least. We both know the theories. The scientific minded – such as yourself – will maintain that the reyaqc and sapiens are offshoots of the same branch. And this would seem likely as we are dependent on their DNA to survive; our basic form at birth is human-like, etcetera. Of course, those with a supernatural bent claim a more elaborate origin; the most common of these being that we are descendents of the Nephilim.

Dolnaraq: The Nephilim being the product of unions between fallen angels and human females.

Cheirves: Yes, yes. Genesis chapter six. The actual term used is not angels, but "Sons of God." So yes, likely fallen angels. The theory is that most of the Nephilim could not reproduce, but that those few who accomplished reproduction sired offspring with defective chromosomes – the reyaqc. But, all of this has taken us far afield of our topic, the current reyaqc population. [*multiple coughs. Cheirves wipes his mouth and drinks a sip of water.*] Yes, Dolnaraq, Africa and South America were once joined. And yes, South America is likely our birth place, but more importantly for today's conversation, it is the home of the Amazon Rainforest. The forest is roughly the size of the continental United States and covers forty percent of the South American Continent, nearly all of it untouched wilderness with sparse human populations. This is a place where the reyaqc may still flourish without discovery, a place that might offer salvation to our depleted species. North America, on the other hand, Europe as well, each has grown in sapien population to the extent where there is very little land left for the reyaqc.

Dolnaraq: Give me some details in terms of population decline, Doctor.

Cheirves: [multiple coughs] Twenty years ago I estimated the worldwide reyaqc population at just over thirteen-thousand. Today we are less than ten-thousand. We've lost roughly one quarter of our overall population in just twenty years.

Dolnaraq: That's obviously devastating. But, can you clarify? What exactly does this rapid decline mean to the reyaqc species?

Cheirves: First, let me explain that demographic models should be used cautiously in Population Viability Analysis. I believe that predictions derived from quantitative models for the reyaqc are unreliable due to the lack of quality demographic data available, difficulties in estimating variance in demographic rates, and lack of information on dispersal. Think in terms of varying habitable areas, mortality, movement patterns. This said, I have utilized several approaches including: analytical, deterministic single-population, metapopulation, and spatially explicit models. [*multiple harsh coughs, accompanied by blood hacked onto Cheirves's handkerchief*]

Dolnaraq: Doctor, would you prefer we continue another time?

Cheirves: No, no, no. Certainly not. Let's be honest, we may not have the opportunity to meet again, you and I. [*multiple coughs and then a weak smile*] You must understand, I've taken many factors into account, including statistics such as the number of reyaqc remaining, the overall decrease in population over time, breeding success rates, known threats such as the expanding human population, and so on.

Dolnaraq: And your conclusion?

Cheirves: On the positive side, we are long lived. Not considering violent death, we live well over one hundred years and are capable of reproducing for nearly all of these. Couple this with our ability to select the gender of offspring, thus birthing a high female population which could then drastically increase our static birth rate, and I believe there is cause for hope. Add to this a strategy to inhabit greater regions of the rainforest, and, eh, we might yet survive. But, make no mistake. We are an endangered species. If this trend does not reverse, we will be beyond the point of recovery within little more than one generation. I fear, my dear friend, we are on the verge of extinction.

PART THREE

THE PACK

Chapter Twenty-Nine

Tresset Bremu stood, brush in hand, glaring at the incomplete painting. Something wasn't right. Perhaps the hue. He normally liked deep blue tones which created moody shadows and rich soulful skies. But this particular work cried for something else, something striking, aggressive. Perhaps more red tones. A sense of heat, of danger, of blood and death.

Tresset exhaled, stepping back from the canvas, seeking a broader perspective. There was a dirt road, bordered by random foliage and stone, snaking its way toward the rising sun. Two reyaqc, silhouettes only, but strong of form and stature, were two thirds of the way up the path, their shadows long, their postures purposeful and true. Hidden behind a large stone were several humans, withered in their frailty, dressed in cumbersome business attire and clutching automatic weapons. Their eyes were wide with terror and their foreheads damp with perspiration. Behind them, in the lower right corner of the work, were numerous reyaqc, caged behind a fence made up of miniature high-rise buildings and automobiles, trains and factories. These reyaqc, molts all, wept and clawed, but could gain no liberty.

Tresset narrowed his lips, cocked his head slightly, and daubed his brush on his palette. More reds. Definitely more reds. And oranges. The sun should appear as a blazing fireball on the verge of nova, prepared to enflame a fallen world.

The reyaqc chieftain dropped his head and placed the palette and brush aside. Too obvious. Everything he'd painted recently had been brash, without subtlety, devoid of mystery and beauty. A pup could read his meaning with little coaxing. Moving to a nearby basin, Tresset dipped his narrow hands in pale yellow water. Using a harsh industrial soap, he washed, scrubbing each hand and forearm up to the elbow as might a surgeon. He scoured between fingers, under the nails, on the dark pads that served as his palms, and within each crevasse of his thick rubbery skin. Afterwards he dried each with a clean towel, and then rubbed his hands with a cloth dampened with a strong disinfectant.

Keeping the damp cloth, he then strolled to the opposite wall of the tiny office and stared at a large map of the region posted there. The map, yellowed and dog-eared by exposure to the elements, pinpointed each of the North American desert reyaqc packs, their chieftain's name, and their approximate number. Much of Nevada and some small areas of both California and Arizona were among the few remaining places with sufficient undeveloped land for reyaqc packs to settle. But even these areas were shrinking and soon, Tresset feared, would be gone altogether. Tresset stared at a spot roughly twenty-five miles to the northwest of his own pack. Bytneht Noavor. Tresset had heard nothing since he'd slain the upstart's whimpering spy. This troubled him. Bytneht would not accept the insult. Without doubt, the smarmy pup would retaliate. But, why no activity? Tresset's spies had observed nothing unusual within the settle-ment, no hushed comings and goings, no furtive meetings with his leadership. Bytneht was known to be rash, vengeful. Tresset had as-sumed—in fact, hoped—this insult would spawn a hurried, ill-conceived attack upon his own compound. Tresset's finely-hewn forces would easily subdue those of his opponent, Bytneht would be slain, Tresset would assume command of both packs, merging them and creating a more formidable force.

Why had Bytneht failed to respond? Was he too cowardly to face Tresset, to risk his molts against a superior force? A low rumbling growl emerged from Tresset's naked throat. Something was not right. His spies must've missed something. Bytneht may be a shortsighted fool, not realizing the danger now faced by the reyaqc species, and the need to unite, but he was no coward. Strategy was a puzzle and Tresset was missing a piece.

He detested missing pieces.

Tresset's nose twitched. There was a scent upon the too-hot breeze. Ordool, the yellow bat, approaching the office. "Enter," barked Tresset before the other could knock. "Tell me something useful."

The brightly-colored molt crossed the threshold, allowing a hot burst of wind to surge into the room through the open door. "There is a vehicle approaching, still some twenty miles distant," offered Ordool. "One reyaqc, two humans."

"One reyaqc?"

"Yes, Chieftain. He's been identified as Donald Baker."

Tresset whirled to face his subordinate. "That is not his name!" barked the angered molt. "He is a reyaqc—despite all he's done, or what he now chooses to call himself. You will refer to him with a name worthy of his true nature." Tresset's glare was intense. Ordool shrank at the outburst, his leather-draped arms coming together before his breast, one narrow hand covering the other in a nervous gesture.

"Come, Ordool. Sit." Tresset's tone was suddenly gentle, reassuring. Ordool could be fragile. Best to soothe, not to anger. "When should I expect him?"

The yellow bat took a tentative step closer, his shoulders hunched forward, his eyes averting those of his chieftain as his ears twitched right then left. "Given the terrain, Dolnaraq should arrive within three-quarters of an hour, sir."

"Dolnaraq," whispered Tresset as he clenched his disinfectant cloth. "Dolnaraq."

Chapter Thirty

Charles Chambers blinked his eyes back into focus as he massaged his throbbing forehead. It seemed he'd been staring at the computer screen for hours. He'd called a friend at the police department, Hal Holmberg, a buddy from his police academy days. Charles had attended the academy before he rerouted his law enforcement dreams toward the litigation side of the equation. His original thought had been to become a prosecutor, putting away the scumbags guys like Hal brought in. That had lasted only until his mortgage went past due a couple of times. Then, Charles had done some moonlighting during tax season with one of his law school pals, and well, the money was too good and Charles' altruistic calling too faint.

He voiced his concerns to Hal that this Donald Baker may have taken Julia against her will. But his old buddy said they couldn't do anything just yet. Julia was a grown woman. Charles was an estranged spouse. She wouldn't be expected to keep him apprised of her every move. In fact, by Charles' own admission, she'd been avoiding him, not returning his calls. And there'd been the text message to both Charles and to her employer indicating she'd be out of town with family for a few days. Maybe she'd just needed some space, time to think things through. She was under considerable stress, after all.

Charles ended the call unconvinced. Julia was with this Baker, and the whole situation seemed squirrelly. He'd tried finding information about Donald Baker online, but the name was too common. Without knowing more about the man, Charles didn't know whether to investigate Baker the plumber, Baker the surgeon, Baker the college professor, Baker the baker, or any other of the dozens of Donald Bakers. The Donald Baker he was looking for did have the title "doctor," but even with this tidbit, it could take days to locate the right man. This Baker was staying at a hotel. That meant he wasn't a Las Vegas resident. He could be from anywhere. Thus, Charles had no starting point.

After continued frustration and three cans of Monster Energy Drink, he switched his focus to the term reyaqc. The young man in Baker's hotel room had asked Charles if he was a reyaqc. What could that mean, and did it have any significance here? Charles wasn't sure how to spell it: rayick, reyack, reyak? He tried every imaginable variation, and was just about to give up when he came across something under the unlikely spelling, reyaqc. "An obscure mythical creature," sited the online dictionary. "In European folklore, the reyaqc is human-like in appearance, but with the ability to infuse animal traits directly from beasts. Reyaqc are said to have no true form of their own and so steal genetic material from their victims. Some claim the legends of vampires and werewolves have their origins in the reyaqc."

"Monsters," muttered Charles through an ironic snort. "They're talking about monsters." He couldn't believe the amount of time he'd wasted on this folly. What frustrated him worse was that he had no other lead to follow. In his gut, he knew Julia was in danger. The woman was too dedicated to her job to disappear with nothing more than an obscure text message to the hospital. Charles had checked. Her superiors had heard nothing more from her. Something was very wrong here, and it seemed Charles was the only one determined to get to the bottom of it.

Grunting at the sheer stupidity of it all, he clicked into a second website dealing with reyaqc. This one featured a chat room where nerds gathered to discuss so-called "sightings." There were a few poor-quality photographs of supposed reyaqc, some eyewitness testimonials and links to several other reyaqc-related sites. The whole thing smacked of Bigfoot. Charles clicked a link which led him to another site and then another. He scanned several articles, getting a feel for the myth of the reyaqc, but felt this was getting him nowhere. How would any of this lead him to Julia?

Another few clicks and he came across a chat thread titled, "Rogue reyaqc in Vegas." Charles clicked into the chat room and scanned through the comments. According to these reyaqc website "experts," a rogue reyaqc had been responsible for a series of bizarre murders committed over the past several weeks. Charles had heard about the murders, of course. That type of thing was front page news. It was nearly impossible to tune into local talk radio without encountering the topic. But, no one thought it was some crazy mythical monster.

It dawned on Charles that this killer, this so-called reyaqc, could be the patient Raul Martinez referred to, the one who attacked Jimmy Harrison before fleeing the hospital. This could be the connection he'd been seeking. But even so, he didn't believe in monsters. This same guy might be the killer and the patient, but Charles couldn't accept that he was something other than human. And besides, none of this got him any closer to finding Julia—and that was his only true objective.

Charles was just about to give up and exit the site, when someone added another post to the thread. "I heard Donald Baker flew to Vegas to find the rogue," is what it said.

Charles' heart tapped out a staccato rhythm. Baker!

Charles was not adept at chat room etiquette or form. He'd never entered one in his life, but here was his connection. This had to be the Baker he was looking for. This was the man who'd taken Julia. Searching around the page, he found an icon that, when highlighted, read "Reply." He clicked on this and found that he needed to create a screen name in order to continue. After a moment's contemplation, he typed the screen name "Searching" in the space provided, selected a password, confirmed the password, and was then rewarded with an empty message box in which to type. Quickly, he posed the question, "Who is Donald Baker?" and then clicked, "Post."

There was a slight pause, and then several responses hit the screen almost simultaneously.

MO—Dude, you're kidding—right?
REYATTACK—LOL!!!
ZOOT—Who is this moron?

Charles sighed. Apparently this Baker was some sort of celebrity to these reyaqc geeks. "Sorry," he typed. "I've just recently learned of the reyaqc and find the concept fascinating. I'm trying to learn as much as I can." He posted the message, hoping his feigned novice curiosity would draw these people out.

There was another slight pause and then responses poured in.

TOGA—Donald Baker is the foremost expert on the reyaqc. He's a Harvard University professor who has written their history.

MO—Welcome newbie to our little band of reyaphites! Donald Baker is a famous reyaqc whose goal is to civilize the species and bring them into mainstream society.

REYATTACK—Actually, it's Yale, not Harvard.

ZOOT—Donald Baker is not a reyaqc! He's a human sympathizer.

REYBOY—Donald Baker, along with other well-established reyaqc, work together to help both individual reyaqc and even full packs to become educated, secure employment within human society, purchase land, etc.

DIGIT—Donald Baker is a wealthy reyaqc who wrote a book called "Histories" which tells the story of the reyaqc.

MOLTY—You're both wrong, it's Princeton.

REYBOY—Histories is not a book! It's a series of three volumes.

REYATTACK—The college professor is just a front for the real Baker. The true author of histories is a molt who cannot be seen in public. FYI—a molt is a reyaqc who infuses stem cells from animals.

TOGA—Harvard!

DIGIT—Baker is not a molt. He detests molts.

MO—I heard he's working on volume 4.

ZOOT—A guy I know told me he had him for a class at UCLA.

REYBOY—Donald Baker is a molt, and he is a professor. He's the molt Dolnaraq from Histories Vol. 1. "Histories" is actually credited to Dolnaraq but uniformed people call it "Donald Baker's Histories," likely because Dolnaraq is a difficult name to pronounce and because so few humans have actually seen the volumes and so don't know any better.

MOLTY—No. Not UCLA. He's Ivy League.

ZOOT—He is not Dolnaraq. Dolnaraq lived in the late 1800's & early 1900's.

TOGA—Harvard!!!!

DIGIT—Maybe I'd know more if SOMEONE would lend me his copy of Histories. It's not like I can find it at Barnes & Noble.

REYBOY—He is Dolnaraq! Haven't you read the account? He and Tresset Bremu fled Europe for America just before WWI. And, no, you can't buy it at Barnes & Noble! The three volumes of Histories were written in order to give the reyaqc a connection to their past, pride in who they are, and a vision for a brighter future. Baker never intended them to be read by humans, at least not until the reyaqc race becomes established and accepted within the mainstream of human civilization.

Charles was losing patience with the online bickering. Obviously, Baker was a man of stature for those who believed in creatures that went bump in the night—though, no one seemed to know many details, and there were obviously conflicting reports floating around. But now there was something else, another piece falling into place. The guy on Baker's phone had said he'd gone to see Tresset Bremu. Charles had been having difficulty recalling the odd name until now. But seeing it on the screen, he was fairly certain that this was the name mentioned. "Who is this Tresset Bremu?" he typed. "Where can I find him?"

There were a couple more posts about which university Baker worked for, and if, in fact, the university professor was actually the Baker or just a front guy, and then the responses to Charles' question appeared.

ZOOT—Tresset was a reyaqc chieftain who lived in the early 20th century.

REYATTACK—Tresset is a fierce molt who drinks human blood.

REYBOY—Tresset & Dolnaraq were close companions. They lived in a wild reyaqc pack as children and fled together when the pack was attacked and decimated.

MO—Tresset's still alive. He and Dolnaraq are mortal enemies.

Charles sighed. There was so much myth. He didn't know where the facts were in all of this—if there actually were any facts to be found. "Where is Tresset Bremu now?" he typed.

ZOOT—Dead. He was born in the 1800's.

MOLTY—I heard he leads a pack in Montana.

REYBOY—He's not dead. Reyaqc live longer than humans.

DIGIT—He's in Pennsylvania.

TOGA—Reyaqc are immortal.

REYATTACK—He returned to Europe in the mid sixties after receiving a revelation from The Beatles White Album.

MOLTY—Reyaqc are not immortal, they just live about another fifty years longer than us.

REYBOY—My sources say he lives in Nevada.

Okay, here was something—maybe. The kid on Baker's phone had said Baker had taken Julia to meet this Tresset. Obviously, he must be in Nevada. "Nevada? Where in Nevada?" he typed.

TOGA—Tresset Bremu lives with Donald Baker at Harvard.

REYBOY—No one knows where he lives. In order to protect their species, the reyaqc are very secretive. That's why there's so much contradictory information floating around.

There were a few more posts claiming whereabouts for Bremu, placing him on nearly every continent, and one crazy actually asserting that he was jettisoned to the moon from Apollo 13. Charles rose, stretched, began to pace. Most of what he'd read was nonsense, but the name Donald Baker fit, as did the term reyaqc, and the name Tresset Bremu. Obviously, none of the myth could be true, but there was a germ of something here, and Julia had somehow stumbled into it. He wondered if the reyaqc was in reality some sort of cult. Maybe they dressed up like animals or lived out in the wilderness. Julia may have stumbled onto some pack of whackos. Maybe they'd abducted her. So much of this made so little sense.

Passing back before his computer, Charles leaned forward, clasping the mouse, with the intent of exiting the site, when a new posting caught his eye.

REYBOY—Police just captured the rogue reyaqc in Vegas!

Chapter Thirty-One

Julia removed the blindfold, squinted at the bright desert sunlight, and then, opening the car door, stepped from the vehicle into the searing heat. The scene was nearly incomprehensible. If there had been any lingering doubts concerning Donald Baker's extraordinary claims, they were erased in that instant. They were at an abandoned mining operation set amidst low-lying foothills of brilliant red and calico tan. The sandy ground was peppered with stones and pebbles, and it seemed to Julia that even the few visible cacti had difficulty making a go of it here. There were a handful of nearly dilapidated buildings, some rusted machinery, a blue Jeep and a beat-up Ford pick-up; but beyond these few anchors to normality, Julia might have been on a different planet. The entire place was populated by what could only be these reyaqc that Donald Baker had gone on about.

They were in various stages of undress. Some were entirely naked, walking about as if this was the normal state of things, which, perhaps for them it was. Many others wore some clothing, but not as a human would see fit. One young male, repairing the Jeep, wore a floppy yellow sun hat and a pair of Nikes—nothing else. His companion—also a male—wore a blue and green housedress that flapped in the hot desert breeze. Several of the reyaqc wore pants but no shirts; others, shirts with no pants. A slender male, relaxed naked on a lawn chair reading *Great Expectations*.

The attire was disturbing, but the reyaqc themselves were of a sort that perhaps Jim Henson and Picasso could have colluded. No two were alike. Some were quite furry and bore varying degrees of animal-like snouts and teeth. Some had ears large and pointed, which twitched at sounds, or lay back against their scalps. Though most had no obvious deformities, many looked as though they could have been rejects of some

Frankensteinian experiment. A nose would be off center, residing more on a cheek than above the lips. Julia noted a female with two hands attached to the same arm. Nothing seemed complete, as if the reyaqc were caught somewhere between a human and an animal existence and couldn't quite commit to either.

Then there were humans. Or, at least, they appeared human. Only perhaps a dozen were visible, all but one male. Their clothing was worn and dirty, but seemed appropriate for both climate and gender. They went about, performing tasks alongside the reyaqc, seemingly entirely adapted to the strange circumstance.

Donald Baker had moved off to the side, perhaps thirty feet from the Hummer. He spoke with a small, bare-chested reyaqc of about five foot three inches in height. The creature had elongated canines protruding from both upper and lower gums. His nose was dark with wide flaring nostrils. The top of his head was covered in a mop of stringy black hair, but much of his form bore the short tawny fur that could have come from a lion. The reyaqc continuously pulled a rag from the right pocket of his green military-style pants, wiping both hands, and sometimes the forearms up to the elbows, then folding the rag in quarters, and replacing it in the pocket. Perhaps thirty seconds or a minute later, he'd repeat the process. It seemed an unconscious act and Julia wondered at the psychology behind it.

Shane had exited the Hummer and now stood beside Julia. "They're staring at us," said Julia in a near whisper.

Shane slipped a stick of gum into his mouth. "Yeah. You're staring at them too. I'm sure this reyaqc community doesn't get many visitors."

Julia gazed about the compound again, taking in the bizarre scene. "I guess I didn't expect them to be so…beastly."

Shane nodded a weary nod. The man seemed entirely void of energy. "Yeah, well, all reyaqc infuse from humans. A lot infuse from animals too. This community gets off on their hybrid characteristics."

"They look like rejects from a bad *Star Trek* episode."

Shane shrugged. "Ever wonder where the idea of vampires and werewolves came from? You're looking at it."

"But human DNA and animal DNA aren't compatible."

"The reyaqc aren't human, Jules."

It seemed to Julia that Shane might well be saying this more as a reminder to himself than as an admonition to her. She wondered what happened during those four days she'd been drugged. She had not known Shane prior to that day, had spoken no more than a few sentences with him. Yet, she sensed a change. The man she'd met at the hospital had been full of youthful exuberance. He'd seemed brimming with energy, nearly ready to burst at the seams. But now it seemed the life had been drained from him, as if it was an effort to move about, to stand even. Surely the death of the girl, Taz, affected him. Julia sensed it was more than this. There was something troubling the young man, something deep, perhaps even life altering.

Perhaps she was simply projecting her own emotions onto him. She had to admit the possibility. Her life was in shambles, why shouldn't everyone else's be the same?

Donald and the short lion-like reyaqc had concluded their conversation and were making their ways toward Julia and Shane. Julia noticed the short reyaqc nod at two others who fell in step behind them.

"So, Dolnaraq," the reyaqc said. "I see you've brought humans. New givers, I hope."

Donald offered a sideways glance at the shorter reyaqc. "These are my companions, Shane Daws and Dr. Julia Chambers. I have promised them safe passage, and hope you will respect that."

The reyaqc said nothing, but continued forward until he stood before Julia. She had to fight the urge to flee as he studied her head to toe, a contemplative grin upon his peculiar face. "A female," he said with an approving nod. "Healthy, tall, dark-of-skin, and intelligent, yes? You are a doctor?" His accent was similar to Donald's, but with less sophistication, his tone authoritative, his voice strangely compelling. Despite his freakish appearance, this creature was somehow charismatic.

"Yes, a doctor," nodded Julia.

"Under my protection," added Donald with an indirect glance at his companion.

"Mmmm, of course she is. The male seems healthy enough. No congenital diseases, I hope."

Shane glanced sideways and took a half step back. "Doc, I think you'd better do something here."

"Tresset," said Donald. "They are under my protection."

"Which means what exactly? You're weak, Dolnaraq. You've forsaken your own kind for the world of the humans." The reyaqc motioned to the two others standing three paces back. "Olac. Berid, take them both. We'll decide what to do with them later."

"Tresset, leave them be. This is not necessary." This from Donald as the two reyaqc stepped forward.

"I decide what is necessary, Dolnaraq. Givers are scarce. The human scent is on the wind. Your companions will be safer in custody."

A tall brutish reyaqc, which may have been part bear, grasped Shane above the left elbow and moved as if to lead him away. Shane glared at Donald, and then allowed his head to drop in defeat. It was at this moment Julia made her move. The Hummer was still only a few feet away. If she could get inside, lock the door, maybe the keys were still in the ignition. She hadn't seen if Shane took them with him or not. But even if she couldn't drive the vehicle, she might still evade the creature's grasp.

She bolted to her right, and then zigzagged left. The other reyaqc, the one that did not hold Shane, swiped at her with claw-like hand, but missed by several inches.

"Do not damage them!" shouted Tresset. "They are both valuable. Especially the female."

The reyaqc was only inches behind Julia when she made the Hummer. She thrust the door open, using it to smack her pursuer in the snout with a loud *thunk*! The thing roared a curse, but Julia had bought herself enough time to hop into the vehicle, and close and lock the door.

There were no keys.

Nothing in the ignition.

Not on the floor.

Julia smacked the steering wheel with the palm of her hand and cursed Donald Baker for ever being born.

The reyaqc pounded on the glass, attempting to break it with his fists. The Hummer shook with each blow. But worse yet was the heat. The outside temperature hovered around one hundred-fifteen. Inside the Hummer it was probably closer to one-thirty. Without the keys to start the ignition and thus turn on the air conditioning, she wouldn't survive for more than a few minutes. Already, sweat poured off of her and she found it hard to breathe the thick searing air.

The pounding stopped.

The reyaqc moved away with a grunt and a stomp.

Donald Baker stood at the door, keys in hand. He inserted the key into the lock, twisted his wrist, and then pulled open the door. "Come out of there before you suffocate."

"You said I wouldn't be harmed," shot Julia in protest.

As per usual, Donald's expression was that of a plastic mask. "You are valuable to them, Julia. Do as they say. You're less likely to be injured."

Chapter Thirty-Two

Tresset looked different, of course. It had been several years since they'd met face-to-face, and the reyaqc chieftain had had numerous infusions since that last encounter. But, like Donald, he tended to seek donors of similar facial structure and form as those of his previous givers, allowing his general "look" to remain somewhat consistent. The face was still round, the skin pale, the hair on his head dark. His lips were thin, his eyes slightly narrow, but alert and bright, displaying a keen intelligence. His nose was somewhat less angular than in previous years, and the nostrils wider. This width, along with the tawny fur about his body, feline-like incisors, and retractable claws, were derived from his sustaining species, the mountain lion.

Donald leaned his head back ever so slightly, sniffing the air. It had been a long time since he'd enjoyed the scents of a reyaqc pack. It filled him with warm nostalgia and brutal memories. As the two strolled through the compound, Donald allowed his gaze to linger on the many animal cages situated toward the southern end of the old mine. There were mountain lions, of course—for Tresset. There were two German shepherds, a half-dozen cats, a brown bear, a few wolves, some bats— and a red fox. Almost unconsciously, Donald glanced at the back of his left hand, at the small tuft of orange-red fur that had clung stubbornly through the years. A century since he'd last received animal essence, and still, despite his denials, he was at some level, a molt. The sins of the past, he'd learned, always visit the present, and most likely the future as well.

Donald inhaled once more, savoring the multitude of aromas and the tales they told. "You do understand," he said. "There was no need to imprison my companions."

Tresset did not bother to look at Donald, but continued strolling, hands clasped behind his back, nodding at various reyaqc whenever one drew near. "Dolnaraq, this is my pack. I'll run it as I please."

Donald sighed, and corrected his companion. "Tresset, my name is Donald Baker. It has been for some time now."

Tresset scoffed and spit. "Donald, yes. And before that, Matthew Greene, and before that Oskar Kohler. You pretend to be one of them, but you and I both know that it's impossible for you to ever truly connect with the humans." The reyaqc chieftain paused, staring at his lifelong comrade. "Look at you. You dye your hair in order to keep the color consistent. You wear a beard to mask the subtle changes in your facial structure after infusions. You wear colored contact lenses behind tinted glasses. I doubt you'd know your true nature if you somehow encountered it in a freak moment of authenticity." Tresset drew closer, his tone sincere, concerned. "Dolnaraq, we are old, you and I. Certainly our frequent infusions of essence have provided us the appearance of youth, but the age span of a healthy reyaqc is but one hundred thirty years—one forty under the best circumstances. Don't you think it's time you returned to your people; finish out your life's work among your own kind?"

Donald met Tresset's gaze, his eyes unblinking, his conviction sound. "I understand my role, Tresset. I am no traitor to our people. We live in a world dominated by humans. We're dependent on them for our survival. Their society thrives, and still you live in deserted mines, running what little electricity you get off of discarded generators, infusing from animals, hunting for your food. The reyaqc have the potential to be a great people, but you and those like you squander our gifts. You blame the humans for your situation, when it is within your own power to affect change."

"No, Dolnaraq. We are already a great people, as a true reyaqc defines greatness. Unlike you, we have no need to be something other than what we are."

"No need? Then why did you require me to negotiate and purchase this abandoned mining site for your pack? Without such aid, humans would have run you off as trespassers. The world has changed, Tresset. There is little unclaimed space. Land must be purchased, not just occupied. There are satellites that can spy on you from the sky. If a reyaqc pack were to occupy such a place as this with no justification or rightful claim, they would be investigated. As it is, I'm forced to give explanations for you and dozens of other packs I've assisted, telling authorities that reyaqc groups are offshoots of the Amish or some other religious order that seeks privacy. Or, such as in your case—that you're a mining company doing preliminary evaluations of the site before commencing to mine. Do you have any idea how much paperwork has been filed on your behalf, how many licenses have been acquired—how much money I and others such as I have invested?"

Tresset spat, and then resumed strolling. "You make my point for me, Dolnaraq. You think as the humans think. You confine yourself by their regulations. You even married a human—married! The reyaqc don't marry. We have no such concept. Yet, you choose to deliberately refrain from strengthening our species by fathering strong specimens for the next generation. Instead, you tie yourself to a frail human woman with whom you can never reproduce."

"You scoff at humanity while living as their leeches," countered Donald. "Not only do we infuse our very essence from their core, but even as you claim your independence from them, you utilize their inventions—those vehicles you own, the generators that power your compound, the air conditioners, the computers, the cell phones, even your paints and canvases—all stuff of humans." Donald paused before adding,

292

"As for the wife, she is dedicated to the reyaqc cause. As well, she allows me a certain social status. Her family is well connected, her father a congressman – one, I might add, sympathetic to our cause. And as to offspring, those I provided in my younger years."

Tresset nodded a subtle nod and gazed at the rock-strewn earth before him. Donald glanced to his right, noticing two fur-covered reyaqc mating, unashamed, in the midst of the populace, the male nearly suffocating the female with his weight and intensity as he served his own lust. Despite his background, Donald couldn't help but think of them as barbaric, as animals even. "The reyaqc have contributed much to human society," offered Tresset as if unaware of the sight before him. "Though, none have received due credit. Aristotle, founder of western thought and early science—a reyaqc. Peter the Hermit, instrumental in the formation of the misguided Crusades—reyaqc. Two signers of the American constitution—reyaqc. Genghis Kahn—reyaqc. Tolstoy—reyaqc. But each was forced to hide behind the mask of humanity for fear that the simple-minded humans would not understand their true nature. But you know this. You've written extensively on each of these men in your ever-so-precious *Histories*."

"What is the common element among these well-known reyaqc?" countered Donald. "None were molts. None lived in animal-like packs on the fringes of civilization. None mated in the streets like dogs. Rather, they contributed to the greater good with the hope that one day our people could come forward as equals and be accepted. Those names, those wonderful names known to both peoples of the earth will be the bridge on which we build our case. Those precious reyaqc will be the witness to humanity that we are worthy of our place."

Tresset cocked his head, offering a wry grin. "Khan was hardly what you would call civilized."

Donald chuckled. "Despite his somewhat barbaric ways, Khan established laws and was even instrumental in creating a standard written language for his people. He instigated a postal system. Even in his brutality, he was a civilizing force."

"And so will I be." Tresset withdrew his neatly folded antiseptic rag from his pocket and wiped his palms and forearms. "But I will not pretend to be human in order to accomplish my goal."

No, thought Donald. *You'll allow me to do that in your stead, and then belittle me for having the foresight to pave your way.* Aloud, he said, "What goal is that?"

Tresset's milky eyes gleamed and it seemed he stood a little straighter as he said, "An established reyaqc territory in the western United States. A recognized people. A nation unto ourselves, with our own laws, our own government."

"How do you hope to accomplish this feat?"

"Why, in the same manner humans have used for centuries—war."

Donald was astonished at his companion's temerity. Though, this, he probably shouldn't have been. Tresset had always had a bit of a god complex about him, never fully understanding—or being willing to understand—the limitations set on him by the world in which he lived. "Tresset," offered Donald, almost as if addressing a child. "The United States boasts a population of over three hundred million. The world contains over six billion humans. The reyaqc number only in the thousands worldwide—not even tens of thousands, but just thousands. Your pack, though large, numbers no more than one hundred. We are not on the brink of dominance, but rather extinction."

Tresset eyed Donald as if he was the child. "Victory no longer need belong to the largest, most well-equipped army, Dolnaraq. Look at nine-eleven. See what Al-Qaeda achieved, or what the IRA accomplished in

Ireland. A small, fiercely-dedicated force might topple a giant. You may not respect our way of life, but that makes us no less formidable."

Before Donald could respond, there came a sudden growling and scuffling from behind. Turning, he saw two adolescent males skirmishing over a slain and bloody coyote. The larger of the two, an auburn-colored molt with an extended snout and a lean muscular frame, wrestled his rival to the ground and pinned his right arm in place by clenching his jaws over the other's wrist. The other kicked and squirmed, raking razor-like talons across his opponent's back. The aggressor screeched, releasing his grip and allowing his foe to flip to his left, tossing the larger molt onto the stony dirt.

"Dolnaraq! Barthoc!" said Tresset. "Enough. You can battle over the carcass later."

Immediately, the two young reyaqc scrambled to their feet. "Yes, chieftain," said one.

"As you say," added the other, his voice winded, and blood dribbling from his back.

Tresset appraised the two nervous molts. "Dolnaraq, have you yet repaired Padnor's vehicle?"

"No, Father. Not yet," said the smaller of the two, his eyes alternating between Tresset and the dusty ground.

"Do it then."

"Yes, sir. Right away." And then they were gone, marching quickly to their right, and then around the side of a small wooden building, and out of sight.

Tresset smiled as he stared at the coyote carcass, now left unclaimed on the rocky ground.

"Dolnaraq?" asked Donald with a curious twinkle to his pallid eyes.

Tresset shrugged. "Over the decades I've sired many sons. I was running out of names. Now, Dolnaraq, why are you here? I can only keep your companions safe for so long."

"There's a rogue in Las Vegas. Four deaths and several near-deaths. There may be others of which I'm unaware."

Tresset chuckled. "A rogue, Dolnaraq. You know my opinion on rogues. They weed the human garden. You worry too much about humanity and not enough about the reyaqc."

Yes, Donald knew all too well Tresset's position on rogues. But this didn't change anything. "Until we can reveal ourselves in a controlled manner, reyaqc survival depends on anonymity. A rogue threatens our secrecy, opens us to dangerous exposure. As usual, you misunderstand my motivations."

Tresset bent and snatched a claw from the ground, perhaps half the span of a finger in length. He turned it from side to side examining it, and then slipped the piece into his left front pocket. "It's not your motivation which is in doubt, Dolnaraq, but your judgment and ultimate loyalties."

Donald hesitated for a moment, thought about his response, and then chose to remain on tack, leaving Tresset to his own biases. "The rogue. Do you have any thoughts as to who that might be?"

Tresset rose. Whatever issue he'd had concerning the claw was not something to be shared with Donald. "You want to know if anyone from this community has recently left for human civilization?" The reyaqc pondered this for a moment. Or, thought Donald, at least he made a show of pondering. With Tresset one could never be certain. So much was done for effect. Despite Tresset's accusations, Donald was not the only one who wore a mask. "There is one," offered Tresset finally. "A male. Treleq. I've known him for over fifty years, and he's always had an unhealthy infatuation with human culture. He left maybe five months ago, seeking to purge himself of animal essence and to become civilized like the great Donald Baker."

Donald ignored the dig. "Did he take willing givers?"

Tresset scoffed. "You know there are none to spare. Maybe he sought to contact other city reyaqc, perhaps to share their givers for a time. And perhaps the radical change to his physiology caused him to lose his mind. These transitions do not always end so well as you proclaim, Dolnaraq."

Chapter Thirty-Three

Julia lay on a metal cot. The thin mattress was stained yellow and brown, smelled of musty animal, and the metal frame was flimsy and ill-balanced. But she had become weary. If ever she were to flee this place, she would need her strength. But flee to where? She was in the middle of the blazing desert, conceivably a hundred miles or more from any true civilization. The heat was merciless—only the small window air conditioner lowered the temperature to merely unbearable. Should she somehow escape this madness, how would she survive? No water, no vehicle, no idea even as to the direction of the nearest town; she'd likely be dead within the first twenty-four hours.

Wiping the dusty sweat from her forehead, she allowed her head to roll to her left. Shane sat against the far wall on the unfinished wood planked floor. His eyes were closed, his head down, but he wasn't sleeping. Whenever there was a sound, his jaw tightened, his muscles flexed. Obviously, he was listening for something. Listening and thinking. But thinking of what?

Julia closed her eyes. She had plenty of thinking to do as well. The reyaqc of this compound, they were disturbing, gross, and yet, amazing. The merging of DNA between species—how was that accomplished? There were genetic defects to be sure. Even in the short time she'd been here, she'd seen disproportioned or missing limbs, malformed digits, any number of minor, and not-so-minor, deformities. But this would surely be expected from a species that collected genetic material from multiple sources. That they were viable at all was the miracle.

She knew from talking with Donald Baker that the reyaqc prefer to draw "essence" from the spine. Julia hadn't yet had the opportunity to analyze this process, but her guess was that the reyaqc drew somatic stem cells from the bone marrow. The plasticity or trans-differentiation of such stem cells might allow them to be manipulated by the reyaqc's system and to somehow be incorporated into the existing genome.

Amazing!

From a medical standpoint, Julia imagined numerous applications, envisioned cures to any number of diseases. Parkinson's, diabetes, maybe even cancer. If this strange ability to incorporate and manipulate cells could be reproduced…

Julia was stunned by the possibilities.

Julia was stirred from her contemplations as the short reyaqc, Tresset, entered the small space followed by a dust-blown Donald Baker. Two additional reyaqc remained just beyond the door. Tresset's bodyguards, she supposed.

"Julia, Shane." Donald stepped forward to the center of the room. His face was dusty, his hair in disarray, but the rubber-like skin was not reddened by the sun. "My intention was not that you should be confined. Our host is rather cautious."

Julia eased herself into a sitting position. "If that was an apology, it's not accepted. You had no right to imprison us."

Donald's nostrils flared, but his face remained impassive. She realized he no longer wore the colored contact lenses and tinted glasses. His eyes were an uneven white, like milk mixed with water. They were unnerving, inhuman. Julia had never felt comfortable with the man, and was now less so.

"Rights are an ambiguous thing," said Donald. "They fluctuate from culture to culture, year to year, even generation to generation." He turned his gaze to Shane, who still sat in the corner, forearms resting on his knees, staring at Donald through dead emotionless eyes. "Mr. Daws, it seems we have one potential suspect as to our rogue's identity. A reyaqc named Treleq. He left perhaps five months ago to live among the humans. He brought no givers."

Shane gave an almost indiscernible nod. Julia had come to realize that the man was in serious mourning. "Okay," he said through a sigh. "Any ideas on how to find him?"

Donald nodded. "Apparently, he's quite handy with machinery. We can begin by checking auto shops located near the earlier attacks. Treleq may have sought employment at one of these." He then returned his inhuman gaze to Julia. "I'm afraid you'll need to endure the blindfold again. The location of this community must remain well guarded."

Tresset stepped forward. His posture was one of confidence, arrogance even. Folding his ever-present sterile wipe cloth, and sliding it into his front right pocket, he said, "No, Dolnaraq. There will be no blindfolds. The humans are needed here."

Julia's heart leaped. She had the nearly uncontrollable urge to scream, but instead, only clenched her fists and leveled her gaze at Donald Baker.

In the corner, Shane dropped his head and muttered, "Oh boy. Here we go."

Donald showed no sign of agitation, but simply addressed his companion in an even, businesslike tone. "Tresset, I promised the humans safe travel. You have willing givers here. There is no need to take these forcefully."

"No, Dolnaraq. We have givers, but not enough. Many are faltering. Too many of us relying on too few of them."

Donald locked eyes with his companion. Neither reyaqc blinked; neither moved for several seconds. Finally, Donald spoke. "Three of my personal givers accompanied me to Las Vegas. They are university students, intelligent, healthy, and enamored with the reyaqc. I'm certain they'd consent to give."

The one called Tresset grunted. "I will accept these, of course. But we have a greater need for female donors. Yours, of course, would be male." He then moved forward and knelt before Julia, placing one paw-like hand over hers. Though his appearance was frightful, Julia once again noticed a magnetism, a charisma in his bearing. "Woman, I understand this is foreign to you. Dolnaraq informed me that you have just recently learned of the reyaqc. You most likely find us repulsive, as honestly, we often do you. But never allow yourself to doubt this one thing—we do have the right to survive."

Julia met his gaze, forcing herself to appear calm. The reyaqc's words had been gentle, respectful. But there was an underlying tone; it was difficult to interpret. Unease? No. Contempt. This reyaqc held her—held all humans—in contempt. He would be cordial only so long as it suited his needs. "How can I know I won't be killed in the process?" she asked.

Tresset offered a subtle smile and a slight nod. How very much like Donald this one was. "I give my word that we will do everything within our power to ensure your safety. Still, I make no guarantees."

With this, Shane finally came out of his haze. "Jules, you don't have to do this. Infusions don't always go as planned. Trust me, I know from experience."

Julia stared at Shane, at his troubled blue eyes, his hollow expression and his mop of white hair, and wondered to what experience he referred. She glanced at the doorway, at the two guards standing just beyond. What choice did she have? This creature wouldn't let her go. She wasn't being given an option. There were dozens of reyaqc here, and only her and Shane to oppose them. Even the human "givers" within the community would likely side with the reyaqc. No, she was trapped. The best she could hope for would be to control the circumstance in which they took her essence.

"No, Shane. If I understand Tony the Tiger here correctly, I either do this voluntarily, or have my DNA sucked from my body while I kick and scream like Mina Harker against fifteen Draculas. Of the two, I'd rather maintain what little control is left me."

"Julia," said Donald. "I had hoped for more civilized behavior from Tresset. I suppose I should have anticipated this."

Julia leveled her gaze at the red-haired reyaqc. "You've drugged me, held me captive, blindfolded me and dragged me into this hell. Why should I expect anything more *civilized* from these reyaqc?"

*****

Donald and Tresset took Shane with them when they left the small room. Apparently, there was information they wanted from Shane concerning the rogue reyaqc. Though Julia tried to relax, tried even to get some sleep, conserve her energy in this ridiculous heat, she found herself incapable of inactivity. She was terrified, plain and simple. She tried not to show this; she would show no weakness to these beasts, but every moment was a struggle to maintain composure.

Julia started. There was a knock on the flimsy wooden door— tentative, almost inaudible above the constant hiss of the window air conditioner. "Hello, Dr. Chambers," came the voice of a young woman. "My name is Minya. May I enter?"

Julia rose to a sitting position on the cot and unconsciously ran her fingers through her jet-black hair. "Do I have a choice?"

There was no response. Julia could see the girl's shadow in the crack at the base of the door. This Minya, whoever she was, shifted from one foot to the other, but remained silent. Julia had the distinct impression she was nervous, that she didn't know how to respond to Julia's caustic question. She wondered if this was one of the human "givers." Perhaps she'd come to prepare her for the taking of DNA. Julia closed her eyes, steeled herself for the coming molestation of her very being.

"Hello," came the tiny voice again. "If I am disturbing you, I can come back another time."

Julia almost accepted this offer, but no. This was going to happen. Why prolong the inevitable? Better now while she still had some small wit about her. "No. Come in. It's not like I'm going anywhere."

The door opened slowly. The girl peeked in before stepping into the room. Julia withheld a startled gasp at the sight of her visitor. This was no human servant. Minya was covered in short golden brown fur. Her nose was tiny, the nostrils upturned. Her ears were somewhat elongated, but not drastically so. She wore a brown, loose-fitting smock, and held her hands together before her ball-like belly. The girl dropped her gaze to the floor and stood just within the doorway.

"You said your name is Minya?"

The young reyaqc nodded. "Yes, Dr. Chambers. Minya."

"And you're here to…?"

"To infuse. Yes."

Julia blew air through her mouth. "Well, if you're going to suck my DNA, we might as well be on a first name basis. Call me Julia."

The girl kept her gaze to the floor. "That is kind, Dr. Julia. I hope I don't frighten you unnecessarily."

"Well, you might kill me or leave me comatose, but I'll try not to act scared. How's that?"

Still, the young reyaqc didn't meet her gaze. "Dr. Julia, obviously you don't want to do this. I will leave." She turned as if to exit.

How very unlike Donald or Tresset. How unlike her current—and very incomplete—perception of the reyaqc. "Wait," said Julia, though she didn't quite know why. "You're barely more than a girl."

The reyaqc turned back toward Julia, but came no closer.

This was not the savage creature she'd expected to find. "Listen, uh, Minya. I'm still grappling with all of this. It's a little beyond the genetics I learned in med school. Just give me a little time to process the idea."

Minya nodded, but still held the door open as if to leave. She seemed nearly as frightened as Julia.

Julia patted the mattress with her left hand. "Come here. Sit beside me. And close the door. I'd like to keep what little cool air we have indoors."

Minya nodded, smiled a timid smile, closed the door, and joined Julia, sitting beside her on the cot. "Thank you, Dr. Julia."

Julia gazed at her and offered a practiced bedside smile. The girl was trembling. Shouldn't Julia be the nervous one here? "You have animal DNA. What species?"

"The house cat, Dr. Julia—for its speed, agility, and soft coat."

Julia studied the girl. "But, my understanding is that you have no control over which characteristics you inherit."

Minya giggled and smiled. The grin was not unpleasing. In fact, despite the weirdness of her overall appearance, Julia found that Minya was rather cute. "No. we cannot choose, but we can hope."

Julia nodded. "Well, your coat does look soft and supple." She paused for a moment, and then added. "Why take an animal characteristic at all? It seems there's a heightened possibility of deformity when adding non-human DNA to the mix."

"There are several reasons," said Minya.

Despite herself, Julia found that she liked the girl.

"Most of us infuse from animals as a way of relying less on human donors. We have so few, and can only take so much without endangering them. Also, there are some advantages in hunting skills, sense of smell, ferocity. Each reyaqc has personal reasons for the choice."

Julia nodded. There was an awkward silence. The two met each other's gaze, and then Minya dropped her focus to her lap.

"So," said Julia. "I'll be honest with you. I'm terrified. A friend of mine fell into coma as a result of an infusion. After that, I saw a girl die."

Minya nodded. "There are risks, yes. But you're referring to attacks by a rogue. Such a one would take no precautions. I will be very careful. The risk is minimal."

"Will it hurt?"

Minya once again looked upon Julia. Her milk-white eyes were moist, her child-like face taut. "There will be some pain, yes."

"As I understand it, you have a bed of hollow spines on your palm."

Minya nodded. "Yes. I will infuse from the back of your neck. As the needles penetrate your spine, you will experience a burning sensation. I'm sorry."

Julia stared at the girl. She was so young, so innocent, so unlike anything she'd come to expect from a reyaqc. And yet, she might very well bring about Julia's own death. For a brief moment, Julia considered fleeing. She could easily overpower this girl. The door was now unlocked, the guards had left with Donald and Tresset. Maybe she could make her way to the Hummer.

And then what? She didn't have the keys. She had no idea where she was. Surely, dozens of reyaqc would see her as she raced through the compound. She was trapped. "Well," said Julia, an uncharacteristic quiver to her voice. "I guess we should get this over with, huh?"

Minya nodded. "That would be best." She paused, and then added, "I will make sure my unborn child learns of your generosity."

Chapter Thirty-Four

Charles Chambers had made a call to his old buddy, Hal Holmberg, at Las Vegas Metropolitan Police Department, after which Holmberg had made a series of calls, and then—finally!—after nearly three hours, he'd gotten back to Charles. "Yeah, Homely, what did you find?" said Charles as he picked up the phone.

Holmberg snorted derisively at the use of his old nickname. "You were right, Chuck. There was a suspect apprehended this afternoon near Sahara and Nellis. And, yeah, we ran his prints against those taken after the attack on the paramedic. They're a match. It looks like we can tie this guy to the string of weird murders, too. I haven't seen him myself, but from what I hear, he's a real lunatic. The mayor scheduled a press conference for three o'clock to announce the capture."

"Any idea who the guy is?"

"Nah."

"He didn't carry any ID?"

Holmberg snorted. "ID? The only thing he had on was one of those silk Hawaiian shirts. Apparently that was all ripped up and covered in blood. The guy's a real freak, Chuck. I bet he'd make Dahmer or Bundy seem stable."

"I need to see him."

"Not a chance, buddy."

Charles massaged his forehead with thumb and forefinger and closed his eyes. "Listen, Hal. This guy is somehow connected to Julia's disappearance. I've got to talk with him."

There was a sigh on the other end of the line. "You don't know that, Chuck. You don't even know for sure that Julia's actually missing. She's probably just off trying to get her head on straight."

Charles shook his head. "No," he said with some edge to his voice. "Trust me, Hal. She is missing. She's been abducted, and I've got to get to her before something terrible happens."

"Listen, all you have is a bunch of wild suppositions you've tied together based on rants from nerdy kids on the internet."

Charles felt like screaming at his old friend. He didn't have time for this. Taking a deep controlling breath, he said, "Yeah, and yet it all fits. Think about it. This guy's fingerprints match those of the patient that attacked the EMT. All of the names fit together. Julia went to meet with a Donald Baker because she thought he'd have insight into what this guy had done to her patient. The guys on the internet claim Baker came into town to find a killer rogue. They also claim he's associated with someone named Tresset Bremu. When I called Baker's hotel room, the kid who answered said Baker had taken Julia with him to see Bremu. Yes, the fringe stuff is wacky, but the core elements all fit. I'm guessing they're all connected to some crazy cult or radical movement."

"You think our guy is this rogue Baker is after?"

"Absolutely. He's probably some random cult member that flipped from some drug-induced mind control mumbo jumbo and this Baker's worried he'll expose the group for what it is."

"I don't know on that one, Chuck. Seems like you're filling in your own gaps. From what I hear about this guy, he's some kind of freak. But listen, I still can't help you. The suspect has killed a cop; he's terrorized the city. This is a big media story. The only people getting to that guy now are the DA's office and his own attorney."

*****

Charles would almost certainly lose his license over this. He'd tried more legitimate channels, had attempted to call in every favor owed in an

307

effort to be assigned as the killer's public defender. But this was a high-profile case. No judge would assign the biggest murder case of the decade to a guy who cuddled up next to a 1040 form every night. So Charles had gone the not-so-legitimate route. No one knew who the killer was. His fingerprints didn't match any within the national database. He had no identification, had refused to give his name or any other pertinent information. So, Charles made up a name for him, claiming to be the "family attorney," and demanding to see his client. He knew the ruse wouldn't hold. At some point, the man's true identity would come out and the whole charade would tumble around Charles' ankles. But, he didn't actually want to defend the guy. All he needed was to see him once, to talk with him, to find out where Baker had taken Julia. After that, the pieces would fall where the pieces fell. Charles didn't have time to waste while the system determined that Julia was actually missing. She could be in real danger, and every hour that went by was an hour that made finding her alive and unharmed less likely.

The Clark County Detention Center was a large, block-like, six-story building located in the heart of downtown Las Vegas only a couple of miles up from the northernmost part of The Strip and only blocks from the Fremont Street Experience. It was unlikely that many tourists knew how close they were to murderers and rapists, robbers and addicts, and this was probably for the best. Las Vegas was, after all, a city dependant on tourism. Upon entering the building, Charles met with some opposition. Playing dumb to the fact that his "client" had not yet revealed his name to the authorities, he'd produced his business card and requested an audience with the prisoner. Of course, he was denied.

"Look," said Charles to the jowly gray-haired desk sergeant. "My client's name is Jake Miller." He'd borrowed the name from his second cousin, an actual client should someone choose to check. "Will you please try again? I'm certain he was brought in this afternoon."

The man looked up at Charles through tired gray eyes, exhaled through his nose, and typed the name into his computer once again. "We don't have him," said the sergeant.

"Yes you do," said Charles. "Listen, this is the guy accused of the murder spree. The mayor's giving a press conference concerning his arrest in another hour. I'm the family attorney, and have been sent here by the suspect's very concerned parents to insure that my client's rights are not violated. As such, it is imperative that I consult with Mister Miller prior to the public announcement of his arrest."

The sergeant gazed at Charles for a long moment, his rheumy eyes seeming to scrutinize him. If he was anything like most law enforcement officials, he wouldn't be a fan of defense attorneys—especially one defending an alleged cop killer. "Word is your client's whacked," said the dreary man.

"Well, thank you for that astute professional diagnosis," countered Charles. "But even mentally ill suspects are entitled fair representation."

A snort, a grumble, and the sergeant picked up the phone receiver.

The battle did not end with the desk sergeant, but Charles continued to hammer his way through the hierarchy, claiming his client was entitled to meet with his attorney prior to the scheduled mayoral press conference, that his rights were being violated, and any delay could give the defense means to have the charges dismissed. The district attorney's office felt his claims were weak, but apparently not so weak as to prohibit him from seeing the prisoner. Using the press conference as a time-sensitive event had been his salvation. If the authorities had had more time to consider the situation he'd surely have been booted out and instructed never to return.

Instead, Charles now sat in a small bleak room on a molded plastic chair staring at an equally bleak room on the opposite side of Plexiglas. The air was somewhat stale and slightly chilly, which, in the Las Vegas summer, could be considered a welcome change. But Charles liked the heat; it made him feel alive, on edge. Cool air caused him to feel tight and off his game. In truth, it wasn't the air conditioning that bothered him, but rather the fact that this was taking so blasted long. Julia was missing. He was convinced she was in danger, and here he sat waiting on bureaucracy to plod along. He was fidgety, nervous. Every few seconds he looked at his watch, not so much checking the time as releasing pent up energy.

Charles rose, moved away from the counter with its clear impenetrable shield. He crossed the room, once, twice, pulled the chair out, sat, glared at his watch, and rose to repeat the process. How could he have let Julia go? If he hadn't been so stupid, if he'd been the husband he was supposed to be, she would have confided in him concerning this patient. She may have sought his legal opinion. Maybe she would have brought him with her to meet Baker. Charles was ready to scream. What was taking so long?

He turned toward the Plexiglas barrier. The door was just closing in the adjoining room.

A room that was no longer empty.

Charles couldn't help but gasp at the sight of his "client."

The man Charles had dubbed Jake Miller was no longer naked, but wore prison orange. Seeing the suspect, the way he flayed about, hopping and stalking, Charles wondered how anyone had managed to get him dressed. "Jake" was a man of about five foot ten or eleven, and was thin to the point of emaciation. There was a lump on the left side of his chest, almost as if he had one female-like breast. There were random patches of hair on his nearly bald head, one here, another there. These stuck out at impossible angles. The man's skin was pale, nearly blue. Charles could actually see the veins of the prisoner's neck and face.

The face!

The forehead sloped back as might a German shepherd's. As to the ears: one was slightly elongated—both were vaguely triangular with wiry strands of hair poking this way and that. The man's nose seemed at a loss for definition. It just seemed a blob of malformed flesh above the slightly cleft mouth. There were no discernible lips, and the mouth itself seemed to pull back into a tight grimace revealing a set of teeth, some broken, many uneven, and all of which seemed unnaturally long. The man's cheeks were mismatched. One was high and bony; the other seemed devoid of structure, as if, perhaps, there was no bone beneath.

Recovering from his initial shock at the grotesque sight, Charles stepped forward, watching the inmate lope from one end of the room to the other and back again. There was a microphone setup and he could hear the man grunt and jabber in a high breathy tone as he paced and spun and hopped. His movements were awkward, an exaggeration of the type Charles had seen with long-term drug addicts or alcoholics. But there was a strange sense of something else as well, perhaps an unusual center of gravity, the way he leaned, almost hunching. His hands were cuffed behind his back, and surely this contributed to his awkward gait. But even so, the desk sergeant's taunt, "Word is your client's whacked," rang in Charles' mind.

"Hello," Charles said, as he stood staring at the grotesquely odd man. "Hello," he repeated, this time louder and accompanied by three sharp taps to the Plexiglas.

The inmate did not respond, but simply pivoted this way and that, grunting and jabbering, spittle dangling from the corners of his mouth like a rabid dog in a Stephen King movie.

"Hello," hollered Charles once again. "I'm Charles Chambers, your attorney. I need to speak with you."

The man twirled in place three times and then sprinted toward the far wall, colliding with it at his left shoulder.

"Hey!" shouted Charles as the man resumed his pacing. "I'm your lawyer. You're being charged with the commission of several murders. Your only hope of getting out of here is through me. We need to talk."

The man blabbered something nonsensical that sounded like, "Baby gumbo Lela tock," and then spit on the tile floor, knelt, leaned forward, and rubbed his forehead in the stuff.

Charles was appalled. It was unlikely he'd get through to this guy. All of his efforts had been in vain, wasted on a dead end.

No.

He had to connect with this man, had to learn if he knew anything of Julia. "Donald Baker!" screamed Charles. "Donald Baker!"

The man paused, lifted his gaze, and glared at Charles.

"Donald Baker flew into town. He's looking for you."

In one fluid motion, the inmate leaped to his feet, marched to the Plexiglas, and pressed his face against the clear barrier, causing his nose and right cheek to spread outward like putty. It was then Charles saw the eyes. Those strange peculiar eyes. One was noticeably larger than the other. Both were round, bulging in sunken sockets. And colorless. Charles had never seen such a thing. At first he thought they were as the eyes of an albino, pink at the iris. But upon examination, there was no iris, not in any traditional sense. There were pupils, but these were small, pin-like, barely discernible, granting the man a bizarre surreal appearance. For an irrational moment Charles almost believed that this could be something other than human, but his mind was too grounded in reality to go there. The man had medical issues, that was evident, both physical and psychological. But that was the extent of it. The prisoner was as human as anyone else. He had to be, if for no other reason than that the alternative was simply unacceptable.

"Donald Baker wants to see you," said Charles.

"Donald Baker," repeated the man in a voice that should have belonged to a woman. "Dol-nar-aq." The face was still plastered against the glass, but the expression was one of… What? Wonder? Anticipation?

"I want to take you to Baker," continued Charles. "But I need your help."

"Dol-nar-aq here?" asked the man with the woman's voice.

Charles recalled the name Dolnaraq from the chat room. It was a name some attributed to Baker. "Dolnaraq's near. He's with Tresset Bremu. I need you to tell me how to get to Tresset Bremu so I can bring Dolnaraq to you."

"Tresset!" screeched the man. He then spit on the clear obstruction and proceeded to wipe his nose in the spittle with a tight circular pattern.

Okay, so apparently the man didn't much care for Bremu. "I need to find Tresset so I can Bring Dolnaraq to you." Charles had moved closer now, his face only inches from his client's.

"Tresset!" howled the man in a shrill feminine shriek. In a sudden rush of motion, he marched away, twirled in the center of the room, and sang, "Silver mine! Silver mine! Silver mine!"

At first Charles thought the inmate had lost whatever tiny thread of comprehension he'd had, but then Charles remembered something he'd read on the internet, something about Donald Baker.

Chapter Thirty-Five

Shane sat beside Julia's cot on a folding metal chair. The small window air conditioner blew his hair gently, but provided only minimal relief from the stifling desert heat. She was in a fretful sleep. Her chocolate skin had paled some, and her features seemed drawn-out and hollow. It had been six hours since the infusion and still she'd only hinted at consciousness. The pregnant reyaqc girl had returned to her own dwelling within an old mine shaft and was doing well. Now, if only Julia would come around. He hated the fact that she'd been pulled into this, that she'd been given no true choice in the matter. He understood the reyaqc's need for human essence—had actually assisted reyaqc in luring unsuspecting people into their trap—but that was a lifetime ago, and now, well, Julia had needs and rights too. Where was the consideration for the humans in all of this? He sighed, ran his fingers through his bone white hair, and stared at her. She was a brave woman. He could see that in her. Brave, beautiful, capable. He only hoped she didn't go the way of Taz.

Taz—young, energetic, quirky, curious, lively Taz.

There were some memories, some events that a man could never leave behind. Some memories could sit on a guy's shoulders like an eighty-pound backpack and remain there until he was firmly planted beneath a headstone bearing the epitaph "monster."

Shane and two of the doc's givers had folded Taz's body into a large black trunk. A bellhop had carted it out and loaded it into a Tahoe they'd rented for this purpose. They'd driven far out into the desert, well past the small town of Pahrump, Nevada, off of any main road, and then even further off of secondary arteries. Finally, they'd dug a deep pit, lowered the body in, doused it in an anonymous and highly flammable liquid the doc described as burning at five times the temperature of gasoline. Then he'd cremated his friend. The smell! Even now, Shane could smell the heavy, greasy, decaying smell of the girl's flesh, of her organs and muscles as they sizzled and popped, shriveling into blackened twists of matter, and finally disintegrating into unidentifiable ash. He doubted he'd ever free that horrid smell from his mind and constantly rubbed at his nose like a frenzied coke addict in an attempt to clear the odor from his olfactory follicles.

Taz had family—a mother, a father, and two siblings. The doc had used Taz's cell phone to text message each of these, indicating Taz had met the man of her dreams and run off to live in Europe. Shane doubted they'd believe the subterfuge, especially as months went by and there was no further word of her. And even if they did believe, Shane had to live with the fact that this girl's family would never know her true fate.

All this simply to hide the existence of the reyaqc.

Shane wiped a curled index finger across the base of his nose and wished there was some place he could buy a pack of smokes. He'd always known of reyaqc brutality. His introduction to the species had hardly been peaceful. He supposed it had always been somewhat about the danger and excitement. Always, right from the beginning, in Paris, with Gisele. But this. This! What if it happened again? What if Julia died? Would he be forced to cremate another woman? Was that to be his purpose, his contribution to the reyaqc species—body disposal?

Shane raised his eyes to the ceiling as if seeking guidance, and then returned his gaze to the unconscious woman before him. To his relief and surprise, Julia's eyes fluttered, her expression changed. She seemed to be working her jaw, grinding her teeth. Her fists opened and then closed. Another few moments and her eyes cracked open. She blinked several times, obviously attempting to bring her vision into focus.

"Hey, Jules," he smiled. "How you doing?"

"Shane?" The voice was dry, weak, nearly inaudible.

"Yeah, it's me." He paused, and then added. "I'm really glad to see you coming out of this. Seriously, you have no idea."

Julia nodded. "Did...they make you?"

Shane shook his head. "Infuse? No. The doc got me out of it. The last time I did it I nearly died. I was out of it for weeks. Something in my system, I guess. I'm just not compatible. That's what turned my hair white, you know. The infusion."

Julia lifted a hand, fished around for a lock of her own hair. Shane chuckled. "Don't worry. Your hair's still black as midnight. It's beautiful. You came through this thing, Jules. You're okay."

Julia attempted a smile, but said nothing. Even speaking seemed an awful chore.

Footsteps approached. Then the flimsy wooden door opened behind him. "How is Dr. Chambers?" asked Donald Baker as he strode across the room. Even in the blazing desert heat, he still wore his tweed jacket. Shane supposed he was making some point to his host. Surely that outfit could be comfortable to no one—reyaqc or human.

"She survived, Doc. Looks pretty zapped," said Shane.

Julia made a weak attempt at speech. "I'm...okay. I jus..."

Shane patted her on the forehead. "Take it easy, now. Rest. Don't rush it."

The doc came forward. Shane stood and moved away, allowing him to examine Julia. He lifted a penlight from his right jacket pocket and then flicked the narrow beam into each of her eyes. Next, he took her pulse by pressing his thumb against her jugular, and gazing at his wristwatch. He rolled her head to one side, examining the back of her neck, then rolled it the opposite direction and sniffed beneath her nose, gaining insight from the odor of her breath. "Mr. Daws is right," he said. "Remain prone for as long as necessary. Drink plenty of liquids."

Julia nodded her agreement, and then slipped back into a fitful sleep.

The doc probed about her abdomen, checked her legs for coloring and circulation, and then turned to face Shane. "There have been three more murders," he said. "Two of which were police officers. After which, our rogue was captured. Judging by the reports, he no longer bears a fully human appearance, though resembles no specific creature. Likely he's infused from multiple and various sources. The process would wreak havoc on both body and mind. If this has been his practice for any length of time, it may explain the mental deterioration leading to psychotic behavior."

It was then Julia began to gasp. Seemingly fighting for air, she thrashed about, legs curling up toward her belly and arms flopping uncontrollably. "Doc, she's in trouble!"

But the doc was already moving. His face impassive, but that meant very little in a reyaqc. Donald was concerned. His actions proved that. "Julia, do you hear me?" he asked as his right hand squeezed her wrist. "Pulse is erratic." He moved forward, and using his thumbs, pried her eyelids open. "Her pupils are non-responsive." His face was no more than two inches before hers. Shane saw his nostrils flare. "Julia, stay with me. Do not allow yourself to fall into sleep." He turned to Shane. "Blankets. Quickly. Prop her feet—now! Stay with me, woman. Mr. Daws, my bag. Here are the keys. Run to the vehicle. We need an I.V. Julia, look at me. Focus, young lady. Focus. Quickly, Mr. Daws. We're losing her."

Chapter Thirty-Six

It was late evening. The sun had gone down perhaps an hour before, and yet the temperature still hung close to one hundred degrees. The absence of light did little to slow the reyaqc community. It seemed nearly as many reyaqc milled about now as had during the heat of the day, perhaps more. Shane knew that some of them had enhanced night vision due to genetic traits gained from nocturnal animals, and that reyaqc in general had slightly enhanced senses in comparison to humans, but perhaps the temperature contributed as well. There were very few air conditioning units in this settlement—three that Shane had seen. Perhaps the inhabitants simply retreated to the coolness of their mine shaft abodes during the searing daylight hours.

Standing outside the small wooden building where Julia still fought for her life, Shane watched swirls of dust and sand dance across the stony ground. Using the back of his hand, he wiped sand and sweat from his forehead. The evening wasn't a comfortable one, but Shane had needed to get out of that tiny room for a while. The doc and the young reyaqc girl, Minya, were tending to Julia, and the doc had finally convinced Tresset Bremu to allow Shane the freedom to roam. He was amazed at what he saw here. Yes, he'd lived among the reyaqc, shared an apartment with them, and even loved one, but those were civilized reyaqc, humanized. Gisele and her companions didn't infuse animal essence; they didn't live an inhuman existence out away from society. True, they were different from human beings. They thought differently, behaved differently, believed differently. Most people would find them strange, off-putting, even bizarre. But still, they functioned within society. Some went to universities, some had jobs, others stole for a living, but wasn't even that a human trait? Here, very few of these reyaqc would be able to walk a street or enter a convenience store without causing a stir. Shane had seen pictures of molts and even a few poor quality videos, but aside from his one brief encounter in Paris, he'd never actually witnessed them first hand. Despite himself, despite his new-found doubts, he couldn't help but to be astonished at these strange beastly creatures. He longed for Taz in that moment, ached for her. Because he knew she'd have thrilled at this experience. And he was disheartened that he no longer felt that same exuberance. Here he was in the heart of a secret reyaqc settlement, and his thoughts kept wandering back to an all-too human, all-too frail girl and how she should have been here as well.

To the south, Shane saw almost nothing but stars and darkness. The mountains had vanished with the sun. There were few electric lights, as the entire compound was run off of generators, and there really weren't enough of those to go around. Still, the moon was three-quarters full, and bathed the area in a gentle glow. Shane could hear the caged animals at the far end of the compound as they paced about their pens voicing various grunts and growls. He smelled them as well, the warm breeze was coming from that direction and Shane was reminded of the reek of a farm or of a zoo.

A loping shadow grew before Shane. It was a young male reyaqc, perhaps ten or eleven years of age. The pup obviously bore some animal's DNA, but for the life of him, Shane couldn't determine what this might be. There were random patches of gray/brown fur about the reyaqc's naked form. One ear appeared entirely human; the other had a flap-like appearance. The fingers and toes were long, the legs willowy. It seemed the face was extended just slightly about the mouth, perhaps the beginnings of a muzzle.

The reyaqc came to a halt perhaps three feet distant, squatted, and stared at Shane. Shane, in turn, stared at the reyaqc. They remained thus for several moments, until finally the reyaqc broke the silence. "What is the city like?" he asked.

Shane sighed. Did he really want to get drawn into a conversation? He'd only stepped out to get some fresh air. But, Shane still had some of his feelings for the reyaqc. Perhaps his devotion and enthusiasm had been dampened, but he found it hard not to reserve at least a little awe for these amazing beings. "The city," said Shane. "I dunno. Crowded, I guess."

"How many people?"

Shane shrugged. "The Las Vegas valley has more than a million-five. Other cities like New York and Chicago have way more."

The young reyaqc stared at Shane for a moment, and then asked, "What does a million mean?"

Shane had to smile. How could he explain this to the boy—this pup—who had probably never seen more than a few dozen of anything in his life? He pondered for a moment, and as he did, he gazed out over the horizon and into the night sky. Out here away from the city lights, the stars were clear shimmering specks splayed throughout the black canvass of the sky. Thousands of them, it seemed. "Look up," he said.

The young reyaqc complied.

"You see those stars?"

"Yes."

"More than that."

The reyaqc pup rose from his squatting position, staring upward, his mouth agape. Slowly, he turned counterclockwise, gazing at each section of the sky, taking it all in, pondering the immensity of it all. The spell was broken by the sound of approaching footsteps. "Kyrl!" snapped a sharp, authoritarian voice. "Away. Do not pester this man."

The young reyaqc scampered away, disappearing into the darkness without another word. "Tresset Bremu," said Shane as the diminutive reyaqc marched forward, his head cocked assuredly, his expression stern. "The boy wasn't bothering me. You didn't have to run him off."

"I wasn't worried about your comfort," said Tresset. "It was that you might contaminate the pup with your tales of humanity and its superiority that concerned me."

Shane nodded. What could he say to that?

Tresset gazed up at Shane through untrusting eyes. The reyaqc must have been six or seven inches shorter than Shane, but still the young man felt as if this creature was staring down on him rather than the reverse. "I understand you lived among reyaqc."

Shane nodded, attempting to avert the reyaqc's gaze by focusing on the darkness beyond Tresset. "Yeah. In Paris. It's been over three years since I left."

Tresset snorted and pulled his cloth from his pocket to wipe his hands. "City reyaqc—like Dolnaraq. You gave essence?"

"Once. It almost killed me. I was bedridden for something like six weeks."

Tresset snorted again. His nostrils flared. "You are a weak specimen. Very little use to us. Tell me about the female. Does she recover?"

"The doc says she's stabilized, but tenuous. Her system didn't respond well to the donor process."

"The doc? You mean Dolnaraq." Tresset finished wiping his hands, and folded his cloth in quarters before returning it to his pocket.

Shane nodded. "Yeah, Donald Baker."

"Has Dolnaraq said when the woman might be able to give again?"

Shane was suddenly furious. All of the pent up emotion from the past several days seemed to rise up and there was no way he was going to hold it back any longer. Despite Tresset's off-putting appearance and dictatorial demeanor, despite his claws and dagger-like teeth, Shane could take no more. "Again?" he screamed. "She almost died! She still might. She should have never been forced into this."

The reyaqc shook his head slowly. "She volunteered. It was her choice."

"Oh, don't even go there. She had about as much choice as a Jew stepping into a gas chamber at Auschwitz. You don't know me. All you see is a human—someone different than you, and therefore lesser than you. But, I've had a love for the reyaqc. I've defended your right to survive. I've even tricked other humans into giving essence, but despite what I've done in the past, despite the need, no one should be forced into this against their own will—no one!"

The reyaqc did not flinch, nor did he rise up in rage. Rather, he moved to within inches of Shane. His breath was hot and moist. It smelled of uncooked meat. His eyes were white, emotionless, but intelligent still. When finally he spoke, his voice was firm, confident, compelling. Shane felt as if he was in this one's spell, that he had no choice but to bend to his will. "I am a reyaqc, Daws. I understand all of this on a level you could never hope to achieve. Still, I know humans well. I live in a world dominated by them. But, understand this. The pack needs female givers. The few that we have are severely depleted and need recuperation before donating yet again. By your woman giving of herself, because of her sacrifice, an unborn reyaqc now stands a chance of survival. And that chance is worth risking the life of one of the more than six billion humans on this planet."

The reyaqc chieftain then turned and marched into the night, leaving Shane alone with the millions of stars. Neither the human nor the reyaqc saw the two merciless eyes staring at them from behind a teetering storage shed.

Chapter Thirty-Seven

Charles Chambers leaned into the sharp, nearly invisible cutback, which was illuminated only by his single headlight. His lime green 2009 Kawasaki Ninja ZX roared and grabbed the road despite the loose gravel splayed across the searing asphalt. Charles' mouth was dry, his lips cracked, and his face – despite his full-face helmet—riddled with sand. He worried about fuel. He'd passed Cactus Range, Golden Arrow, Tybo, and all other remotely populated areas far behind. Sure, the bike got better than sixty miles to the gallon, but the tank only held 4.5 gallons. He was now off of anything resembling a major thoroughfare and was flying down unlit rural back roads and sometimes dirt pathways in search of an abandoned silver mine owned in part by Donald Baker.

One of the fanatics on the reyaqc-themed website indicated that Baker often invested in property for reyaqc communities. When Charles' "client," the rogue, began chanting the words "silver mine," Charles phoned his assistant and asked her to research Baker's name in relation to any silver mine holdings in Nevada. The research had taken longer than anticipated. There were several "front" corporations and layers of diversion to muddle through, but in the end the connection had been found. Now, aided by his BlackBerry Smartphone's Global Positioning System (GPS), Charles was racing through the ink black night toward the site, hoping against hope that his street bike could handle the increasingly rocky terrain, and that once he arrived, Julia would be alive and unharmed.

He knew he was asking for a lot. But, he was an attorney. That's what he did for a living.

Chapter Thirty-Eight

Julia blinked. Her eyes were dry as was her mouth. Working her tongue, she attempted to produce saliva, but was for the most part unsuccessful. It seemed her body could not generate enough liquid. From a medical standpoint, this was confusing. Over the past several hours, she'd consumed copious amounts of water, produced very little urine, and had no noticeable sweat. Where had the liquid gone? She wasn't bloated. She felt none of the typical symptoms of over hydration—she wasn't confused or inattentive; she had no paralysis, no rapid breathing or vomiting, no shouting or delirium. She hadn't taken her blood pressure, so couldn't know if that was elevated, but her sense was that it was not. As such, she could only conclude that she was not over hydrated, so once again—where had all the liquid gone?

She blinked again, attempting to moisten her eyes, then sighed and stared at the uneven lines of the ceiling. She'd been in and out of consciousness for the past several hours. Initially, Donald Baker tended to her, but for the past two hours, she'd been alone with the young reyaqc woman, Minya. The girl had a sweet and caring disposition. Despite the circumstances, Julia couldn't help but like her.

There was a coolness, almost a tickling sensation on Julia's legs. Tilting her head up with some effort, she glanced down to see the girl rubbing some sort of gray/green paste below her knees and down toward her ankles.

"Minya," she said through a dry and raspy throat. "What are you doing?"

The girl smiled. "It's an herb compact, Dr. Julia. The mixture is believed to help stabilize your system."

Julia allowed herself a weak chuckle. "Well, I certainly wouldn't want my system unstable." Though, to herself she thought everything else in her life was instable, why not her system? "How's the baby, Minya? Healthy?"

"Kicking," smiled the reyaqc girl as she rubbed the last of the salve into Julia's leg and then picked up a frayed green dishtowel and wiped her hands.

"That's a healthy sign," said Julia. "When are you due?"

"Two months."

Julia began to ask her how long a reyaqc's pregnancy typically lasted, but it was then that the lights and air conditioning went out. Five seconds later there was a horrible scream followed by shouts and clamoring. Minya's ears twitched, her nose flared, she stood rigid for only a moment and then she was beside Julia, whispering in her ear, and tugging at her arms. "Hurry, Dr. Julia. We must flee downwind."

Rising unsteadily to a sitting position, Julia mumbled, "Why? What's going on?"

"Raid. Now, hurry. Stay with me."

Did she say "raid?" What kind of raid? Had the police somehow found out about her abduction? Had some authority learned of the reyaqc community and now attempted to round them up? "What do you mean, raid, Minya? What's happening?" Julia's head swam. This sudden movement was unsettling.

"Another reyaqc pack, Dr. Julia. Please, we must get downwind before they find us."

Julia had dozens of questions. Why would one reyaqc pack attack another? Were they in some kind of war? What would happen to her if captured? But she understood that she could ask none of these now. In truth, just standing upright was challenge enough. Minya pulled her forward, cracked the door open, and sniffed at the night air. Julia could now hear the sounds of steady conflict—harsh guttural growls, the thuds and scuffles of hand-to-hand combat, the shrieks of agony.

"There is a small shed about fifty feet to our right," whispered Minya. "Just beyond that is a pile of discarded wooden pallets. We'll move first to one and then to the other. Once we feel it safe to move again, we'll climb the hill behind the woodpile. If we get separated, find the metal tracks leading out of the mine. Follow those into the cave entrance and keep going as deep as you dare. It will be utterly dark. You'll need to feel your way. But do it anyway. It might be your only hope."

Julia scanned the night, but saw little more than the occasional shadowy form race one direction or another. Still, she could hear the fighting, could hear the barked orders and quick military-like responses. "Why?" she asked in a stark whisper, "What will they do to us if we're caught? What do they want?"

Minya turned toward Julia, her expression firm, her face seeming years more mature than it had only two minutes before. "Me, they will use for breeding and sport; you, as a giver, and not gently. Most likely, four or five females would take your essence in the space of a day. You wouldn't survive. Now, come. We have no time."

With that, Minya tugged Julia's hand and they were through the doorway, slinking between ramshackle buildings. Julia's head seemed to sway this way and that in sloshing waves. Her legs quivered and she seriously wondered if she had the strength to make it the few dozen feet to the next structure, much less up the side of a steep, rock-strewn foothill. Slipping behind a small wooden hut, Julia bent, placing her palms on her knees for support, and gasped in huge gulps of the hot night air. Waves of nausea assaulted her and she closed her eyes, willing herself not to vomit.

Moments later, when Julia had temporarily stayed the rising bile, she opened her eyes to see Minya standing tense, her back slightly arced, her head tilted back, and her nose flaring. "Do you see them?" whispered the reyaqc girl.

Julia squinted, staring into the darkness of the foothill rising behind the building. She didn't have Minya's cat-like eyes. All was black with only sporadic slashes of gray. "I don't see anything."

"They hide about three quarters of the way up the slope—a secondary raid party. Their purpose is to capture or kill any who seeks to flee. We'll need to find another way."

There was a sudden crash and clatter. Julia turned to see two reyaqc, both beastly, both naked, not twenty feet away. One had thrown the other against the small mountain of discarded wooden pallets and now thrust his face into the base of the other's neck, ripping and tearing. The pinned reyaqc clawed at his attacker's back but the other merely intensified his attack.

"Come," said Minya. "We must keep moving or the raiders will catch our scents."

A commotion erupted from a large, corrugated, building to the north. Flames shot out of the few small windows and smoke seeped through the arched roof. There were shouts and screams, roars and howls. "They're setting fire to the settlement," shouted Minya as she grabbed Julia's hand and pulled her toward the south. "This is how they drive inhabitants out for the slaughter. Hurry! Run for the animal cages. Our scents may be lost to the raiders as we get close to the beasts."

Julia did as she was told, still fighting nausea and quite possibly un-consciousness, she willed herself forward, slinking along a jagged row of small structures that lined the east side of the compound. But she doubted they could make it to the far side of the place. There were only sparse buildings to hide behind. Much of the area was wide open and barren. Chaos erupted on all sides. A barn-like building to the west was now engulfed in flames. Julia saw forms grappling with one another, could hear the slashing and rending of flesh, the agonized cries of the dying. No matter which direction she turned, shadowy reyaqc raced about tumbling and fighting. Torches bobbed in the night as raiders went from building to building igniting the compound. The hot desert air became heavy with glowing soot. It was nothing short of pandemonium.

Julia's stomach twisted. She gasped, fell to her knees. Nausea overtook her like a thundering wave against a worn and rotting dock. She leaned forward, palms flat upon the gravel-strewn ground, vomiting like a dog that had eaten chicken bones. She heard Minya's frantic voice as the girl urged her to rise. Julia lifted a hand, waving her forward, but the young reyaqc came back for her.

The assailant seemed to rise up out of the night, his powerful body glowing reddish yellow in the flickering firelight. The reyaqc's forehead was domed, his face sweeping into a long muzzle, and framed by shots of short wiry hair. The eyes were round, as were the black-furred ears. The arms were broad and seemed perhaps more powerful than the legs. Julia tried to scream a warning through her horrific retching, but it was too late. The thing swiped a claw across Minya's back, sending her sprawling to the ground.

"No!" cried Julia as she launched from the ground, heedless of the spasmodic jerks still racking her form. Grabbing a softball-sized rock, she hurled it at the thing, striking it on the left shoulder.

It turned, growled, and then grinned. "A human female," it said. Its voice was low and beastly.

Still dizzy, Julia turned to flee. The thing laughed, but didn't follow as she'd hoped it would. Instead, it turned its attention back to Minya, who was still writhing on the ground. Julia cursed. The girl was pregnant, injured. Julia had wanted to draw the beast away. Minya screamed as Julia reached the tall mound of discarded wooden pallets where two reyaqc had battled just minutes before. Quickly, she found a broken pallet, pulled a plank free with a sharp crack. Two rusted nails protruded from the far end.

Minya clawed and kicked as her assailant dragged her across the stony ground. Julia's first strike connected with the reyaqc's right cheek. The nails first punctured the skin, and then ripped it as Julia followed through like a major league slugger. The reyaqc twirled and roared, but Julia was already into her second swing. This one connected with the upper chest. Julia tried to pull the board free for a third blow, but the frenzied reyaqc ripped it from her hands, heaving it to the ground.

Before the assailant could advance on Julia, Minya launched onto its back, her long claw-like nails penetrating his upper chest, her legs wrapping around his torso, and her sharp, needle-like teeth ripping at the exposed flesh of his neck. The reyaqc twirled and flailed, his arms reaching wildly back in a crazed attempt to dislodge the young girl. But his limbs were too thick, too inflexible to find the mark. Retrieving her fallen weapon, Julia clubbed the beast on the side of the head again, again. Each time the nails shredded more flesh. She heard the awful popping as an eyeball burst. Still, she struck him yet again. Now he staggered. Minya bit deeper. Julia drew her arms back and swung with all her might. "Go directly to hell. Do not pass Go. Do not collect two-hundred dollars, freak face!"

The blow connected with a sickening crack. The reyaqc toppled backward, landing squarely on Minya, who shrieked in pain. Dropping the wooden plank, Julia grabbed a now-limp arm of the unconscious reyaqc, and with three sharp tugs, pulled him off of the girl. Minya gasped, her eyes wide. Blood and water poured from between her legs drenching her simple brown smock. "Dr. Julia!" she shrieked. "The baby! The baby!"

Chapter Thirty-Nine

At the faint sound of the first strike, Tresset Bremu rose from his seat, ears twitching and nose flaring. "Dolnaraq," he said. "It seems you've distracted me from a much larger problem than a single rogue terrorizing a human city."

The doc rose as well, also sniffing at the air. "Who are the intruders? What's the situation?"

"Bytneht Noavor, a young upstart chieftain. I found a claw earlier and recognized it as from a jackrabbit molt. Bytneht uses these as spies because they hear well and flee quickly. I have anticipated this assault, but apparently misread the timing." The lights went out then, along with the air conditioning. Immediately, Tresset marched through the doorway, barking orders to his pack, the doc following at his heels.

Stepping through the doorway, Shane saw Tresset stride into the darkness, calling out names, ordering reyaqc into predetermined positions. There was a certain glee to his voice as the first sounds of battle ensued. Shane's gut tightened. What kind of lunatic got off on the slaughter of his people? He'd heard of pack raids, read of them in Donald Baker's *Histories*. They could be brutal things.

No, not could be. They were outright savage—always.

The raiding party would seek to kill all males, for they wanted no further opposition from the pack. The females were dragged away to be passed among the ranks. They would find a place in the new pack as breeders, little more than slaves, but at least they would live. The human givers would be treated similarly. Shane's only small encouragement was that these reyaqc packs shunned the use of weapons. It was a matter of pride that these death battles be done hand-to-hand. The only exception was the use of fire as this drew the sleeping community out of their homes and into the fray.

Stepping forward, Shane grabbed the doc just above an elbow. "We've got to get Jules and get out of here. If we're captured, they'll drain us both till we're dust."

The doc nodded absently. "You have the keys to the Hummer. Get Julia. Take her away. I'll contact you in the morning." He paused. "That is, assuming I've survived."

"Come with us. This isn't your fight."

The doc shook his head slowly. "There you are wrong, Mr. Daws. This is very much my battle. If ever the reyaqc are to rise above savagery, if ever we are to escape extinction, these petty slaughters must cease. I hope to be a voice of reason amidst insanity. Now, go. Julia is in peril. Get her away—the young pregnant molt, Minya, as well." He turned, vanishing into the darkness. It was the last time Shane would see Donald Baker.

Clinging to the shadows, Shane slipped quietly around the low narrow building housing Tresset's office. The hut where Julia rested was not too far distant, but he needed to be cautious. The reyaqc had keen night vision and sense of smell. Shane was at a distinct disadvantage and could be of no help to Julia if he was captured or killed.

Figures raced in every direction; reyaqc rolled about the rocky ground clawing and biting at one another. There was a loud whoosh from the north. Shane turned to see a large corrugated building ablaze. Flames and smoke shot out from the windows and doorway. Reyaqc raced from the inferno into the waiting mob.

Shane sprinted to the next building; a small shed similar to the one occupied by Julia. Hers was now the next to the south. Glancing in each direction, he made his way to his intended destination and peeked around the front of the hut. The door was closed. There was a rush of activity to his right, but he couldn't distinguish the action. Another building went up in flames. Already, the air tasted of bonfire. Five quick steps and Shane slipped around the corner and in through the unlocked door.

Empty.

Now what? Where had Julia gone? Had she been caught? Shane cursed himself. If on their first meeting he hadn't encouraged her to seek the doc's help, she never would have become involved. If she died it would be his fault. Hearing the harsh sounds of battle, Shane wondered how he had ever found the reyaqc romantic or noble. Had he been so blinded by the mysteries of this race that he'd failed to see the reality of their condition? How could he have been so gullible?

Loneliness, he supposed. A need to belong. He wondered how many were led down similar paths of destruction by these simple human desires.

But, Julia?

Where to find Julia.

None of this was her fault. Unlike Shane, she wasn't a willing participant in the matters of the reyaqc.

There was a sharp thud at the side of the building, growls, the sounds of battle. Two figures snarled and slashed just beyond the doorway. And then, abruptly, there was a soft thud and the brawl was at an end. Who had been the victor? One of Tresset's molts, or the invader? If it was an assailant, Shane was likely in serious trouble. He stood silent, breath held, eyes focused on the thin wooden door. What should he do if a raider came through the doorway? He had no weapon and doubted his strength would equal that of a battle-tested reyaqc.

Five more seconds, now ten. Shane released his breath in a slow silent stream and then inhaled with similar care. Was the victor still beyond the door? He hadn't heard departing footsteps, but reyaqc could be stealthy.

A sound.

Had the handle just turned?

Shane swallowed. His fists clenched. And now, yes, the knob was turning, the door swinging open.

A great form moved confidently into the room. The reyaqc must have been six-five, three-fifty, with the bulk and form of a brown bear. As the molt bared its teeth and stepped forward, Shane grabbed the only possible weapon available—the cot on which Julia had lain. It was awkward but, having an aluminum frame, not heavy. Holding it before him like a shield, he charged the startled molt, hitting him just above the waist. The charge did not harm the reyaqc. It didn't even cause him to step backward or lose his footing. But it had surprised him. As the roaring molt tossed the cot aside, Shane raced through the doorway, turned right, and then right again, racing into the darkness, away from the compound, and toward the foothills bordering the eastern side of the settlement.

Shadowed forms loomed above, blocking his escape, advancing on him even as he made the incline. Over half of the complex was ablaze and numerous eyes glowed an eerie yellow-white in the flickering firelight. Shane cut right, racing along the eastern slope. Footsteps loomed close behind. His left foot connected with a low-lying shrub, he nearly tumbled forward, but righted himself at the last. He had no choice. To stumble now would mean to die. Veering west, he darted between two small structures and onto more level ground. There came a horrific howl from behind. Shane cut left and rolled just as a dark form lunged to where he had been only a second before.

A piercing sound rose above the cacophony of battle. Something familiar, yet too faint to distinguish. There it was again. Even as he raced across the uneven ground, he cocked his head to the left. There were two shapes, just to the southwest. Was that Julia and the young reyaqc girl, Minya? It seemed the girl was in labor with Julia crouching over her to deliver the pup. But even this momentary distraction was catastrophic.

Shane felt warm breath beside his throat, and then there was a sharp puncture and ripping.

Chapter Forty

"Shane!" cried Julia, though it was doubtful he could hear her amidst the screeches and howls of battling reyaqc. He'd appeared from between two buildings, racing as if the devil himself was at his heels. And the demon lord might well have been, for three dark and savage forms bounded after him. They would be atop him in seconds, maybe less. "Shane!" she shouted again, but then stopped herself mid-cry. To distract him was to kill him. Though, truthfully it seemed the outcome was a given.

His head snapped in her direction—only for a moment. There was recognition. But then the nearest aggressor was upon him, its jaw clamped tightly to Shane's neck. There was no cry of pain, no prolonged struggle. The two simply tumbled to the rock-strewn ground, rolled twice, and came to a halt. The reyaqc leaped to his feet, felt about in his mouth as if picking something from his teeth, and then rejoined his companions. Shane lay motionless in the dirt, a dark puddle spreading beneath him.

Julia's heart thundered. Shane was her only human connection to the outside world, the only one who, like herself, might seek to flee this madness. Even more, despite his connection to Donald Baker, she suddenly realized this was someone she might one day have called friend. They'd developed something of a bonding during their confinement. He might not yet know it, but Shane was a man of character, someone with a deep and caring heart, and a desire to do what was right. Julia patted Minya on the cheek, whispering that she'd return in a moment, and then, keeping low, Julia managed an uneven jog to where Shane lay. Her head swam, her vision dimmed, and it seemed she might pass out from the exertion. But somehow she made the trek and knelt beside Shane. The damage was bad. Already, he'd lost significant blood. There were several jagged wounds about the area of the carotid triangle. At least three of these were critical. A sharp curved razor-like tooth, perhaps three inches in length, protruded from his neck just beside the subclavian artery. Julia was hesitant to remove this for fear she might release another flood of bleeding. He was in and out of consciousness, his breathing labored. Even with proper medical care, it was unlikely he'd survive more than minutes. Still, Julia kicked into trauma mode: applying pressure, assessing vital signs.

And then Minya cried out in pain.

Reality.

Even in the flickering firelight, Julia could see a fresh flood of blood gush from the reyaqc girl. Her body shuddered and bucked. Julia glanced down at Shane's still form. Basic triage. The choice was really no choice at all, or so the textbooks would tell her. Shane was too far gone to mend. But Minya and her unborn child—these, Julia could at least hope to save. In an almost indiscernible whisper, Julia leaned forward and said, "I'm sorry, Shane." With one last sorrowful glance at the dying man, she returned to her duty.

Minya was gasping, her breathing labored, her contractions sharp and uneven. The blood loss was astounding. Julia didn't know reyaqc physiology, but most mammals were similar in the birthing experience, and this was obviously an emergency situation. "Hang in there, Minya," urged Julia as she wiped Shane's blood from her hands onto her pants and repositioned herself between the young mother's legs. "Don't fall asleep. I need you with me through this."

Minya nodded with a grimace, but remained silent. Her eyes fluttered. It seemed she strained to maintain consciousness. To the west, a flaming building succumbed, collapsing in upon itself. Reyaqc ran to and fro, seemingly oblivious to the life and death scene just a few yards distant.

Or perhaps, Julia and Minya offered no threat, and thus could be attended to later.

Uneasy that she was not remotely sterile, Julia pressed Minya's legs further apart, reached inside the girl, and muttered a string of syllables, which may have served as a curse or a prayer. The child was a footling breech, both feet presenting. To complicate matters further, the umbilical cord was prolapsed, the umbilical vein obstructed. The risk was that the fetus would continue to pump blood out of the placenta, while getting nothing in return, causing hypoxia and hypovolemia—shock from decrease of accessible blood volume. Immediate delivery was a necessity. If Julia didn't get the baby out of the mother now, she'd likely lose them both.

Delicately, and with great skill, Julia reached deeper, clasping the cord between her thumb and index fingers. She felt the soft throb of the child's pulse, but it was weak, erratic. Carefully, Julia endeavored to reposition the child, but with no success. The fetus was too far down the birth canal to maneuver, was lodged tight, and in such a position as she could not extract the child vaginally.

Julia heard a loud crackle and only then realized that the structure nearest her—perhaps thirty yards distant—was now ablaze. Already, the increased heat seared the air. Sweat dripped off of her brow and onto Minya's swollen abdomen. The girl gazed at her through gritted teeth, her white featureless eyes fearful and moist. "Dr. Julia, my baby?" Her voice was weak, pained. It was obviously a great effort to utter even these few words.

Extracting her hands from the birth canal, Julia inched closer to Minya's head. "Can you hear me?" she asked.

The young reyaqc girl nodded as she gritted her teeth at the onset of yet another brutal contraction.

"There's a problem," said Julia. "The baby is facing the wrong way. It's stuck and I have no means of moving it forward. The umbilical cord is prolapsed. No fresh oxygen is getting to your child. It's imperative we birth now if the baby is to survive."

"My baby!" gasped the girl.

Julia sighed and nodded. "This gets worse, Minya. I need you to listen very carefully. The baby's only hope is that I perform a cesarean section. That means I'll cut here and pull the baby out through the opening." Julia drew a line with her finger just above the girl's pubic bone. "Minya, I have no anesthesia to diminish the pain."

The girl looked at Julia through moist child-like eyes. "I will deal with the pain, Dr. Julia. Rescue my baby."

Julia nodded, drawing in a long breath. "Minya, I have no medical supplies. I have no way to suture you back together. You've already lost an amazing amount of blood. That combined with the shock the cesarean will cause to your system…" Julia hesitated. "Minya, there's very little chance you'll survive."

The girl stared at Julia, apparently processing the information. "If you do not perform this ce-ces…?"

"Cesarean section," offered Julia. "If not, your baby will most certainly die, and likely you as well. I'm sorry, Minya, but there's very little choice."

Minya nodded and clasped Julia's hand. Her childlike face was pale and fearful. Her lips quivered as she spoke. "Save my baby, Dr. Julia."

"I'll do everything I can, Minya. I promise." Julia paused for just a moment and then asked. "The baby's father, who is he? I'll need to bring the baby to him." Though, Julia wondered if the father was even still alive at this point. The entire compound now seemed strewn with bodies.

"Dolnaraq," said the girl. "Dolnaraq is the father."

"Dolnaraq?" Wasn't that the name Tresset Bremu used when addressing Donald Baker? "You're saying Donald Baker's the father?"

Minya forced a weak smile that quickly transformed into a grimace of pain. "No," she said through clenched teeth. "Tresset Bremu has a son named Dolnaraq. It is he. But, the baby will need a mother. The males, they teach the young to fight and to hunt, but they don't tend to their needs."

Julia understood. In this society that would seem natural. "Then who?" she asked. "Who should get your baby?"

"You, Dr. Julia. Raise her. Teach her."

"Her? You already know the gender?"

Minya shook her head. "Reyaqc are born without gender. They require an infusion soon after birth. This initial infusion determines the sex."

"You want her to infuse from me?"

Minya nodded. Her skin was losing color, her features seemingly less defined.

"You want me to adopt her as my own?"

Minya nodded again, but was suddenly racked by intense pain. There was another surge of blood. "Minya, I've got to perform the procedure. We're running out of time."

A tear escaped the corner of the girl's eye, and yet she tried to be so brave. "Promise me, Dr. Julia. Promise you'll take care of my baby."

Julia met the girl's pleading gaze and nodded. Despite Minya's odd appearance, Julia now knew within the deepest recesses of her being that this girl was as human as any person on the planet. "Yes, Minya. I'll take care of your baby." This promise, made so hastily, with no time for consideration, terrified her more than anything had in her entire life. But somehow, deep within, Julia knew it was right that she raise this child, this pup, not even human, as her own.

She had no scalpel, but already she'd come to a solution. Racing across the rocky ground, she came once again upon Shane. He was dead now, but Julia had no time to mourn. Quickly, she withdrew the sharp, curved tooth from his neck and wiped the blood from it with her shirttail. Yes, it was as she'd remembered it, thin and very, very sharp. It might cut almost as well as a razor blade. Retuning to Minya, she sliced some fabric from her sleeve and wrapped this around the base of the tooth creating a makeshift handle. This would be an awkward instrument, but Julia believed she could manipulate it adequately.

Moving into position, Julia said, "I'm ready to proceed, Minya. This is going to hurt terribly. I'm sorry."

Minya nodded. It seemed she might be trying to think of some brave final words, but nothing presented itself. Julia gave her a quick squeeze of the hand and went to work, making a small horizontal incision in the skin just above the pubic bone. Minya screamed and writhed, but Julia sought to steady her with her left hand, while cutting with the right. The tooth was sharp, and cut the tissue well enough, but the cuts were more jagged and uneven than had Julia used a scalpel. Still, it would need to suffice. Now she was slicing through the underlying tissue, gradually working her way to the uterus. Still, Minya screamed, but these seemed weaker, less frantic. Wiping sweat from her brow, Julia then separated the abdominal muscles with her fingers. This caused her some difficulty, and she wished for clamps—and while she was at it, a whole surgical team along with a sterile environment to boot.

Julia found it necessary to make two insignificant cuts in the musculature in order to achieve the space required to work on the uterus. Minya bucked again, causing Julia to drop the tooth. Quickly, she retrieved it, wiped it once again on her shirt, and then proceeded to make a low transverse incision. Minya was almost entirely quiet now and Julia almost wished for the bucking and screaming. Somehow, some impossible way, she hoped against all logic that the girl would come through this alive.

Julia reached into the uterus, found the child, curled her fingers about it and gently pulled it free of its mother's womb. The child was a strange looking thing. The nose was nothing more than two slits above a lipless mouth. There were no ears, but rather small crescent-shaped holes on each side of the head. The skin was a transparent blue, wrinkled and cold, the eyes tiny and colorless. Julia moved to present the child to Minya, but the girl was dead, her pale white eyes staring sightless into the smoke-filled sky. Julia was surprised to find she was crying. She was a medical professional, an emergency room physician. She'd lost patients before. But this girl, this precious young girl, caught amidst this insanity. It seemed so unfair.

Then there was a voice. That all too familiar voice that in no way belonged in this place. And it was panicked, frantic even as it called her name.

It was then Julia realized she was under attack.

Chapter Forty-One

Charles Chambers came upon the reyaqc settlement from the north. Though it had probably been something less than two hours, it seemed he'd been traveling for days—racing through the dusty desert, winding down forgotten roads, squinting into the night for fear he might miss a sudden turn and go tumbling off of some cliff or embankment. Fuel had been a concern as well. He still had some, he was sure of that, but definitely not enough for the return trip. Now, gazing down upon chaos from the crest of a rise, he wondered what his wife had stumbled into.

As expected, it was an old silver mine. Most of the few remaining structures seemed decades old and in need of repair. But nearly half of the compound was ablaze. Shadowy forms ran from building to building, igniting them with torches. Figures darted this way and that: fighting, brawling, slaying. Bodies, both dead and near-dead, littered the ground and it seemed there was no near conclusion to the scene.

Julia was down there—somewhere. He was sure of it.

How was he to find her? Did she still live? The only thing he could think to do was to ride into the madness and search. If he found her, he'd throw her onto the back of his bike and put as much distance between them and this place as possible. If they ran out of gas, well, he had his cell phone. He'd call Triple A.

So Charles slipped the Ninja into gear and followed the uneven dirt road into the compound. He found it difficult to accept the scene before him. These were not human beings racing about, fighting, setting the place ablaze. These were something else, some monstrous race of half-beasts.

Reyaqc.

He remembered the term from the web sites. But that had been pure nonsense.

But it hadn't.

Donald Baker had proved to be real. So had Tresset Bremu. Each was named on legal documents connecting them to this place. The inmate had been real as well. Those strange white eyes—the same eyes he now saw all about him—had been real. The elongated teeth had been real. The strange loping gate. The fur-like shots of hair. Oh, he'd been strange looking, true. But Charles had never once—not seriously at least—considered that the man was anything but human.

Charles motored past a forest green Hummer on the northernmost edge of the compound and wondered if this belonged to Baker. There was a metal building ablaze to his left and two wooden structures to his right likewise engulfed in flame. These were now nothing but ruined frames. Charles shuddered as he recognized the odor of burning flesh. A naked figure raced by, its hunched form covered in blood-matted fur. Its snout seemed canine, though its anatomy was more or less human. Another shadowy form loomed ahead. It rose to upright, the severed arm of its fallen foe clutched in its taloned hand, its muzzle rife with red pasty matter. Charles veered left, accelerating as best he could on the loose sand and gravel surface. He had no desire to come within reach of that thing. A flaming form bolted from the left, shrieking a haunting screech of pure agony and impending death. "Dear God," whispered Charles as he continued forward. He had no idea if there was anything he could do for the fiery figure and feared attack should he stop to help.

Now, slowly moving along the east side of the compound, he scanned the grounds, hoping against all odds that he could find Julia alive and unharmed amidst the insanity. Smoke hung in low wispy billows and glowed orange in the firelight. Tilting his visor back so he could be heard when shouting Julia's name, he immediately felt the sting of burning ash upon his cheeks. "Julia!" he cried into the fiery night. "Julia! Where are you?"

A figure stepped out before him. Charles maneuvered to his right, but found another beast coming at him from that side as well. A glance to the left and he knew he was surrounded. With no hesitation, Charles gunned the throttle, aiming for the space between the two forward-most reyaqc. But instead of evading his charge, the beast to the right came directly on him, head lowered like a linebacker. The reyaqc connected at Charles' ribcage just above mid-chest. For a fraction of an instant, Charles dared believe that he may remain upright, but then the tires slid out from under him and he hit the ground hard, his helmet taking the brunt of the impact, a sharp pain shooting through his left shoulder.

The thing dove upon him—its face! This beast was nothing resembling human. Its jaw was long and narrow, nostrils wide and flaring, its ears slender and tapered. And it had horns. The type one might see on a ram. No, these were nowhere near the size, but the general shape and look was the same. The thing pummeled him in the gut causing Charles to curl into a tight ball. Then it tugged at his helmet, most likely wishing to rid the thing so as to attack the face or head. He had only seconds to act—or seconds to die—Charles fumbled a hand into his right jacket pocket and withdrew a tiny Glock .40 caliber M-27. He'd only used the pistol once, on a firing range just after he purchased it for protection. But at this short range, he didn't think he'd have much difficulty hitting his target.

The beast struck again. Charles fumbled the pistol, his fingers dancing in an effort to control the thing. No! This was his only hope. He couldn't let it go so easily. He caught the handle, but tentatively. The beast smacked him across his helmeted face. Once again, the gun bobbled. Charles' heart raced. Somehow retaining his grip, he managed to flip the safety and to then press the small barrel into his assailant's abdomen. The report was a muffled pop. At first Charles wondered if the Glock had fired at all. Yes, he'd felt the recoil. Yes, there'd been a sound, however muted. But the reyaqc continued to pound at him. Just as Charles was about to squeeze the trigger again, the reyaqc stiffened as if only now coming to the realization that it had been shot. Its pallid eyes went wide, its too long jaw dropped open. Using the butt of the pistol, Charles slammed his right hand into the side of the beast's face, causing it to tumble off of him to the left. Now he saw the tiny hole in the abdomen, the seared flesh, the spreading crimson ooze across the lightly furred belly.

Holding the Glock out before him, he rose unsteadily to his feet, his side burning, and his gut feeling like recycled mashed potatoes. The other two reyaqc obviously recognized the gun for what it was, and backed away, retreating into the night without sound or threat. Charles released a sigh. He was far from an expert shot. If both reyaqc had chosen to charge, he doubted he could have felled even one of the two.

With an eye out for further attackers, Charles glanced at his Ninja. Lying only a few feet away, the motor still hummed. Quickly, Charles marched to it, killed the engine, and then pocketed the key. He couldn't ride the bike and hold the gun. Right now, the gun seemed the better choice. Once he'd found Julia, they could return to the bike. As well, Charles removed his helmet, setting it beside the Ninja. That thing, though offering some protection in the event of an attack, could be a hindrance.

My God, how was any of this possible?

Charles scanned the area, still trying to comprehend the scene. All around, voices belted out orders; small groups rushed one way or another, engaging other similar groups in hand-to-hand combat. The battles were fierce and bloody. But one thing brought a wry grin to Charles lips. It seemed he was the only one to bring a gun to the party. He squeezed the

345

thing, felt the forward cant of the grip in his palm, admired the military matte finish. He had only eight rounds left. But eight rounds might cause sufficient fear amongst these unarmed beasts for two humans to escape into the night.

An uneven row of small huts and sheds sat off to his left and to the south. Several had been set ablaze, and bobbing torches moved in his direction. Though his side stabbed with burning pain—he was convinced now that he'd broken a rib in his tumble from the bike—Charles jogged forward, threw open the door to the next shed and, gun held at the ready, peeked inside. Empty. He decided to repeat the process, hopefully staying ahead of the fire starters. There was a fierce cracking sound to the west and Charles turned to see a large wooden building collapse in upon itself amidst hungry flames.

"Julia!" he cried as he went from one building to another. "Julia!"

Now someone had begun setting fires from the south, heading north. Charles could only pray Julia was not in one of these. She was an intelligent woman. Surely she'd realized what was happening and fled to open ground.

Another thirty yards forward, he saw two forms, one kneeling, the other on her back, legs spread wide. Birthing? In the midst of all this chaos! The kneeling shape was familiar in form.

His heart leaped.

Julia!

Yes, crazy. But something Julia might just do. Stop to assist in a birth though the world collapsed about her. Could it be? Could that really be her, or was he just seeing what he wanted to see?

There was another form as well, not five feet to the side—large, inhuman. It was rising slowly, as if injured, possibly just regaining consciousness. The birthing pair didn't take notice. They were too involved in the delivery. Charles raced forward, gun held before him, crying

Julia's name. The shadowy form of the reyaqc was almost upon them. Julia turned toward the thing. Yes, it was Julia. He was sure of it. She held an infant in her arms and was trying to shelter it.

Charles fired once, twice. The lumbering form glanced in his direction but showed no sign of injury. Apparently both shots had gone wild. Charles stopped, planted his feet wide as he'd been taught at the firing range, held the gun steady with both hands, aimed, and then fired a single shot. The reyaqc jerked to the right. Charles fired again. The creature went down like a marionette with the strings cut free. The gun dealer had been right when he'd claimed the Glock packed a lot of stopping power for such a tiny weapon.

As Charles drew near, Julia looked up at him. She was a bloody mess, her hands and forearms dripping red from the elbows down, her clothes splattered and stained with the stuff. She registered no surprise at his being there, but simply said. "Give me your jacket. I've got to wrap the infant."

Chapter Forty-Two

Donald rushed through the darkness, his keen night eyes taking in the scene, his head slightly cocked as he sniffed at the subtle breeze in search of Tresset's scent. He'd already addressed his friend once since the onset of hostilities, but had been brushed away as a nuisance. Now, it was time to try again. Perhaps Tresset would see logic as the true fighting was underway. The scenes about Donald tore at the core of his being—reyaqc slaying reyaqc. Mutilating. Cannibalizing. Repeatedly, he sought to intervene, to force these molts to think, to understand what they were doing and of how senseless it was to slaughter one another. But though none attacked him—perhaps out of deference for Dolnaraq's standing within reyaqc society—neither did they heed his pleas.

Donald came upon a young reyaqc girl of perhaps five or six years old. She was huddled beneath a pushcart as, ten feet away, three invaders raped her mother. Donald shouted at the attackers, demanded they cease, but only one even bothered to glance in his direction. This one, a coyote-like molt of perhaps sixteen years in age, said, "I know who you are, so I won't kill you, but don't try to stop this." And though Donald pleaded for sensibility and restraint, the three simply howled and ravaged with an increased ferocity. Donald stepped forward, laid a hand on the coyote-molt's shoulder. The youth whirled on him, his teeth bared.

Donald was frightened to his very foundation.

For deep within, he knew that if he dared intervene further, these youth would kill him. So he took the child from her hiding place, carrying her in his arms while attempting to shield her from the horrible sights about them. She cried, of course, called for her mother, but all Donald could offer was a simple, "There, there," and a promise that things would change someday.

Coming upon two molts, each circling the other, each preparing to engage in battle, Donald shouted, "There's no need to do this!"

Neither responded, but rather growled at one another, their circle drawing tighter, the moment of engagement drawing near.

"We can negotiate. Find a reasonable settlement. Address your grievances."

One of the two, a lanky molt with large pad-like paws at the end of each arm, glanced only momentarily at Donald. "No disrespect, Dolnaraq, but you don't live the life of a molt. You don't know."

"I don't know!" shot Donald as he pulled the trembling child closer to him yet. "I was a molt. I was raised in a pack such as this—and saw it brought to ruin on a night such as this. I tell you, there's a better way."

But as Donald was yet finishing his statement, the two lunged at one another; blood was drawn, the moment lost. And Donald felt a lurch in his chest, a shudder through his frame. For the reyaqc, his people, his family were destroying themselves and he was powerless to effect change. Yes, he had a certain stature within the greater reyaqc community; in some ways he was nearly revered. But he saw now that this clout extended only to word and not to deed. Like wayward teens when confronted with parental wisdom, the reyaqc might nod in agreement at all Donald brought forth, but ultimately he was no more than background noise.

Donald caught Tresset as he marched along the west side of the compound barking orders, directing combatants, and coordinating the evacuation of the females and small pups. Leaving the trembling child with a young female, Donald approached his lifelong associate. "Tresset, we need to speak."

The chieftain stood erect, chest thrust forward, eyes glimmering in the firelight with a fierce passion known only to those who thrill at the heat of battle. "I've no time for discussion, Dolnaraq. Narrish! Lead this group of females to cave seven. Take two additional males with you and leave one there as a guard when you return. Hurry. I'll need you here." The slender molt to which Tresset spoke, nodded and hurried off to perform his duties.

"Tresset, this is insane. The reyaqc already face extinction. Are you trying to hurry the process along?"

"Survival of the fittest. Isn't that what Darwin—one of your precious humans—called it?" Tresset cut to his right. "Mardo, join with Jymis and his group. Work to drive the invaders from the northeastern perimeter. Instruct Hennia to secure the food storage building. We'll need our provisions once this is concluded."

Donald followed closely on Tresset's heals. "Think this through. By engaging in battle, you're decreasing an already emaciated population."

Tresset jerked his disinfectant cloth from his pocket and cleansed his hands. They appeared raw from the constant friction. "Dolnaraq! I am not the aggressor. We are attacked. I am coordinating a defense, and in so doing, facilitating less loss of life."

"We could talk with Bytneht Noavor. Reason with him. Perhaps he'd call off the attack."

"You're naive, Dolnaraq. You've spent a century studying both human and reyaqc history and yet you are too blind to recognize the nature of both species." Tresset paused, gazed at Donald for a moment, his expression firm, but not absent compassion. Donald sensed the onset of emotion from his former pack brother, a softening, however insignificant, as their eyes locked. Tresset sighed and nodded. "Speak with Noavor if you please. And pray he doesn't execute you on sight. But leave me alone. I've no time for distractions. Tehmys! Take three molts to the northeast side. Slay those with torches. Quickly. Do you hear me? Go!" Tresset rubbed furiously with his rag.

Naive, thought Donald. No, he was all too aware of the reyaqc condition, the propensity toward violence, the pack instinct, the perpetual aggression of molts. No, his flaw was not in naivety, but in that he yet hoped for change. Would this occur this evening? Of course not. But if these two factions could take even one step away from their barbaric ways and toward a more civilized existence, could this influence other packs? He could hope so, and would continue to hope, for without it, there was little reason to continue.

*****

Donald located Bytneht Noavor on a low rise just to the southwest of the compound. In truth, only calling his own well-regarded name allowed him to pass through the ranks unmolested. Bytneht stood amidst a small group of followers, barking orders and adapting strategies much as did Tresset. Donald was surprised at the chieftain's youth, for he could be little over twenty years of age. Donald thought of Tresset at that age and hoped this one carried a more rational perspective than had his friend. Like Tresset, Bytneht had chosen a feline as his sustaining species, Donald suspected a cougar, but jaguar was also a possibility.

Bytneht was slender and most likely agile. His muscles, taut and ready to spring, rippled beneath his bare flesh. He had shoulder-length blond hair, human-like in appearance, but knotted and ratty. His head was round, ears erect, his teeth white and without fangs. He had a powerful looking neck and jaw. His back, arms, and legs bore no fur, but a short silver-gray coat covered him from the chin down to his upper abdomen. His legs were thick and powerful and his hands and feet large. Even in the uneven light, retractable claws bulged just beneath the surface. The young chieftain laughed as Donald approached. "Dolnaraq! That's right, isn't it? You're Dolnaraq! They told me you were here but I thought it

351

was a rumor. Ha! This is perfect." Bytneht had a cocky swagger about him that Donald found unnerving. This one would be slow to negotiate.

"Bytneht Noavor, I'm pleased to make your acquaintance. May I have a word?"

Bytneht laughed and in doing so prompted those about him to do likewise. "'Make my acquaintance?' 'Have a word?' I didn't know this was a formal occasion."

"Formal, no. Urgent, most assuredly." Donald's tone was even, his expression neutral.

"Stiff! This one is stiff," shouted Bytneht. "Too many years behind the desk. Ha!" The young molt moved close to Donald, his pale eyes locking onto the elder reyaqc. "Did Tresset Bremu send you to negotiate surrender? Is he afraid to meet me face-to-face?"

"I represent nothing more than myself alone and nothing less than the reyaqc species as a whole."

Bytneht clapped his hands in amusement. "Oh, this one is priceless! I think we should keep him."

Donald glared at the foolish youth. "Bytneht, the reyaqc are endangered. The human world continues to encroach on our minimal territories as our numbers decrease. Soon the human race at large will learn of our existence. It's amazing that so few have done so already. These ridiculous raids, this senseless taking of reyaqc life doom us all. Our only hope of survival is to unify our efforts, to adapt, to grow as a people so that as the humans become aware of us, we do not appear frightening and barbaric. We cannot be perceived as a threat or we will be slaughtered or caged."

Bytneht smiled. "But, we are a threat."

"No. It is we who are threatened. Our very existence as a species lies in the balance, yet you continue with this folly."

Bytneht cocked his head and offered a low purring chuckle. "You are a self-important old molt, Dolnaraq. I don't get it. You know that? I don't get it."

"What is it you don't understand?" Donald's tone was terse, humorless.

Bytneht laughed. "I don't understand why everyone makes such a big deal out of you. Because all I see is a narrow-minded old molt who thinks he has all the answers. I see a fool of a reyaqc who doesn't even have the common sense to realize the trouble he's found." Bytneht turned his attention to those about him, a cocky smirk on his narrow lips. "Dolnaraq seeks to be a savior to the reyaqc. I say we treat him as a proper savior should be treated."

With that, Bytneht's lieutenants were upon Donald.

Chapter Forty-Three

Two guards hustled the jackrabbit molt to stand before Tresset, the captive trembling to the point of near nausea, his short gray fur on end, his small white eyes darting from side-to-side. Tresset turned, glaring at his people as if they might just be fools. "It took two of you to bring a bunny rabbit forward?" The compound was burning down around them and they wasted their time with this?

The senior of the two molts mumbled an apology and then both scampered away at Tresset's terse command.

"So," said Tresset as he moved toward the molt. "You are again brought before me as messenger. Or is it that you were again caught spying?"

The jackrabbit shuffled in place, his right foot thumping involuntarily upon the ground. "I am a messenger only."

Pathetic. Tresset would never allow one such as this to exist within his ranks.

"Noavor surrenders?" mused Tresset, though he knew better. His compound was falling. Though his molts would likely drive Bytneht back, their settlement was in ruin. It would take months to rebuild. No, Bytneht was playing his advantage, possibly toying with Tresset, attempting to rile him further, hoping he'd make a catastrophic mistake. Whatever the message was to be, it was a ploy, a maneuver.

"Bytneht Noavor does not surrender," offered the jackrabbit molt in response to Tresset's question.

"Then what?" asked Tresset. Already he was playing through possible responses to each imagined scenario. Battles were won by words as well as by bloodshed. He wondered what information he could glean from this cowering molt, if he might best secure information through torture or through guile. Neither, he surmised. It was doubtful that Bytneht would entrust any but the most rudimentary tidbits to such a cowardly creature.

The messenger seemed certain to flee, his legs jerking, nose twitching; but somehow he managed to stand his ground. "I bear a demand for your immediate surrender."

Tresset nearly lunged at the trembling molt, but restrained himself only because the jackrabbit had use as a messenger. No, the battle had not gone well, but they had been caught unawares. Now that his pack had assumed formation, the tide would turn. "You expect me to surrender to that—pup?"

"Bytneht Noavor promises that upon your surrender there will be no further loss of life. Your pack will be absorbed by ours, and you, being the only true liability, would be exiled."

Liability! Bytneht was audacious, that was a certainty. Pulling his cloth from his pocket, Tresset paced before the molt, rubbing the sterile cloth furiously between his hands. "Noavor does not seriously expect me to accept such an offer." Of course he couldn't think that. He was goading Tresset, seeking to enrage him. He hoped Tresset would behave rashly, deviate from his strategy. No. Bytneht was yet a young fool. Did he really believe Tresset might be duped by such a simple maneuver? Madness. The thought was madness.

"There is another aspect to our position as well," offered the trembling messenger. And here he stood just a bit taller, his twitching lips curling almost imperceptivity at the corners.

"Yes?" asked Tresset as he stepped one way and then the other, his hands rubbing harder, harder against the cloth.

"Dolnaraq is our captive."

*****

Tresset marched forward, five of his best lieutenants following close behind, the jackrabbit molt leading the way through Bytneht's ranks. Even now, Tresset saw the figure upon the rise just south of the compound. They had stripped Dolnaraq naked, and, using wooden beams from a dilapidated building, had fashioned an x-shaped cross on which to hang him. And though this cross was not the more traditional T, still Tresset knew enough of human history to recognize the imagery. If the circumstances hadn't been so grim, he might have found the scene amusing. Yes, Dolnaraq did have a bit of a messiah complex at that. But the old fool was well intentioned, he always had been. It was just that his academic mind had difficulty grasping the real world. What made perfect sense in theory did not often play out well in practice. Now here he was, a fool tethered to rotting pieces of wood—bargaining fodder for two warring factions. Pathetic.

Still, he could not pull his eyes from Dolnaraq. His friend's face was bruised and swollen, his limbs bloodied. A patch of his beard had been ripped free. Even in the dim light of the flaming compound, Tresset saw the way his chest heaved, could almost hear the labored breaths and tight agonized gasps. Dolnaraq was conscious, as was evidenced by the periodic tightening of his arms as he sought to heave himself up on the torturous planks in order to better breathe. But otherwise his chin rested on his breast, his tangled red hair clumping loosely just above his eyes.

"Dolnaraq is not of my pack!" shouted Tresset as he drew close to his adversary.

"Yet you come running to protect him," smiled the young Bytneht as he made his way down the uneven slope to meet his foe.

"No, I came to see a pup who fancies himself a chieftain," answered Tresset. Already, he'd pulled the disinfectant cloth from his pocket.

Bytneht swaggered forward, his lieutenants close behind. "I'm young. So what? Can your old brain even remember your youth?"

"I remember being a fool."

Bytneht laughed. "Then, maybe you haven't changed as much as I thought." Bytneht's companions howled in exaggerated laughter at this middling joke.

Tresset glared at the other. "Dolnaraq was right in one aspect. If we are to survive, the reyaqc do need to unite. I offered an alliance. You responded with a raid."

Bytneht chuckled. "That's a simple way of looking at it." He stepped to within ten feet of Tresset, stood straight, his head cocked just slightly to the left. "In your plan, you became the leader and I the follower."

Tresset squeezed his cloth. "My experience is far greater than yours, my long-term strategies sound."

"My drive and energy make you look old and pathetic. Look at this place, oh great strategist. Your pack is beaten. For every minute we stand here yakking, more of your people die."

"As do yours, Noavor. Look closer. It is not we that near defeat."

The young chieftain chuckled.

Dolnaraq lifted his head. It seemed a great effort for him to draw breath, but with obvious pain, he hauled himself up and shouted, "Stop the fighting! While you're negotiating, stop the fighting." Then he slumped down again, his lungs heaving, bloodied spittle dripping from swollen lips. It seemed that in such a position, arms extended, head down, his entire weight supported by his wrists, that breathing had become an extreme burden.

Tresset despised weakness, and surely asking a favor of his enemy would be just that. But Dolnaraq suffered, and despite all that had come between them, this agonized the senior chieftain at a level much deeper than conscious thought. "Release Dolnaraq. He has nothing to do with this."

Bytneht smiled. "I thought you said he was not of your pack."

"He came only earlier today on another matter. Release him. His wisdom may not be as infallible as he would like to believe, but he's done much for the reyaqc. There's no need to make a spectacle of him."

Bytneht seemed to contemplate this for a moment, and then, smiling, he turned, strolling up the dusty incline to where Dolnaraq hung, and before Tresset realized what he was doing, he'd freed his claws, raking them across Dolnaraq's chest.

With a roaring howl of utmost agony, Tresset burst through Bytneht's startled lieutenants and fell upon the smarmy chieftain.

Chapter Forty-Four

Julia cradled the infant as she and Charles slinked through the shadows along the southern end of the compound. Though Charles urged her to leave the child behind, she staunchly refused to do so. He'd grumbled and groused, but he knew her well enough to realize she wouldn't be persuaded on this. But the addition of the child negated his Ninja as a means of escape. There was no way she could hold the infant while squeezing against Charles' back as they road over rough terrain.

Charles found the keys to the Hummer in Shane's pocket. They crept through darkness, moving past the multiple animal cages. The beasts were in a state of panic. As yet, no fire had reached them, but ash-filled smoke filled the air and each breath burned as it went down. The caged creatures raced about their confines, pawed at the walls, growled and whimpered. A spider monkey clung to the wire bars of its pen, shaking furiously and screeching in a terrified falsetto. A red fox paced one direction and then another, back forth, back forth, its nose twitching, its tongue hanging limply out of one side of its muzzle. Julia felt bad for them, and if there had been time, she might have even released the non-threatening breeds.

She looked away from the caged beasts and into the smoke filled night. The moon glowed red as its rays pierced the fiery sky. The smoke irritated her eyes, dried them, caused them to feel scratchy each time she blinked. The baby stirred in her arms and she pulled Charles' jacket back to peek at the strange child she'd claimed as her own. Her life was suddenly inverted. This was now her first responsibility, the safety of the child. All else was secondary.

They made their way past the cages. There was a small wooden shed ahead and then, just beyond, a larger building, single-story, old and surely rotted. Their plan was to skirt the southern end of the compound and then sweep north, working their way along the western outskirts of the place and toward the vehicle.

In truth, Julia was amazed that Charles had found her, or, if not that he had found her, that he had gone to such great lengths to find her. He hadn't yet had the opportunity to share the details, but clearly he'd expended some effort in locating her. When they got out of here—if they got out of here—then what? Charles wanted another chance with her, that much was clear. But did she want him? Was there anything left of the love they'd shared, or had the twenty-pound sledgehammer of his sudden rejection shattered all hopes for them? Could the relationship be repaired, and maybe even more importantly, should they even try?

Charles paused, cautioning her to stay low. There was some sort of commotion up ahead. They were behind the tiny shed now, and she peeked around the corner to the southwest. A cluster of reyaqc stood there, three held torches illuminating the scene. Two beastly creatures rolled about the rocky ground slashing and biting at one another as the others stood watching the brawl. Another form, perhaps fifteen feet further up the rise, hung strapped to wooden planks—crucified. Julia squinted, attempting to draw the figure into focus, but the torches caused him to appear more as a silhouette than anything else. Though every few seconds, each time the breeze moved from east to west, it seemed a truer light flashed across his face. All at once, the features seemed familiar.

Remaining firmly in the shadows, Julia stepped around Charles, attempting to gain a clearer view of the scene.

"Julia, what are you doing?" Charles' voice was a sharp hiss.

"The man on the cross, I need to get a better look at him."

Charles cursed as she stepped further from him, crouching beside a ten foot high mound of gravel to her left. Gaining a different angle, she hoped to achieve a clearer view. Charles had followed, and probably for fear of discovery remained silent. Still, Julia sensed his anger. Of course, he thought her foolish. Perhaps she was. But she had to know. Moving just a little further now, she peeked around the gravel mound and up to the left...

It was him.

Donald Baker.

Julia held the infant closer, her arms trembling as she considered the situation. She'd not cared for Donald. He'd proven devious, single-minded, and outright criminal. Kidnapping, after all, was a federal offence. That said—everything he'd done was to the goal of aiding his species. He wasn't antagonistic to Julia, or to any humans. As far as she could tell, it was simply that he had a burning passion to aid the reyaqc. Based on the deference she'd witnessed the reyaqc showing him, she surmised that he had a certain clout among them, and without a doubt he was the most civilized reyaqc she'd encountered. She clutched the infant closer. What would happen should Donald be killed? What other reyaqc could she trust to guide her in raising this unique child? What other reyaqc would even allow her to keep the baby? As illogical as it might seem, she was keeping the child. Minya had given her that charge, and Julia accepted. She believed Minya wanted more for this baby than life in the barren desert, that she saw in Julia a greater hope for that child. Likewise, Julia saw Donald Baker as her only means of succeeding in this mission. She might be wrong on this last count, but she didn't think so. Donald was key, both to her adopted child, and to the survival of these other reyaqc.

"We've got to rescue him."

Charles jaw nearly dropped to the dirt. "Him? The guy on the cross? Julia that's insane."

"That's Donald Baker." Julia said this as if this information alone was all Charles would need.

"Okay, that's Baker—so what? Didn't he kidnap you? Isn't he one of *them*?" With the last word Charles waved his arm in a wide arc, indicting the entire compound.

Julia turned to face her husband. "Charles, we need him. He's important, both to the reyaqc as a whole and to the safety of this baby."

Charles stared at her, his expression one of exasperated disbelief.

Julia glanced up at Donald again. His chest heaved. His limbs quivered. "I know this is insanity to you. It is to me too. But our chances of survival are much greater with him than without him." She paused, scanning the shadows, surveying the terrain. "Even without Donald, we can't continue in this direction. We'd be walking right in front of that brawl." Julia pointed to her left. "If we swing around this way, behind the cages and then up the back side of that rise, I think we can sneak up behind Donald, untie him, and then maybe slip down the back. After that, we can make our way to the Hummer."

Charles stared at her for a moment before speaking. His Adam's apple bobbed, his jaw tightened. She was asking him to further risk his life. "You sure you want to do this?"

Julia gazed down at the infant in her arms, at the two pearl-like eyes staring up at her in perfect innocence. As strange as it seemed, Donald Baker was the only one she trusted where this child was concerned. "I'm doing it, Charles, whether you come with me or not."

He nodded. There wasn't much else for him to say.

Chapter Forty-Five

Donald gritted his teeth, flexed his biceps, and arched his back, pulling himself up in order to gain a gulp of fiery air. It seemed the stuff was mostly soot, but still, it filled his lungs, eased the need for breath. Relaxing now, he allowed his head to slump forward upon his chest. Breathing was near impossible with his arms spread to support his entire weight on this rotting wooden structure. In another thirty seconds or perhaps a minute, he would pull himself upright again in order to gain his next gulp of life. He would again feel the muscles of his upper arms tear, would endure the coarse and splintering wood scraping against his bare back, would suffer the ropes rubbing against his wrists wearing the skin raw and bloody.

His gaze fell upon the scene several yards below. Tresset and Bytneht Noavor thrashed and rolled about, each injuring the other with every slash and bite. Bytneht was larger, younger. He was defter of movement. His agility far surpassed that of his opponent. But Tresset was tested. He possessed a patience born of experience. His instincts were sharp, his every strike masterful. Still, he tired. Even through the smoky haze, even amidst his own suffering, Donald saw his age-old companion faltering and his emotional anguish at the thought of Tresset's impending death far surpassed his physical torment.

Donald lifted himself once again, gathered a breath, and attempted to shout to the combatants. "You are not so different as you think. Talk! Not battle!" But his warnings were naught but the feeble croaking of a used-up reyaqc tied to a wooden frame. It was doubtful that any heard his words. If anyone had, well, not one pair of eyes turned in his direction.

As Donald watched through bleary eyes, Tresset kneed Bytneht in the groin, and then quickly tossed him to the left. Springing to his feet,

Tresset huffed, his lungs heaving at the exertion. But still he leaped forward just as his opponent sought to right himself. But Bytneht anticipated the lunge, sidestepping Tresset and gaining the upper hand.

Donald tensed, once again lifting himself to breathe.

There was a sound from behind. Whispered voices. He turned his head but could see nothing from his angle. Yet, there was a scent on the air—two actually. Humans. "Julia?"

"Yes." Her voice was but a whisper. "Don't draw attention to yourself. We're here to free you."

Who was the other one, the male that he smelled? Clearly he was not one of the pack's givers. His scent was too civilized. Even through the perspiration, Donald smelled musky cologne and the sweet odor of hair product. Not Shane. The scent was different. Who was this man?

The frame shuddered. He'd been crucified upon an x-shaped structure. Support beams ran from the ground to the top of each arm of the "x" where Donald's hands were strapped. Another plank rose to the center point where both lines of the "x" converged. These boards were being pulled free, one at a time. The male supported the structure with his back as Julia pulled and twisted at each support until the nails were freed and she could drop the boards carefully to the ground. Now, as Julia held the board on Donald's left, the male inched to the right, clasped the plank just above Donald's right hand, and they lowered the frame. Donald now laid on his back staring into the smoke filled sky.

"Hurry. I must intervene before Tresset is killed."

"We're doing what we can," said the male. "Just stay still while I untie these straps."

Julia's face loomed above Donald. She'd just retrieved something that had been lying perhaps five feet off to the side. She cradled a lime green and black riding jacket. Donald smelled the infant reyaqc within. "The girl, Minya, her child?"

Julia nodded. "We need to get the baby to safety. We're going to take the Hummer. Come with us. After the battle's done, we can return."

Donald's right arm and leg were free. He took a deep breath. His lungs still ached, but breathing was easier now. "I can't leave, Julia. Not now. Take the car. Gain some distance from the battle. But don't stray too far. That baby needs the care of a reyaqc."

"I promised Minya I'd raise the child."

Donald stared at her for a long moment. There was a determination in this woman, a will that he'd sensed earlier and now proved strong and unshakable. He nodded. She offered a weak smile.

An agonized screech pierced the night air. At the same time loping footsteps drew near.

Leaving Donald's left wrist strapped, the human male rose to his feet, fumbled in his right pants pocket, and then withdrew a small handgun. "Stop right there. I will shoot."

Donald tilted his head so that he could see the scene before him. Two reyaqc had noticed the activity upon the rise and had come to investigate. Below, Bytneht straddled Tresset's bloodied form, his jaws clamped upon the chieftain's neck as Tresset thrashed about in pain and terror. "Julia, untie my hand—quickly!"

The woman placed the infant on the ground and began working on the thick leather strap that bound Donald to the board.

"Quickly!"

He felt a tug, a pull, a tug in another direction and then his arm was free.

He was to his feet. His muscles burned, his throat was raw, and he could barely stand upright for the pain, but these things were inconsequential. As he stumbled down the slope, Tresset lifted his right arm as if to pull Bytneht's jaw from his neck. His head rolled in Donald's direction. Their eyes met. "Dolnaraq," gasped Tresset. "He is worse…" There was an exhalation of breath. Tresset's arm jerked and then fell limp. Donald closed his eyes. His emotions swirled—his duty, his promises, his life's work—his rage. He knew what Tresset had wanted of him. He knew how he would respond.

"Noavor!" screamed Donald, seeing the young chieftain rise, his hands held high in victory and Tresset's limp and lifeless form at his feet. He raced forward heedless of all. One molt made to intercept Donald, but the human male warned him off with the gun.

The young chieftain turned, muzzle bloodied with Tresset's life fluid, and grinned a broad, self-satisfied grin. "He's dead, Dolnaraq. Too bad for you."

Donald knew rage as he had not known in a century's time.

Blinding rage.

All-consuming rage.

He welcomed it.

Beckoned it.

Embraced it.

No longer did he hold it in check.

No longer did he quash that which cried to be free.

The self-assured Bytneht didn't fully realize he was under attack until Donald fell upon him. Every ache was dismissed, every injury forgotten. Philosophy evaporated. A lifetime of learning and hope crumbled away as dust, and Donald knew nothing but murderous rage. Though he had no fangs, he clamped his jaw on Bytneht's neck while simultaneously clawing his eyes with his fingernails.

He tasted flesh. Thick salty flesh.

He tasted blood. Copper and iron. Sweet, sticky, flowing.

He bit harder, tearing, grunting, ripping the surface tissue free, and then burying his face in the musculature beneath.

He lunged again.

Again.

Again.

Bytneht's eyes went glassy, his limbs limp, but still Donald ripped and tore and chomped.

Then, suddenly, with no apparent reason or prompting, Donald came to himself. His vision cleared. His mind swept away the low-hanging clouds of rage. There was flesh still caught between his teeth. Moist spongy matter obstructed his nostrils. He sensed the injuries inflicted upon him by the struggling Bytneht's claws. He saw the jagged chunk bitten out of his left forearm, perhaps two inches in diameter and nearly an inch in depth. Had he even felt Bytneht bite him? Looking down at the ravaged form of the young molt, he felt his abdomen tighten and turn. Donald tumbled off of the lifeless form as his stomach gave up its bloody contents on the hot stony ground.

Epilogue

Donald was a chieftain. Or rather, Dolnaraq Bytneht was chieftain. He had slain the upstart ruler and so must now attach Bytneht's name to his own as a reminder of his responsibility to Bytneht's pack. It was not a position to which he'd aspired. Nor was it a position he desired. But it had been thrust upon him by his own irrational actions. By reyaqc tradition, the one who slew the chieftain assumed the role. Bytneht Noavor had slain Tresset, and thus earned the position over the two packs. Donald had likewise slain Bytneht and so the burden of leadership now rested with him. He knew this was what Tresset had wanted, knew that in the end, Tresset realized that should Bytneht attain dominance, that he would perpetuate only savagery, that the reyaqc would never ascend to their true potential.

Or had Donald simply inserted his own fears into the emotion of the moment? He supposed he would never know. But truly, his greater concern was the pack, these molts, these reyaqc. They looked to him for guidance and direction. What was he to tell them? He abhorred their lifestyle. Was it possible to educate them—all of them—to such an extent as they could enter society? What of the molts? What if he could not convince them to give up their beastly essence? What if they preferred to live a wild, unhindered existence? Or, what if, like Treleq, the Las Vegas rogue, they sought to divorce themselves of animal essence, and then went insane for their efforts? Not every molt handled this transition without complication. He had nothing to offer these reyaqc, for he understood so little of their needs and motivations.

And credibility.

Donald had succumbed to rage, had murdered Bytneht Noavor in a savage haze of blood. How could he then stand before the reyaqc and proclaim civilized behavior and education as their true salvation? Perhaps he was the fool Bytneht had thought him to be. He'd spent a lifetime studying the reyaqc, but though he'd uncovered volumes worth of facts, could it be that he'd never touched the soul of his own race?

Donald closed his eyes, drew a deep breath, and then stared at the small patch of reddish orange fur on the back of his left hand. Did he even know his own soul? He had sworn, a century ago, that he would never behave as a beast again, that he would be an example of a refined, well-educated, civilized reyaqc. But when he'd seen Tresset lying dead in the dirt, when he'd seen Bytneht's haughty grin and heard his smarmy gloats, all that Donald had sought to be, all he had claimed of himself, had been swept aside in a rush of animalistic rage. He was once again the savage molt who had loped about the edges of civilization, naked and wild.

Who was he really? Which was the true Dolnaraq?

Footsteps approached from behind. Donald turned to see Julia. She wore blue jeans and a green pullover blouse. A wide-brimmed straw hat shaded her face and neck from the brutal Nevada sun. She cradled the bundled infant in her arms, three weeks old now and already alert. She'd allowed the child to infuse from her on two occasions. The child was healthy and Julia had shown little signs of distress after each drawing of essence. An infant's need was much less than that of an adult.

"The rebuilding goes well," she said as she stepped to alongside him.

Donald nodded. "Tresset was a capable leader, but he focused too strongly on ambitious strategies for battle—both against human and reyaqc. Most of the burned structures should have been leveled and rebuilt soon after I purchased this old mine. Tresset's pack is obviously eager to rebuild their home and Bytneht's followers were nomadic and anxious to have a more stable existence. The act of working together on construction is helping to form a bond between members of the two packs. I think the union goes well."

"I've been meaning to ask you something. You own the mine."

"I and two other financially secure reyaqc."

"But, you don't support the existence of packs. You think the idea outdated, that it hinders the intellectual and emotional growth of the reyaqc."

Donald attempted a grin, though he knew this gesture irritated the woman. "Sometimes in the interest of a greater good, we are party to things we find adverse to our sympathies." He paused. "Have you heard news from Charles?"

Julia kissed her child on the forehead and then responded. "Yes. Your connections at the state level were a great help. He had the rogue declared mentally unstable and unfit to stand trial. He'll be transferred to a mental facility within forty-eight hours."

"Very good. We'll have better access to him this way. Perhaps we can even affect an escape before his true nature is realized."

"Charles was reluctant to become involved." Julia smiled as the baby burped and then cooed.

"He had already involved himself prior to my making his acquaintance. But by accepting my offer to provide documentation as to the rogue's identity and thus the ability to maintain his pretext as the rogue's attorney, he was able to avoid inevitable disciplinary action, possibly even disbarment."

"He became involved in order to rescue me—from you." She added the last with a broad grin.

"And, I suppose his continued involvement is meant to win your favor."

Julia's grin faded. She dropped her gaze, now stroking the child's head.

"I won't pry," said Donald.

Julia expelled breath in a long sigh. "Maybe I'd feel better if someone did pry. It seems everyone's afraid to touch the subject—except Charles, of course."

"And?"

"I don't know. I've got a child now. A child that has very specific and specialized needs. One of the reasons Charles nearly strayed was because he was tired of waiting for me to decide to have children. But this isn't the type of child he wanted. Charles is still very cautious about the reyaqc."

"Of course he is. And with good reason. But I'm more curious about you. It's been nearly a month that you've lived among us. How do you now feel about the reyaqc?"

Julia chuckled. "I'm the adoptive mother of one. What choice do I have?"

"You could give the child to a reyaqc female. She would be raised with care."

Julia shook her head. "No. Not an option."

"Your promise to the birth mother?"

"Yes… No. More than that." She gazed at the child with a tenderness that went beyond words.

"You love the child," offered Donald. "And in doing so, you've decided to remain here among the reyaqc, regardless of the consequences to your personal and professional life."

Julia nodded. "I suppose I'll figure it all out as I go along." She readjusted the child, resting the infant's head on her left shoulder. "It will either work out with Charles or it won't. I guess he'll always be a part of my life, but I'm in the process of change. Maybe the change will draw us back together, maybe not." She turned her full attention to Donald and he knew she had something on her mind. "I'm not the only one facing change," she said.

"No. I suppose not."

"You took a sabbatical from the university, but you're not comfortable here, not as a chieftain."

Donald gazed out upon the devastated community below. "Like you, I've had responsibility thrust upon me. And like you, I refuse to run from it."

"But?"

Donald hesitated before speaking. Did he really wish to share his inner struggles with this young woman? Was he comfortable with that level of honesty? Yes, he decided. He supposed it best that he did. His wife was still in Boston and would not be joining him to live within the pack. Hers was a civilized existence. She would wait patiently for him, but she would not consent to dwell among a pack of molts. But, Donald was chieftain here and so here he must remain, at least in the short term. And chieftains didn't share their problems with their followers. It caused concern among the ranks, a lack of confidence. Julia wouldn't harbor such notions and so might be the only being to whom he could speak freely. Turning to face her directly, he said, "Through my writings, through my research, I've tried to offer the reyaqc something better, something more in keeping with the true greatness that I know lies within. There are many reyaqc who live as I have among human society. But many more are savage. They have no desire to learn, to grow. With our numbers so few, and with human population growing and technologies advancing, it's only a matter of time before we are discovered by society as a whole. I feel the burden of our survival as a species."

Julia paused for several seconds before responding. "Donald, a leader can't save his people. Though, God knows if you listen to campaign speeches, they all seem to think they can. But in reality, the best they can do is to offer structure and direction. In the end, each of us, either reyaqc or human, is responsible for our own destiny."

Donald smiled, a true smile, not one fabricated to mimic that of a human. "You're trying to free me of my burden."

"It's not your burden, Donald. It never was."